Fire on the Fells

ALSO BY CATH STAINCLIFFE

DETECTIVES DONOVAN & YOUNG
Book 1: The Fells
Book 2: Fire on the Fells

DETECTIVE JANINE LEWIS MYSTERIES
Book 1: Blue Murder
Book 2: Hit and Run
Book 3: Make Believe
Book 4: Desperate Measures

STANDALONE
The Lost Girls of St Ann's

Cath Staincliffe

FIRE ON THE FELLS

JOFFE BOOKS

Joffe Books, London
www.joffebooks.com

First published in Great Britain in 2025

Cover art by Nick Castle

ISBN: 978-1-80573-094-1

For Tim. Again. Always.

PROLOGUE

He walked quickly, up the sheep track and through the moorland. His spine tight, hands curled, fingernails pressing into the palms of his hands.

Were they following him?

His breath was uneven, hard to catch. The air dry and thin in the heat of the evening. The sun was an orange ball nearing the horizon. The sky above a stunning, summer blue.

Flies pestered him, drawn to the sweat on his face, on his bare calves. He swiped them away.

Searching the hillside, he saw no movement. Everything petrified in the sullen heat.

His eyes filled with sudden tears, a sharp sting.

He closed them for a moment, rubbed at his chest, trying to soothe himself. Taking deep breaths, he focused on the smell of baking earth and dried grass.

There! A jolt of fear. *No, no, it's all right . . . Just a rock. A rock, that's all. Not a person.*

He sniffed hard, squashing the urge to cry. Took a drink from his water bottle and then shook out his hands as though he could fling the anxiety away.

Walking further up the hill, he spotted scattered bones on the path, a rabbit skeleton, shreds of fur and tiny white ribs. The skull had gaping eye sockets, large curved teeth.

An outcrop of small boulders provided a stopping point. The stone was warm to the touch, limestone pitted by centuries of weather. He ran his fingers over it, feeling the grainy bite. Letting it ground him. Solid. An anchor.

At the base of one rock, in a shady nook, he noticed a smear of green. Crouching down to look, he found moss. *Sphagnum fallax.* He opened his camera app. Close up, the plant looked like a tiny rainforest, furry trees lush with life.

The setting sun was too fierce to photograph, unless he did it with his eyes closed, so instead he turned and framed a picture of the moors to the east. His shadow lay elongated in the view but could be cropped out afterwards. The heather rolled away, a thick purple blanket. Blanket bog. He heard the chuckle of a grouse but did not see the bird.

A fly landed on his lips, startling him; he spat it away.

Climbing further, he saw a clump of yellow tormentil. *Thrives on acid soil.* The knowledge was a comfort. He knelt to take a picture.

He drank, resisting the temptation to douse his head and cool off a little. *You can shower later.*

He busied himself with his camera roll. Selecting then discarding a number of shots he'd taken.

Seagulls crossed high above, their cries echoing round the plateau.

He covered another quarter-mile; dust coated his boots.

The sun had slipped now, half below the horizon, picture postcard style. The burnished light spilled across the land and reached up to paint the underside of a single feathered cloud with carmine and orange.

He got a good shot.

All this . . . His heart grew full. *All this to live for. To fight for.*

His gaze swept over the land, the grass and the heather, the gulleys that pleated the slopes, the ancient stones.

A cry drew his eyes upwards. *Oh God!*

Delight blossomed through him. He swung his phone up, pressed record.

Beautiful.

'No!!!' A scream ripped from the core of him.

And the world turned red.

CHAPTER ONE

Wednesday

Leo

Leo couldn't breathe.

Luke stood in the dock awaiting sentence. In the weeks since his son had pleaded guilty to racially aggravated criminal damage, he'd been plagued by dreams of *this very moment*.

In Leo's nightmares the facts warped, distorting so that Leo himself was sent down or Ange led away, or the charge became murder, treason. The sentence — death by hanging. Leo had woken from those dreams in a clammy sweat, his heart thudding, knowing he would not sleep anymore. He'd lain awake, listening to Ange breathing for as long as possible, then quietly made his way downstairs. Sat in the armchair with a mug of tea and watched the dawn arrive.

Ange, beside him now, was gripping his hand so tightly it had gone numb. She was strong, her work as an artist often manual, physical. Shaping stone and metal and wood to realise her vision.

Leo didn't look at her, couldn't face seeing her sorrow, her distress. That would undo him. Already he struggled with the pressure behind his eyes, the raw ache in his throat.

Luke affected a blank expression, eyes a thousand miles away. But the pallor of his complexion, the way he picked at his nails, the ripple of his throat as he swallowed, showed how scared he was.

Leo had attended Crown Court on many occasions for his work. Jury trials often, charges of murder or manslaughter. Leo's role as detective was to lay out the evidence acquired during an investigation, build the story of timelines and eye-witness testimonies, forensic evidence, of motive and opportunity and responses in interview. To defend the integrity of that evidence and explain to the jury how it amounted to proof of guilt. Doing his best to address any doubts the jurors might harbour.

But now, here, today, he was simply a father waiting for the judge to make her decision. Feeling helpless, mute, with no power to affect the outcome.

How has it come to this? he asked himself for the umpteenth time. How did his child, their child, who'd always been loved and sheltered and cared for, who had changed them from a couple into a family, who'd been raised to question, to learn, to create, to understand; how did this child become a vandal and a hater? At only twenty-one.

Yes, Luke was groomed. Along with his friend Jack, who was up on the same charges. Jack's parents, Rose and Trevor Sherringham, were sitting on the row below. Rose had greeted Leo with a look of bitter animosity, eyes flinty and mouth screwed up tight, when they'd arrived in the court foyer. Her husband had placed a restraining hand on Rose's shoulder and steered her aside. Avoiding an ugly scene, Leo guessed.

The two lads had been recruited by an older man, Christopher Hirst. Fed a diet of misinformation and conspiracy theories, directed to websites where they could 'learn the truth' about their country, the threat to their white race and how to act as patriots. This worldview casting them as victims, feeding their insecurities, offering brotherhood and a common cause.

All those years when Leo would catch sight of his boy and his heart would swell, his spirits rise. But more lately that initial leap of joy had been followed by a lurch, stomach plummeting, because things weren't right. Luke had changed. Withdrawn. Luke was angry, dismissive — cruel at times. He railed against everything they valued. And Leo had no idea how to fix it.

The judge was speaking. 'Your actions at both the taxi firm and the mosque caused significant distress and harm to the people there. I am aware this is your first offence and you are very young . . .'

Leo clenched his jaw. Would she suspend the sentence? Give Luke a chance to repair his ways?

'However,' the judge continued, 'you planned these attacks with others. You daubed grotesque racist and Islamophobic slurs on the properties in question. And we have seen evidence that you were also planning a further attack on a synagogue. The nature of these offences, the intention to spread fear, hatred and division, is sickening and of deep concern. People in this country are entitled to feel safe in their places of work and worship, in their communities and their homes.'

Leo grabbed a breath.

Ange turned to him, her cloud of red hair visible out of the corner of his eye. But Leo didn't reciprocate, he watched Luke instead as the judge continued, 'And consequently the court is sentencing you to twelve months in custody.'

Luke flinched as if he'd been slapped.

Ange moaned. *It'll destroy him, Leo. Jesus. They'll eat him alive.* Her words when Leo had told her what Luke had done and what the consequences might be.

Luke looked directly at Leo, mouth tightening, and slowly, almost imperceptibly, shook his head. Leo couldn't read his expression. Derision? Resignation? Loathing?

6

'Take him down.'

Leo wanted to run across the court, break into the dock and rescue his boy. Drag his son from the dark, spirit him away. Save him.

He bit down hard on his tongue.

Luke crossed to the stairs that led down to the cells, the limp from his motorbike accident evident.

Ange began to cry. Leo held her. His own eyes stinging.

He grasped for hope. *Twelve months. A year. Then he'll be home. This time next year he'll be home.* The assertion rang hollow.

They'd lost him.

The police had already been on Luke's trail after the graffiti attacks but when Leo stumbled upon proof of his son's involvement, he had had to pass the information on.

'You dobbed me in, you bastard!' Luke had raged at him. Then shut him out. And Leo didn't know if he'd ever be forgiven.

* * *

Thursday

Shan

Shan arrived at work before Leo. Increasingly the case. Not because he was late but because she found being at home unbearable. Since she'd lost the baby, she and Erin were at sea. Every interaction was awkward, clumsy, tainted with words unspoken. As if the magnetism that had once drawn them together was now reversed, forcing them apart.

These days Shan chose to get up early, grab a quick breakfast before Erin surfaced and head into work. Then linger late at the office. They'd not talked, not properly, about the rupture to their lives. Shan wouldn't know where to begin. She didn't know what she wanted. Could barely decipher how she felt.

Not good, that's for sure.

7

The sadness between them was like some bog of despair. *What?* Shan almost laughed at herself. *A slough of despond.* Where the hell did she get these phrases from?

She greeted Lily, the cleaner, who was mopping the hallway, and climbed the old wooden stairs up to the third floor where Leo and she had adjoining offices under the eaves.

Sunshine flooded through the skylight and the air, stirred by her opening the door, filled with shafts of dancing dust motes.

Golden Magic Dust, she'd named it as a child. *From dragons? For dragons?* Dragons were involved somewhere along the line. Shan had been crazy about dragons. Her collection spanned Beanie Babies and other stuffed toys, plastic moulded figures, numerous books, pyjamas and hats, and a Chinese red dragon stick-puppet that could be made to prance and weave.

Shan had chosen the puppet on a trip to the Chinese New Year celebrations in Manchester with her parents, who'd adopted her as a baby from China. They were Yorkshire born and bred but did their best to make her aware of her cultural heritage. They regularly cooked Chinese meals, bought her lucky Chinese knots to decorate her bedroom and copies of the *Mulan* and *Kung Fu Panda* movies as soon as they were released. A delight to actually see characters like herself.

Shan had been the only Chinese student in her primary school class, but Chinese New Year was celebrated there in the same way as organised festivities for Eid, Diwali and Christmas.

She made a cup of tea and set to work but was interrupted by the sound of Leo climbing the stairs — his uneven tread and the familiar grunts he made as a result of his joint pains.

Her door was open, in the faint hope of allowing some air to circulate, and he stuck his head round it.

'Morning.'

'How was yesterday?' she asked. Although she could already tell — from his expression, the weary look in his eyes, the downturn of his mouth.

Leo took a breath to speak, then his phone rang.

'Matthew?' he answered. Their senior officer, DCI Matthew Booth.

Leo listened, his eyes on Shan.

'Swaledale . . . Syke Moss . . . Post me the grid reference . . . And the coroner? . . . CSM already there? . . . Got it. Will do. Thanks, Matthew.'

Shan felt the prickle of adrenaline flash across her shoulders, up the back of her calves.

'Body found on Syke Moss,' Leo said.

'I guessed as much.'

'Shall we?' He tilted his head in invitation.

Shan drummed her palms on the desk, a quick six beats. 'Yep.' She pushed herself up.

Leo gave a nod. '*Avanti*,' he said. And led the way.

* * *

Leo

They left Shan's car at the station, and Leo drove. Settle was busy. Always. But especially now, September still high season. The market town in the national park drew coach parties, holidaymakers, tourists, overseas students, motorbike clubs, cyclists, scouts and guides, all thronging to play in the Dales.

Shan had taken her sunglasses off, was checking the location on her phone.

'Best way's up to Hawes and over Buttertubs Pass,' Leo said. He'd lived here all his life, place names and the routes between them second nature. Not that there were that many roads to choose from.

'Right. You don't need the satnav?'

'No.' Leo yawned. God, he was tired. Yesterday he and Ange had come back to their house alone. Ange had sat at the kitchen table, head in her hands, while Leo made mugs of tea that went cold before they could drink them.

Their conversation had been staccato, fragmented. Phrases begun without the need of completion, understood in the shorthand that came from a twenty-five-year-old marriage.

'I just can't imagine . . .' Ange.

'We can get on the visitors' list . . .' Leo.

'If only . . . if we'd known . . .'

'Armley has a first-night unit.'

'I'd best check his room.' Ange had stood. 'Old pizza boxes and — oh, Leo.'

They'd cried together. Then Ange had wiped her face roughly, almost angrily. 'Right. No wallowing. And you . . .' She lifted her hands, held his shoulders, eyes on his. 'Don't you disappear on me. I need you now, Leo. I need you present.'

'I know,' he'd said.

She'd not been referring to his physical presence but his emotional one. To Leo's propensity for depression and the miserable, paralysing sense of futility that overwhelmed him at times. That was the withdrawal she feared.

'I get that you can't control it,' she'd added. 'Maybe I'm not being fair, but please promise me you'll get help if you feel it coming on.'

Now he yawned again, stretched his neck, hearing it click.

'Keeping you up?' Shan joked. He was trying to come up with a suitable riposte, when she yawned too. 'You got me doing it now!'

The road ran through the valley alongside the River Ribble and criss-crossed the railway line at points. The sun was strong. A few high cumulus clouds coasted overhead, spreading shadows that rippled slowly over the flanks of the fells and the pale drystone walls that stitched the fields together. Heavy rainfall in spring had allowed a lush explosion of greenery. Welcomed by many. But it led to flooding in some villages and calls yet again for better land management. Since then the county had been plagued by drought. The heat unrelenting.

'Luke — he got twelve months,' Leo told Shan.

'Oh. I'm sorry.'

He gave a shake of his head. 'And a referral to Prevent.' The antiterrorism programme. 'Rehabilitate?' A bitter taste in his mouth. 'If only, eh? The whole bloody system's broken. Education? Recreation? It's a joke. Overcrowding, staff shortages . . .' He knew he was ranting but he couldn't stop. 'Teach him a lesson? The only lesson he's likely to learn in there is the next chapter in the far-right playbook. Any white supremacists in there will be on him like flies on . . .' He groaned.

'Depends where he is, I guess,' Shan said. 'Some places still manage to help people, against all the odds.'

Leo looked at her, sceptical.

Shan shrugged. 'Here and there.'

'Don't you go all Pollyanna on me,' he said.

'Say who now?'

'Behave!' He tried not to smile.

Shan laughed. He liked it when she laughed. There hadn't been enough of that recently. He knew she was struggling in her home life, not that she confided much in him. And of course it wasn't that long since she'd had the miscarriage. Leo had been with her when it had started, trying to persuade her to go to hospital and then reluctantly agreeing to drive her home.

They passed a snack van, selling burgers, drinks and ice creams, flying a Yorkshire flag, the white rose.

'Look at this idiot,' Leo said. A large white SUV was tailgating them. The road, like most in the fells, was narrow, winding, only suitable for overtaking on a rare, long straight stretch.

As Leo rounded the next corner, the SUV roared out past them, pulling sharply back into the left just in time to avoid an oncoming delivery van whose driver was leaning on his horn.

Shan had her phone up, filming. 'I could send this through,' she said. 'Ruin his day.'

'Teach him a lesson.'

They both laughed.

* * *

11

The road twisted its way along the small dale, narrowing as they neared their destination. The grey drystone walls on either side were stippled with lichen. Sheep grazed in the fields and Shan caught sight of a rabbit darting for cover — startled by the noise of the car, she guessed.

A farm came into view, the farmhouse on one side of the road and a yard with a large barn and several smaller outhouses on the other. A squad car guarded the approach.

Leo pulled in and the officer stationed there came to meet them.

Shan took in a breath; the reek of silage was pungent in the air. A horse fly landed on her arm and she swiped it away.

'DI Donovan,' Leo introduced himself.

'DC Young,' Shan said.

'We're here to meet Tom Bairstow,' Leo said.

'Yes, sir.' The constable made a note in her tablet. 'You can park in the yard.' She pointed. 'And I'll let them know you're on the way. Do you need transport? We've a Land Rover. I can ask them to send it down.'

Shan was happy to walk but Leo was the one with dodgy knees.

'How far's the walk?' he said. 'A mile or so?'

'About that.'

'We'll walk,' Leo said. 'We can always grab a ride back. Downhill's the worst. Arthritis,' he added for the benefit of the PC, who nodded.

A mewling above and they all looked up.

'Buzzards,' Leo said.

Shan watched the two birds, broad rounded wings silhouetted against the sky, wheel and peel away. Their sharp cries echoing along the dale.

'You follow the farm track from the yard up to open country, then bear right and eventually you'll be able to see the location to the east,' the PC said.

'Do we have an ID?' Shan asked. They'd been given no information about who'd been found. A farm worker or fell walker? Man or woman? Old or young?

'I've not heard, ma'am.'

Shan smiled. She didn't warrant the title. They were peers, at the same level. One in uniform, one not. 'Shan's fine,' she said.

'Yes. Right. Kara.' Kara grinned.

'And Leo,' Leo said.

They retrieved their protective clothing from the car boot. A rucksack apiece. They'd change at the inner cordon if they were OK'd to enter. Sometimes the crime scene manager wanted to limit the numbers present, especially if the initial documentation and recovery was ongoing.

At the far side of the farmyard they crossed a cattle grid onto a track between two fields. Cows in one of them. No break in the wire of the fence that Shan could see.

'Don't make eye contact,' Leo half whispered.

'Hilarious,' Shan said. 'You're wasted here, you know. You should do stand-up.'

He gave a small bow.

Still, when they reached the next meadow, which only had sheep grazing among spikes of thistle and rusty brown dock, she felt her shoulders relax and the tightness in her spine ease.

Ahead the change in terrain was abrupt, striking. The green pasture giving way to moorland, brown and purple and tan flecked with green. Swathes of heather in full bloom.

A sign at the boundary proclaimed access land.

'Privately owned?' Shan asked Leo, once they'd climbed over the stile.

'Most of this area is. One of the estates.'

After several minutes she noticed Leo had fallen behind. She heard him huffing. He'd turned, facing back the way they'd come.

'Breather?' Shan said.

'A minute.' He panted.

Her own heart was pumping faster with the climb and she was aware of a light film of perspiration around her forehead. She dragged her fingers through her hair, lifting it away from her scalp to cool down. Then drank some water from her bottle.

The farm and the yard, the road they'd driven along, were all obscured now by the hump of the hill they'd climbed.

Shan watched moths dip and fuss about the heather. Saw a shiny black beetle scuttle across the path. She could smell the vegetation baking in the heat, a honey scent underlaid with bitter notes.

Erin. Erin in her head. All the walks they'd done like this. Come rain or shine. And now? Everything sour, spoiled.

Maybe we should take a break, have some time apart? The thought, unbidden, sent a chill through her, a wave of guilt and fear.

She drank again. Blinked fast. Raised her face to the sky, eyes closed, savouring the warmth, and tried to clear her mind.

Resuming their ascent, they skirted a shallow pool in the track, flies busy on the surface of the dark water. The ground to the side was spongy beneath the plants. Peat bog. Further up the moor was scarred by grids of scorched heather, the vegetation stripped away and the tar black peat exposed.

'That looks awful,' Shan said, pointing.

'Grouse shooting,' Leo said. 'They burn the heather so the birds can eat fresh shoots. There's a voluntary agreement in place to reduce it on blanket bog like this.'

'Going well, then?' Shan said. 'Surprised much?'

He gave a laugh. 'You should hear our Ange on the subject.'

Shan knew Leo's wife was a keen environmentalist and her artwork centred on nature and landscape.

They pressed on and reached the crest of the moor.

'There!' Shan pointed, her pulse quickening. Close to the eastern horizon, where the magenta and brown land met the blue bowl of the sky, were a cluster of off-road vehicles, a white forensic tent, stick figures — some in white suits.

She could feel the nerves in her stomach, apprehension mixed with vital curiosity. To know, that's what drove her. To hunt the truth and find answers. *Who? How? Why?*

They picked up pace, almost on the level now, eager to reach the scene.

***

Leo

The tent was pitched on a steep slope, falling away from the plateau. Stepping plates led from the cordon across the heather to the scene. Two crime scene investigators were crouched over, combing the area within the cordon in a fingertip search. Beyond, heading north where the land rose, Leo could see several yellow numbered markers, placed there by the forensics team to identify items or features of interest.

Three men in civilian clothes stood together outside the cordon. One with a dog on a lead. *Witnesses? All in good time.*

Informed of their arrival, crime scene manager Tom Bairstow sent word they could view the body in situ. Suited, booted, gloved and masked, they went through a gap in the police tape that hung unmoving in the still air, and crossed the stepping plates to the tent.

'Leo, Shan,' Tom greeted them as they entered. 'Watch your balance.' On such uneven ground, it would be easy to pitch over and disturb vital evidence.

Through the centre of the tent ran a gulley, perhaps three feet wide and two feet deep, fringed by dried rushes. In the rains, run-off would flow through here. One of the many streams that zig-zagged down from the tops.

In the channel lay a body.

Leo moved closer, taking in the sight before him. The victim lay on their back. Male, Leo thought — that's what his guts told him. Head lolling to one side. Face, what was left of it, a mess of bloody craters, same down the neck. A fly there, bluebottle. Leo fought the impulse to swat it away.

One eye obliterated. The other milky, a mix of white and crimson, a sinister marble. *Playing marbles with Luke on the rug in the living room. Luke locked up now. Staring at cell walls.*

Shiny jet-black hair, like Shan's, grass seeds and heather fragments tangled in it. Brown skin. Slim build. Left hand across the stomach, palm upright at an ungainly angle, also peppered with shot. A tattoo on his wrist, a ring of leaves. The other hand lay by his right hip. Smooth, Leo noticed. None of the prominent veins or liver spots or swollen knuckles that come with age. *Young, then.* A couple of bracelets on that wrist, plaited threads strung with beads. Orange T-shirt, khaki shorts. Blots of blood speckled the T-shirt, the cotton punctured. Walking boots. Scratches and scrapes on his arms and legs. Torn skin around the elbow of his left arm.

Leo considered his height. Guessed at five foot seven, eight. *Teenager?*

To be dead like this. To be dead so young. The terrible waste of it. Luke might be in a bad place but at least he was alive.

'Shotgun?' Leo said.

Tom agreed.

'You find a weapon?' Shan said.

'Nothing yet.'

'So not self-inflicted?' Shan said.

'Highly unlikely. We'll move him now, see if there's anything underneath him. And check for ID. We'll need some space.'

'Of course,' Leo said. 'And who called it in?'

'The man out there with the lurcher. Simon Lloyd.'

'And the other two?'

'One's the head keeper at Patefield Grange, the other's the estate manager, Phil Beaumont. This is Patefield land. We rang to alert them and they arrived just after we got the tent up. They'd a shooting party up here yesterday.'

'Got it,' said Leo. He looked again at the figure in the gulley. Someone's son.

It was pity Leo felt at times like this. Pity and sorrow, a loosening in his chest and an impulse to rail at the injustice of a life so brutally ended. Feelings he swallowed in order to do his job. Retaining compassion but detaching himself from the pain as much as was possible. This lad, his loved ones, needed a detective not a fellow mourner.

* * *

It was stifling in the tent and Leo pulled his mask down as soon as he stepped outside, welcoming the fresher air. Not that there was much in it.

Simon Lloyd was understandably shaken. Thin faced and tow haired like his dog. Twitchy too. The dog sitting to heel, sentinel. Eyes snagging on one thing after another. Hypervigilant. A sight hound. Not that they didn't have a decent sense of smell, like any dog worth the name. But their vision was extraordinary.

'We were walking over to Thwaite,' Lloyd explained. 'And Roxy, she hared down here. Wouldn't come back to me.'

'She a hunting dog?' Leo asked.

Lloyd scowled with distaste. 'No. She's a rescue. A pet.'

'She's lovely,' Shan chipped in, and Lloyd gave a faint smile.

'When I saw . . . it's terrible,' he said.

'Yes,' Shan said.

'Well . . . I rang 999 and they said to wait here.'

'Did you touch anything?' Leo said.

'Yes. I thought I should check. See if they were breathing, if I could help even though . . . it looked—' He swallowed, overcome. Rubbed his fingers over his mouth.

'So I knelt down and felt for a pulse in the neck. But he was cold and hard, stiff, you know?' He broke off, shook his head. Roxy looked up and began to rise. Lloyd patted her head and she sat.

17

'And Roxy, did she touch anything?' Leo said.

'She was sniffing around. I called her away. But I can't be sure if she actually touched anything.'

'Thank you.'

'I thought maybe it was a fox or a hare caught in a trap or something. But—' The man's dark blue eyes held a raw, pained expression.

'Thank you for everything you've done,' Leo said. 'It's a shock, something like this.' He gave the man a moment to settle. 'We'll need to come and take an official statement, plus fingerprints and a swab so we can identify you in our forensics tests. That'll probably be tomorrow.'

'Yes.'

Lloyd gave them his address and phone number.

'And you didn't see anyone else?'

'No.'

'We don't have any identity for the person at this stage and of course we haven't been able to inform next of kin, so we'd ask you not to post anything on social media or speculate with people. Did you take any photographs or videos?' Leo said.

'No. I can't believe people do that.' He was scandalised.

'People think they're helping,' Shan said.

'Occasionally, that's the case,' Leo said. 'Anyway, are you and Roxy OK to get yourselves back home?'

'Yes.'

'Sure?' The man looked sick with shock.

'Yes, thanks.'

'Leo? Shan?' Tom called from the tent.

They said goodbye to Lloyd, pulled their masks back up and went to join Tom.

The body had been lifted from the ditch and placed on a body bag. It remained in exactly the position they'd seen.

'Rigor mortis is present and seems complete,' Tom said. 'So we're looking at death occurring at least eight hours ago. The process from death to the rigor completely disappearing can be anything from twenty-four to thirty-six hours. We'll observe when the rigor dissipates and that'll give us a window, but it's not going to give us an exact time of death. Only a ballpark.'

'OK,' Leo said. 'So sometime *before* the early hours of this morning?'

'And while cause of death is likely a result of shooting, that needs to be clarified at a forensic post-mortem,' Tom added.

'Sure,' Leo said, knowing there were occasions when the pathologist found the cause of death to be something other than the obvious.

'We've checked his pockets and there's no identifying information,' Tom said.

'Nothing?' Leo was surprised.

'Nowt,' Tom said.

'Phone?' Shan said.

'No.'

Leo looked at the figure. The scratches on the arms and legs were the sort of scratches you'd get scraping on the ground. Luke used to be decorated with similar marks in his skateboard phase.

Leo had seen the yellow markers heading up the hill.

'He wasn't shot here?' Leo asked. 'Those are drag marks.'

'Think so. And there aren't pellets scattered here. And not as much blood as we'd expect. It's likely he was pulled down from higher up the hill.'

'To hide him,' Shan said.

Tom gave a nod. 'We'll try and establish the route and confirm where he was shot.'

Leo summarised Simon Lloyd's account and how they'd follow up. 'We're going to speak to the estate manager and keeper now. Do you need them here for anything else?' Leo said.

'No. Their shooting party is still booked in at the Grange,' Tom said. 'I told them that isn't going to happen today and to keep everyone there in case you want to speak to them.'

'Thanks,' Leo said.

'Who doesn't have a phone?' Shan said to Leo as they emerged into the open air.

'Precisely,' Leo said. 'So where is it now?'

CHAPTER TWO

Thursday

Shan

The two men still waiting at the cordon were the estate manager, Phil Beaumont, and the head keeper, Jason Tattersall. Beaumont was the older, solidly built with close-cut receding hair and rimless sunglasses. Red bands of sunburn ran across his forehead and nose.

After expressing his shock and concern at events, Beaumont suggested they take the Argocat back to the lodge.

'Argocat?' Shan said, looking over at the vehicle. It was like something from a video game, a cross between a tank and a jeep with eight wide tyres.

'All-terrain vehicle. Better than a four-by-four on boggy ground,' Beaumont said.

'Amphibious,' Tattersall added. Shan guessed he was a few years older than her, late thirties perhaps. His face and arms were tanned, probably from being outdoors in all weather. Hollow-cheeked, with a sharp nose, he had an alertness to him that put her in mind of Roxy the lurcher.

Leo logged them out with the officer staffing the cordon and they walked over to the vehicle.

'Before we go,' Shan said. 'Were any of your group in this immediate area yesterday?'

'No,' Beaumont said. 'Our butts are further up, half a mile or so over the top. We've cancelled this morning's drive at your request.'

'How many people are there?' Leo asked.

'Eight Guns.'

'Guns?' Shan said.

'Members of the shooting party,' Beaumont said.

'Call 'em Guns,' Tattersall added.

'And after yesterday's shoot, was everyone's accounted for?' Leo said.

'Of course . . .' Beaumont sounded puzzled. 'Oh, I see . . . No, everyone's there.' He started the engine.

'Our dogs would have found . . . it, if he'd been here when we were,' Tattersall said, twisting round from the passenger seat.

'Even at that distance?' Shan said.

'Oh, aye,' he answered, as if it were a daft question.

'And your staff?' Leo said. 'All accounted for?'

'As far as I know. We can check as soon as we get back,' Beaumont said.

The vehicle jounced over the moor, clambering uphill.

When they reached the top of the ridge, the land sloped very gently down the other side until it plateaued out. Moorland ran to the horizon, aglow with purple heather.

Shan could make out the line of grouse butts below. Three-sided structures spaced across the heath.

'That's where you were shooting?' She pointed.

'That's right,' Beaumont said. 'Beaters drove the birds from the east to fly over the Guns.' He waved a hand to indicate.

Shan noticed Tattersall, sitting in front of her, knocking his fist on the side of the car. Could you call it a car? She tried to figure out if there was a pattern to his tapping. Perhaps a

21

song in his head? But she couldn't discern any rhythm to it. Probably just nervous energy.

After a mile or so Beaumont took a track down to the right, where a small plantation of conifers and a group of buildings nestled in the valley. Patefield Grange stood at the centre. A country house with steep pitched roofs and generous windows. The limestone glowed in the late summer sun. To one side of the house were terraced gardens and a vivid blue swimming pool with sunloungers dotted around it.

Shan smelled the medicinal tang of pine sap as they skirted the trees. They didn't enter the complex through the main gate but Beaumont drove around the side and into a large yard where several other vehicles were parked. A barn held farm machinery. There were stables and workshops and other outbuildings around the perimeter.

'What do you need?' Beaumont asked, jumping from the driver's seat. The man had an energy to him, a sort of can-do, let's-get-on-with-it vibe. He reminded Shan of her last PE teacher.

'Talk to each of you in turn. And check no one's missing from your staff,' Leo said. 'A list of employees and rotas would be helpful.'

'Sure thing,' Beaumont said.

'And then we want to establish the movements of everybody yesterday.'

'Everybody?' Beaumont frowned. 'Well, people were out on the shoot during the day then back here.'

'People ate here?' Shan said.

'Dinner at eight. Five courses, fine wines.' He caught himself and cleared his throat. 'I mean, I'm pretty sure no one would have been out after tea at five.'

'We'll need to verify that,' Leo said. 'Find out if anyone saw anything, heard anything at all.'

Beaumont looked as though he was about to object. Then, in an abrupt change of mood, clapped his hands together.

'So! Who do you want to talk to first?'

22

Somewhere a dog barked, and another joined in.

'You,' Leo suggested. 'Mr Tattersall, we'll see you afterwards.'

'Fine.' Tattersall nodded.

'We can use my office.' Beaumont gestured to a long low building at the bottom of the yard closer to the main house. 'Tea, coffee? Soft drinks?' he asked.

'Tea, please,' Shan said. 'No sugar.' The heat made her thirsty.

'The same for me,' Leo added.

'Jason, will you let Anita know?'

'Will do.' Tattersall left them.

Shan and Leo followed Beaumont to the office.

The building had been refurbished but still had the original flagged floors. There was an eclectic mix of furniture. A traditional mahogany desk had pride of place facing the row of small windows that looked back across the yard. The wall behind the desk held a mix of shelving and metal filing cabinets. On the gable end, above the door they'd come through, hung a stuffed stag's head, antlers resplendent, above two crossed rifles. Opposite the desk was a brown leather chesterfield sofa, a coffee table and two old wooden armchairs set around a faded Turkish rug.

'I'll just fire this up for those records.' Beaumont moved behind the desk and switched on a computer. Took off his sunglasses. 'Please pull up a seat.'

Once they were settled, Shan said, 'What does your job involve?'

'Estate manager?' He blew out a breath, shaking his head. 'I oversee everything. Manage the buildings and the land, oversee maintenance and development. Hire and fire. Health and safety. And, of course, I manage the budgets. We're a major player in the local economy, bringing money into the area, creating jobs. A leading employer.'

Shan recognised the key argument for grouse shooting, trotted out to answer any opposition, to rebuff concerns about natural diversity and conservation.

Leo asked Beaumont to take them through the timetable of the previous day.

'Certainly. Briefing straight after breakfast at eight forty-five.'

'Who did that involve?' Leo said.

'All the Guns, keepers, loaders. The beaters are briefed by the keepers separately. First drive was at nine thirty and then the second at eleven. Lunch back here until one thirty.'

'There'd be waiting staff and kitchen staff here for that?' Shan asked.

'Yes and again at dinner. Third and fourth drives were at two and three. Eighty-seven brace downed by the end.' He caught himself boasting, dropped his smile, presumably remembering the reason for their interest. 'Picked up and back here by half past four for tea. And dinner was at eight.'

'Until?' Leo said.

'Liqueurs and coffee served at ten thirty. The bar remains open as long as the guests require.'

'How many people were at dinner?' Shan said.

'I think it was sixteen; we have visitors with the Guns who don't attend the shoot. I can get that checked for you.'

She nodded.

'And if people had left the lodge before dinner or after, would there be any record?' Leo asked.

'No,' Beaumont said.

'Not even in case of fire?' said Shan, thinking of hotel regulations and occupancy rules.

'You have to understand . . .' Beaumont began.

I don't have to do anything.

'. . . we're catering to an exclusive clientele. No expense spared. People don't want to feel they're being monitored. We pride ourselves on creating a discreet—'

Shan interrupted, 'So there's no way of knowing if any of this party left the Grange?'

'That's right,' he said crisply.

'And staff?' Leo said.

'Some are on shifts, some live in, those with more senior roles.'

'You do?' Leo said.

'Yes, the wife and I have one of the houses, a pair of semis, beyond the cottages the far side of the yard.' He gestured in that direction. 'Jason and his wife have the other. His brother Niall and Ian Kerrigan, underkeepers, and Carrie Crowther, our house manager, are in the cottages. Casuals, that's the beaters and kitchen staff, chambermaids, come and go as needed.'

'The beaters and the loaders, when do they leave?' Leo said.

'The beaters leave immediately after the drive. The loaders come back here to clean and service our guns, prepare for tomorrow and so on.'

'Where are the guns kept?' Leo said.

'We have a gun safe in each room for guests' own use. We also have our own gun room, over there.' He pointed up the yard.

'Do you keep a record of what's taken out each time?' Shan said.

'Of course.' A spark of irritation in his eyes matching his tone. 'Was he shot? The man who was found?'

We haven't said it's a man, Shan thought.

'We can't divulge that information at present,' Leo said.

Beaumont looked momentarily sceptical then backpedalled. 'Right. Yes. Of course. Of course. Awful. Terrible.'

There was knocking at the door.

'Come in,' Beaumont called.

A young woman, blonde hair pulled back in a ponytail, dressed in a short-sleeved black shirt and skirt, came in balancing a tea tray. Three cups and saucers, two small china teapots, a milk jug. A cafetière. A plate of oat biscuits.

Shan's mouth watered.

'Thank you,' Beaumont said.

'Pleasure.' She smiled. 'I'll get you a table,' she said to Shan and Leo. 'Easier.' She stopped by the coffee table, put the tray on it and lifted the whole thing over to place between their seats. Shan noticed the darker brown lines in the crook of her arm. Fake tan.

'You're the Americano?' she checked with Beaumont.

'Thanks, Anita.'

Smiling again, she took one cup and the cafetière to his desk then left.

She was very smiley, Shan thought. Probably a hospitality thing. *Applicants must be able to smile genuinely and regularly in a consistent fashion.*

Shan tested the tea, pouring a little to see if it needed to brew longer. Usually the case. But this was a perfect colour. She filled her cup, took a biscuit.

Beaumont said, 'Perhaps I can ask Carrie to speak to the guests and let you know if any of them went out last night? Carrie's our host, she's forward-facing hospitality. Keeps everything running smoothly.'

'Thank you for the offer but we'd like to address the party directly. Could you ask Carrie to assemble them after we've spoken to Mr Tattersall?' Leo said.

Like Poirot! Shan thought irreverently. Then she saw the figure in the ditch, the awful loneliness of that, the horror of it, and felt a flush of shame.

'Of course,' Beaumont said with a tight smile, and returned his interest to his computer.

'As well as the list of staff, we'd also like a record of the members of the shooting party and guests,' Leo said.

'I'm not sure that data protection laws allow that,' Beaumont said.

'We're investigating a suspicious death. We're fully aware of data protection legislation. We won't be asking you for anything that isn't permitted,' Leo said. 'And any records will be removed at the conclusion of our enquiries.' Shan could hear the steel in his voice.

A pause, and then Beaumont said, 'Sure thing.' He clicked his mouse, typed some words. 'So here's a list of per-manent staff. I'll print that out?'

'Thanks,' Shan said. 'Could you also email me a copy?' She stood up and reached over to give him her business card.

'Will do. And the rota for the ground staff and those working on the shoot yesterday. I'll ask Carrie to provide you with the house staff rota. Jason's the best man to ask about the beaters.' He clicked the mouse again. 'And finally our Guns and guests.'

The printer whirred and spat out several pages.

'Is that everything?' Beaumont said.

'Thank you,' Leo said.

'Anything else you need from me, just shout,' Beaumont said brightly, but Shan sensed antipathy beneath the words.

'I'll fetch Jason.' Beaumont turned off the computer and reached down to gather the printed pages together and passed them to Shan.

'If we get confirmation that this was a homicide, we'll be launching a murder enquiry,' Leo said. 'We'll need to establish a mobile incident room close by. We have a Portakabin we can bring up, put it in the yard or the car park.'

'We could provide space,' Beaumont said quickly. 'That's the sort of size you need?' He picked up his sunglasses.

'And an electricity supply,' Leo said.

Beaumont clapped his hands. 'The old Dairy. Of course! We're converting it for an Airbnb. It's not furnished yet, but I'm sure we can rustle up tables and chairs and the like.'

'Thank you.'

'Helpful of him to suggest the Dairy,' Leo said after Beaumont had left.

'You know why, though?' Shan said.

'Do I?'

'He didn't like the idea of a police prefab ruining the ambience. His face!' She laughed. 'He assumed it was a man, our victim?' Shan said.

'I'd put money on it,' Leo said.

'Yes but you saw him,' Shan said. 'Beaumont didn't.'

'Default position?' Leo said.

'Yep.' *A man's world. Still.* 'How long would it take to walk from here to the scene?' she asked.

'Twenty minutes? Thirty? We should check that.'

'And what time does it get dark?' She launched her browser. 'Eight o'clock.'

'You think that's a factor?' Leo said.

'Well, harder to find and shoot someone in the dark.'

'Or easier to do it by accident? Poor vision. Anyway, you've heard of lamping?'

'What?' she said.

'Using off-road vehicles in the dark. The headlights show the quarry — shines in their eyes and the dogs are set after it.'

It was an image she'd rather not have stuck in her head. 'That's gross.'

'It's legal — for foxes, hares and rabbits. But they reckon some lampers kill badgers.'

The door opened and Jason Tattersall came in.

'You want a seat?' Leo gestured to the one at the desk.

'You're all right,' Tattersall said with a shrug. There was a pause, then he said, 'OK, then.' But he moved to perch astride the arm of the leather sofa, and they turned their chairs to face him.

He wore a green polo shirt with a crest embroidered on it, a white rose, flanked by two birds — grouse, Shan guessed — and the letters PG entwined. The logo for the estate. Cargo pants and walking boots.

He was fidgety, pinching the beading on the sofa then moving his hand to worry at the collar of his shirt. A restlessness to him that made Shan take note, wondering if it was something significant or just his temperament.

'You're in charge of looking after the grouse?' Leo said.

'That's right.'

'But the grouse live on the moor all the time?' Shan said.

'Yes. Completely wild. They roam free.'

'So what's your job consist of?' Shan said.

'Head keeper's responsible for predation, protecting the birds from stoat, weasel, crows, foxes.'

'How's that done?' Shan said.

'Snares, shooting, poison. That's all legal,' he added quickly. 'Then managing the habitat.'

'Burning it?' Leo said.

'Controlled burning, encourages new growth. It's a unique ecosystem. We maintain the balance of the environment.'

Sounds like a pamphlet, Shan thought.

'Then there's training up underkeepers. Two of them at the moment.'

'And on shoot days?' Leo said.

'I'm running the beating line, making sure that goes smoothly.'

'How many beaters do you use?'

'Usually a dozen. They just work the day. Most'll come up from the villages hereabouts.'

'Nothing untoward happened at yesterday's shoot?' Leo said.

'No. Great day, challenging bag.' Tattersall nodded for emphasis.

'Challenging? How do you mean?' Leo said.

'Plenty of birds, moving at speed. They reach a hundred and thirty miles an hour, you know. Kept the Guns busy. It's a very skilful sport. They don't expect it to be easy but they do expect it to be plentiful. A good supply, right? That's our selling point.'

'And it's pricey?' Shan said.

'Oh, aye,' he admitted. 'The Guns are after a superior experience. And they're happy to pay for it.'

'So what sort of rate for a weekend like this one?' she said.

'You're talking upwards of three thousand per day with the accommodation.'

Whoa!

'Did you or anyone you know about return to the moor after the drive was done?' Leo said.

'No,' he said.

Shan heard a clip-clopping sound and looked out to see a large, chestnut horse ridden by a woman in all the gear.

29

'Mr Beaumont said you could give us details of the beaters hired yesterday, and phone numbers for them?' Leo said.

'Sure,' Tattersall said. 'I can send you the WhatsApp group.'

'Are they mainly youngsters?' Shan was thinking of the likely age of their victim.

'Mostly. One or two older folk but mostly teenagers or early twenties.'

'And no one's missing that you're aware of?' she said.

'No idea. I messaged them all to cancel today. No one's rung looking for anyone. It's public access land,' Tattersall said. 'Anyone can come and go. No reason to think it's someone from here.' He picked at the sofa beading again.

'Have you worked here long?' Shan said.

'Since school. It's a great job if you like the outdoor life. My dad was a keeper.'

'And your brother.'

'Yeah,' he said.

Like doctors, Shan thought. Or farmers. Or those military families. Some police she knew had followed their fathers (and it was invariably fathers) into the job. Shan often wished they hadn't. It only prolonged the culture of a boys' club, of us (the police) against them (everyone else), reinforcing the sense of exclusion, entitlement. So that anyone like Shan, anyone not white, not male, would only ever be an outsider.

Tattersall sent Shan the WhatsApp group info and they concluded the meeting. Tattersall took them through the guest car park, where Shan paused to watch a white SUV park up. A man, stocky, sporting dark blonde hair and wearing wraparound shades, stepped out.

'Leo, it's racer boy,' she said quietly.

'Well, well,' Leo said, raising an eyebrow. 'Small world or what?'

* * *

The country house was three storeys high with wings at either side and dormer windows set into the steep roof. A semicircular stone portico with columns framed the front entrance, either side of which stood large box trees trimmed into spirals. Waste of a good shrub, as far as Leo was concerned.

Inside, the vestibule was large enough to accommodate two lounging areas. The floor was tiled in Victorian-style checkerboard. A wide stone staircase led up to split at a balustraded gallery above.

Paintings of hunting scenes and landscapes adorned the walls. Above the stairs hung a huge modern tapestry which looked like Hardraw Force to Leo, the tall column of water tumbling over the cliff. Ange would probably know who'd woven it.

Beaumont waved them to the back of the space. 'We're through in the Orangery,' he said.

'Ah, Oliver,' he called. Leo glanced back to see the man from the SUV. 'Can you join us? The police want to speak to everybody.'

'Absolutely.' He strode forward. 'Is this about cancelling the drive?'

'We'll explain to everyone together,' Leo said.

'Give me five!' He splayed his hand — five digits, as if they couldn't count — then hurried up the stairs.

The hubbub of chatter died down as they entered the room. True to its title, the Orangery held three fruiting trees sporting dark, glossy-green leaves, flower buds and ripe oranges, under a glass and iron canopy.

Leo did a sweep of the assembled party, estimating thirty or so people, all seated at round tables. The staff were distinguished from the guests by their polo shirts. The garments varied in colour but all were emblazoned with the Patefield crest.

Jason Tattersall sat at a table with two other men, all in forest-green shirts. Leo assumed these to be the keepers. One of them was huge, built like a rugby prop with a lumberjack beard, but he guessed the other man, who had a wiry frame and sharp nose, must be Jason Tattersall's brother, younger by the look of him.

The guests were much of an age — forties, early fifties at a guess. A couple of the women were younger. All were well-dressed, well-groomed, well-heeled.

Beaumont led them over to a woman wearing a beige pantsuit with short sleeves, her hair in a French plait.

'Carrie Crowther,' Beaumont said.

Leo gave their names and the three shook hands.

Crowther handed Leo a spreadsheet. 'The rotas for yesterday's hospitality and in-house team. Phil said you wanted them.'

'Thank you.'

'What a terrible situation,' she said. 'So very sad.' She had warm, brown eyes and a spray of freckles over her nose and cheeks.

Shan took the sheets from Leo and scanned through them. 'So most of the waiting staff left at eleven and the kitchen staff were here another hour?' she said.

'That's right,' Crowther said.

'No one missed a shift?' Shan said.

'No.'

'And no one absent this morning?'

'No.'

'Is everyone here?' Leo asked her.

'Yes. Apart from Oliver — ah, he's here now. Yes.'

Leo watched the SUV driver slip into a vacant chair.

Leo straightened up and turned to the room. 'Thank you for your time. I'm Detective Inspector Leo Donovan, and this is my colleague Detective Constable Shan Young. As you may have heard, we're investigating a suspicious death on Syke Moss.'

Sombre faces greeted him.

'We don't yet have an identity for the victim. If anyone here was out in that area after the conclusion of yesterday's final shoot, we'd like to hear from you. If anyone saw anything unusual or has heard anything that might help us, please wait behind now to talk to us. And should anything occur to you later, we can be contacted via Settle Police Station.' It was always important to give people a confidential route for talking to the police.

'Does anybody have any questions?' Leo said.

A man with chiselled cheekbones, dark hair and beard, and unnaturally bright teeth spoke up. 'What about this afternoon? We'll be able to shoot then?'

'No,' Leo said. 'The moor is out of bounds.'

'Oh, for f— All of it?' The man's eyes flashed. He shook his head with impatience. He'd make a good actor, Leo thought. A diva.

The woman beside him murmured a deprecation.

'It's a crime scene,' Shan pointed out.

The man glared at her. 'The whole bloody moor?'

'Rafe!' his companion hissed.

'Until we've completed all our searches.'

Beaumont looked flushed. 'We'll look at providing alternative activities.'

'We came here to shoot grouse,' Rafe continued. 'Not to fanny about with . . . Are we insured? We'll get compensation, yes?'

Leo heard intakes of breath from several people in the room. At the rudeness or the mention of money? Crass at such a juncture.

'I'll come back to you on that as soon as possible,' Beaumont said brightly.

'Are you talking to everyone else in the area?' Rafe said.

'What?' Leo said.

'Well, you're asking us if we've seen anything, if we've been up there. But what about all the farms and villages over the way? You'll be talking to them too?'

What was the man getting at? Feeling aggrieved? Unfairly singled out?

33

'If we decide that's appropriate,' Leo said steadily.

'This suspicious death — was it a shooting?'

'I can't comment.'

The man gave a hooting laugh. 'Ha! It was. They were shot, so you lot hone in on us. Shambles.' He threw himself back in his chair.

'That's not fair!' a woman across the room protested.

Carrie Crowther intervened. 'In the light of such a tragedy, I'm sure we all want to give any help we possibly can,' she spoke smoothly.

'Someone has lost their life,' Leo said plainly. 'We strongly suspect foul play. We are here talking to you as potential witnesses because you were known to be in the vicinity yesterday afternoon. And this is the nearest property in the area.'

'Fair enough.' Rafe showed his palms in a gesture of surrender, but it felt half-hearted. Disingenuous.

Leo drew the meeting to a close and Carrie Crowther announced drinks, including tea and coffee, would be available in the bar. And that drinks could be delivered poolside if anyone wished.

Leo had hoped someone might have hung back with information but was disappointed as the room emptied, leaving them with Beaumont and Crowther.

***

In the vestibule, they were approached by one of the guests. The woman who'd been sitting with Rafe. She was petite, wore her mahogany hair in a sleek bob; her eyes were pale, like sea ice.

'Excuse me.' She looked around, and instinctively Leo suggested the three of them move outside.

'I'm sorry about my husband,' she said, a groove of worry in her forehead. 'He's . . . well . . .' She gave a shake of her head, exasperated. 'Anyway, I went out last night before dinner. To walk our dog, Pippin. She'd been with us on the shoot, picking up.'

'The birds?' Leo said. He had a rough idea of how shoots worked but wanted to make sure he understood.

'That's right. But I took her for a run anyway.'

'What time was this?' Shan said.

'About quarter past seven. It was still light. Well, the thing is, I heard shots.'

Leo's interest sharpened and he sensed the same from Shan at his side.

'Pippin froze. They're trained to be still when the guns are firing. It didn't really strike me at the time. There's always gunfire somewhere like this, it's sort of background noise really. If I thought anything, it was probably that a keeper was dealing with a fox. Or a farmer was. I just felt I should mention it.' She gave an apologetic smile, taking in Shan as well.

'Where did you walk?' Leo said.

'Towards the butts, perhaps halfway there?' she said uncertainly.

'Thank you. Could you tell how far away the shots were?' Leo said.

'They weren't *close*, close. But they weren't as far as the next dale over, either.'

A burst of laughter from inside and she glanced back, tension in her stance. *Living on pins.*

'How many shots?' Leo said.

'I think there were four. But not all at once. Because Pippin stopped again. So two and then a gap of . . . I don't know . . . not long, maybe a minute, ninety seconds, and then two more.'

'Coming from which direction?'

She thought for a moment, the furrow in her brow deepening. 'From the West, nearer the butts.'

'And how long had you been walking when you heard the first shots?' Leo said.

'Fifteen minutes or so.'

'Did you see anyone?' Shan said.

'Not a soul.'

'That's very helpful. Thank you, Mrs . . . ?' Leo said.

'Duvall, Helena.'

'We'd like to get that written up as a formal statement. We can do it here with you now. I'm sure Mr Beaumont can find us a quiet space.'

Her face flickered with apprehension but she nodded agreement. Her unhappiness was palpable. Leo imagined she walked her dog simply to escape from her husband for half an hour. Idle speculation, he chided himself. Not germane. *Not for now, anyway.*

But given what Tom Bairstow had said about rigor and time of death, Helena Duvall could well have heard the shots that killed the young lad on the moor.

CHAPTER THREE

Thursday

Leo

When Leo arrived home, he sat outside in the garden for a
few minutes to decompress. His head was full of the day's
work: the lad in the gully, beads on his wrist, ragged holes in
his orange T-shirt; the arrogant Rafe Duvall; his wife Helena's
testimony; and Tom Bairstow's call at the end of the day to
say they'd moved the body to the mortuary and located the
site of the shooting — one hundred and fifty yards uphill from
where the victim was found.

Leo breathed in the scents of twilight, the pine trees
releasing their aroma, honeysuckle and night-scented stock
fragrant in the warm air. The stone bench still held the heat
of the sun.

The hamlet was quiet, no sound from any neighbours, as
if the heatwave had exhausted everyone and they were resting
inside.

He twisted his neck side to side, feeling the tug where the
muscles were locked in tension.

A faint noise by the pond caught his attention. He put on his phone torch and ran the light over the ground. A toad. Enormous, the size of a side plate. Leo smiled. The toad hunkered down. Leo killed the torch.

When he rose to go inside his knees protested, the creak audible in the quiet.

The house smelled of warm bread.

In the kitchen, Ange was pulling a batch of loaves from the oven. 'It's too hot for this,' she complained. She looked tired. Shadows under her eyes, face even paler than usual.

'Hi. You eaten?' Leo said.

She nodded. 'Yours is ready to zap.' Divested of the bread, she pulled the oven gloves off and moved to hug him.

'Any word on the visiting order?' Leo asked.

'Nothing yet. Did you sleep?' Ange had been up and out of the house before Leo had risen.

'On and off. You've flour . . .' He dusted her chin.

He took the portion of homemade lasagne that had been defrosting in the fridge and put it in the microwave, set it to heat through.

'Can we ask for one ourselves? A visiting order?' Ange said, draping tea towels over the loaves.

'No,' Leo said. 'Has to come from the . . .' *Inmate? Prisoner?* Luke's new status floored him, even though he'd known it had been on the cards. '. . . person. But we can write, send him a letter.'

'Yes,' she said. 'I'll do that. Will first class still get there the next day?'

'Not a clue,' Leo said. When had he last posted a letter? 'And the staff'll have to read it, vet it, first.'

The microwave pinged. With a cloth he carefully removed the container, tipped the contents onto a plate. The smell of garlic, oregano and tomato made his mouth water. He hadn't eaten for, what . . . six hours? His last meal a ploughman's at Patefield Grange.

'I need to turn things off out there,' Ange said, untying her apron and hanging it by the door.

'Out there' was her studio, a converted chapel at the rear of their garden.

Leo burned the roof of his mouth with the first forkful, ate the rest with plenty of blowing and mouthfuls of water.

He made a mug of tea and helped himself to a slab of flapjack from the tin. Time to make another batch. Maybe half a batch; he didn't eat it as often in hot weather. But Luke liked . . . *Luke's not here. Luke's in a cell. Sharing? Alone? Which was better?*

In the night, Leo had woken and instinctively listened to check if Luke was home, scanning for tell-tale noises: Luke's tread on the stairs, water running in the bathroom, the snick of his door closing. Then remembered that Luke wouldn't be back, not tonight, or next week, or next month.

Perhaps there would be some relief, he thought as he sipped his tea. For him and Ange. A respite from the stress of the last few years. From the battle lines of family discord. From the endless arguments with Luke, the shouting, the sulking, the tears and worry. A breather now the worst thing had happened.

Not the worst thing, he chided himself, thinking of Syke Moss and the lad there.

And they'd yet to see what prison might do to their son.

Ange came back as he was wiping down the worktop.

The landline began to ring. Leo cocked an eyebrow at Ange — barely anyone used that number anymore. Mainly scammers pretending to be the bank or their internet provider, or people pushing smart meters.

Leo answered.

'You proud of yerself, are you?' A woman's voice, venomous. 'What sort of a man are you?'

'What?' Caught off guard, Leo was trying to work out both who it was and what she was on about.

'Grassing up yer own son. Yer not fit to be a parent, ya fucking snitch.'

Leo felt his heart clench and his cheeks heat under the onslaught.

'And it's not just your lad, is it? Sitting in a fucking cell.'

Jack Sherringham's mother. Of course. Rose had rung him when Jack was charged, claiming it was all ridiculous — hadn't the police enough to do with drug gangs and terrorists everywhere? Leo had tried to set her straight; their sons were being drawn into terrorist activities. She'd not cared for that.

Now she hissed, 'You think you're safe cos yer a copper? Well, you've got that wrong, pal. You'll find out soon enough. Grass like you, you want to watch your back. And I'll tell you now—'

Leo hung up. He was shaking.

'What?' Ange said. 'Who was it?'

'Rose Sherringham.'

'Oh, Leo.'

'Not happy,' he said.

'I can imagine.'

'Threatening a police officer,' he said.

Ange's expression sharpened. 'Do we need to worry? Should you report her?'

'Hey.' Leo held up his hands. 'Let's not overreact. The woman's venting. Talking shite.'

'Leo, it's not shite if it ends up in you being hurt.'

Or you. The thought was a knife to his gut.

'This is what they want,' Leo said. 'To frighten us. It's how they work.'

'You think she's caught up in all this far-right bollocks?' Ange pressed her hands to the table, leaning towards him.

'Not necessarily, but she's a believer. She definitely never saw what Luke and Jack and Christopher Hirst did as problematic.'

'You should tell them at work.'

Leo wasn't convinced.

'Think about it, please? I've got enough to worry about,' Ange said.

'I know. I will.'

'I'm going to watch an hour or so then go up,' she said. 'What about you? How was today?'

'Suspicious death. We're pretty sure it's murder. You know Syke Moss?'

'No.'

'Above Thwaite, in Swaledale.'

'OK.' She went to fill the kettle. Gestured. Leo shook his head.

'Body there, a young lad. Well, young man. Asian, I think. Maybe. We've no ID. He's got tattoos, so—'

Ange's mouth opened, the colour drained from her face. Her arm shook and she set the kettle down.

'Ange?'

'The tattoo?' she said, touching her own wrist. 'Leaves, a bracelet of leaves?'

Leo felt the room tilt. Ice up his spine. 'You know him?'

'There's a lad working with us on the protest. Ty. Tyler Prasad. He's camping near Keld. That's not far from Thwaite, is it? I've not been able to get in touch with him today. I kept trying his phone. I thought that was a bit weird. Leo, he can't, he . . .' She was snatching for breath, gasping.

'Hey, hey.' He moved over and eased her into a chair. 'Take it easy, slow breaths.'

She calmed a little. 'Please Leo, it's not him. It's not, is it?' Hands pressed to her cheeks.

'How old's Tyler?'

'Eighteen.' Ange reached for her phone. Fingers trembling as she scrolled through her files and found what she was looking for. She showed the photo to Leo. A group posing for the camera. 'That's Ty, in the middle.'

A beautiful boy, grinning, fingers in a peace sign. Bucket hat on his head. The bracelets, the T-shirt, the tattoo all the same.

'Tell me it's not him,' Ange said. 'Please, Leo. Tell me it's not him.'

* * *

Shan had messaged Erin, *Don't know when I'll finish. I'll get take-out*. Added two kisses after dithering for a moment. She didn't know how to *be* anymore. Work was fine, work was safe, she didn't have to second-guess herself in the job. But home . . . Erin . . . love . . . babies . . .

Erin replied, *Cool xx*

She missed Erin. She missed how they'd been together. The powerful desire that had prompted her to approach Erin in a club one night, their first kiss halfway down some rank steps, the stone sweating with condensation, splashed with spilled drinks. The blaze of Erin's blue eyes.

And everything that followed. The passion and the laughter, moving in together, the long journey to getting pregnant. The future unrolling. A red carpet. A yellow brick road.

And now what? A dead end.

There'd been stupid squabbles. Erin blowing up over housework, Shan arguing for a cleaner. Then the reality that Erin's hours were regular, unchanging; Shan's going from nought to sixty whenever a case broke, meaning home and Erin had to take second place to the investigation. And finally the shock of the miscarriage.

Shan braced herself for the door, key in hand. *This should be my sanctuary*, she thought, her stomach knotting.

Erin was in the living room, the TV on, some legal drama, the smell of alcohol strong in the air.

Shan saw the bottle of vodka. 'I could do with one of those,' she said, keeping it light.

Erin shrugged. 'Help yourself.' She turned off the TV.

'You don't need to—'

'I know.' Erin's voice was low, strained.

'Noodles?' Shan held up the carryout.

Erin shook her head.

I don't need this, Shan thought. *I can do without this*. But she pretended everything was normal, that the atmosphere wasn't thick with resentment and bitterness.

She grabbed a tumbler from the cupboard and helped herself to a slug of vodka, added cranberry from the fridge. She took a swig before unpacking her meal. Then sat beside Erin. *See? I'm not avoiding you.*

The food was good, hot and salty, plenty of mushrooms and tofu.

'How was work?' Shan asked, wiping her mouth with the paper napkin.

Erin turned, such sadness in her gaze that Shan felt her insides lurch.

'When are we going to talk?' Erin said.

'Isn't this—'

Shan tried to object but Erin cut her off, pain tugging at her mouth, puckering her forehead. 'It was my baby too, Shan.'

'I know,' Shan said.

'I wanted it so much.' Erin was on the brink of tears.

'And I didn't?' Shan's anger was electric, an exposed wire, raw.

'I don't think that! I didn't say that,' Erin insisted. 'I never said that. But I need to talk about it, to share.'

'I can't,' Shan said.

'Why?' Erin hit her own thighs with balled fists.

'Because I'm a mess, because I don't know what I feel from one minute to the next.' *I'm drowning.* Her throat closed.

'So tell me. Anything. All of it.'

'I need time. I need more time.'

'No,' Erin said. 'You're putting it off . . . and the more time passes, the harder it gets, the worse it is. I can't reach you.'

Shan felt trapped, hunted. 'Please.' She grabbed her glass, drained it. 'I'm tired, today's been—'

'Don't! Don't tell me about work. Not now.' Erin took a breath. 'Let me tell you how I feel, then. What all this is like for me.'

Shan stood. 'Erin, please.'

Erin rose, pulled Shan into an embrace.

Shan's muscles tightened, her back stiffened. The desire to draw away, to escape, almost overwhelmed her. She could feel the heat from Erin's body, the familiar shape of her, smell her rosemary shampoo and the scent of her skin, the tang of vodka, count the rise and fall of her breaths.

'I can't,' Shan said, pulling away. 'I'm sorry, I just can't.'

'Shan?' Erin was crying, her face flushed.

Shan wiped her nose, shook her head.

Her phone rang, splitting the air.

Erin locked her gaze. A plea. A challenge. *Don't answer.*

Shan turned away, sniffed and wiped at her nose again.

A beat.

Two.

The phone rang on. Then she raised the handset to her ear.

'We got an ID,' Leo said.

'What?' *Stupid.* She knew exactly what he meant.

'Ange knows him, she described him. She has a photograph. He's been working on a project with her.'

'Oh, Leo. Is she OK?'

He gave a heavy sigh. 'He's from Lancaster. His family are there. Ange thinks she has an address somewhere. She's looking now. If not, we can try the electoral roll.'

'What's his name?' Shan heard movement, glanced back to see Erin climbing the stairs. *Oh God.*

'Tyler Prasad,' Leo said. 'Sorry, hang on . . .' She could hear murmuring, then Leo came on the line again. 'We've got it. I don't want to leave it overnight, so—'

'Pick me up,' Shan said. 'Or we can take my car if you want. I'll drive.' She'd only had one drink.

'It's late,' Leo said.

'I'm coming,' Shan said.

'I'll be there in forty,' Leo said.

* * *

44

Washing her face, she was aware of Erin in bed in the adjoining room. She considered telling her she was going out to work again but couldn't face the likely response.

She brushed her teeth and then decided to bring her toothbrush with her and the pile of clean laundry that she'd not yet put away. *Just in case I don't get chance to come back before the morning,* she told herself. Knowing it was not just that.

Her holdall was under the bed, so instead she used two shopping bags from the kitchen and packed her things in there along with her laptop. She grabbed a carton of cranberry juice and her phone charger. Noticed that she was holding her breath.

She sat on the sofa, head in hands. *What are you doing? Sneaking off like some . . . thief.* Was she a thief? What was she stealing? Their happiness? Their future together? But that had gone already, hadn't it? Soured, fractured.

Oh, Mum. If only she could ask her advice. Her mum knew her better than anyone. Always offered sound words of counsel.

'You find it hard to trust, Shan. Maybe you always will.'

'You were left, Shan. You were abandoned. Whatever good reason your birth mother had, that doesn't change your experience. But don't stop trying. Don't give up on trust. Don't cut yourself off from all those possibilities.'

'Be honest with yourself, with others. If you don't know what's going on, say that. None of us have all the answers, not all the time. Never, actually.' She'd laughed.

So why couldn't Shan follow that guidance now?

Shan fetched a sheet of paper from the pad on the fridge. Wrote, *I need a break, Erin. Some time on my own. To sort myself out. I'm so sorry I can't talk about it. Not like you want. Not yet. I'll keep in touch.* She groaned. It sounded so remote, cliched. But she had no idea how to make it any better. *Love, Shan.* She did still love Erin, didn't she? Did she?

She heard a car pull up outside, left the note on the kitchen counter, picked up her bags, turned off the lights and left the house.

* * *

It took just over an hour to reach the address in Lancaster, traffic on the A65 quiet. En route, Leo told Shan what he'd gleaned from Ange.

'Tyler had a place to study climate science in Liverpool, starting later this month. He's been up here for the past week, working on this event they're holding. Free the Fells — a big picnic and march, a trespass.'

'Trespass?' Shan said.

Leo sighed. 'Yep. Peaceful trespass. All about restoring blanket bog. To help with climate change. Ange is liaising with the local force over the route and traffic measures and so on.'

'They're marching on Syke Moss?'

'No, a similar estate. Craven. Also used for grouse shooting,' Leo said.

'Where's Tyler been staying?'

'Campsite outside Keld.'

'Is that near Syke Moss?' Shan said.

'Not far.' Leo blinked hard several times. He wound his window down. Passing lights in the dark was hypnotic, making him even more sleepy.

'Does he have a car?'

'I don't know. They've been meeting in the arts centre in Muker. Ange wasn't sure what he might have been doing on Syke Moss. It wasn't anything to do with the project.'

He related the news from Tom Bairstow about locating the site of the shooting.

'So Tyler was shot and then moved and hidden, like we thought,' Shan said.

'There's something else,' Leo said. 'Carrie Crowther called me. The list of dinner guests . . .'

'Yes?' Shan looked his way.

Leo slowed where the road zig-zagged, the black-and-white chevron signs coming thick and fast.

'Anita had spoken to her. The one who brought us coffee,' Leo said.

'The smiley one,' Shan said.

'Was she? Anyway, Oliver Peel had been booked in for dinner but cried off. He wasn't feeling well and planned to rest in his room. So he wasn't there yesterday evening.'

He watched Shan, her interest piqued, as was his.

'And yet he was on the road back to Patefield Grange this morning. So he sneaked off and spent the night somewhere else? Why? What for?'

'A liaison?' The most obvious explanation.

'Ooh la la,' Shan said. 'Do you know when he cancelled? Was he still around at seven thirty when Helena Duvall heard shots?'

'We need to find that out. Ask Anita.'

'Is the moor clear for access now?' Shan said.

'Tom says yes. I've emailed Beaumont to let him know. And taken up his offer for use of the old Dairy. We'll set up shop there.'

'We can't talk to Oliver Peel if he's off shooting,' Shan said.

'We'll ask him to come back at lunch.'

'OK. Suppose he did use that as an excuse to go back to the moor, what possible reason could he have had to shoot a kid like Tyler?'

'What reason could anyone have?' Leo said.

'Maybe it was just some horrible accident,' Shan said.

'Then why cover it up?' Leo increased speed. *Where are all the moths?* he thought. Once upon a time, driving at night like this, every light source would be mobbed. The windscreen smeared with casualties.

'What do we tell his parents?' Shan said.

'Only the hard facts.' *Oh, and they are hard.* 'Nothing else, not until we know more.'

* * *

The Prasads lived at the far end of a stone-built terrace on a cul-de-sac. Handsome three-storey houses with sash windows and wrought-iron fencing. Lights glowed at some of the properties in the row but theirs was in darkness.

There was no available parking space, so they left the car in the adjoining road and walked back. The neighbourhood was quiet, slumbering.

'Fox.' Leo pointed. They watched as the animal slipped behind a bunch of wheelie bins at the end of an alley.

'So cool,' Shan said.

'We've had one with kits out the back at home,' Leo said. He thought of Jason Tattersall, his mission to kill them. *'Stoats, weasels, crows, foxes . . . snares, shooting, poison.'* Leo remembered stoats from his childhood but the last time he'd seen one was years back.

The Prasads small front garden was full of wildflowers. In the streetlight Leo could make out daisies and cornflowers, clover and poppies. A row of drunken-looking sunflowers teetered at the boundary fence.

Leo imagined the family inside, in bed already perhaps, or watching television with the curtains drawn. Oblivious.

He hated this. Hated to be doing this. Crashing into their lives with the worst of all possible news. A wrecking ball. He hated it but at the same time needed to own it, to witness it with them, to forge a terrible connection. He could have left it to local officers, someone unconnected to the enquiry, to do the death call, and on occasion he had. But most times it was a task he claimed, saw it as his duty.

'OK?' he checked with Shan.

She looked sad, resigned, an unfamiliar heaviness in her eyes. About the task in hand? She gave a nod.

Leo rang the doorbell.

A moment passed then they heard movement within the house. The hall light snapped on, illuminating stained-glass panels in the door. Green leaves and round fruits. Reminiscent of Tyler's tattoo.

A shadow approached the door, then bent down. They heard the sound of a bolt being drawn back. The shadow rose again and the door opened.

The man was tall with fair hair, thinning on top. He looked at them warily, frowned a little.

'Mr Prasad?' Leo said.

'Who are you?' he asked. He had an American accent, or Canadian maybe.

'I'm Detective Inspector Leo Donovan and this is my colleague Detective Constable Shan Young. My identification.'

The man took off his glasses to read Leo's credentials.

'You are Mr Prasad?' Leo said.

'McKenzie,' he said. 'Randall. My wife's name is Prasad. Eesha Prasad.'

'Her son is Tyler?' Leo asked.

'Our son.' Confusion in his eyes gave way to the glassy glint of fear. 'What's wrong?' he said. 'Is Tyler in some sort of trouble?'

'Randall?' A woman's voice came from further inside.

'May we come in?' Leo said.

'Sure . . . er . . . yes.'

Leo glimpsed a collage of photographs on the wall. Most of them featuring Tyler at various ages. The same face as in the photo Ange had shown him, now copied to his phone.

They met his wife at the doorway into the back room.

'It's the police, about Tyler,' Randall said.

'Tyler?'

'Can we sit down?' Leo said gently.

'Oh God.' Eesha Prasad put her hand to her heart, her expression stark with apprehension.

The couple took the sofa, hands clasped. There was only one other seat, a large armchair. Shan nodded to Leo to take it. She stood to one side.

'Can I ask you to look at this photograph. Is that Tyler?' Leo said.

'Yes,' they said in unison.

'I have some very bad news about your son,' Leo said. 'I'm so sorry, Tyler was found dead this morning.'

Eesha made a strangled sound, her fist pressed to her mouth.

'*What?*' Randall blurted.

Leo repeated himself.

'Oh sweet Jesus.'

'No, no. No.' Eesha was shaking her head. 'That can't be right. We just spoke to him yesterday.'

Leo noted that. Something to come back to at a later stage.

'What do you mean dead?' Randall demanded. 'How?'

'Tyler was found on moorland a few miles from where he was camping in the Dales.'

Randall's eyes reddened.

His wife's grip tightened, she bowed forward.

'Was it . . . ? I don't . . . This is crazy,' Randall said.

'I'm sorry,' Leo said again. The atmosphere in the room was thick with shock and confusion. He saw Shan's toes flex and relax in her shoes.

Leo waited, giving the couple as much time as they needed to absorb this initial blow. An earthquake, he thought. The first massive hit, the ground torn up, foundations ripped asunder, a world turned to rubble. Then the aftershocks. Tremors through the years to come. Their lives irreparably ruptured.

It was Eesha who broke the silence. 'I don't understand. Was he taken ill? It could be his heart. My brother, remember my brother? And my uncle as well.' She looked up at Randall, who nodded.

Oh Christ.

'I need to tell you something else, something very difficult. We have reason to believe that Tyler didn't die from natural causes. There is no easy way to say this but Tyler was the victim of a shooting.'

'What?' Randall said. 'A shooting?'

'With a shotgun.' The ruined face, the bloody eye.

Randall gasped. His eyes filled, and he covered his face with his hand, tears spilling through his fingers.

'Shan, please could you make some tea?' Leo said. 'Is that all right?' he asked the couple.

Eesha didn't respond. She was shuddering.

'I'll show you—' Randall began.

'I'll manage, thanks,' Shan said.

Eesha moaned, 'Tyler. Not Tyler. Not my baby.' She burrowed her face into her husband's chest. He rested his chin on the top of her head.

After a while, Eesha stirred. She blew her nose and screwed the tissue up in her fist. She stared at Leo. 'Who did this? Who?'

'We don't know, but I give you my word we're doing everything we can to find out.'

No one spoke for a few minutes. The only sounds were the stuttering breaths of Eesha and her husband and the chink of crockery, the bubbling of the electric kettle, as Shan made drinks in the kitchen.

* * *

An hour and a half later, having explained the protocol for a forensic post-mortem and for one of them to officially identify their son, Leo and Shan took leave of Randall McKenzie and Eesha Prasad.

A crescent moon, sharp, magnesium white, hung above the house amid a dusting of stars. The night was still warm.

'You OK?' Shan said when they reached the car.

'Sure. You?'

'Yes.'

'Home, then.'

'Ah . . .' Shan looked uneasy.

'What?' Leo said.

'I . . . erm . . . I'm not staying at home for a while.'

'Oh . . . right.' Leo felt awkward, unsure how to respond.

'So if you could maybe drop me at a Travelodge or a Premier Inn or something. There's one near—'

'Stay at ours,' he said.

'No, I couldn't.'

'Shan, one night. We've a spare room. Easier all round. And it'll save me the extra driving.'

'Well . . .'

'No arguments. Just say yes. Please?' He was so tired he could drop.

'Yes, please.' Shan gave a wan smile. 'And thank you.'

CHAPTER FOUR

Friday

Shan

It was an early start that morning, on the road before eight. Ange, Leo's wife, appeared as they were preparing to leave.

'You sleep OK?' she asked Shan.

'Yes, thanks,' Shan said. She'd not expected to sleep at all, a strange bed and the mess with Erin on her mind, as well as the buzz of questions she had about the case. But in the end she'd fallen off immediately and woken after a dreamless few hours to the sound of her alarm.

'You knew Tyler?' Shan asked.

Ange nodded. 'Briefly. He was lovely. Bright. And kind and—' She dragged her hands through her hair, a mass of ginger curls. 'His parents. I can't begin to . . . I'd like to meet them,' she said to Leo, who looked taken aback.

'Well, I'm . . . not sure . . . procedure . . .'

'Sod procedure, Leo! Ask them. They'll want to meet me. Ask them. Or I can. Give them my number.' She spoke heatedly and Shan wanted to hide.

'It's just—'

'I was with their son three days ago. He was here, work-ing, planning. Happy and excited. We went for a pint after the workshop. If that was Luke, I'd want to talk to whoever had seen him recently. To know how he was. To find some good memor—' She broke off. Sniffed hard.

'This was Tuesday?' Shan asked.

'Yes,' Leo said. 'Ange is going to give us a statement.'

'Was it just the two of you at the workshop?' Shan said.

'No. Eight in all.'

'Visiting students, like Tyler?' Shan said.

'Mostly local people, activists, Green councillors, couple of sixth-formers. There was one other student visitor, a film-maker. Lydia. She's up from Manchester. In fact, she's staying at the same campsite. I can give you her details.'

'Please,' Shan said.

'Her name is Lydia Siemens. She's Deaf. She can lip-read and she's got a transcription app for calls but you might be best texting first.'

Shan took the number. 'Did Tyler have a car?' she asked Ange.

'No. Not here, anyway. He had a bike he used to travel about.'

'OK. Thanks,' Shan said.

'Will you see them today?' Ange said. 'His parents.'

'Yes,' Leo said.

'Please, just give them my number. Let them decide if they want to talk to me or not.'

'OK.'

'And the group. We've another session today. I don't want to cancel — people will need to come together. Can I tell them what's happened? No way can I stand there and pretend I don't know anything.'

'When is it?' Leo said.

'Three o'clock.'

Leo looked at Shan.

'We'll be going public as soon as we've got formal ID and the PM report is in. That should be before three,' she said.

'Hang fire till you hear from me?' Leo said to Ange. 'I'll message.'

'OK.'

Shan phoned Oliver Peel once they were in the car but he didn't pick up. 'He may think it's a spammer,' she said, so she rang reception at Patefield Grange and spoke to the house manager, Carrie Crowther. 'Please could you ask Mr Peel to call me as soon as possible. He's not answering.'

'I will. He's in having breakfast,' Carrie said.

'Is Anita there?'

'I can find her.'

'Thank you.'

When Anita came on the line, Shan thanked her for correcting the list of dinner guests and asked what time Oliver Peel had cancelled his dinner reservation.

'Half past five,' she said. 'I'd just had my break and chef was pleased because he wouldn't be losing a cover last minute when the food was already prepped.'

It was sweltering in the car already. 'Can I put the aircon on?' Shan asked.

'You can — not sure it's fit for purpose,' Leo said.

He was right about that. She held her hand over the vent on the dashboard and there was no way you could call the weak stream of air that came out anything close to cold. At least she wasn't stuck in uniform in this heat. Instead she wore a light cotton shirt and linen trousers, the coolest things she owned that were suitable for work.

Ten minutes later, Oliver Peel rang. Shan asked if he could meet them back at the Grange at lunchtime.

'Why's that?' He sounded discomfited.

'Just part of our routine enquiries,' Shan said.

Leo gave a thumbs-up. The bland statement meant there was no risk of tipping him off when he just might turn out to be a suspect.

* * *

The campsite was in a valley to the west of Syke Moss. Two fields, part of a farm, now given over to tents and campervans.

An annexe to the old farmhouse housed the reception. Signs warned about barbecues and wildfires, gave a list of emergency numbers and local services, a schedule of charges and a notice about noise nuisance on site.

Shan had a flashback — she and Erin camping up in the Lakes, near Keswick. A rare clear night after days of rain, when they'd lain on the ground and counted stars. Talked for the first time about starting a family. The ways they might do that. 'I'd like to carry the baby,' Shan had said. 'The first one, anyway.'

Erin had laughed. 'I am *so* glad you said that.'

'You wouldn't?'

'No way. I'd love us to be mums together but I don't ever want to be pregnant.'

'Perfect match,' Shan said.

Then Erin had yelped. 'Mossie! I'm getting eaten alive here.'

Shan shelved the memory as the owner came through to the counter. A woman with iron-grey curls and silver-and-pink-framed glasses.

'We're investigating a serious incident involving Tyler Prasad,' Shan said after making introductions. 'He was staying here?'

'That's right.'

'I'm sorry to say Tyler's been the victim of a violent attack.'

'Oh no!' she said. 'Is he all right?'

'I'm afraid not. He didn't survive,' Shan said.

'Oh good God.' Shan could see the shock on the woman's face. She shook her head, hand covering her mouth. Sudden death rippled out like this, affecting so many people.

The bell over the door clanged and a woman carrying freezer packs came in. 'Morning, Mandy.'

'Sheila.'

'Didn't sleep a wink, boiled alive in that van. Just goes on and on, doesn't it? I'll just stick these in here.' She put the packs in the chest freezer at the side of the room, paused on her way out as if to ask a question, but apparently sensing the tension in the atmosphere thought better of it and left. 'We'd appreciate it if you'd keep that to yourself for now. Until identity has been officially confirmed,' Shan said.

'Yes, of course. How awful.' She looked from Shan to Leo. 'But where?'

'Up on the moor,' Shan said.

'I can't believe it.'

'When did you last see Tyler?' Shan asked.

'Wednesday, I think. Can I . . . ?' She gestured to the computer. She looked something up, then said, 'Yes, Wednesday. I checked his friend in earlier and I saw them talking by the bike store.'

'His friend Lydia?' Shan said.

'No, Molly. Molly Unwin? Lydia arrived last week, like Tyler.'

'What time did you see them on Wednesday?' Shan said.

She thought about it for a moment. 'Six thirty. About then. Molly's in the second field. Her car's not there at the moment, so she must be out.'

'OK. Can you ask Molly to call us when she's back?' Shan passed her a card. 'And we'll need to look at Tyler's tent. And can you keep it off-limits for now?'

'Yes. His pitch is number eight. It's on the far side of the field, a green dome tent.'

'And if we want to talk to Lydia?'

'She's at nine, the next one over.'

'Thank you.'

They walked across the site. Sheep bleating in the next field. The smell of frying bacon and dung mingled in the air. Shan could feel the sun on her scalp, fierce already.

A message came through from her dad. *Sunday? xx*

Her stomach flipped. She'd have to tell him about Erin. Explain that the monthly Sunday get-togethers would just be the two of them. For now, anyway. Forever? She felt sick at the thought.

Rain check. Will call later xx

Shan had already missed two calls from Erin. She was relieved that her phone had been on silent and she hadn't needed to make a decision about whether to answer. Erin hadn't left a message, so it couldn't be anything urgent, not some crisis with the house or a medical emergency. *I'll text her later*, Shan thought. *Saying what, though?*

A red admiral dipped among the nettles by the wall and landed, opening its wings wide. A pop of black and red and white on the green.

They found Lydia outside her tent, seated in a low camping chair, bent over a laptop. She wore short brown dungarees, a lime-green T-shirt. She glanced up and scrambled to her feet as they approached. 'You texted me about Tyler?' A slight thickness in her voice.

'Yes,' Shan said.

'He wasn't here yesterday, didn't come back last night. I tried his phone but it was off. I thought maybe he'd stayed with one of the others but his bike's still in the shed. Has something happened?'

'Lydia, I'm so sorry,' Shan said, 'but Tyler has been killed.'

'What? No!' Alarm and disbelief flooded her eyes.

Shan kept herself calm, steady.

'But how?'

'He's been shot.'

'No.' Lydia covered her eyes for a moment. 'Is it a hate crime?'

Shan's mind flew to Luke and those like him. She looked away, preparing her next words, but remembered to face Lydia when she did speak. 'We don't know, we've a lot to find out. You can help us?'

'Yes, yes. Anything,' Lydia said.

'When did you last see Tyler?'

'Wednesday, we were both at the arts centre, we'd done a workshop there the day before and agreed what we'd be making. So we were there, then Ty rode back here. I was going to get some things in Hawes and call at a launderette then get a meal.' She paused, obviously trying to concentrate while knocked sideways by the grim news. 'I got back later, had a shower, and Tyler's tent was already zipped up. I thought he was in bed.'

But he was already up there on the moor.

'I haven't seen him since. I thought he might be at the session today and if he wasn't I could ask the others.'

'Did you ask Molly?'

'Who?'

'Tyler's friend — she's camping here.'

Lydia frowned.

'Arrived Wednesday,' Leo prompted.

'I don't know her.'

'Was he planning to go anywhere on Wednesday evening?' Shan asked, then realised Lydia wasn't watching her, wouldn't have caught the question. Shan waited for her to look up, then repeated it.

'No, but he liked to walk when he could. Taking photos.'

'Anywhere in particular?'

'Just round here, there's paths in every direction,' Lydia said.

'And he wasn't worried about anything? Nothing out of the ordinary had happened?' Shan said.

'No, nothing. He was great. He was really—' She stopped again. The reality of the situation breaking over her afresh.

'We've not found Tyler's phone,' Leo said. 'It might be in his tent.'

'He'd never leave it. He's got a really good camera on there.'

They turned their attention to Tyler's tent.

Shan took photographs first of the untouched tent, then again once they'd opened it. There was nothing remarkable to see. Sleeping bag and pillow, bag of clothes. Toiletries. A basic camp kitchen, small enough for him to fit into panniers. A laptop, mouse and headphones.

But no phone, no wallet, no keys.

They put the laptop and mouse into an evidence bag.

'What's this?' Leo showed Lydia a black rectangular device.

'A power bank, charger for his phone and laptop.' Her mouth worked and she rubbed at her forehead.

'Are you going to be OK?' Shan said.

She shrugged. 'I didn't even know him very well but I just . . . It's not real.'

'I know,' Shan said. 'It's a terrible shock. An awful thing.'

'The workshop today . . . I don't know whether Ange and the others . . .'

'We've spoken to Ange and she'll let everyone at that meeting know what's happened.'

'You've seen her?' Lydia said.

'She's Leo's wife,' Shan said.

Lydia blinked. 'Donovan. Right.' She obviously remembered his name from the text they'd sent asking to talk to her. 'OK. Oh God.' She looked away across the field, arms wrapped around herself as if for protection.

When she looked back, Shan said, 'We need to leave his things here for now and not disturb them. The campsite know. Thank you again for your help. And if this all feels too difficult, maybe get in touch with someone you can be with?'

'Thanks,' Lydia said, her eyes glistening.

* * *

Leo

When they arrived at Patefield Grange, Carrie Crowther took them to the old Dairy. It was painstakingly renovated and retained a rustic feel with lime-washed stone walls and black wooden roof beams. Leo breathed in the chalky smell of paint.

'We've rigged up some tables and chairs,' Carrie Crowther said. She gave them the Wi-Fi password. 'Let me know if you need anything else.'

'Thank you,' Leo said.

'Is there any news?'

'We know who the boy was. We hope to be releasing that information later today.'

'Right.' She hesitated. 'Is it someone local?'

Leo wondered what lay at the root of the question. A concern that she might know the victim? General curiosity? Or something to do with the estate's reputation — would it be better or worse if the victim was from the area?

'No, not a local,' Leo said.

Until lunch, they spent time working on their laptops collating and updating all the information on the case.

A video call came through from the pathologist, Dr James. Shan stood to watch over Leo's shoulder.

'An otherwise healthy adolescent male,' Dr James said after the preliminaries. 'Extensive external lacerations and penetrating wounds from lead pellets fired from close range. Puncture of the carotid artery, resulting in severe haemorrhage. Three pellets lodged in the frontal lobe entering through the orbital cavity, the eye, precipitating severe cerebral oedema. This swelling coupled with the blood loss is your cause of death.'

'Close range?' Leo said.

'A matter of feet.'

'Thank you.' Leo ended the call. He turned to Shan. 'I don't think you accidentally fire a gun so near to someone. Whoever pulled the trigger did it deliberately. They were close to Tyler, they could see him, talk to him. It's not like he was shot at a distance by mistake.'

'But the only people Tyler knew up here were the campaign group,' Shan said. 'And he only met them last week. So it's not like he's any enemies or history here.'

'OK.' Leo pushed away from his desk so he could look at her straight on without aggravating his neck. 'A stranger, then? A chance encounter?'

'Yes. Because if he'd planned to meet someone I reckon he'd have mentioned it to Lydia at least.'

'Unless he was meeting them for dubious reasons.' Important to consider every possibility.

A knock at the door interrupted them.

'Come in,' Shan called and racer boy Oliver Peel appeared wearing a khaki shirt and gilet, cotton trousers and leather boots. He carried a gun case. Gun inside, presumably.

'Have you eaten?' Leo asked, aware he was peckish himself and wanting the man to be as comfortable as possible so he couldn't later claim he'd been poorly treated.

'I'll grab a bite after this.'

'It may take a while,' Leo said. 'If you'd like to fetch a sandwich.'

'No. No.' He set the gun down and settled into one of the spare chairs. Gave them a brief smile. 'So?'

'As you know,' Leo said. 'We asked anyone who left the Grange at any point after the final shoot on Wednesday to tell us.'

'Yes.'

Leo paused, waiting to see if the silence might pressure him into a response. Nada.

Leo looked at Shan.

'You weren't at dinner,' she said.

'Oh that, yes. Feeling a bit iffy. Thought I was coming down with something.' He rolled his eyes, mocking himself.

'Where were you?' Shan said.

'In my room.'

'You missed breakfast too,' Leo said.

'Slept late. Must have needed it.' Peel grinned.

'Still in your room?' Shan said.

'Yes.' A sliver of irritation in his reply.

'Can you recall when you last saw anyone on Wednesday?' Leo said.

'Tea after the shoot, I suppose.'

'When was that?'

'Half past four, five,' Peel said.

'And yesterday, when did you come out of your room?' Leo said.

'Late morning. I got a message saying the morning shoot was off so I just hung around until we were all asked to go to the Orangery.'

'You're telling us that between five o'clock Wednesday and midday yesterday you were in your room?'

'That's right.'

'You're sure about that?' Leo said.

'Yes.' A spike of annoyance.

'You see, Mr Peel, we have reason to believe you weren't here yesterday morning. That you were actually on the B6479.'

'What? That's ridiculous.' He gave a humourless laugh.

'Your car registration number?' Leo said.

'What exactly is going on?' Peel said.

'That's what we're trying to establish,' Leo replied. He could feel himself growing hotter, exasperated. The air in the room seemed to have thinned, the atmosphere now oppressive. Leo nodded to Shan, who opened the video on her phone of Peel's dangerous driving and turned the screen to show him.

He watched, lips compressed, a flush reddening his cheeks.

'That was at eight forty-five yesterday morning when you claim to have been in your room,' Shan said.

'I . . .' He inflated his cheeks, exhaled. 'I was just . . . This is nothing to do . . . Really, I . . .' He was flailing.

'Shall we start again, Mr Peel?' Leo said. 'With the truth this time?'

He bristled. 'And I have to answer these questions, do I?'

'No. No, you don't,' Leo said. 'But that might give me reason to think that you're hiding something. And if that was the case, given I'm investigating a murder—' Leo saw Peel swallow at the word — 'I could arrange for a formal interview under caution. You would obviously be entitled to legal representation.'

'No!' he said. 'Christ, no! Look, I went to Morecambe, right? I drove to Morecambe. OK? I stayed over. Drove back in the morning.'

'Why?' Leo said.

Peel sighed. Crossed his arms.

'You'd paid to stay at Patefield Grange, so why travel to Morecambe and stay there?' Leo's money was still on an affair, though he'd no idea if Peel was married or single. 'Were you visiting someone?'

'No!' As though that was a repulsive idea. 'I went to the casino. The Empress Hotel.'

'Can anyone corroborate this?'

'The hotel will.'

'We will check,' Leo said.

'Do. I've nothing to hide.'

Moot point.

Leo waited a moment, hoping the man's irritation would subside. 'And what were you doing at the casino?' Leo said.

'Blackjack. Some roulette.' He wasn't smiling now. Face grim, resentful. Pale blue eyes drilling into Leo's.

'What time did you leave here?' Shan said.

'Eight o'clock.'

'And what were you doing between five o'clock and eight o'clock?'

'I was. In. My. Room.'

Leo could feel the man's temper bubbling.

'You didn't return to Syke Moss?' Shan said.

'No! No, of course not. Fucking — no!'

Leo could imagine Shan's hypothesis. Peel goes onto the moor with his gun, meets Tyler and shoots him, conceals his body, taking anything that might identify him, then drives to Morecambe in an attempt to distance himself and create an alibi. So why not tell them from the outset that he wasn't on the premises?

'No one can vouch for your whereabouts between five o'clock and your arrival at the Empress?' Shan said.

'No, but I'm telling you the truth.' Something dawned on him. He raised his chin. 'Look, ask the keeper. I was getting into my car and I saw Jason. I saw Jason in the yard. He probably saw me. I think he saw me. Ask him.'

'This was at eight?'

'Yes. There's no way I could get that vehicle onto the moor, not without wrecking the suspension. And I had no reason to go tramping about in the dark anyway.' He was anxious to prove he'd left in the car and not on foot but he didn't seem to be aware that the critical time period was before eight. Was that because he didn't know when Tyler had been shot? In which case, he wasn't their perpetrator. Or was he being clever in feigning ignorance?

'There's nothing you can think of to place you in your room in the couple of hours before you left?' Shan said.

Beads of perspiration ringed his forehead. 'No. Can't you check my phone, the GPS?'

'That wouldn't narrow it down enough,' Leo said.

'I was there. I swear. Then I drove off.' He gestured, palms up, fingers curled — *look, nothing to hide*. 'The courier!' he almost shouted.

'Courier?' Shan said.

'At the bottom of the lane. I wasn't expecting any traffic and this guy on a motorbike appears out of nowhere, comes round the bend and I only just miss him.'

'He was a courier?' Shan said.

'Yes. One of those people who bring takeaway. They have those big square boxes for the food.'

'Like Deliveroo?' Shan said.

'Exactly. But not that. Different colour. Purple and white stripes.'

'We'll speak to Jason Tattersall and ask if he saw you. And we'll find this courier,' Leo said.

'Sure. They'll tell you the same.' His shoulders dropped, a sign of relief.

Leo caught a whiff of the man's sweat, rank. A marker of the stress he was under.

'Is there anything you wish to add?' Leo asked.

'No. That's everything.' He made to pick up the gun, then stopped. Sat forward, hands on his knees. 'Look, this . . . it doesn't need to go any further, does it?'

'This?' Shan said.

'The visit to the casino,' he said tightly.

'Not if everything you tell us can be verified,' Shan said.

'Right. Good.'

Once he'd left, Shan said, 'Why is he so bothered about people knowing he went to the casino?'

'Gambling problem? Feels ashamed?' Leo suggested.

'But who is he worried might hear about it? Is he married?'

'Don't know.'

'You know what else is weird?' Shan said, leaning back in her chair. 'They're all sitting down to a five-course meal. Then who orders takeaway?'

'Staff?' Leo said.

'Most kitchen and waiting staff would be fed, it's a perk of the job. I did two years at a French place in Leeds.'

'Nice food?'

'Put me off croque monsieurs for life.'

He laughed. 'Could be the ground staff, or someone in the cottages, getting a pizza. One of the keepers?'

'It'd be easier to ask the courier than go all round the houses,' Shan said.

'Cottages.'

'Nitpicker.' Shan shook her head. Leo pretended to be wounded. 'Look, the takeout place will have a record. If we can find the company. Let's go grab some lunch and ask Carrie Crowther if she knows them. If not, we can google it. There can't be that many places do takeaway in striking distance. Not up here.'

CHAPTER FIVE

Friday

Shan

From the vestibule in the big house, Shan could hear a wall of sound: a hubbub of voices and the clatter of cutlery coming from the Orangery, where the shooting party were having lunch. Swapping stories of prowess, no doubt. Who shot the most birds.

'We could order at the bar,' she suggested to Leo. 'And eat on the terrace.'

'Good idea.'

She glimpsed racer boy Oliver Peel and petite Helena Duvall by one of the alcoves near reception. An unexpected intimacy in the way she touched his arm, the inclination of his head towards hers.

'That looks cosy,' she said, drawing Leo's attention to the couple.

'You think there's something going on?'

'You don't?'

Helena pushed Peel away, hand on his shoulder. A playful move, laughing. Perhaps she was just flirting, a respite from the sour company of her husband.

'Question is, does it have any bearing on the investigation?' Leo said.

'You're no fun at all sometimes,' Shan teased him.

His mouth twitched into a smile.

The bar was busy too but Shan saw it was mainly staff. A lot of youngsters — the beaters she guessed — and two of the keepers sitting with them: Ian Kerrigan, who towered over his companions and had a booming voice to match his size, and Niall Tattersall but no Jason.

'We should catch Jason Tattersall before they start again,' she said to Leo as they waited to order. 'What if he hasn't come back for lunch? I'll check if he's around. Can you get me the goat's cheese salad and a tropical smoothie and an espresso?'

'Hedging all bets?' Leo said.

'Something like that.' The heat was making her feel more lethargic than she liked. The espresso would give her a boost of energy after her food.

The group erupted at some punchline of Kerrigan's. Shan found the way it was business-as-usual disconcerting. There didn't seem to be any of the dislocation and concern that most communities feel when someone is killed in their midst. But perhaps this was a show for the paying guests, and behind closed doors these local kids and their families were as disturbed by Tyler's death as anyone else.

Kerrigan's grin faded and he stiffened, stroking his wide beard, when he saw her approach.

A ripple of curiosity ran round the circle. They wouldn't all necessarily know who she was, not the casual workers who'd had their shifts withdrawn when yesterday's shoot was cancelled. Some of them swapped glances, sharing the unspoken question.

Shan bent besides Kerrigan so she could make herself heard. 'Is Jason about?'

'Yes. Somewhere.' His voice was deep, rumbling.

'We'd like a word with him,' Shan said. 'When do you start back?'

'Leaving in forty-five.' He nodded to the clock above the bar.

'Thanks. If you see him before I do, can you let him know we're on the terrace?'

She straightened to go and one of the group, a girl with a shock of vivid crimson hair and a pierced septum, said, 'You the police?'

'That's right,' Shan said, wondering if there was a follow-up question.

'They're saying it's murder.' She swung her phone round to show her peers.

So, the press release was out. Tyler's parents must have done their ID.

'That's right,' Shan said. She looked round them all and added, 'If anyone can help us in any way at all, please call one of those numbers. Or come find me, Shan Young.'

The mood among them had turned sombre, but a snatch of song and a burst of laughter from the other end of the bar broke the spell.

Niall Tattersall edged his way out from the middle of the group.

'How's it going?' he asked.

She appreciated the enquiry. But what to answer? 'There's a lot to do.'

'Right.' He gave her a look of sympathy.

'Have you seen Jason?' she said.

'He might be outside. I can look. I need to . . .' He had a cigarette in hand.

'That's OK. I'll come out with you.'

A quick scan showed the yard was empty, though Shan could hear a dog barking and the natter from a radio somewhere.

'You want one?' he offered. He was relaxed. A noticeably different energy to his brother, who always seemed wound up tight and about to explode.

'I don't smoke,' Shan said.

'What was he doing up here, then?' Niall asked. 'The lad. Holiday, was it?' He flicked his lighter, sucked at the flame.

'Volunteering. A nature project.'

Niall shook his head. 'Somewhere like this — we never have that sort of trouble.'

'Jason said your father was a gamekeeper here.'

'Yes. It was the only work he could find. We had a farm. On the southern stretch.' He thumbed over his shoulder. 'Foot and mouth did for that, 2001. The estate offered to buy us out. Cheap as chips for them. Dad refused at first but when they offered him the job and one of the cottages, rent free. Well . . .' He shrugged.

He dragged on his cigarette. 'Never saw myself staying. My dad, Jason, they took to it. Never tried owt else. Thought I'd strike out on my own. Did for a while. Bar work, driving — even so, rents are that high I had to live at home. Drive back late at night, set out early in the morning. Keep a car on the road an' all. Then a job came up here. No-brainer.' He shrugged. Shan found it hard to tell whether he was pleased about that or simply resigned.

'You're not from round here?' he said.

Shan waited a beat. 'Leeds.'

'Different growing up there,' Niall said. Shan relaxed. 'We'd go into Leeds, clubbing and that. Worked there once, packing at a warehouse.' He grimaced.

'You didn't like it?' Shan asked.

'It was shite.' He gave a grin. 'Least this is outdoors.'

She nodded. 'If you do see Jason, tell him we're having lunch outside.'

'I will.'

***

Shan found Leo out on the top terrace; he'd picked a table with a parasol.

The pool was sited at the bottom of the terraced gardens. It was decorated with a large floor mosaic of Yorkshire's white rose. A yellow centre with five white petals and five green sepals on a blue background. Shan remembered the word sepals from biology. A couple of the sunloungers were occupied, guests making the most of the good weather.

Shan fantasised briefly about going for a dip. Imagined the bliss of sinking into cold, clear water.

'The news is out,' Leo said. 'I've rung Randall and Eesha to tell them we'll be over this afternoon.'

Shan pulled up the press release, brightening her display to counter the brilliant sunlight. It was important to know exactly what the public were being told.

Yorkshire police have today launched a murder enquiry and released the identity of a man found on Syke Moss moor on Thursday. Tyler Prasad, an eighteen-year-old student from Lancaster, was visiting the area and died from shotgun wounds. Police are appealing for help, asking anyone with information to come forward. Tyler's parents, Randall McKenzie and Eesha Prasad, describe their son as a gifted, compassionate person who cared deeply about climate justice and would go out of his way to help anyone. DI Leo Donovan, leading the investigation, described the crime as a brutal tragedy, devastating for Tyler's family and friends, and a shock for all in the local community. He appealed for anyone with any information to contact the police.

Anita brought their food.

'That's great, thanks,' Shan said. 'Anita, do you know of a takeaway round here that uses purple and white boxes?'

'Oh, that'll be Vinnie's. They're down in Reeth.'

'They any good?' Shan asked.

Anita creased her nose. 'This is better.' She tipped her head towards their meals.

'I'm sure it is,' Leo said.

'Anita? A word.' It was Beaumont.

Anita flushed. Shan wondered if she'd done something wrong. Let the side down.

Beaumont caught sight of Leo and Shan. 'Ah.' He waved. 'Everything all right?'

'Good, yes,' Shan said.

'Dairy OK?'

'Yes, thanks,' Leo said.

'I'll get on.' Anita smiled. 'I'll find you later about those shifts?' she said to Beaumont.

'Sure.'

When they were alone, again Shan said, 'This is bizarre.'

'This?' Leo said.

She waved her hand, taking in the idyllic setting; the beautifully served food; the bright, clear day; the lavender, box and rosemary hedging busy with bees and butterflies; the pool (the colour of Erin's eyes, she thought with a thump to her gut). 'And they're all carrying on like nothing's happened.'

Leo took a sip of his tea. 'Life goes on.'

Shan ate a forkful of beetroot and cheese, the salt and tang, the earthy taste making her mouth water.

Below, one of the sunbathers, wearing a neon orange bikini, rose, ditched her sunglasses and walked to the pool. She dived in, shattering the white rose, twisting the bloom into a thousand glittering diamonds.

* * *

With minutes to go until the party left for the grouse moor, there was no sign of Jason Tattersall, so they went in search.

Leo pointed him out in the yard, in conversation with the other keepers.

Shan wondered whether Niall had passed her message on. And whether his brother had ignored it.

'Mr Tattersall,' Shan said. 'You have a moment?'

'Not really, no. We're heading out.'

'It won't take long,' she said.

'I'll catch you at tea,' he told her.

Shan hardened the tone in her voice. 'We don't want to wait.'

He looked like he was going to refuse, agitation in the set of his jaw and an intake of breath, but he moved out of earshot of his workmates and said, 'What is it, then?'

'Wednesday night. Do you recall seeing anyone out here around eight o'clock?' Shan said.

'What? No.' His face creased in irascibility.

'You sure?'

'I wasn't here at eight. I was on my way to Richmond.'

'Why?' Shan said.

'To pick up parts for the car.'

'At that time of night?' Shan asked.

'It's my cousin's place, Cooper's. No problem for him.'

'And before that?'

He gritted his teeth. 'At home.'

'Between what times?'

'Christ! Six till seven.' Everyone was short-tempered with the incessant heat but was there more behind his outburst?

'Can anyone confirm that?'

He looked furious. 'The wife.'

Shan could see Ian Kerrigan glancing their way, the big man's face hard to read.

'Is she here? Can we speak to her?'

'Christ sakes,' he said.

Beaumont started the Argocat, ready to ferry people to the butts, calling to the guests. The PE teacher rounding up his team. Rafe Duvall stood with his wife and two other visitors. The men were wearing tweed flat caps, like Shan's grandpa had done. Helena was speaking to one, smiling and nodding, but there was something off about the man's body language. A rigidity in all three men, in fact. Perhaps Rafe was being a dick again.

'Come on, then,' Tattersall said tersely. He signalled to his colleagues, raised his voice. 'Give me ten.' Then strode across the yard to the lane leading to the cottages.

There were half a dozen homes, in two terraced rows facing each other. Two larger houses, semi-detached buildings, sat beyond. One of these was Tattersall's.

He opened the door and called, 'Bex? Becky?' He turned. 'She'll be round back.'

Shan and Leo followed him along the side of the house to the rear, where a woman was sitting reading in a recliner under a huge beech tree. She was heavily pregnant and wore a loose white sundress.

Shan's response was visceral, a lurch of envy and a backwash of grief making her feel weak, her bones softer but her guts tense. Would it always be like this? Haunted?

'Jason?' Becky said, putting her paperback down.

'It's the police. They want to ask you—'

'DC Young, Mrs Tattersall,' Shan interrupted. It was important Tattersall shouldn't give too much away. He could be trying to tip her the wink, if he wasn't being straight with them. 'Can you tell us where you were at eight o'clock on Wednesday night?'

'Here.' Her ankles were red and badly swollen, the creases white. They looked tight and hot.

'Was anyone with you?'

'No. Why?' Her voice wobbled.

'It's all right,' Tattersall said.

'What time did your husband get in from work?' Shan said.

'Just after six.' She looked from Shan to Jason, apparently puzzled by the questions.

'And did he go out at all that evening?' Shan said.

'Yes. He'd gone to collect some parts for the car.'

'When did he leave?'

'About seven. Why are you asking me this? What's going on?' She rocked side to side, trying to get up. Her breath uneven.

'It's all right,' Tattersall said again. 'You stay put.'

'Jason?' She sounded tearful.

Tattersall turned to Shan. 'Satisfied?' he said hotly. 'She's not meant to get stressed. She's on bed rest.'

Shan's eyes prickled. She was too hot even in the shade of the tree. The calculator at the back of Shan's head was always

74

ticking over. She'd be six months along now if she hadn't lost the baby.

'Thank you,' Shan said to Becky Tattersall, fighting to keep her voice level.

'Yes, thank you,' Leo said. 'When are you due?' he said warmly.

'Two weeks.'

'Your first?'

'Yeah.'

'They're usually late,' Leo said. 'Ours was.'

He was trying to calm her, Shan saw that, but she wanted to disappear. To stick her fingers in her ears and close her eyes and shut it all out.

'We tried all sorts,' Leo said. 'Curry — and swimming.'

'They'll induce me if I go over. 'Cos of the swelling.'

'Good luck with it,' Leo said. 'All the best.'

'How many have you got?' Becky said.

'Just the one.' He spoke as though nothing was wrong, no hint of the trouble his son was in.

Shan felt weepy. *Stupid! Concentrate. Do your job.* She cleared her throat. 'We'll leave you be,' she said. 'Thank you too, Mr Tattersall.'

Tattersall gave a curt nod, his eyes full of resentment.

'So, are the Tattersalls lying?' Leo said as they walked to the Dairy. 'Or is Oliver Peel?'

'Or all three of them?' Shan said.

* * *

Leo

Leo messaged Ange to tell her it was fine to talk with the campaign group about Tyler, and if anyone knew anything that could help the investigation to encourage them to get in touch.

Unlocking the car, he noticed movement in the sky over the moors. A drone. Always something insect-like, creepy, in the devices.

He drew Shan's attention to it. 'That'll be the press.'

'You think?'

'Yes. Word's out — there's going to be a lot of interest.'

As they set off for Lancaster, Shan called Cooper's garage, who confirmed that Jason Tattersall had collected parts for his car on Wednesday and had arrived sometime after eight.

She then rang the Empress Hotel in Morecambe. Leo listened while she argued with the receptionist about giving out personal information. Her voice tightened with impatience as she asked to speak to the manager. Then, 'I *will* put it in writing. Your email, then? . . . And address it to . . . ? Thank you.'

She typed fiercely, then groaned and sat back.

'Jobsworth?' Leo said.

'Data bloody protection.'

'How're you doing?' He could sense she was troubled.

Shan sighed, raised her hands to grip the headrest. 'I'm fine,' she said, sounding anything but. Leo wondered whether to probe any further, ask where she'd stay tonight or if she'd spoken to her partner. She pre-empted him. 'On the way back, can you drop me at mine? I want to collect my car and pick up some stuff.'

'Sure. You can always stay—'

'No, I'll see my dad tonight, stay there. Thanks, though.'

Leo's phone rang. Matthew Booth, his senior officer.

'Matthew?'

'What can you tell me?' DCI Booth said.

Blimey! Give us chance! Leo thought. 'We're waiting on forensics. We've a person of interest among the guests at the grouse shoot but nothing solid yet.'

'This is a disaster. For the tourists, the local economy, the reputation of the area, but particularly for the force. We have to be seen to be giving it a hundred and ten percent, especially as the victim is a person of colour.'

Especially given our dismal track record on racist policing, Leo supplied silently. He resented the implication that he and Shan were not already working their arses off, doing the best job they could.

'You know how easily the media could spin this,' Matthew went on. 'We have to wrap it up pronto. Keep me posted.'

'Will do,' Leo said curtly. He turned to Shan and rolled his eyes. Booth wasn't a bad boss, wasn't great either, and Leo could imagine their chief super had been breathing down Booth's neck and he was just passing the message down the ladder.

* * *

Tyler's parents bore the stunned, drained look of the recently bereaved.

'Eesha's sister's here,' Randall said. 'We're in the yard. Where do you want to—'

'Out there is fine,' said Leo.

The back garden was a riot of greenery. A bright green hop plant scrambled over the pergola directly outside the house, providing shade for the seating area. The planting was dense and varied. Grasses, shrubs, wildflowers and herbs with a path of stepping stones meandering between. An apple tree stood at the bottom, laden with fruit.

'They're here,' Randall said.

Eesha was sitting, leaning into her sister, head on her shoulder. She'd been crying. She straightened up. 'Padma, this is . . . erm, oh God—'

'Leo and Shan,' Leo said.

'Listen,' Padma said, 'if you can spare me for half an hour, I'll go get the milk and bread.'

'And brandy,' Randall said.

'And brandy and beer, OK.' She tried to smile but her lips trembled. She drew a quick breath, kissed Eesha on the cheek and left.

Randall took her place and Leo and Shan sat on the other bench seats. Reclaimed wood, Leo saw, with bright batik cushions.

'This is beautiful,' Shan said.

'Tyler designed it,' Randall said.

'With your help,' Eesha said. 'A garden for the wildlife.'

Goldfinch and great tits darted about the apple tree and small honeybees drowsed among the flowers.

Leo spotted the straw cone in the far corner. 'Is that a bee skep?'

'Eesha's the beekeeper,' Randall said.

There was a moment's silence. Leo let it settle. He wouldn't rush them. He was acutely aware that they'd come fresh from identifying their son's body. He pictured Luke on a trolley, still, waxen, lips tinged blue. Pushed the thought away.

He could smell fennel, a spicy aniseed scent and something sweeter, perhaps from the honeysuckle that scrambled through the hedge.

'So what now?' Randall said.

'We'd like to talk to you and find out more about Tyler, especially over these last few days,' Leo said.

'Oh, do you want a drink?' Eesha said in a rush as though she'd just noticed afresh that they were there. 'We've no milk.'

'No, thanks,' Shan said.

'We're fine,' Leo said. 'You mentioned you'd spoken to Tyler on Wednesday?'

'That's right,' Randall said. 'He rang us . . . me . . .'

'Was that unusual?' Leo said. When was the last time Luke called him? At best he'd get a text: *out of petrol, can you come get me, I need £20 for tonight.*

'Not unusual but not frequent either. Tyler needed cash,' Randall said.

'Much?' said Leo.

'Oh no, just to get by for the next week or so. He's not working while he's doing the campaign—' Randall stopped abruptly. 'Was doing,' he amended. He looked down, fists balled, knocking his knuckles together.

'What time did he call?' Leo said.

'Six-ish, half six?' He looked to Eesha for confirmation.

'It'll show on your phone,' Shan said.

Randall took it from his pocket, checked it. 'Eleven minutes past.'

'How did Tyler seem?'

'Great. He—' Randall raised his face up to the roof of the pergola, blinking. Then resumed talking. 'He said the project was going great and the people were good and, yeah . . . That was it, really.'

Leo told them Ange had been working on the Free the Fells project with Tyler and had asked him to pass on her number and the invitation to talk.

Eesha didn't hesitate. 'Oh, yes. Randall, we should, we must.'

Leo gave them the details and Randall keyed it into his phone.

'Do you know where he was calling from?' Leo said.

'The campsite, I think,' Randall said.

'Yes,' Eesha said. 'And he was going for a walk to get some more photos.'

'He was on speaker,' Randall said.

The *chop-chop-chop-chop* sound of a helicopter grew louder, making it impossible to keep talking. Leo watched it fly overhead. Air ambulance. Likely someone in trouble at the coast. People heading to the beach unprepared for mercurial conditions. Morecambe Bay was especially treacherous with its fast tides and quicksands.

Leo let the noise recede. 'What was he photographing?'

'The landscape,' Eesha said. 'Wildlife when he could, and mosses. He loves moss. He has some Insta accounts. Environmental stuff, climate justice.'

'It would be great to get those details,' Shan said.

'Sure.' Eesha gave her the names of three different accounts.

'But he's not posted anything since that call,' Eesha said. 'I checked. If you look on his phone—'

'His phone's missing,' Leo said. 'Could you tell us the make and model?' Leo noted them. He already had the number from Ange. 'We have got his laptop. That's password protected. Do either of you know his password?'

'We have it somewhere,' Eesha said. 'We wrote it down, remember?'

Randall frowned. 'I don't know where we put it.' He sounded anxious. 'Where did we put it?'

'We can look for it,' Eesha reassured him.

'So someone took his phone?' Randall said.

'Or it was lost,' Shan said.

'Did Tyler carry a wallet?' Leo asked.

'Yes, a brown one,' Eesha said. 'Canvas.'

'And keys?'

'Of course,' Eesha said.

'We've not found those either,' Leo said.

'You think he was robbed?' Randall said, his voice rising.

'Possibly,' Leo said. 'But it could also be that someone wanted to make it hard for us to find out who Tyler was.'

'So they shot him first, that's what you're saying? They shot him and then they try to cover it up by taking his things?' Randall sounded outraged. 'His face, his—'

Leo saw Tyler, the wounds peppering his skin. The remaining eye, white and crimson. The bluebottle he'd wanted to brush away.

'Honey,' Eesha said, 'they're trying to help.'

'I know. But I can't do this. I can't.' Randall stood abruptly, tense, anguished.

'Let's take a break,' Leo said.

'Randall,' Eesha said, 'it's all right.'

But he stood shaking his head, eyes brimming with tears.

'It's not,' he said. 'It will never be all right.' His voice broke. 'Never.'

'Let's take ten minutes,' Leo said. Randall went inside and Eesha went after him.

Leo watched a trio of bees working their way around a tumble of nasturtiums. The bright orange blossoms bouncing with each visit.

When the meeting resumed, Leo asked if Tyler had any trouble with anyone.

'What, like enemies?' Randall said.

'Yes, or strong disagreements. Bad blood.'

'No,' Randall said.

'Not unless you count the police,' Eesha said.

'The police?' Shan said.

Leo's gut tightened.

'Tyler's been cautioned for criminal damage,' Eesha said. There was a defiance in her tone as if she expected them to criticise her boy's behaviour.

'What did he do?' Shan said.

'Threw red and black paint over Barclays Bank at a climate change protest.' Leo saw she was proud of Tyler's action. He envied her that. 'He gets angry,' she said. 'You'd be mad not to.'

'Look,' Randall said, 'this whatever or whoever . . . . it's senseless. Some random fucking nightmare. You can't make sense of it, eh? So don't try looking for some rhyme or reason. Don't go asking about enemies—' He was shouting. Leo recognised the shift in emotion, from numb grief and shock to anger, an urge to lash out no matter the target. The need to blame.

'I understand what you're saying. But it's our job to try and find out everything we can, to understand what happened to Tyler and hold whoever's responsible to account.'

'Molly!' Randall said suddenly, turning to his wife, his rage draining away.

'Come on,' Eesha said dismissively.

'Molly Unwin?' Leo asked. *From the campsite.*

'You've spoken to her?' Randall sounded surprised.

'Not yet. We understand she's a friend of Tyler?' Leo said.

There was a laden silence.

'You can't possibly—' Eesha said to her husband.

He cut across her. 'Molly and Tyler were dating for a year or so in sixth-form. Then Tyler ended it. Molly found it hard to accept.'

'She's vulnerable,' Eesha added.

'She's obsessed,' Randall objected. 'That's what she is. Bombarding him with messages, stalking him on social media. She made his life a misery. Showed up here twice demanding to see him. She even had a copy of his tattoo done on her own wrist, without asking him. She's a nightmare.'

'She's a kid, Randall. She's a mixed-up teenager. We all do crazy things at that age,' Eesha said.

'Like shoot someone?' The shocking words resounded round the space. Randall crumpled. The stark fact of Tyler's death blindsiding him again.

'I'm sorry,' Leo said, needing to acknowledge their loss. The pain. 'We can come back later.'

'No,' Randall objected. 'We do it now. Whatever it takes.'

Eesha laced her fingers through his, put her other palm to his cheek for a moment.

'When did Tyler and Molly split up?' Shan asked.

'Just before Easter,' Eesha said.

'And was the intrusive behaviour ongoing?' Leo said.

Randall looked to Eesha for an answer.

'We thought it had calmed down,' she said. 'Tyler hadn't said anything recently. Molly had gone travelling with friends once college finished. She might still be away.'

Leo glanced at Shan, warning her not to disabuse them of that notion. Not while so much was still unknown.

'Do you have any contact details for her?' Leo asked.

'No. Well — just her address. Her family live near the castle.' Eesha gave them the road and house number.

'You really think she could be involved?' Eesha asked, brow creased in incomprehension.

'We want to talk to her as a potential witness,' Leo said. 'We believe they may have been in touch earlier this week.'

'A witness?' Eesha said.

For now.

* * *

As they left, they were met by camera crews arriving. Vans crowding into the narrow roads. Leo doubled back to the house and warned Randall. 'You don't need to speak to them. You may want to close the curtains, for privacy. Consider asking friends and neighbours to run errands.'

'Why are they here?' Randall asked. He looked exhausted, eyes haunted.

'People are shocked. It's a story of interest—'

'A story!'

'I know,' Leo said. 'But people want to help, and the press want to publicise what's happened.'

'And they can just do that, can they? Camp out here, eh? Put us under siege?'

'They can,' Leo said. 'If you decide at any point that you want to talk to them, give an interview, we can get advise on how to approach that.'

Randall shook his head sadly. Looked over the road where a woman was rigging up a tripod. 'It's crazy,' he said. 'It's all just crazy.'

CHAPTER SIX

Friday

Shan

Shan rang the campsite to ask the owner if Molly was back.

'No. It's very odd,' she said.

'Odd how?' Shan tensed up. Her heart skipped a beat.

'Well, it seems she left yesterday morning. Only stayed one night. If she'd let me know, she could've got some money back — she was booked in for the week.'

'And the tent's gone as well as the car?' Shan checked.

'Yes. I didn't realise when you were here. I'm sorry.'

'Do you have her registration?'

'I do. Here we go.' She read it out and Shan copied it down.

'I don't like the sound of that,' Leo said. 'Let's see if she's at home.'

* * *

Lancaster's medieval castle was infamous as the place where the Pendle witches were tried and sentenced to death in the

84

1600s. Ten of them hung at Gallows Hill, on the moors above the town. Still used as a Crown Court but no longer a prison, the Castle now offered guided tours to the public.

The stereotypical image of women on broomsticks with black hats and black cats adorned tourist trinkets, pub signs, even a bus company's fleet in Burnley. Shan had always thought that there was something weird about the way the area celebrated that violent history. Misogyny and persecution served up as entertainment. Occasional petitions to pardon those killed had got nowhere.

There was a skip outside the driveway at the Unwin's house, full of broken chipboard, scraps of vinyl flooring, lumps of rubble, a stainless-steel sink.

The front door stood ajar. A radio blared from the back of the house, an advert for the National Lottery.

Leo knocked and shouted. When there was no response, he stepped inside and Shan followed. Heavy dust sheets covered the floor. The air smelled of raw plaster and fresh timber.

Ahead Shan saw movement, a plasterer at work in the kitchen. Up on a platform, he was sweeping the thick, caramel-coloured porridge across the top of the wall with a rectangular trowel. Spatters rained down. The radio launched into some piece of yacht rock that Shan couldn't christen.

Leo banged on the open door, which was covered with plastic sheeting. The plasterer turned. Held up a finger, asking for a moment, then smoothed the rest of the load over the wall.

Job done, he jumped down and switched off the radio.

He was spackled in drips of plaster, fresh brown clots and older pale blotches, and a patina of fine dust coated his boiler suit, his hair, even his eyelids.

'Mr and Mrs Unwin?' Leo asked.

The man pointed. 'In the living room.'

'Thanks.'

They turned to follow his direction and the radio blared back to life.

'Can you leave that off for a bit?' Shan called. 'We need to be able to talk.'

'No problem,' he said, and hit the button.

This conversation, the shift in noise, must have alerted the Unwins because the living room door opened and a woman with tousled blonde hair wearing navy linen shorts and a sleeveless Breton top greeted them with a scowl. 'Who are you?'

Leo gave their names. 'May we come in?'

'Why?'

'It's in connection with Tyler Prasad.'

She dipped her head. 'We just saw. I can't, I don't . . .' Her lip trembled.

She didn't wait for an answer but turned and led them into a small living room. The blinds were closed against the heat and a floor-standing fan oscillated in the corner. Next to it, a makeshift kitchen had been set up on a Formica drop-leaf table: kettle, toaster, pile of crockery, box of groceries. A cool box sat on the floor below.

The TV was switched to the twenty-four-hour news channel and Tyler's murder was the breaking news headline scrolling across the bottom.

'Nick, it's the police,' she said to her husband. 'About Tyler.'

He turned off the TV. He was seriously overweight, filling the armchair he sat in. He'd a large moustache and long hair, which didn't look as though it'd been trimmed for decades. Tattoos marked his forearms and his neck. He wore a Whitesnake band T-shirt. Pretty different style to his wife, Shan thought. Often couples came in matching pairs.

'Please sit down,' Mrs Unwin invited them. She sat beside her husband on the arm of his chair.

Leo and Shan took the sofa, a black leather effect piece that squeaked as they sat.

'Is Molly here?' Leo asked.

'No. She's away camping. We don't know if she's even heard yet. I've been ringing but she's not picking up. She'll be devastated,' Mrs Unwin said. 'That poor boy.' Her eyes watered.

'Where's she gone camping?' Leo said.

'The Lakes. Keswick, I think.'

Molly's cover story, Shan assumed.

'On her own?' she asked.

'No, with friends from school. They went up Wednesday. She'd only just got back from Portugal. I said, "Can't you just stay here for five minutes?" But then . . . with all the work going on. And now this—' Her voice rising, she broke off.

'Jules.' Nick patted her hand.

'Sorry. Sorry.'

'Can you give me Molly's phone number?' Shan said.

'How come?' Nick said.

'We'd like to talk to her.'

'Why?' he said.

'As a potential witness,' Shan said.

'Witness? To what?' Jules said in alarm.

Parents protect their children. Some will do anything to shield them from harm. Lie, conceal, give false evidence, even when they've broken the law. At this stage, Shan knew the Unwins should be told as little as possible.

'Molly was seen with Tyler in Swaledale on Wednesday evening,' she said.

Jules was momentarily speechless. She made a scoffing sound. Then, 'That can't be right.'

Shan quoted Molly's car number plate.

'Oh God. You think she's hurt too? Was she with him when he was shot? Did they kidnap her?'

'No. We have no reason to think Molly is in danger,' Shan said. 'She left Swaledale yesterday morning. We want to find her, to see if she can help us.'

'Tyler and Molly had been close?' Leo said.

Jules sighed, shoulders slumped. 'Love's young dream. He broke her heart.'

'Jules.' Nick gave her a gentle reproach.

'Well, it's true. She loved him to the moon and back and he strung her along.'

'Be fair,' Nick said.

'You never stick up for her,' Jules said.

'These things happen,' he said reasonably. 'They're kids. Babies. You don't settle for the first person you get together with at seventeen.'

'We did.'

Shan saw him bite his tongue.

'Did Molly and Tyler ever argue?' Shan asked.

'No. Not that she said,' Jules answered.

'He's a good lad,' Nick said.

His wife cut him a look.

'Was there ever any violence?' Shan said.

'No!' Jules drew back, scandalised by the thought.

'Was Molly angry with Tyler?' Shan said.

'What are you getting at?' Jules said.

'Was she?' Shan persisted.

'She was hurt,' Jules said. 'She adored him and then—' Lips compressed, she gave a swift shake of her head.

'Is it true that Molly found it hard to accept the relationship was over?' Shan asked.

'She was heartbroken. What do you think?' Jules said.

'And she kept contacting Tyler afterwards? Texting, messages, liking all his posts?' Shan said.

'That's not against the law, is it?'

'Harassment—'

'She wasn't harassing him,' Jules argued, her voice rising. 'You make her sound like some sort of stalker. She—'

'Jules! Jules.' Nick tried to calm his wife.

'We're trying to understand the dynamic between Molly and Tyler,' Shan said. 'We need to speak to Molly, to find out how they left things on Wednesday. And if she saw anyone, noticed anything, that might help us.'

'We'll keep trying her,' Nick said.

'As soon as she knows, she'll want to be here. She will,' Jules tried to convince herself.

'Might there be other friends, family she's staying with?' Shan asked.

'No. Her close friends are the ones she said were going to the Lakes with her. When she hears, I don't know what she'll do. Oh God.' She gripped her husband's arm.

'Do you think that Molly may be a risk to herself?' Shan asked.

'No. Well . . .' Jules was at a loss. 'She talked about it. After the break-up. But that's what people say, isn't it? "I wish I was dead."'

'Has she ever made any attempts to harm herself?' Shan asked.

'Nothing like that,' Nick said.

'We'll put out an alert and track her car, try to find her and bring her home,' Leo said.

'OK. Thank you,' Nick said.

'There's one more thing,' Leo said carefully, aware of the need for delicacy. 'We have to ask this, to rule it out as a possibility, that's all. But did Molly have access to any firearms?'

'Firearms? No.' Jules scoffed again.

She looked to her husband for confirmation, but he looked uneasy. 'Nick?' she said. Jules flung back her head. 'No, don't tell me. You promised! You were going to hand it in!'

Shan felt the hairs on her arm prick.

'I meant to. I just . . . I never got round to it.'

She jumped to her feet. 'You bloody idiot! Christ.'

'What are we talking about here?' Leo said.

'My grandad's shotgun,' Jules said. 'We found it when we were clearing out my dad's house. But Molly would never, not in a million . . . What you're suggesting is fucking ridiculous. Go get it, Nick, show them. Get it now.' She trembled with outrage.

Shan kept her face neutral as Nick got up and went out of the room.

He came back five minutes later, his face drained of colour.

'It's not there,' he said. Eyes wary. 'It was in the shed at the back of an old wardrobe. But it's gone.'

* * *

'It's very rare, a woman, a girl, carrying out a homicide,' Shan said in the car.

'True. Tiny numbers. But it looks like she had the means, the opportunity and a possible motive — jealousy, revenge over being dumped. Put out a "BOLO" and check cameras for ANPR, see if we can find her driving,' Leo said.

Shan relayed the request to Control, the information to be shared with colleagues far and wide. She asked Leo to drop her home so she could pick up her own car and she'd meet him at the Grange.

The shift in perspective, the opening up of a promising lead, left her feeling nauseous, giddy with anticipation at the prospect of a hunt.

She imagined Molly Unwin, out there on the run, a broken-hearted teenager with a shotgun. Where would she go? What might she do now?

* * *

As soon as she stepped inside the house, Shan could tell something was wrong. It was a mess for a start, the vodka bottle and glasses still on the table. Erin loathed a mess. It was one of the things they had argued about most. And the TV was on. Erin would never go out and leave the TV running. She should be at work. Why wasn't she at work? The thought of suicide slithered into Shan's brain, a dark coil of fear. *Don't be daft.*

Shan switched the TV off and heard movement above.

'Erin?' she called.

Erin came to the top of the stairs. She was in her pyjama shorts and T-shirt. She looked ill.

'Hi,' Shan said, feeling idiotic. Guilty.

'What do you want?' Erin said flatly.

'I just . . . I . . . I came to get some things. Pick up the car.'

Erin didn't respond. She plodded downstairs and filled the kettle.

'You're not at work?' *Duh.*

Erin didn't answer.

'Are you OK?'

Erin turned to face her. 'What do you think? You won't talk to me. When I ask you to — when I fucking beg you — you do a runner. I call you and you ghost me.'

'I . . .' She wanted to say sorry. She wanted to hug Erin and make it all better but she couldn't.

'I just need—'

'Time? Yes. Space? Yes. Meanwhile, you expect me to just roll over and take it. I have no clue how long this . . . whatever . . . soul-searching will last. Will you keep paying the bills? Do we need to put the house on the market?'

'No!' Shan felt the jolt of shock. 'I'm not leaving — I just don't know.'

Erin gave a sigh. She stared at Shan. Blue eyes burning. 'You're not leaving? You sure about that?'

'No . . . but—'

'Right. And what if I don't want you back?'

Iced water ran through Shan's bowels.

'Erin—'

'What if I'm not prepared to take this, being strung along?'

'It's not—'

'It's not fair,' Erin said. 'It's all about what you feel, what you want, what you need. Where am I in all this?'

Shan didn't know what to say. She was cold inside and out. Shivering.

'Tell me when you've decided,' Erin said. 'Unless I tell you first. Don't bank on me, Shan. I don't know if I can ever trust you again.'

There was a pause. Shan swallowed. She felt dizzy.

'You'd better get your stuff,' Erin said, turning her back and reaching for a mug.

* * *

All the way back to Swaledale, Shan wanted to cry. There was a pressure at the back of her eyes and a constriction in her throat but she couldn't let go. The beauty of the afternoon, the blue, blue skies, the sweep of the hills, the golden sun shimmering across the heights, the sweet smell of hay, the landscape that usually brought her peace and comfort only served to highlight her misery.

She arrived back at the old Dairy to learn a video call was imminent with Tom Bairstow. 'Good timing,' Leo said. 'Forensics are in. Tom's going to talk us through.'

Shan pulled up the report that had come through on her laptop and logged into the video app.

Tom appeared on screen. 'You can hear me OK?'

'Yes,' they said in unison.

'Good. So, the highlights. From the scene where Tyler was shot we have a substantial number of lead pellets but no cartridges.'

'So they cleared the cartridges away,' Shan realised. 'But won't there be tons of lead shot everywhere up there?' Shan said. 'From the shoots?'

'Oh yes,' Tom said. 'The whole moor's drenched in it, lead gets in the water, poisons wildlife, scavenging birds and the like. But the concentration in this particular location is consistent with the recent discharge of a shotgun. The lab also identified blood traces. Some matched to Tyler and some distinct.'

'You think the assailant was hurt?' Shan said.

Tyler fought back? Struggled with his attacker? With Molly?

'It's animal blood — avian,' Tom said.

'Grouse?' Shan said, disappointed.

'Probably. We've sent it for DNA testing, that should tell us what breed it is.'

'It could be a bird of prey,' Leo said, raising his eyebrows at Shan, inviting her opinion. She signalled understanding: this might give them a motive. Someone illegally hunting crossing paths with Tyler.

'A raptor?' Tom said. 'Maybe. You'll hear as soon as we know. And if it is a protected species, then the wildlife crime unit will get involved. There's breeding programmes up and running for eagles, hen harriers, peregrine, but they're still targeted, especially on shooting estates.'

'Not officially,' Leo said.

'Never officially,' Tom said deadpan.

Shan recalled both Phil Beaumont and Jason Tattersall stressing how their work conserved a unique landscape. *Yeah, right.* Strange to think raising thousands of birds to be shot, burning the peat, poisoning and trapping other wildlife that hunted the birds, had anything to do with conservation.

There's more,' Tom said. 'On page four.' He waited while they scrolled through the document. 'Tests on Tyler's body and clothing have come back positive for DNA traces in several places. On the socks and shins, and under the arms.'

'From moving the body.' Shan could see the attacker hauling Tyler by the feet down the uneven ground, lifting him under the arms to drag his body into the gully.

'The dry weather has helped preserve those,' Tom said. 'There should be more than enough to work up a profile.'

A breakthrough. 'That's mega,' Shan said. 'If we get that . . .'

'You just need to match it,' Tom agreed. 'How's it going your end?'

'We know Tyler spoke to his parents at eleven minutes past six, and after that he was seen talking to an ex-girlfriend who had followed him up here. She's yet to be located. That's the last contact with anyone we've established so far. An hour later, a guest walking her dog on the moor heard shots and that meshes with what you've told us about time of death,' Leo said. 'We've also a member of the shooting party who's been leading us a bit of a dance. And the ex — seems she could have accessed a shotgun.'

Tom nodded. 'Good work.'

'The shooting party leave tomorrow,' Shan said. 'So we need to move as quickly as we can on that front.'

'DNA tests are going in as a priority, urgent case,' Tom said. 'But they can't give us a timescale.'

A volley of barking came from outside and Shan checked the time. 'They're back,' she said to Leo. The exhaustion she'd carried after the encounter with Erin had evaporated. She felt a fizz of energy. They were making progress and she was eager to see them make even more.

'Anything else?' Leo asked Tom.

'That's it for now. I'll keep you updated.'

'Day or night,' Shan said.

Tom smiled, saluted with one finger. 'On it.'

* * *

Leo

'Let's find Peel,' Shan said. Her mood had definitely shifted with the forensics. She'd looked tired, drawn when she first came back from collecting her car, but now she was alert, engaged, dark eyes shining, like the Shan he knew best.

Leo stood. 'Lead the way,' he said.

The party were milling about outside. The Argocat had discharged some of the guests. Jason Tattersall shot Leo a filthy glare as he passed carrying gun cases.

Peel was standing with Rafe and Helena Duvall and two other men. When Peel glanced up and spotted Leo and Shan heading towards him, he raised his hand to his companions, pointed to the car park and moved away. Leo saw Rafe Duvall turn to call after him, his face contorted in seeming outrage, distorting his leading man looks. Did he know Peel was speaking to the police? Was that a problem for him? A look of irritation or annoyance passed between the two other men, one of whom took off his flat cap and batted it against his hand.

Helena Duvall said something and gestured, inviting them to go into the Grange.

'Mr Peel,' Leo said. 'If we can have a word.'

'Not here,' he said crisply. 'We don't need a bloody audience.'

Shan slid her eyes at Leo. 'The Dairy, then?' she said.

'I just . . . I'll see you there.' Peel kept moving.

'Mr Peel.' Leo sounded a warning note.

He whipped off his wraparound shades. 'I need a piss. Is that OK?' He was flustered. Cheeks glistening and red from time in the sun.

'Of course,' Leo said.

Walking to the Dairy, Leo's attention was drawn to an altercation in the entrance to the barn. The Tattersall brothers squaring up to each other. Jason spitting insults, low enough not to be overheard, shoving Niall in the chest. Niall pushing back.

Leo felt his pulse jump in response.

'Trouble?' Shan murmured.

Phil Beaumont marched over, hissed something, and the men drew apart and dispersed, heading in opposite directions.

'Looks like it,' Leo said.

Beaumont saw them watching. He gave a weak smile and crossed to meet them. 'Everyone's on edge,' he said. 'Tempers are frayed. I'm sure you understand. Excuse me . . . I must get on.' And he hurried off before Leo could say anything in return.

Peel joined them ten minutes later. Leo noticed he'd shed the gilet. Patches of sweat were visible under his arm and the smell, sharp and oniony, was overpowering in the still air of the room, despite the sickly note of sandalwood cologne that accompanied it.

'We've spoken to Jason Tattersall and he tells us he wasn't in the grounds on Wednesday evening,' Leo said.

'But I saw him. Maybe he didn't notice me? He was working, in a rush. I thought he'd seen me but maybe not.'

'He wasn't in the yard,' Shan said.

Peel fixed his attention on her. 'I. Saw. Him.'

'He says not,' Leo said.

'So it's my word against his?' His eyes on Leo were hard, his gaze piercing.

'We have confirmation that he was elsewhere, with someone else,' Leo said.

'Oh, for pity's . . . I'm telling you the truth. I don't know what else you expect.'

Leo said nothing, just watched Peel, who maintained eye contact for a second or two more then turned his face away. 'What about the courier?' Peel said.

'We'll be speaking to them soon,' Leo said. 'But if there's anything you wish to add or change, now would be a good time to do it.'

Peel gave a bitter laugh, shook his head.

Leo decided to press a little harder. 'Mr Peel, did you go up to Syke Moss at any time after five on Wednesday?'

'No. No! How many more bloody times? I was *in* my room, I *left* at eight. I *saw* Tattersall, I nearly *totalled* the courier and I *drove* to Morecambe.' He slapped his knee on each stressed word. 'That's it. That's all.'

Leo left a beat before saying, 'We now have forensic evidence from the crime scene which should enable us to identify the perpetrator.'

'Good. Great! Bully for you.' His face grew even redder, slick with perspiration. 'Because it's nothing to do with me. And maybe you should be casting your net a bit wider because you are wasting your time with this.' He flung a hand gesturing between them and himself.

'Would you be prepared to voluntarily offer us a DNA sample, a simple cheek swab, for purposes of elimination?' said Leo, calling his bluff in effect. It was a risk — if he refused, Leo couldn't compel him, not without much stronger evidence.

Peel said nothing for a moment, jaw fixed and eyes boring into Leo's. Then, 'Yes, and then maybe you'll get off my back and leave me the fuck alone.'

Shan flicked a look at Leo and went to fetch the kit from their box of supplies. Wearing nitrile gloves, she took the swab from its wrapping and asked Peel to open his mouth.

Swiftly, she passed the bud over the inside of his cheek, then withdrew it, thanked him and placed it in the container. She labelled it carefully.

'We done?' Peel asked.

'Yes, for now,' Leo said.

Peel left, slamming the door as he went. The stag's head shook with the impact. Leo waited a moment to see if it would fall off the wall but it held.

He got up and set the door ajar to try and air the room. But it was like opening an oven door. Unprecedented high temperatures for September. Records being broken every month, every year.

'We should ask them if they can spare us a fan,' Leo said.

'I never thought he'd agree to the swab,' Shan said.

Me neither.

'He's confident.' And the fact that Peel complied so readily made the likelihood he was Tyler's killer recede. Did that increase the odds that it was Molly Unwin?

'We should see the courier anyway. Vinnie's,' Shan said.

'Oh yes. Vinnie's Victuals,' Leo joshed.

'It's not called that.'

'They missed a trick there.'

'You ever thought of working in marketing?' She picked up her bag.

'Can't say I have.'

'Best not, eh?'

CHAPTER SEVEN

Friday

Shan

Fastening her seatbelt, Shan saw Niall Tattersall heading towards the cottages. Something snagged in her mind.

'Leo,' she said slowly, 'what if Peel didn't see Jason Tattersall that night but Niall? He's not as tall but he's a similar build, wears the same gear. It was dark. We should ask.'

She got out of the car quickly and ran a few steps to be in earshot. 'Niall?'

He turned, squinting into the sun. 'Hi,' he smiled.

'Just a question,' Shan said.

'Sure.'

Leo joined them.

'On Wednesday evening at eight o'clock, were you out here?' Shan said.

'Yeah, 'bout then. Going to check the snares.' It *was* Niall! Peel hadn't invented the sighting, just mixed up the keepers.

The sting of his cigarette smoke caught her eyes. She took a step back.

'Did you see one of the guests going to his car?' she said.

'Might have. Don't remember, to be honest.' He gave an apologetic shrug.

'You were checking the snares?' Leo said.

'For foxes,' Niall said. 'Vermin, rabbits.'

'Where do you set them?' Leo said.

'All through the wood.' He pointed towards the conifer plantation. 'Some further out. Around the edge of the grounds as well. Check them every night.'

'And how long does that take?' Leo said.

'Good hour.'

'Did you see anyone else around at all?' Shan said.

'No. Everyone was inside.'

'What about before then — between seven and eight, where were you?'

'At our Jason's.'

'From when?'

'Just after seven. I dropped in to see Becky. She's stuck there. In this heat.'

'And when did you leave?'

He considered. 'Ten to eight, five to? Something like that.'

'You and Jason, we saw you having an argument earlier?'

He gave a short laugh. 'It were nowt. Don't always see eye to eye, that's all.' His tone changed. 'This kid — his poor parents.' He looked about. 'You never think something like that could happen round here. So peaceful.'

Shan wouldn't have called shooting days peaceful but she knew what the man meant.

'Who'd do a thing like that?' Niall said. The question they were all asking, and she wondered if they were any nearer to finding an answer.

* * *

The village of Reeth was nine miles to the east. The road followed the course of the River Swale, the waterway mostly hidden from sight a couple of fields away. They crossed it twice over stone bridges. The water level was low and a pungent chemical smell reached Shan when she leaned out of the window to get a better view.

Vinnie's was housed in an old weaver's cottage on the corner of a cobbled street, the sign in purple and white.

Inside, chalkboards advertised the pizzas, side dishes and drinks available. Aromas of herbs and garlic filled the space. An old church pew provided space for customers to wait. The TV was showing some reality show — scantily clad people, spray-tanned, lounging in a jacuzzi.

The bell on the door had rung as they entered and a woman came through to serve them. Blonde hair in a topknot, glasses and lipstick in the same purple shade as the signage.

'What can I get for you?' An accent, Eastern European was Shan's guess.

Shan introduced herself and Leo and asked for the courier who was working on Wednesday evening.

'Oh.' She looked disconcerted, her cheeks pinked up. 'Milo does all that. Is something wrong?'

'Is he here?' Shan said.

'He's in the back. I show you.'

She waved them round the side of the counter then through the kitchen lined with pizza ovens, one of them in use, the smell of baking stronger here. There were prep tables, piles of flatpack boxes and takeaway containers, a huge fridge. Beyond that was a room filled with more packaging, another fridge and chest freezer, cool boxes, packages of canned goods and drinks, and padded bags with the Vinnie's logo.

'Milo?' the woman called.

The door to the yard was open and there they found a young man — late twenties, Shan estimated — sitting in a chair playing a portable games console, headphones on, a can of energy drink at his side. A motorbike with the carrier described by Peel stood by the back gate, a leather jacket draped over the handlebars.

'Milo,' the woman called again.

He looked round. Took his headphones off. He had short blond hair, and dense tattoos sleeved his forearms.

'It's the police,' the woman said.

A shudder ran through his body. The sort of movement someone makes immediately before bolting. Shan tensed too, ready to chase, but the man stayed put.

'Police?' he said.

'DI Donovan, DC Young,' Leo said.

'What's going on?' he said.

'Could I take your full name?' Shan said.

'Milo Carr. Sophia, you get back,' he said to the woman. 'It's cool, go,' he added when she hesitated.

'Date of birth?' Shan said.

'Eighteenth of June, 1995. Why?' There were visible tremors flickering under his skin. What was he so worried about?

'You made a delivery to Patefield Grange on Wednesday evening?' Shan said.

He shrugged with his mouth. 'Maybe.'

'You keep records?' Shan said.

'We do the accounts.'

'Wednesday evening, Patefield Grange?' Shan said.

He didn't say anything.

'You had an order?'

'Yeah.' But he didn't sound sure.

'For who?'

He stalled, blowing out his cheeks. 'John, I think.'

Two wasps had landed on his drink can and he flicked them away with his fingers.

'John?' *Seriously?*

'Yes.'

'John who?' Shan said.

'Dunno.'

His evasion felt a hundred ways weird. 'We think you arrived about eight o'clock.'

'Right.' Saying as little as possible. He swallowed, shifted in his seat. Glanced back into the building.

'Do you recall seeing any other vehicles on your way up the lane to the Grange?'

He looked confused, distracted, blinking as though it was a trick question.

'Vehicles?' he said.

'Vehicles,' Leo answered impatiently. 'On the lane.'

Carr's face cleared with relief. 'Yeah,' he said. 'Some white SUV gunning it.' So, Peel had told the truth. About this, at least.

Shan tried to figure out Carr's response. He was edgy about the delivery, the reason for his visit to the Grange, but relaxed about other questions. Why?

'What was the order for John?' she asked.

'I . . . the special.'

Sophia called from inside. 'Milo, you ready?'

'I've got a delivery now, actually,' he told them. He lifted his helmet from the table beside him.

'What's the special?' Shan said.

'Double cheese meatballs.' His eyes flicked again to the back room, low down. 'I gotta go.' He stood. Why was he so freaked about the delivery? Or did he know something about Tyler's death? When Peel almost crashed into Carr, had the courier already been up on the moor? Could the motorbike tackle the rough, heather-clad slopes? It wasn't the type used for scrambling.

'And "John's" contact number?' Leo said.

'I don't know if I've still got it.'

'That'd be bad for business, not keeping track,' Leo said.

Sophia came out, carrying a pizza box.

'Perhaps you can help?' Shan said to her. 'There was an order on Wednesday evening for Patefield Grange?'

Sophia looked anxious. 'Milo?'

'Leave it,' he said. 'I'll sort it. It was just visitors,' he said to Leo. 'No need to keep the number. Not like there's any repeat business.'

'John' was one of the guests, then.

'This delivery?' Sophia said, lifting the box.

'We haven't finished,' Leo said.

'Just keep it in the warmer,' Carr said roughly.

Sophia tutted and disappeared.

'Were you on Syke Moss at any time that evening?' Shan said.

'Syke—' The penny dropped. 'No, man. Tyler Prasad. No way. No. I went from here, straight to Patefield and back. Swear.'

'With double cheese meatballs?'

'Yes. I said, didn't I?' There wasn't a shred of credibility in his tone. He tried to hold Shan's gaze but she could see him struggling not to look away — and, more accurately, not to look back at the doorway. Shan couldn't see anything there except the cool boxes.

'Do you own a shotgun?' Shan said.

That brought him to his feet. 'No!'

Realisation struck Shan like a wave of cold water. An explanation for what might be going on. It would make sense. She signalled to Leo — *a word?* — and gestured to the doorway. Inside, she turned away from the yard and said quietly, 'I think he's dealing.'

'What?' Leo mouthed.

'It adds up. He's frantic about something.' She paused. 'Unless it's Tyler's death?'

'Based on?' Leo scrutinised her.

The fact he was nearby shortly afterwards? It was paper thin. She tilted her head in acknowledgement. But drugs — that felt way more plausible.

'I want to search,' she said under her breath. Suspicion of possession of controlled drugs was grounds for a search with no need for a warrant.

But would Leo trust her? She was going on gut feeling, and she couldn't think of anything else that would account for Carr's behaviour.

'You sure?' Leo said.

Am I?

'No,' she admitted. 'But a visitor at the Grange ordering weed or ecstasy at dinner time would make way more sense than a pizza. And if it *was* only a pizza, why's he being so weird?'

Leo considered it. She thought he'd decline, but finally he said, 'OK,' and she breathed again.

She stepped out into the yard.

'Mr Carr, we're now going to carry out a search of the premises on suspicion of possession of controlled drugs with intent to supply.' And if she turned up anything else — Tyler's phone or wallet — even better.

'No!' he said. 'Man, no! Look, I'll give you the number. He'll tell you it was just a pizza.' He thumbed through his phone. 'See, ring him. Ask him. It was just a pizza.'

Shan took a picture of the number. 'We will. But first we search.'

'There's nothing here,' Carr said. 'I swear.' He looked close to tears. He swung his head, one hand at his temple.

'Will you wait with Sophia?' Shan asked Leo. They didn't know if she was aware or involved, but they shouldn't give her any opportunity to hide or destroy evidence.

Shan pulled on clean gloves — she'd learned early on it was essential to always carry a good supply — and began systematically searching. Two of the cool boxes that Carr had been glancing at held ice packs, cold to touch. The third was empty.

Shan looked through the fridge, behind blocks of cheese and containers of sliced onions and peppers, olives and mushrooms. Then through the chest freezer, her gloves sticking to the bags of frozen vegetables and meat. Nothing. Steel cupboards held other goods but no drugs. She searched round the catering-size tins of passata and olives. Then through the kitchen, among the pizza trays and in the drawers of cutlery, the heat of the ovens making her sweat. A small desk held some papers, invoices and receipts, but she imagined most of the business would be conducted online.

Carr watched. 'There's nothing here,' he said. 'I told you.'

At the thought that she'd been mistaken, her stomach dropped. She'd messed up. *Upstairs?* But why had Carr been focusing on the back room? She hadn't imagined that, those anxious glances, had she? She hadn't.

'Shan?' Leo came through from the shop. Curious to see whether she'd found anything. She shook her head.

Should she give up?

Looking at Carr, she could see he'd lost some of the tension from before. Did he think he'd got away with it?

'A minute,' Shan said to Leo. She returned to the boxes near the back door, looked through the ones holding ice packs again, examining the packs more carefully. Nothing unusual. She lifted the empty box and felt a shift of weight somewhere, something moving. Her pulse ramped up.

She turned the box over but it was intact. She turned it back and set it down on the flagged floor. The box was constructed of an inner and outer shell, rigid plastic, the air between the two insulating the contents. She put her fingernails under the edge of the inner lining at either end and tugged. The inside slid up effortlessly. In the bottom sat several glassine bags, each containing off-white powder, and a slice from a brick of what she assumed was cocaine wrapped in cling film.

'Shit, man,' Carr said.

Totally, Shan thought.

Sophia appeared behind Leo.

Shan took shots of the drugs and their container then placed the contraband in an evidence bag.

'Milo Carr, I am arresting you for possession of suspected Class A drugs with intent to supply,' Shan said. 'You do not have to say anything. But it may harm your defence if you do not mention when questioned something which you later rely on in court. Do you understand?'

'You try making a fucking living round here. My mam's sick, we've two kids, and the landlord's talking about eviction,'

Carr railed. Shan felt a pinch of pity for him. It was hard and getting harder for so many people. Most of them scrabbling to get by.

'This isn't the answer,' Leo said.

'What the fuck is then, eh? You tell me. What is?' He kicked out at a chair, sending it crashing over.

'Do I have to cuff you?' Shan said.

He was shaking with rage, eyes glaring, but he contained himself. 'No,' he spat.

'Where are you taking him?' Sophia said.

'The police station. He'll be booked into custody and up before the magistrates in the morning,' Shan said.

And he'd be swabbed when they processed him. So if by any chance he was also involved in moving Tyler's body, they'd be able to match the profiles when the lab came back with them.

* * *

On the drive back from booking Carr in, Shan went through the details they had for visitors at Patefield Grange, looking for a match to the phone number for 'John'. She scanned down the list searching for the same last three digits, 403. Her eyes lighted on the number.

'Got it! Yes! Guess who.'

'Go on,' Leo said.

'Rafe Duvall.'

Leo laughed. 'Pretty boy? No wonder he was so belligerent when we pitched up.'

'But wouldn't you keep quiet, though? Not draw attention like that?' Shan was puzzled.

'Not that sort,' Leo said. 'Entitled. They think they're untouchable. Rules don't apply. And not without reason sometimes.'

'If he's still got any in his possession, we'll set him right,' she said.

'He got any form?' Leo said.

Shan logged in and checked the police database. 'No. Nothing.' Then she typed his name into Google and pages of results loaded. 'Duvall infrastructure and property investment. Worth eleven million,' she summarised. Her eyes jumped down the page. 'Reported losses post Brexit. Restructuring. Restructuring?' she asked Leo.

'Rest of us know it as tightening our belts or downsizing. Check Companies House,' Leo said.

'OK.' She navigated to the website and found the company listing. 'Registered office in Gerrard's Cross, Buckinghamshire. Officers . . . three directors: Rafe Duvall, Eleanor Duvall and Oliver Peel. They're in business together!'

'But presumably Peel doesn't know about Duvall using the local takeaway to deliver cocaine or he wouldn't have told us about the courier,' Leo said.

'And I bet you the Duvalls don't know Peel snuck out for a night on the slot machines either,' Shan said. 'And Rafe doesn't know his wife and Peel are mixing business and pleasure.'

'*If* that's what's going on — you're making assumptions,' Leo said.

'True.'

She watched the sweep of the fells going past, sheep browsing on the lower slopes. Saw a pair of ramblers near the tops.

'Look, if you're tightening your belts, how come you splash out on a shooting holiday?' she said.

'Appearances. Maintaining confidence. You don't ditch the lifestyle, sends the wrong message.'

Shan sat back. 'Trouble is, none of this really gets us any closer to finding Tyler's killer.'

'It doesn't look like it. Carr corroborates Peel's account.'

'But Niall Tattersall doesn't. Well, he couldn't be sure,' Shan said. 'That leaves us with Molly.' Their progress felt uneven, two steps forward then as many back. 'We need that DNA profile.'

'It'll be a day or two.'

There was a sheep in the middle of the road. Leo slowed to a stop.

The sheep turned its head, stared balefully at them.

'The profile doesn't get us very far unless we have samples to compare it to,' Leo said. He gave the horn a toot and the sheep skittered to the verge.

'We'll have Peel and Carr,' Shan said. 'We should get something of Molly's from her parents.'

'OK. But all a bit of a reach from where I'm standing,' Leo said, resuming the drive.

'Maybe. Though at least with Molly we have a possible motive. There's a previous connection, they knew each other. It makes more sense to me than either Carr or Peel.' Or was the culprit someone they hadn't even identified yet? 'The lab will automatically check the database too.'

'And if the person in question hasn't got a record.' He was right, but it wasn't what she wanted to hear. She knew they couldn't ask all the guests, all the workers, all the local residents to voluntarily submit DNA. That sort of mass fishing expedition was only sanctioned on rare occasions when all other avenues had been exhausted.

They crossed a stone bridge, calendar pretty. Passed a pub set back from the road, whitewashed walls and planted mangers, picnic tables full. A B&B sign read, *No Vacancies*.

Her phone alerted her to an email. She opened and scanned it. 'The Empress,' she said to Leo. 'Confirming Peel stayed there on Wednesday night.' Another bit of his story held water.

Minutes later Leo pulled into the Grange, parking near the old Dairy.

'Let's verify Niall Tattersall's movements before we find Duvall,' Leo said.

Shan's heart sank at the thought of facing Becky again.

This time Becky answered the door herself. 'What's wrong?'

'Nothing,' Leo reassured her. 'We just need a word. Do you want to sit down?'

Becky took them into the front room, settled herself into an armchair with a padded footstool. She was red, perspiring, looked very uncomfortable.

'After Jason left on Wednesday evening to go to the garage, did anyone else visit you here?' Shan said.

'Niall,' she said.

'You didn't mention it before,' Shan said.

'You didn't ask. They . . . they'd had a big barney earlier. Jason was steaming. He wouldn't like Niall coming round. Please don't tell him.' She was nervous, blinking frequently and licking her lips.

So the spat we saw today wasn't the first time the brothers had argued, Shan thought.

'What was the row about?' Leo said.

'Work. Jason says Niall's sloppy, cutting corners, that he doesn't concentrate. Niall says Jason's picking on him. It's six of one and half a dozen of the other.' She shook her head.

'Can you tell us when Niall arrived and when he left?' Shan said.

'He got here just after seven and went about quarter to eight.'

* * *

'It feels a bit weird,' Shan said once they were outside. 'Your brother-in-law visits in secret.'

'You've seen what the two of them are like,' Leo said. 'Families, eh? Where there's a family, there's a feud.'

'Where's that from?' Shan asked.

'All my own work,' Leo said.

'Okaaay,' Shan said. 'Now the heat really is getting to you.'

* * *

Leo

At reception, Leo asked Carrie Crowther for Rafe Duvall's room number. 'The Fairfax Suite, number seven in the East Wing.' She pointed up the stairway to the right. 'But if it's

Mr Duvall himself you want, I saw him going out to the gardens.'

'Thank you.'

They made their way through the bar, quiet now the beaters had gone, just a couple of tables occupied.

Through the open French doors, Leo could see Rafe Duvall and Oliver Peel on one of the terraces below arguing, Helena Duvall between them, trying to keep them apart.

'Looks like that particular cat's out of the bag,' he said. Shan had been right.

'No, listen,' Shan said. 'It's not that.'

Duvall's words carried, amplified by the bowl shape of the gardens. 'You're fucking useless. The invisible man. You know how much we've had riding on this. But you're a no-show.'

'Look—'

'You disappeared after tea Wednesday and you blobbed dinner then breakfast. You leave it all on my back. With the shoot cancelled we needed to *up* the charm offensive, go for the hard sell.'

Charm? Leo thought. Not a word he'd associate with Duvall, though presumably he could summon it up when required. And his leading man looks would be an asset.

'It's not my fault some kid got murdered,' Peel said.

'Oliver!' Helena exclaimed.

'They've left!' Duvall shouted. 'They've gone, Oliver. Couldn't even be arsed staying tonight. You've blown it. You know what they said? They'd *consider* the opportunity. You wanker!' Duvall, face livid, shoved Peel, who stumbled and fell into one of the hedges, losing his sunglasses.

'Rafe! Stop it,' Helena said. She bent to tend to Peel.

'You useless waste of space. You shitting fuckwit.' Duvall stormed off, climbing the steps and ignoring Leo and Shan as he passed.

'I'm fine. It's fine. I'll talk to him,' Peel said to Helena.

'Don't. Wait,' she called.

But Peel ran up after Duvall. He started when he saw them but didn't say a word.

Leo and Shan headed after the pair and were close behind Peel when he reached the Fairfax Suite. Peel knocked on the door. There was no response from inside.

'Mr Peel,' Leo said, reaching him. 'If you'll step aside.'

'It's nothing,' Peel said. 'I'm not hurt. I'm not pressing charges.'

Leo looked to Shan. *Shall we?*

'That's not why we're here,' Leo said. He hammered on the door. 'Mr Duvall, DI Donovan here. Open the door.'

Heavy footsteps reverberated from the room and Duvall flung open the door.

'What?' Then he glared at Peel. 'If you've—'

'Mr Duvall, we are carrying out a search under the Misuse of Drugs Act, on grounds of suspicion of you being in possession of a controlled Class A drug.'

Duvall made a spluttering sound. 'Get a warrant,' he snarled, a blaze of white teeth.

'We don't need a warrant,' Shan said. Leo could tell she was enjoying this.

'Stand back,' Leo said sharply.

With a snort, Duvall raised his palms and backed into the living room.

'You both wait there,' Shan said to Duvall and Peel as soon as they were over the threshold.

The suite was lavishly decorated. Thick brocade curtains with exaggerated swags framed the mullioned windows. High ceilings boasted plaster cornices and a huge chandelier. A large over-mantle mirror hung above the marble fireplace. A chaise longue, a sofa and easy chairs were grouped around a sizeable glass-and-bronze coffee table. Richly patterned wallpaper, a repeated watercolour of willow leaves, ran above the wooden dado. Reminiscent of Tyler's tattoo, Leo thought. Another wall tapestry, crafted like the one in the foyer, depicted Aysgarth Falls, with its three stepped waterfalls. An enormous TV screen in one corner with various digi-boxes was almost incongruous.

'I'll take the bedroom,' Shan said. She pulled on fresh gloves. Leo did the same.

'Rafe?' Peel said, sounding bewildered.

'Shut it,' Duvall said.

Leo looked over all the surfaces first, then methodically searched through all the furniture. The antique mahogany sideboard, drawers and cupboards. He examined the shelves of leather-bound books. He looked in the bar housed within a wooden cabinet with its selection of spirits and wines and in the fridge beside it, where champagne, white wine, mixers and a range of craft ales chilled. Leo promised himself a cold beer when he got home — whenever that might be.

He'd almost completed the search and was wondering if Rafe had used up whatever drugs he'd bought and cleaned up after himself, when the door opened and Helena Duvall came in, key card in hand.

She stopped in her tracks. 'What's going on?'

'Leo.' Shan appeared, eyes dancing. 'The bathroom.'

He went through. There was a gigantic claw foot bath-tub, his and hers marble sinks and vanity units, a mirror the size of a bus, a rainfall shower enclosure. Shan indicated the drawer in the right-hand vanity. Leo spied a loose razor blade, a small bottle of beard oil. *Beard oil?* A bottle of Acqua di Parma cologne. And a glassine bag of white powder, just like the ones at Vinnie's, sitting on a rectangle of mirror.

'Jackpot,' Leo said. Shan grinned.

Leo prepared an evidence bag while Shan photographed then removed the items and dropped them inside it. They returned to the living room, Leo holding up the evidence.

Duvall laughed and shook his head. 'I've never seen that before. It must have been left by previous guest.' He smoothed his beard.

'Really?' Leo said. 'Only, we know via phone records that you ordered it on Wednesday.'

'Rafe, you idiot,' Helena said.

He shot her a murderous look.

'It's just a bit of blow. Personal use only,' he said to the police. He gave a blinding smile, devoid of warmth.

'No defence,' Leo said.

'You've been coked up?' Peel said disapprovingly.

'Like you never touch it? At least I was here.' Duvall stabbed fingers at his own chest.

'Stop it, both of you,' Helena said.

'You had it couriered here on Wednesday evening,' Leo said.

'Oh Christ,' Peel said loudly.

'Oliver?' Helena said.

'I'd no idea.' Peel flung out his arms and spoke to the room.

'What on earth is going on?' Helena said.

Peel's shoulders slumped. He sat down on the edge of the chaise longue. 'The police were . . . I never meant for this.'

'What have you done?' Duvall said dangerously.

Leo kept quiet, interested to see what would emerge.

'The police were asking me about . . . Wednesday, because I wasn't at dinner and the boy they found—'

'Tyler Prasad,' Shan said determinedly. 'His name is Tyler Prasad.'

'Oliver?' Helena's voice shook.

'Oh, for God's sake, Helena, don't be dense. That had nothing to do with me but I had to . . . Oh shit. I had to give them an alibi.'

'You were sick?' Helena said, puzzled.

Peel gritted his teeth, face puce. 'I saw the courier down the lane. I was in the car.'

'But you were ill. What were you doing in the car?' Helena said.

Rafe Duvall flexed his fists. Leo could hear him breathing more heavily.

'Where were you going?' Helena looked at Peel. 'Oh, no. Tell me you didn't. Oh God. You went gambling. You *promised*.'

'We were entertaining clients and you went gambling? Potential investors. We're haemorrhaging funds and you went to some fucking casino,' Rafe Duvall said.

'At least that's legal,' Peel said.

With a roar, Duvall flew across space and punched Peel in the face, knocking him from the couch to the floor. He raised his fists to hit out again but Leo and Shan pulled him away.

'Rafe Duvall, I am arresting you on suspicion of possessing a controlled substance, a Class A drug,' Shan said.

'Your fucking brother,' Duvall said to his wife, pointing at Peel, who was wiping blood from his nose.

Helena Duvall and Oliver Peel were siblings!

Didn't see that coming.

'You brought this on yourselves,' Helena said. 'You're no better than each other. You took the family business and trashed it.' Her icy blue eyes flashed. 'Never mind the pandemic or Brexit or anything else. You two, the pair of you, you've pissed it away. Stupid schemes and vanity projects, getting greedy—'

'Don't talk to me like that,' Duvall said.

'Oh, piss off. Could he go to prison?' she asked the police.

'Unlikely. Unless he denies the crime,' Leo said.

'Shame,' Helena said. And Leo felt like clapping.

'More likely to get a conditional caution for a first offence. But that would rest on accepting guilt,' Leo said. 'Now, Mr Duvall, you must accompany us to the police station and make a full statement.'

'I want my lawyer present,' Duvall said.

'What lawyer?' Helena said scathingly.

'Cameron.'

'Cameron deals in company law.'

'Get Cameron. Or at least ask him if he can find me someone,' Duvall said.

'We can supply a duty solicitor, though there might be a wait,' Shan said.

Duvall ignored her. 'Talk to Cameron,' he said to his wife.

'You couldn't even keep off it for three days?' Helena said. 'When you knew—' She shook her head, her neatly edged hair swinging.

114

'Helena, everyone does it. Open your eyes. Grow up. And get a fucking life.'

'Maybe I will. Anything would be better than this one.' She turned on her heels and walked out of the room. Peel twitched as though he'd follow but then settled back on his seat and returned to blotting his nose.

Leo signalled to Shan, who nodded.

'Let's go,' she said to Rafe Duvall.

CHAPTER EIGHT

Friday

Leo

Leo was finishing up at the station when news came through regarding Molly Unwin.

Shan had already left, so he called to let her know. 'Traffic police have found Molly Unwin. She's been involved in an RTC on the M6.'

'Oh shit. Is she—'

'She's OK. No other vehicle involved. I've asked them to wait for me at the scene. I'm going to pick her up. Can you let her parents know and meet me at the house in about an hour?'

* * *

The small Hyundai had collided with the barrier at the start of the exit slip road. The bonnet was concertinaed, windscreen crazed, passenger door buckled.

Molly was in the four-by-four traffic patrol vehicle.

Leo's first impression was of a lost girl, woebegone, her face muddy with misery. She wore jeggings and a cropped, tie-dye

T-shirt that revealed a piercing in her navel. Her black hair was long, in loose waves. A brightly woven backpack sat at her feet.

He told her he'd speak to her in a minute. She tucked her hair behind her ear and he saw the tattoo on her wrist. The identifying feature on the dead lad's body. Something sinister about that juxtaposition.

Leo asked one of the officers to step out for a word. They stood behind the car. The motorway traffic roaring past meant they had to raise their voices to be heard and Leo was forced to concentrate to catch replies. They were buffeted by gusts of hot air. The smell of scorching tarmac, metal, petrol fumes and burnt rubber was thick, choking. Leo could feel the grime coating his tongue. Inhaling the dust made him cough.

'Was she in the vehicle when you arrived?'

'Yes. Just sitting there.'

'Has she said what happened?'

'She's not sure, she thinks she dozed off.'

'Did you give any first aid?'

'We checked her over. Ran it past the paramedics. They agreed if she experiences any dizziness, visual problems or confusion she should go to A&E. The breathalyser was clear. Seatbelt on.'

'What about the doors, were they closed?' Leo asked.

'Yes. Took some pulling to open the driver's door.'

'Windows?'

'Closed.'

'Any sign of a weapon?'

Surprise flared in the other man's eyes. 'No.'

'I need to search the vehicle,' Leo said, pulling on a pair of gloves.

'Sure.' He passed Leo the keys. The fob was busy with knickknacks, a tiny silver guitar, a fluffy owl, a wooden fretwork tree, a ceramic sunflower and miniature silver wind chimes that tinkled as Leo opened the driver's door.

A thorough search through the footwells, on the seats and through the camping gear in the boot failed to turn up the missing shotgun.

Leo also checked the hard shoulder and walked a few yards in the scrub over the barrier, hunting among the litter and weeds. He reasoned that in order to jettison the weapon from the car and away from the traffic, she'd have had to lower her window and hurl the gun over the roof of the car, which was hardly likely. So perhaps she'd discarded it somewhere between Syke Moss and here.

He walked back to the officer. 'Is there anything else you need from her?' Leo asked.

'No. We're done.'

'OK.'

Leo climbed into the traffic car. 'Molly, have you heard about Tyler?'

She gave a nod, eyes bright with tears.

'We're trying to find out what happened to him. Talking to people who knew him, or saw him recently. So we'll get you home. Sit down and have a proper talk, OK?'

* * *

Shan

Shan waited outside the Unwins' until Leo arrived with Molly.

The same raw plaster smell greeted them as they went in but there was no sign of the workman.

'Tyler,' Molly said and began to cry as her mother pulled her into an embrace.

'I know, love, it's terrible.'

'It can't be true, Mum, it just can't.'

'I know, love, I know.'

Nick hovered behind them, and as soon as Molly and her mother parted, he hugged her too.

'You hungry?' he said.

'No.'

'Smoothie?'

'OK.'

'Why don't you have that drink and jump in the shower and freshen up, then we can talk,' Leo said.

'And Molly, please can you put the clothes you're wearing in here and give them to us.' Shan held out a clean evidence bag.

'My clothes? Why?'

'We may need to examine them,' Shan said.

'What?' Molly scowled.

Jules stared at Shan, wary.

'And Molly, can I check your bag?' Shan said.

'Why?'

'Some items of Tyler's are missing.'

She curled her lip. 'You calling me a thief?'

'May I look?' Shan said, reaching out her hand.

'Mum?'

Jules gave a helpless shrug, looking away.

Molly thrust her backpack at Shan, who examined the contents. Nothing of Tyler's there.

Nick came back with a mug of frothy yellow liquid and handed it to Molly. 'Go on,' he said, tipping his head to the stairs.

Molly trailed upstairs and Nick busied himself making drinks for them all, while Jules fired questions at them: Where was the crash? Should Molly go to hospital? Was she speeding? Has she said anything?

Molly came back wearing a short-sleeve, orange towelling robe, hair dripping. She dropped the bag of clothing at Shan's feet, a gesture that was resentful, defiant, but Shan saw a bead of fear in her eyes.

Jules patted the sofa and Molly sat down beside her, hunched forward like some wounded animal.

Nick had brought in two moulded plastic chairs for Leo and Shan.

'Are you feeling OK after the crash?' Shan said.

Molly shrugged. 'Yeah.'

'OK. Tell us how that happened.'

119

'I'd been driving . . . I just . . . I couldn't sleep and I must have been tired. I didn't realise—'

'It was an accident?'

She nodded. Shan caught a glimpse of the fine ladder of scars on the inside of her forearm, silver lines.

'Are you sure about that?'

'I said, didn't I?' A flare of temper.

'Moll,' Nick said gently. 'It's OK.'

'Next question?' she said, aggressively.

Shan and Leo shared a look. Shan nodded for him to pick up the reins.

'You're aware that Tyler was shot and killed on Wednesday evening?' Leo said.

'Yes,' she said, her voice breaking. She pushed her hair, tucking it behind her ear.

A beat, then Leo said, 'And you saw Tyler on Wednesday.'

Alarm flitted across her face. 'Who told you that?' When Leo remained silent, she eventually said, 'Yes.'

'Where was this?' Leo asked.

'You obviously know,' she retorted.

'Sweetheart,' her mum chided.

'In the Dales, a campsite.'

'What were you doing there?' Leo asked.

'Visiting Tyler.'

'Was he expecting you?'

'No. I just wanted to see him. I'd been away and . . . Just wanted to catch up.'

Her father blinked very slowly, drawing in a breath, but she didn't notice.

'And what was Tyler's reaction?' Leo said.

'He was surprised,' she said, trying to smile but striking a hollow note.

'Good surprised or . . . ?'

Molly scooped at her hair again. 'He wasn't expecting it, that's all. He'd have come round if he'd only . . . But now he's dead.' Her face crumpled. Her mum moved to put an arm around her but Molly pushed her away. 'Don't!'

120

Jules raised her hands in surrender: *Look, I'm backing off.*

'What did you say to Tyler?' Leo asked.

'How it was good to see him and I'd heard about the workshop and I'd love to help.'

'And how did he respond?'

She bent her head, tracing the leaves of the inked bracelet with her forefinger.

'Molly?' Leo prompted.

'He said they had enough volunteers. And I said we could just hang out. I'd booked a pitch and we could go to the pub or . . .' She faltered. Shan heard the echo of desperation, imagined the toe-curling embarrassment and hurt of his rejection.

Molly added quickly, 'He was tired, he must have been tired. He didn't mean it.'

'He didn't mean what?' Leo asked.

She twisted in her seat, trying to escape the memory.

'What did Tyler say?' Shan leaned back, not wanting to appear like she was pressurising the girl.

'He told me he was busy. I asked him why he'd ignored my messages. Ghosted me. Why was he doing that?'

Jules mouth was crimped tight. Shan imagined the Unwins had heard some version of this many times before, going by what the Prasads had described.

'We could have worked it out,' Molly insisted. 'We were so good together. We were so happy. You fight for your dreams, don't you?'

'Fight?' Shan said carefully.

'He didn't mean it,' she said again. Her thumb was pressing into her forearm now, over the top of one of the scars.

'What did he say?' Shan repeated.

'He said I shouldn't have come. He didn't want to see me.' She grew tearful. 'He said he couldn't do this anymore. He was sick of it, sick of me.' She raised her face, looking directly at Shan. Her nose running, tears on her cheeks. 'He told me to leave him alone.' Her face darkened with emotion, bitterness in her voice.

'Did you?' Shan asked.

There was a long pause.

'Moll?' her dad urged, gentle concern in his voice.

'I left the following morning,' she said.

Not answering the question.

'Did you follow Tyler out of campsite up onto the moor?' Shan said.

'What?' Her voice wobbled. 'No!'

'Did you see anyone else go with Tyler? Or go after him?'

'No.'

'Did you hurt Tyler?'

'He hurt me!' she insisted.

'Did you hurt him back?'

'No!'

'There was a shotgun, your great-grandfather's, in the shed here. It's missing. What can you tell me about that?' Shan said.

'What?' She recoiled. 'You're off your head!'

'Molly!' Jules cried.

'Moll!' Nick said.

'I loved Tyler. He was everything to me. I'd never . . . I'd never do anything. How can you say that?'

Shan kept quiet, letting her talk.

'If he'd listened to me he'd be alive now, wouldn't he?'

Shan felt a chill at the nape of her neck. 'If he'd done what you wanted?'

'Yes.'

'But he didn't. So, what? You were angry, you—'

'No! But if we'd gone together to get some food or coffee, had a drink, that's what I mean . . . He'd have come round. Everyone knew we were meant to be together. But now it's too late. I love him. I'll never stop loving him. If he'd stayed with me then none of this—' She broke down, sobbing. Her dad reached over and passed her some kitchen roll.

'Molly, if what you say is true—' Shan said.

'It is!'

'We need to prove it. That's why we're going to be examining your clothes, and we want to take a DNA sample from you. That will help prove you weren't there when Tyler was shot.'

'I wasn't!'

'Did you touch Tyler on Wednesday?'

'We hugged,' she said, but her gaze wavered, a sting in the memory.

Shan could see it, Molly launching herself at Tyler. Tyler ambushed, stiff, perhaps pulling away.

'And that was it?' Shan said.

'Yes.'

The DNA traces on Tyler were under his arms, on his socks and around his shins. If Molly was being honest about the limit of their contact, it was unlikely to be her DNA.

'It's just a simple cotton swab,' Shan said, getting out the kit.

'No! I don't have to do that, do I? I want a lawyer.' She was on her feet. 'You can't make me.'

'It's voluntary at this stage,' Leo said. 'But if we arrest you . . . then you'd be obliged.'

'Go on, then.' Chin jutting out. Eyes flashing.

'Molly!' Jules gasped.

'Don't be daft,' Nick said.

Was she telegraphing her guilt, unable to face it directly?

'If you're innocent—' Jules said.

'*If* I'm innocent.' She rounded on her mother. 'Jesus! Listen to yourself. You think I could do that? I loved him. He's dead and I loved him. Can't you understand that?' She was raving, spittle flying as she shouted.

'Molly,' Shan said softly, 'sit down, please.'

She didn't want to arrest a distressed teenager but perhaps she'd have to.

'He shouldn't have said that,' she cried. 'If he'd just stayed with me. Talked to. Listened to me. He told me to go, to leave him alone. He was sick of me. He shouldn't have said that!' Her face was contorted, a look of spite. 'So arrest me.'

Shan turned to Leo. *Do I?* Leo signalled yes with a dip of his eyes.

'Molly Unwin, I am arresting you on suspicion of the murder of Tyler Prasad . . .'

Her mother wailed. Her father stood, protesting, 'Please, wait? You can't do that!'

Molly glared at Shan, mouth screwed tight, as Shan completed the caution.

'Where are you taking her? What's going to happen?' Jules asked.

'She'll be taken to the police station and booked in,' Leo said. 'She'll be interviewed under caution with a duty solicitor present, and then if we bring charges, she'll appear in the magistrates court the following morning. The case will be referred to the Crown Court.'

'No, no.' Jules had her hand over her mouth. 'Don't, please?' She begged them. 'She didn't do it. Nick, tell them!'

'She wouldn't,' Nick said. He looked broken.

'We'll need your phone as well,' Shan told Molly.

Molly waggled it at her, still seething. Shan reached out to take it.

'I'm not going like this,' Molly said, looking down at her bathrobe.

'You can change your clothes,' Shan said. 'But be quick, please.'

Molly walked upstairs, deliberately slowly, head held high.

Shan pondered her attitude. If Molly had killed Tyler, was this her savouring the notoriety? Did she view it as some romantic tragedy? His murder a grand gesture. Proof of a love so all-consuming that she'd taken his life knowing she would lose her liberty as a result.

* * *

Leo

They were almost done booking Molly in with the custody officer — she'd answered the medical questionnaire, had her mugshot taken, and given fingerprints and a DNA sample — when Leo's phone rang: Nick Unwin.

Leo stepped away to take the call.

'We've found the shotgun,' Nick said, voice shaking with relief. 'Our lad had it. Molly can't have used it. It's been at his mate's all summer.'

'I'll be there shortly. Is he with you?'

'Yes.'

'Keep him there and don't let him contact anyone.'

Leo beckoned to Shan and they moved into the corridor. He explained the situation.

'You're kidding me!' Shan said.

'You stay here, will you? I'll go see what's what and we'll decide how to proceed.'

'Sure.' He saw her disappointment. If it was true that Molly had no access to the weapon, then the probability of her being the culprit shrank considerably.

* * *

Molly's brother Joel looked sick with anxiety when Leo got there.

A lad in a Liverpool shirt and racer shorts. Face dimpled with acne. He was pacing around the living room.

Fifteen years old, Leo gleaned when he took his date of birth.

'Tell him,' Jules said. 'Tell him what you told us.'

'I borrowed the gun. Me and my mate. There's rats at the canal, see.' The tips of his ears were blazing red, the colour of his shirt. 'We were just messing.'

'When was this?' Leo said.

'At the start of the summer holidays.'

'And where is the gun now?' Leo said.

'Still at his.'

'Have you spoken to this mate today?'

Joel shook his head.

'Right, I need you to take me there. And don't tell him we're coming.'

Leo drove Joel to his mate's house. The lad corroborated Joel's story, and the shotgun, which he was keeping under his bed, was confiscated.

'You were in possession of an illegal weapon. We take that very seriously.' The boys looked chastened, anxious. Joel had tears in his eyes. Leo issued them both with a warning.

He told Joel to wait in the house while he made a call.

'Did you find it?' Shan asked.

'Yes. Their story adds up. No way could Molly have used that gun.'

'Shit! So what now?'

'De-arrest her,' Leo said.

'But she still has a credible motive,' Shan argued. 'And she was the last person to see him.'

'Only if *she* shot him. And as of now we've no evidence supporting that.'

'But Leo—'

'Listen — we have her DNA. Those profiles from the scene should be ready sometime soon. If it's her, we pick her up. But we haven't grounds to hold her now. Trust me on this.'

Shan groaned.

'Shan?'

'OK. I'll run her back and explain the situation.'

'I'm taking Joel home. I'll probably be there first, so I can fill them in.'

Silence.

'Another day tomorrow,' Leo said by way of encouragement.

'Yeah, right,' Shan said and hung up.

* * *

He descended Buttertubs Pass at the end of a long, hard day.

The evening sun was low in the sky, the valleys below already dipped in shadow. The light made the colours sing: the heather a vibrant purple and some of the drifts of bracken already flaming orange, taking on their autumn colour. Wisps of cloud like swags of sheep's wool were tinged rose and mandarin. Would Luke have been outside at all today? Kickabout in the yard? An hour perhaps.

The increasing savagery of conditions in prisons, the hacking away of resources, of programmes for rehabilitation and training, had left Leo feeling dismay and anger in equal measure over the years. But now he imagined the effects of that up close and personal.

A trio of cyclists passed on the opposite side of the road, tackling the steep incline.

Ahead of Leo a coach navigated the twists in the road with caution, and behind that a delivery van kept edging out looking for an opportunity to overtake.

He caught sight of a hawk circling high over the fells to the east. Couldn't tell what type. *Avian blood.*

At home, Leo's neighbour, Billy Ollershot, was sitting out front of his house on his captain's chair, mobility walker beside him. He waved as Leo got out of the car. His heart sank. Could he pretend he hadn't noticed? Then he felt guilty for thinking that.

Leo crossed the narrow lane.

Billy looked all of his ninety-five years. The last months had seen him in and out of hospital. Ange and Leo did what they could to help out. Billy was adamant he'd stay in his own home. 'Only way I'm leaving here is in t'box.'

'How do, Leo?'

'How do.' Matching his traditional greeting. 'Taking the air?' Leo asked.

'Like a boiler room in there. This side of 'ouse is OK at t'moment.' Billy shifted in his chair. 'I were reet sorry to hear about your Luke.'

'Yes,' Leo said, stiffening.

'Ange told us. Be a heck of a shock to t'lad.' Billy shook his head.

'We hoped it'd be a community order.' Leo heard rustling in the hedge, little animals foraging or perhaps birds settling in to roost.

'Twelve month?' Billy said.

'Aye, twelve months. How you doing?'

'Fair to middling. Nowt's changed — well, apart from the eyes. Time was, I'd have my nose stuck in a book but now . . .' He blew out a breath.

'Is it the font?' Leo said.

'The what?'

'The size of the letters.'

'Mebbe,' Billy said.

'Just, you can get e-books now and make the writing as big as you like.'

Billy grunted.

'I'll get Ange to show you sometime. It might help.'

'You did the right thing, you know,' Billy said. 'Wi' Luke.'

'Ta.' Words caught in his throat. 'Doesn't always feel like that,' he said finally.

'Aye,' Billy said.

'Best get on,' Leo said.

'See you later.'

A few steps away, Leo turned back. 'What do you do if you can't read?'

'Sit here and wool-gather.'

'Fine Yorkshire pastime,' Leo said.

* * *

Ange was out, a note on the table. *Doing an extra couple of hours for the food bank. Tea in the fridge. I've had mine.* xxx

Leo dished up some potato salad and emptied the bowl of mixed greens onto his plate. He heated a chicken fillet in the microwave and opened a bottle of pale ale, then put everything on a tray to take out onto the patio, where the last of the day still lightened the sky in the west. The gloaming.

The light from inside was enough to dimly illuminate the seating area.

He drank some beer, savouring the crisp, hoppy taste, the chill of it. He ate quickly and, still hungry, fetched himself a portion of blackberry and apple crumble.

He felt leaden. Tired and close to tears. *For no particular reason*, the voice in his head said. *Not true*, he argued with himself. The senseless murder, dealing with other people's grief — he couldn't completely isolate himself from it. And Luke, missing Luke, still feeling culpable for reporting his son.

'You should cry,' Ange had told him more than once over the years. 'It's natural.' But if he started, how would he ever stop? That was his fear. *Be in the moment.* That was meant to help too.

He watched the stars glimmer, heard a snatch of laughter from one of the other gardens, sounded like Jill down the road. He breathed in the sweet evening air. Someone nearby had cut their grass.

He heard Ange arriving back. She came to find him.

'Hey,' she said. 'You want another one of those?' Pointing at his bottle.

'At least,' Leo said.

She came back out brandishing a beer, a glass of white wine in her other hand.

'Nice chicken,' Leo said.

'Lemon and cardamom.' She sat beside him. 'I froze the others.'

She edged off her sandals and took a drink. Leaned her head back.

'How you doing?' Leo said.

She sighed expansively, bent forward and put her glass on the table, the piece she'd built from reclaimed timber. He remembered the benches at the Prasads'. Had Tyler made those? With his dad?

'The visiting order came through,' Ange said.

His heart rose. *Thank God.* He could see his boy. Start building bridges, a way back. 'Great. When for?'

She turned and took his free hand in hers.

'Leo,' she said. 'It's just for me. He's only invited me.'

'Ah, Christ.' His eyes burned. The stars and the garden all blurring. And his heart tearing for the loss of his son.

* * *

129

At her dad's house, Banjo came bounding out to greet her. Shan bent to fuss the dog, telling him he was a good boy, rubbing the scruff of his neck, suffering the wet lap of his tongue on her chin.

'Work bring you down here?' her dad asked, once they were inside. 'Only, I thought you'd be on that Tyler Prasad case. Your DI's running that, isn't he?'

'Yes.'

'Main story on the news. Terrible thing. That poor lad.'

'Yes.'

'And his family.'

'I know.' *Where to start?* 'I am on that but I'm not here for work exactly.' She changed the subject. 'Have you eaten?'

'Waited for you. It's only pasta.'

'Sounds good. I'll take my bag up.'

Banjo followed her upstairs, still thrilled at her arrival, tail thumping, practically tripping her up.

'We're not going out,' she warned. 'Don't get your hopes up.' Banjo stared at her, eyes limpid, whined and beat his tail some more.

She wanted to lie down and sleep for a week.

The velvet curtains in her old bedroom were closed. To keep some of the heat out, she guessed. The decor was still the same as when she'd last lived here, minus the posters and pictures. Pale violet walls and bare wood skirting boards, purple curtains. A fitted grey wool carpet. The old stone house could be bitterly cold in winter.

'Your purple phase?' Erin had teased the first time they'd stayed over.

'At least it's not black. Imagine if I'd been allowed free rein in my emo phase.'

'Did they stop you?' Erin sounded surprised because Shan's parents had been pretty laid-back.

'No. I just didn't have the energy for stuff like paint and rollers.'

'Too busy emoting?'

Oh, Erin. Would she be OK? Would she go back to work on Monday? What was going to happen to them? Erin had been hurt, she'd made that clear. *'Don't bank on me, Shan. I don't know if I can ever trust you again.'*

'Shan?' her dad called.

'Coming.'

They ate at the table in the kitchen, Shan asking questions to keep the conversation focused on him. His new glasses, where he'd bought the sun-dried tomato pesto, the hosepipe ban, how his pub quiz team were faring, work at his printing firm.

She loaded the dishwasher and made tea, took it through to the lounge. The familiarity was comforting, her graduation picture on the wall opposite two watercolours of the Dales that her dad had bought for her mum. The cast-iron fireplace with tiled panels. Photographs of the three of them on the mantlepiece.

A fine layer of dust coated everything. Erin would be irked by that, but dust wasn't dirt as far as Shan reckoned, and her dad managed well enough in the years he'd been alone. The place was never pristine but it was clean.

Banjo whined.

'Let him out in the garden, will you?' her dad said.

She did, looking out at the tangled patch of wildflowers and long grasses that he'd let take over the lawn. They'd thrived in the drought. One lot of neighbours had objected to the change, claimed it looked 'messy'. 'Better than sterile,' her dad had said when he relayed the substance of the set-to. The complainants had tried to enlist other residents to their cause, protesting that the weeds would sow seeds in their gardens, but hadn't found any takers.

Shan left the back door ajar and went back.

Expectation hung heavily in the atmosphere. Or was she imagining it? She fished for something to say, something innocuous, but he got in first, 'So you're here because . . .'

Shan sighed. 'We're just . . . we're having a break. Erin and me.'

'A break?' He looked concerned. 'How come?' He was always direct.

'Things haven't been very good. Since the miscarriage.' She felt heat glow in her cheeks.

'I'm sorry, love.'

She hoped he'd leave it at that, dared to feel relief, but he shifted in his chair and said, 'It's not been very long, though, has it?'

'No,' she said. Clenching her teeth, suddenly tearful, a stinging behind her eyes, but determined not to break down.

'Who suggested the break?'

'Dad, I . . . I don't want . . . Me.'

'You think it might help?' His eyes fixed on her.

'I don't know. Can we talk about something else?'

'It's just, you seem—'

'Dad!' She was a teenager again, a mutinous fifteen-year-old.

'I'd like to help,' he said gently.

'You can't. Nobody can.' Her throat ached. She was too hot, her skin sticky. Would it ever rain again?

'What will the break give you?' He sipped his tea.

'Breathing space. To decide what to do.' She stared out of the window at the darkening sky, the vivid licks of turquoise and lilac that streaked the thin clouds above the houses opposite.

'What to do about . . .'

'Me and Erin.'

'And whether you try again for a baby?'

'No! Yes. I don't know.' She wiped away a treacherous tear. Just the thought of it had her drowning. The procedures, injections and tests, the money, the debates about donors, the stress.

'Well, do you know what Erin wants?'

'Not really.' Her irritation at the probing gave way to a feeling of hopelessness. *What does it matter? Any of it? It's all a mess.*

The dog slipped into the room, accepted a stroke from her dad, then jumped up beside Shan on the couch.

'Look,' her dad said, 'sometimes you need a . . .' He was blushing. 'Someone objective to—'

'You?' she squeaked.

'No. Not me, you daft thing.' He laughed and she felt a little bubble of mirth rise in answer.

'Listen, when your mum and I realised we couldn't start a family, it was really difficult. I wanted us to try IVF. Your mum was clear that she wouldn't go there. And I was equally sure that I wanted children any which way. That had always been the plan. Maybe that was weird — me, a bloke, feeling so strongly about wanting to be a dad.' He paused, clearing his throat. 'We couldn't see any way through. And she took that to mean that she wasn't enough for me. That I'd leave and find someone else.'

Shan had known all about her parents choosing to adopt her, getting approved, then matched, their journey to China to bring her back, but only the bare bones of what came before. And certainly had never heard about this.

'It was like we were on different sides. I don't know . . . talking different languages.'

Shan found it hard to watch the emotion on his face and bowed to scratch Banjo's head.

'Honestly, I thought we were done. I was furious at her for being so inflexible, even though I knew intellectually, emotionally, on every level, it had to be her call. She was the one who'd have to go through the procedures and the drugs and what have you. It all sounded pretty brutal. And no guarantee of success.' He took a breath. 'Anyway, she asked me to go to counselling with her. So I did. I thought it was a waste of time, to be honest. I was already thinking about where I'd live next, but I wanted to show willing.' He gave a sniff. 'It was a bloody lifesaver, Shan.' She glanced over at him, saw the sheen in his eyes. He drew his hand over his mouth, studying her.

His message couldn't have been more obvious. 'I'll think about it,' she said, reaching for her cup.

'Good,' he said.

She would. She would think about it, she told herself. It didn't mean she actually had to *do* it. And besides, there was no room for anything but the investigation at the moment. She had to concentrate on that. Just that. For now.

* * *

She couldn't sleep. She'd opened the window as wide as possible to let in some air. It was a clear night, the sickle moon visible but few stars, too much light pollution in the city.

It was noisy too, noisier than Settle, with the blare of emergency sirens coming at regular intervals, the drone of traffic, the squeak and bang of doors being opened and closed, and trains rattling and clacking over the nearby junction on the way into Leeds.

She was sweaty, then itchy, insects crawling over her arms, her calves, the top of her back. When she did finally succumb, she was startled awake by a bunch of prats singing 'Bohemian Rhapsody' at the top of their lungs.

She turned the pillow over to the cooler side and stuck her feet out of the bottom of the sheet. She drowsed again, then there was knocking and Erin was at the door. Shouting at her. Red-faced and spitting anger. The house filled with police and they were searching. Tossing everything aside, tugging out drawers, ripping up the mattress.

Shan was frightened, a terror, cold and dark, stealing through her.

'I don't know,' she kept telling them. 'I don't know. I don't know.' But they were digging. The ground was soft, the soil black and crumbly. A baby there in a purple box.

Still.

Horribly still. Pale.

Erin screamed at her.

'I didn't!' Shan said. 'I didn't hurt it. I didn't.'

'Look,' her dad said. 'Just look.' He was pointing, jabbing a finger.

The baby had been shot, a spray of tiny holes across its back. A constellation of red stars.

'Shan!' her dad shouted, still gesturing to the baby. 'Shan!'

She reared up, heart thundering, mouth dry as dust. She heard the call again. Not her name but Banjo barking. The start of the day. *Just a dream.* She stared at the ceiling. At the paper globe lampshade. *Just a dream.* But the feelings of shame and fear and guilt were lodged in the pit of her stomach and the bones of her jaw.

CHAPTER NINE

Saturday

Leo

Leo was finishing breakfast, having his coffee prior to driving into work, when a call came in from their chief superintendent, Ken Quigley.

'Leo, we need to meet. Can you come in?' Quigley said. No preliminaries.

'Today?' Meetings were rare, scheduled weeks in advance. Most of the time Leo was supervised by Matthew Booth, his line manager.

'ASAP. You and DC Young.'

'Is something wrong?' Leo asked. His mind lighted on moments from the last few days: arresting and de-arresting Molly Unwin, interviewing Oliver Peel, busting Rafe Duvall for possession. Had the Patefield estate objected to the way they'd conducted themselves?

'Nothing that can't be sorted out,' Quigley said. Which didn't really answer the question. 'I'll see you soon.'

Perhaps it was something closer to home, Leo wondered. Concern about Ange knowing Tyler Prasad — did someone think that might prejudice Leo's handling of the enquiry? But then Quigley wanted to see Shan too. *So what is it?*

His stomach churned and he couldn't finish his coffee, the taste in his mouth suddenly acrid.

He phoned Shan and asked her to meet him at headquarters, explaining he'd no idea why the superintendent had asked to see them at such short notice.

On the drive his mind worried away at the question. The roads were busy, legions of tourists in their luxury vehicles in among the delivery vans, tractors and runarounds going about their working days, and dozens of bikers wearing elaborately designed leathers, many on the big Easy Rider–style machines. Pennants flying as they streamed past him. Probably some rally or race on today.

Roadkill dotted the tarmac at regular intervals. Mainly rabbit. Crows trying to feast on it whenever there was a gap in the traffic.

Shan was already there, waiting in reception, when he got through security.

'I'll just . . .' He pointed to the toilets.

The shiny office block held the stale chill of air conditioning and Leo wished he'd brought a jacket.

Chief Superintendent Quigley greeted them at the lift on the first floor and took them into his room. It was a spacious glass cube with dado walls. The venetian blinds were lowered but not fully closed on the external side. Bright strips of light seared the carpet.

The air was viciously cold in here too, and Leo felt his knees ache when he took a seat.

Shan seemed nervous, sitting with her hands clasped, and he wished he could reassure her but he'd no clue what was going on.

Quigley was a large-framed man with apple cheeks and big, brown eyes. He undid his jacket button and edged his chair up to his desk.

'I've asked you to come in today in connection with the Tyler Prasad enquiry.' He took a breath, rubbed at the base of his nose with a knuckle. 'The family are dissatisfied.'

Dissatisfied! Leo felt his stomach drop. This he was not expecting.

'What do you mean?' Shan said.

Leo's mind leaped through the steps he'd taken, informing the next of kin as soon as possible, giving them some time after that before interviewing them as witnesses. They'd been distraught, of course, heartbroken, but still Leo hadn't sensed any problem. They'd cooperated as much as they could. Was it because he'd given them Ange's number? But they'd seemed so keen to speak to her.

'Dissatisfied with what?' Leo said.

'Specifically with your role, Leo.'

He felt sick.

Shan looked at him, her face creasing in concern.

Quigley cleared his throat. 'The family have been made aware of your son's conviction.'

Luke!

'In particular, the fact that the offence was racially aggravated.'

'What?' Leo said, incredulous. *Tarred with the same brush?* 'And they think because Tyler's mixed race and Luke—'

Quigley held up a hand. 'Let me finish.'

'Sir,' Leo said, biting his tongue.

'They have requested that we find a replacement officer to continue the investigation.'

'No way!' he protested.

Shan was trembling, her face pale with anger. 'You can't replace him, sir!'

'I have explained to the family that's not feasible. Least of all because we've a chronic shortage of detectives and it would take months to find someone.'

'And people can't pick and choose which officers work on their cases,' Leo pointed out. 'Same as you can't ask for a different teacher or . . .' Leo felt rage boil through him, hot and violent. Containing himself as best as he was able, he said tightly, 'I am not my son. I hope to hell you also told them that. My record . . . my work—'

'They're grieving. They're all over the place,' Quigley said.

'They're wrong,' Shan asserted. 'If every officer who had a connection to people who are racist or homophobic or misogynistic was written off, you'd have practically no police force. And that's without the ones who are actually paid-up bigots themselves.'

There was a stunned silence.

'Let us remain with the issue in hand,' Quigley said coldly.

'Guilt by association?' Leo said.

Quigley sent him a sideways glance but ignored the comment. 'This is a high-profile case. Eyes are on us. There is a compromise. A way of moving forward without undermining the work already done while still reassuring the family. Diplomacy. DC Young takes the lead. You take a back seat.' He locked eyes with Leo. 'Behind the scenes but still in charge.'

'But that makes it look like Leo — like DI Donovan is guilty of something. That they have grounds to doubt him,' Shan said.

'Not at all,' Quigley argued.

'This is because of Greaves and Irving, and the Foster case, isn't it?' she said, referring to the recent scandals involving racist officers.

And countless other failings going back forever, Leo thought. The police not only reflecting the prejudices in society but often condensing them, a culture allowing them to flourish, a petri dish. Was it any wonder people mistrusted them?

'DC Young!' Quigley said sharply.

'We shouldn't do that, sir. I'm not prepared to do that,' Shan said.

'This could be—' Quigley began.

'I won't. I won't do that,' she said, grit in her tone.

All the air seemed to leave the room.

Insubordination. Christ, Shan was going to get herself disciplined at this rate.

'Let us talk to the family,' Leo said. 'Clear the air, address any concerns they have face to face.'

'I don't think—' Quigley said.

'This is my reputation. And I don't want sticking in the back seat like some embarrassment. If they had all the facts . . . I deserve that. They deserve that.'

'It's a very delicate situation.'

'Let us talk to them.'

'They might refuse.'

'We can ask.'

'It could be seen as undue pressure.'

'The truth is, sir, that you can't replace me, we've no staff — even if you judged that was an appropriate thing to do, which it isn't. Not unless I've failed in my duties. So, I'm continuing to lead the investigation. To pretend otherwise is scarcely transparent or honest. Not really in the spirit of our anti-racism action plan. In fact, it could be seen as misleading.'

Quigley didn't like that, true though it was. His round cheeks bloomed red. 'And if at the end of the day they're still antagonistic?'

Leo wouldn't entertain that. 'Let's talk to them. Let's see.'

Quigley regarded him for some time, chewing his lip before apparently coming to a decision. 'Very well,' he said curtly.

Leo was shaken to his marrow. He felt like he'd been in a car crash. Hollow. Stressed. Adrenaline and cortisol coursing through his veins like bleach.

His mouth was dry, his pulse uneven, as he rang Randall's number.

'Hello?' Randall sounded wary.

'Hello. I'm in a meeting at the moment with Chief Superintendent Quigley. I appreciate that you and Eesha have some concerns about my continuing to work on Tyler's case. I'd like to come and see you both, myself and DC Young, to discuss it. Answer any questions you might have. And explain my personal situation.'

There was a pause. Leo could hear Randall breathing. He waited, Shan and Quigley watching.

Leo could just make out a muffled exchange, presumably Randall relaying his request to Eesha.

Leo hung on. More indistinct conversation. It sounded like there were two women speaking. Eesha's sister Padma was there, presumably.

Finally, 'OK.'

'We could be there within the hour,' Leo said. 'If that's convenient.'

'That should be OK.'

'Thank you. We'll see you later.'

* * *

Shan stared at him in the lift down and shook her head. '"Have been made aware of"?' she quoted Quigley. 'Who's made them aware?'

Leo had wondered that himself, briefly. 'It doesn't matter. It's public knowledge anyway.' The local press and media had covered the arrest and conviction of the far-right cell.

Luke. Bloody Luke.

Ange was visiting him today. She'd promised to try and persuade him to add Leo to his visitors list.

'I'll write anyway,' Leo had said. 'I'll write to him.'

'And bare your soul?' Ange said.

'Something like that. What else can I do?' What if this was it? What if their estrangement, Luke's rejection of him, was permanent? His throat had locked, eyes stung at the prospect.

'Something to eat?' Shan asked as they left the building. 'There's a place round the corner.'

Leo hesitated.

'We have time,' she said. 'And you look like you need it.'

The cafe had tables and chairs outside, bordered by planters sprouting grasses and spikey succulents. Hanging baskets spilled fuchsia and nasturtium and ivy. The shop front, canopy and furniture were styled in lime-washed pastels, giving it a seaside feel. Like the ice cream Luke liked. Neapolitan. *Stripey-icey*, he'd called it.

Most of the seats were taken by groups of mums with children in strollers but Shan found a free table on the edge.

Eating a chicken salad roll and drinking a mug of tea helped settle the frazzled feeling torturing Leo's guts. Eased the chill that had burrowed into his bones during the meeting.

Shan seemed hungry, munching away on a rainbow salad bowl with all sorts of vegetables and beans and seeds in it.

She'd been fierce with Quigley. Almost reckless. He was proud of her, but still. 'You need to be careful,' Leo said.

'I couldn't just sit there and say nothing,' she objected.

'Look, I'm grateful but I'm just saying—'

'I know what you're saying.' She met his look, smiled.

'Right, then.' He screwed up his serviette. 'Better make tracks.'

* * *

Shan

Shan parked around the corner from the Prasads' house and texted Leo: *Just arrived.*

She watched a couple down the road unpack their shopping, carrying bags and boxes in from the car boot. A toddler in a floppy sun hat was helping, tottering with a pack of kitchen towel in through the gate.

Her eyes stung. Stupid! All those fantasies she'd had of her and Erin and their baby. *You never even picked a name,* came the nasty little voice in her head. *Erin asked you to. She bought you a book. You barely opened it. The child knew it wasn't welcome. You didn't really want it.*

'Fucksake,' Shan said aloud and banged her head back on the headrest, trying to silence the nagging chatter.

In the rear-view mirror, she saw Leo's car enter the street and pass by looking for a place to park. She took a swig of water and picked up her bag, got out and went to join him.

Reporters and camera crews were clustered outside the house. Shan wondered how they coped with the heat. Did they take it in turns to nip away for a break, a cold drink in the shade somewhere?

Their attention swung to Shan and Leo and the cameras started rolling while they bombarded Leo with questions.

'Can you give us an update, DI Donovan?'

'Have you made any arrests?'

'Was there a racial motive?'

'DI Donovan have you a quote for the public?'

Leo said, 'No comment today,' just the once as they edged their way through to the house.

Eesha's sister, Padma, answered the door to them. Unsmiling. 'We're in the living room,' she said tersely, leading them into the first door off the hall.

Three small sofas, draped with covers, formed three sides of a square with an open fireplace on the fourth side.

There was a huge glass jar in the hearth, full of ferns and moss. Shan knew there was a word for the bottle and for that type of garden but couldn't remember either.

Eesha and Randall sat on the far couch in front of the bay window. Leo and Shan took seats on the one facing them. Padma on the one between.

The room was rich with colour, peacock-blue walls, a white ceiling and touches of pink and green in the fabrics. Pieces of driftwood, large pine cones and dried seedheads served as ornamentation among the books on the shelves. Framing the bay window was a trailing philodendron plant in a macrame hanger and a large pink-glazed pot with a tall umbrella plant and a peace lily, like the one Leo had in his office. Gauzy curtains were closed, allowing light in but shielding them all from view of the press outside.

'Thank you for agreeing to see us,' Leo said. 'I understand you have some concerns because my son, Luke, has recently been convicted of a crime.'

The couple looked guarded, ill at ease. They were wearing the same clothes as yesterday. Shan felt for them, their world shattered, unfathomable.

'We have,' said Padma sharply.

'I'd like to tell you what happened, if that might be helpful, and then you can ask me whatever you like. But is there anything you'd like to say first?' Leo asked.

Eesha glanced at her husband, then said, 'Tyler was picked up by the police on several occasions. Picked out sometimes because he was Asian. Indian, a brown boy. He was treated differently. We weren't surprised.' She gave a small shrug, her face an expression of exasperation. 'So when we heard about your son, I think you can see why we would feel uncomfortable.'

'With me?' Leo said.

Shan swallowed.

'Yes,' Padma said.

'Yes,' Eesha echoed.

'Let me lay out the facts, then,' Leo said. He spoke quietly, hands on his knees.

'Over the past few years, Luke has become increasingly withdrawn from me and his mother — Ange, who Tyler was working with,' he added.

Randall dipped his head.

'He began to talk about conspiracy theories, ridiculous stuff. We tried to challenge him, fact check, but everything we said was "fake". *We* were the ones being brainwashed. He repeated racist ideas too,' Leo said. 'Far-right sentiments. We hadn't raised him like that, we didn't — we don't agree with those views. We tried everything. He lives . . . was living with us. He's just twenty-one. It was toxic.'

The family were listening intently but Shan could read their body language. Eesha had her arms folded in defensive mode; Randall had his head cocked, reserved and sceptical; Padma wasn't even looking at Leo but up at the ceiling.

'This year, I suspected Luke was lying to us about where he'd been, what he was up to. I thought he might have been involved in spray-painting graffiti on an Asian taxi firm.'

The atmosphere was claustrophobic. Shan consciously tried to relax her back, lower her shoulders. A peal of chimes from an ice cream van sounded, 'The Teddy Bears' Picnic', incongruous alongside the grim story Leo was telling.

'Shortly afterwards, Luke was injured in a motorbike accident. I was called to the hospital. While he was in surgery—' Leo's voice tightened, he coughed and continued — 'I looked at his phone. I found evidence — pictures, group chat — that proved he was involved with two other people in a far-right cell.'

'God,' Randall said.

'They were coordinating attacks. Hate messages graffitied on the taxi firm, on a mosque, and they'd been scoping out a synagogue.'

Shan thought Randall looked sympathetic now. Eesha was staring at her lap. Padma, lips pursed, face averted, appeared unconvinced.

'I passed on that information, photographs and screenshots of the messages, to the police.' Leo paused, blinked. His mouth worked.

Was he going to cry? Shan couldn't breathe. She pressed her fist to her chest.

Leo inhaled briskly, smoothed the fabric of his trousers over his knee. 'Luke was arrested and charged on release from hospital. The others too.'

'You helped convict him?' Randall said.

'It was the right thing to do,' Leo said. He sounded crushed. A pause, then, 'And I want to do the right thing by Tyler. By you. I'm committed to it. This is my job. This is what I do. I am not my son. I need your trust.'

No one spoke until Eesha broke the silence. 'Does he know, your son, that you did this?'

'Oh, yes,' Leo said. 'He hates me for it. He won't allow me to visit him. Only his mum. She's there today.'

Shan was shocked. She imagined how deeply that must cut.

'Would you want to visit?' Eesha asked, frowning.

'Yes,' he said without hesitation. 'I have to believe there's some hope. And I love him.' He paused to clear his throat.

'He's my son. I loathe what he says, what he believes, what he's done, but—'

'You think he can change?' Eesha said.

'I don't know.' Leo rubbed his forehead. 'I really don't know. I hope so.'

Randall turned to his wife. Some communication was exchanged wordlessly.

Eesha said, 'Thank you. We were worried.' She raised her shoulders, let them drop.

'Do you have any questions?' Leo said.

'No,' Randall said.

'Are we OK?' Leo said.

The couple nodded. Padma opened her mouth to speak but a glance from Eesha stopped her. Padma seemed unhappy but sat back, resigned to their decision.

Shan felt something in her loosen in relief. 'We'll be in touch,' she said, getting to her feet. 'As soon as there's any news.'

'What about Molly Unwin?' Padma asked.

'We've spoken to her. We're making further enquiries, that's all I can say for now.'

Eesha gave a slight shake of her head. Shan saw she was still unwilling to believe Molly might be responsible.

Outside, the heat was like a wall. They moved through the scrum of the media.

Shan parted from Leo at the corner.

'You OK?' she said. She sensed the sorrow in him, wide and deep.

He pulled a rueful face, gave a shrug. 'You?'

She smiled. 'No, not really.'

'You still at your dad's?'

'Yes.' She sensed he was expecting her to elaborate. 'I'll see you in the morning.'

'Bright and early,' he said.

'Well, early anyway,' Shan said. A burning at the back of her eyes. 'Take care.'

* * *

Leo was almost home when Randall McKenzie rang him. 'We've found Tyler's password. We think it's still current.'

'Thanks, that's great,' Leo said.

'It's "chipko" with a "k" then "xoxo". All lowercase.'

'Can you text me that, please?' Leo said. He wanted to be sure of the spelling.

'Sure thing. Some of Eesha's relatives were active in the Chipko movement, back in the day.'

'What was that?' Leo said. A motorbike appeared in his rear-view mirror and he slowed so it could overtake.

'Tree huggers,' Randall said. 'Literally. They attached themselves to trees to prevent logging in the Himalayas. Started back in the seventies.'

'Tree huggers, eh?' Leo said.

'That was our Tyler.' Randall's breath hitched. 'Something in the genes. I'll text it now.'

'Thanks very much,' Leo said. 'And if Eesha or you have any other questions, or any concerns, please get in touch.'

'We will.'

He was passing Snaizeholme, part of the red squirrel reserve, when his phone went again. Not a number he recognised.

'Leo Donovan?'

'Yes.'

'I'm with the Counter Terrorism Unit.' A Geordie accent.

'OK.' Leo's mind scrambled, racing to guess why they were contacting him.

'I know you contributed evidence in the prosecution of Christopher Hirst, Luke Donovan and Jack Sherringham.'

'That's right.'

'The men have been referred to the DDP, the Desistance and Disengagement Programme.'

Leo knew this. He also knew there was little evidence as to how effective the deradicalisation programmes under the Prevent umbrella were.

'I wanted to make you aware that there's been chatter among some groups and individuals online about the case.'

'What sort of chatter?' Leo said.

'I can't go into specifics but we're seeing images of that graffiti being shared and the crime held up as an example to follow. It's a pattern we're familiar with. Information is also being shared naming you and your role as a police officer. Stating that you turned your son in.'

Not exactly but near enough. Uniformed police had already found incriminating CCTV footage of Luke carrying out one of his crimes before Leo shared what he knew.

'Is this a warning?' Leo asked, thinking of the call from Rose Sherringham.

'It's a courtesy call.'

'Are there any credible threats?' Leo asked. It'd be easy enough to find out where Leo lived. The reports in local news had said that Luke was from Yockenthwaite. The hamlet was tiny. But surely even the most fanatical of actors wouldn't risk the fallout of coming after a police officer.

'Not in our estimation, but it wouldn't hurt to be vigilant.'

And what about Ange? All the time she spent on her own, working in her studio. His blood chilled. He must tell her. Decide what 'vigilant' meant.

When he reached home she was watering the garden with grey water from the washing machine. She'd rigged up some extra piping to divert the outflow to a big container. The water butt had run out weeks ago. Most of the plants they'd left to take their chances, many had been chosen for their drought resistance, but the vulnerable ones, the sweet peas, and the pansies and petunias in the trough, couldn't survive without a regular drink.

The creatures in the pond had to fend for themselves, like those in the river nearby, the levels at a historic low.

Ange put the watering can down when she saw him. Wiped her forehead with the back of her hand.

'You look like I feel,' she said.

He opened his mouth to ask about Luke but she headed him off.

'Get a shower. I've made tea.'

148

'What are we having?' he asked.

'Tapas.'

'Ooh, tapas.'

She inclined her head. '*Si. Es muy bien.*'

He ran the shower barely warm while he soaped himself and washed his hair then turned it cold, gasping at the sensation. He tried to concentrate on that feeling, the tingling in his skin, in an effort to quieten the clamour in his mind.

Afterwards, dressed in baggy shorts and a T-shirt, he found Ange in the kitchen putting the finishing touches to their meal.

'Stick the flatbread in, will you?' She gestured to the microwave. 'And there's a bottle of white in the fridge.'

Settled at the patio table, Leo's mouth watered at the smell of food and he wasted no time taking helpings from the various dishes: patatas bravas and aioli sauce, tomato, basil and onion salad, roast halloumi, mushroom croquettes, and garlic and chilli prawns.

'Blimey, Ange,' he said after a few mouthfuls. 'You've surpassed yourself. What's this in aid of?' He knew she didn't enjoy cooking as a rule. It was a chore they shared based on a few well-worn standbys that were quick and easy to make and to freeze.

'Had a craving. And I thought we could do with a change. I bought the croquettes, mind. Life's short.'

He speared another prawn, relishing the bite of garlic and the burn of chilli, then the sweetness of the meat.

When he'd eaten his fill, he wiped his mouth, drank some wine then sat back.

Ange had already finished eating and was sipping her drink. She put down her glass.

'So,' she said.

'So,' Leo echoed. He took a breath, gearing up for whatever was to come.

'I got there in good time and went through all the security.' She gave a shudder. 'Patting me down and everything. There were lots of visitors, women with kids and—' She faltered. Leo understood. Ange had never been inside a prison

149

before. It was not a nice place for anyone. Whenever he'd visited in the course of his work, it was a huge relief being allowed to leave, to walk away, exit the gates.

'How was he?' Leo said.

'Bit quiet. He complained about the food.'

'I bet.'

'He said it was all a bit weird and he was sharing with an older bloke but said he was OK. He'd shown the ropes to Luke. There's a gym on the wing and Luke'll be able to use that to help with exercises for his leg and his collarbone. And we can do calls and video calls. I need to put my number on the system.'

Leo was aware he was eager for her to get to the part where she'd asked Luke to consider seeing his father. Leo rebuked himself. Selfish. He should be thinking only of his boy.

'He didn't look great, to be honest.' Ange had another drink. 'He's going to send a list of things he wants us to buy. And we can send some money in too.'

A bat streaked past. They roosted in the woods behind. Leo pointed and Ange made a noise of appreciation.

'What about work or training?' Leo said.

'He said that's not been settled yet but he'd rather work than study. Although he didn't seem particularly keen on either.'

Nothing new there, then. 'Long as it gets him out of his cell. And he's probably still . . . knocked sideways.'

'Yes.' She refilled her glass. 'So, when I was going, I told him you'd like to see him but I didn't push it. I didn't say more than that.'

'Did he react?' Leo gripped his glass.

'Not really.'

'OK.' Leo swallowed his disappointment.

While they'd talked, dark had fallen. Leo could hear the soft ticking of wood releasing heat. Stars pricked the night. Leo stared up at them. Could Luke see out of a window in his cell? Could he see the sky? The new moon over to the east? Would he be able to sleep with a stranger in the room and the unfamiliar noises of the old Victorian building, crammed full of men? Sealed in with metal bars and blocks, bricks and stones. Incarcerated.

He should tell Ange about the Prasads and their request to the chief super. It wouldn't be fair if she heard about it second-hand. And he should tell her about the warning to be vigilant. *Oh Christ.* He hadn't the energy to get into all that now. He'd tell her tomorrow.

CHAPTER TEN

Saturday

Shan

'You should go to the pub,' Shan told her dad. 'I'll be fine.'

'You could come with.'

'Please, no.'

He laughed. 'Well, I could join them lot later. You and I could eat first?'

'No, it's OK.'

'Only, I'm driving down to Bristol tomorrow, staying with Dean and Viv. I won't be back till Wednesday.'

'I'll survive. I might see if Suze or Harry's around tonight.' Old friends from Leeds. Shan had no intention of getting in touch with either, but it might work as a get-out for her dad. 'I'll take Banjo out soon anyway,' she said. 'It'll be good to get some exercise.'

'What about your tea?' he said.

'Am I seven?'

'Sorry,' he said. 'But you are, some of the time — seven. In my head. Or fourteen. Twenty-one.'

'Stop.'

'I'm stopping.' He backed out of the room and she poured herself a glass of water. Drank it down then went to change into a loose cotton shift that she'd had the foresight to stuff into her bag when she fled from Erin.

It wasn't far from the house to the canal, and Shan welcomed the shade from the trees that lined the footpath. The trail was popular; families with kids on bikes mingled with dog walkers and runners and cyclists. She passed two narrowboats, gaily painted, pots of geranium and a wigwam of runner beans on one. A little further on she took the track that led up into the woods. Off the lead, Banjo hoovered up smells, picking his way through the tangled undergrowth.

The light slanted through the tree trunks, illuminating the dance of insects and pollen. Shan felt the prick of midges at her neck.

Underfoot the leaves had dried to a crisp, making a crunching noise as she walked and raising up little puffs of dust.

Robins and great tits were flitting from branch to branch. She heard a wren — she thought it was a wren, a long, bubbling song.

Even after this prolonged heatwave there were pockets of damp below the trees where fungi and mosses and ferns thrived. She stooped to photograph a cluster of tiny white mushrooms. *Send it to Erin.* Then she remembered, felt a wave of sadness.

When she reached an old stone slab, a remnant from the industrial past, she sat there to eat the apple she'd brought with her.

Banjo continued his snuffling, looping back to check on her now and again.

A beetle scuttled by her feet, black with a blue sheen on its back like it had been sprayed with metallic car paint.

The stone seat was between two birch trees. She craned her neck back to see how high they rose, and noted the blue sky above was softening as the day grew nearer its close.

The leaves hung still and so when she saw movement on one, she investigated and found a shield bug, triangular and a rich green, the same as the moss she'd photographed.

She caught a splash of candy pink through the trees — delicate herb-Robert flowers. Her mum had loved wildflowers. Some of what she taught Shan had stuck.

'Oh, Mum,' she whispered. The longing to see her mum, to talk, to touch, to have one more encounter swept through her. *Twelve years*, she thought. She'd grown used to these moments and imagined now that she would always have them.

And if her mother was to appear, come and sit beside her now, what would Shan say?

I don't know what I'm doing, Mum. I'm lost. I've messed up.

And what would her mum say? *You'll find your way. Go easy on yourself, Shan-Shan. Listen to your heart.*

Shan was startled by the sudden clatter of a wood pigeon bursting from the canopy above. A fine sweat broke across her skin. Her pulse jumped. She gathered her breath then called for the dog. 'Banjo? Come on now. Come now.'

She ate in front of the television, veggie Pad Thai. Then showered and went to bed. She made a wish as she lay down: *No more dreams, please. Just sleep. A good long sleep.*

* * *

Leo

Leo had not expected to sleep much — too tense, too stressed — but when he'd got into bed Ange had snuggled close, kissed his neck, his cheek, his lips by way of invitation. Their love-making had been slow, languorous in the heat of the night. He had lost himself to her touch, to the steady rhythm of their pleasure, to the passion that built and built and left him gasping and free.

Lying back afterwards while Ange went to wash, he let the tears slide silently down the sides of his cheeks, for all he had, and for all he'd lost, and he listened to the owl calling, calling, calling.

* * *

Sunday

He filled Ange in on the complaint from Eesha and Randall while they made breakfast.

'*What?* They never said a thing. They rang me Friday afternoon after you passed on my number.'

'And before they got wind of Luke.' Still bitter that Luke's crime had almost cost him the case. And, if he was honest, disappointed that the Prasads had been so quick to judge him and find him wanting.

'I arranged to see them on Tuesday. They've not cancelled.'

'I think we resolved it. But if I hadn't insisted on seeing them . . .' He flung up his hands.

'I hate that,' she said. 'That people could think you had any truck with what Luke did.'

'I'm not sure they really thought that, they're intelligent people. It was maybe a heat-of-the-moment thing.'

'I sort of get it, though,' she said. 'I mean, your lot aren't exactly a shining example of a multicultural institution. And after those guys—'

'I know.' Leo cut her off; she was referring to the same scumbags that Shan had seized on in yesterday's meeting. The disgraced officers were despicable, and their behaviour only served to further alienate some communities from the police.

'There's something else,' he said. 'I had a call from Counter Terrorism, apparently there's been some chat among the far-right groups.' He sighed. He really did not want to tell her this, but he couldn't keep her in the dark.

'What is it?'

'My name's being bandied about, my part in the Crusaders being sent down.' No doubt the chat rooms were referring to Luke and the two others by the moniker they'd chosen for their cell, trying to glorify what they were doing. 'We've been told to be vigilant.'

Her face fell. 'Bloody hell, Leo.'

'I know.'

'What does that even mean?' she demanded. She was angry but he saw she was fearful too.

He couldn't tell her he didn't really know, so he rolled out the advice they regularly gave out to people under threat. 'Keep the doors locked. Don't answer unless you know who it is. Don't open any packages you weren't expecting. And we should probably check under the cars.'

'Jesus!'

'To be safe,' he added. It sounded lame.

'I don't even know what should be under there,' she said. 'How the hell am I supposed to recognise—'

'Hey. Hey.' He moved in, held her. 'We'll work it out. I'll show you.'

'It's not fair,' she mumbled into his shoulder.

'I know,' he agreed.

She pulled away and went upstairs.

Leo was eating his toast with one eye on the time when she came back in. 'I don't believe it!' She was staring at her phone.

'What?'

'Next Sunday. They've withdrawn permission for the protest.'

They being the police, Leo assumed.

'*We can no longer guarantee the safety of attendees or the general public*,' she quoted. She looked across at him, aghast. 'We've spent *weeks* talking to them. It was all sorted. They can't do this.'

He swallowed. 'I think you'll find they can. And maybe now with Tyler's death—'

'No!' She cut him off. 'No. Don't you dare use that as an excuse. This is the last thing Tyler would want.'

'And his parents?' Leo said.

'They'd want us to go ahead.'

Of course they would.

'And they want us to help with a vigil for Tyler. Or maybe the bloody police will ban that too.'

'Ange.'

'Don't *Ange* me!'

Leo swallowed a sigh.

She stood still for a moment, hand clutching at her hair, then dropped her arm. 'Right,' she said, as if she'd reached a decision. 'They can't stop people protesting.' There was iron in her voice. She snatched up her car keys. 'I might be late tonight.'

Alarm bells rang. 'What are you doing?'

'The food bank,' she said, as if he was an idiot.

That only took up the morning. 'Ange. After that?'

'You don't want to know.'

'I'm asking.' He could feel his temper rising.

'And if it involves breaking the law?' she challenged him.

Oh Jesus.

'Best stay in the dark, then, eh?' she said, hands on hips, head cocked.

And if she did tell me? What then? Turn her in like I did Luke? Not the same, he reassured himself. Luke's actions were despicable, intended to spread fear, hatred and division, like the judge said. Whatever Ange was planning would be driven by a sense of justice, a desire to unify, to protect, to prevent harm. *To save the planet.*

He watched her watching him, still fizzing with fury. He couldn't tell her what to do. Wouldn't try. Much as the impulse was there. They were adults. Equals.

'Be careful,' he said.

She shrugged and turned away.

'I love you,' he said.

She looked back. Face rueful. 'I love you too,' she said, as though it was a sad, inescapable fact.

* * *

Another warm day but a wind was blowing, a southerly bringing heat from Africa and dusting everything with Saharan sand. As soon as he stepped outside, Leo tasted a gritty deposit in his mouth, like brick dust. His car was coated.

His phone rang then. Tom Bairstow. 'I wanted to give you a heads-up. The samples you sent through for DNA testing . . .'

'Yes?' Leo's hopes rose. Molly Unwin or Oliver Peel? Was today the day everything slotted into place?

'Neither's a match to what we recovered from Tyler.'

Damn.

'I'm putting the full report together now. What I can tell you is that the traces are from the same person and that person is male.'

'That'll narrow it down,' Leo said sarcastically. 'But thanks, Tom. I'll message and let them know.'

He stood a moment, feeling the anticipation drain away and then turned his attention to the car. Used screenwash to wipe away the orange powder on his windscreen before driving off.

He got stuck behind a horsebox early on, fought to dampen his irritation. He recalled Oliver Peel and his reckless overtaking. The man now exonerated from any involvement in Tyler's murder.

A funeral party had assembled outside the church in Arncliffe. The church resembled many others in the area, built in limestone with a crenellated square tower at one end and a slate roof over the nave. The coffin was being moved from the hearse onto a trolley. Leo wondered if it was anyone he knew. Growing up in the area, living here most of his life, and working with the public meant he'd a wide web of connections.

He wondered what Tyler's family would do for his funeral. The body should be released to them in the next few days.

Approaching Malham Tarn he hit a queue of traffic, tourists for the most part, on their way to visit the glacial lake. A couple of miles south there'd be plenty more of them visiting Malham Cove, the huge natural amphitheatre that was one of the biggest draws in the national park and popular with climbers too.

When he finally reached work, their rooms on the top floor of the police station were stifling. He called through to Shan, 'You see the DNA report?'

'Yes. Square one,' she said.

'In better news, I've got Tyler's password.'

'Yes!'

He rolled up his sleeves. 'It's like a furnace in here.'

'We could try this.' She came through carrying a large electric fan. 'Found it in the downstairs office.'

She plugged it in, turned it to high speed and switched it on. Papers on Leo's desk were whipped up into the air and sailed around the room. Leo swore and grabbed at them.

'Sorry,' she squealed, hitting the switch and doubling over with laughter. 'It's like a snow globe,' she managed, still giggling.

Leo laughed too, a sweet release.

They collected the documents up, sorted them, then Leo weighed them down with the spider plant and peace lily from the top of his filing cabinet, and some box files. Shan put the fan on again.

She pulled up a chair and they sat side by side so they could both see Tyler's laptop. Leo typed in the password when prompted and the home screen loaded. A photograph of leafy woodland for the wallpaper, dotted with icons for his apps.

Leo opened Tyler's email. The inbox was uncluttered, only a dozen or so messages. All had been read. Several referred to the Free the Fells project. Three were from Ange, who was coordinating the workshops.

'When did he last send anything?' Shan asked.

Leo checked that folder. 'Tuesday. Message to Liverpool University about accommodation.' He felt a pang of sorrow. Tyler Prasad would never be an undergraduate, never get a degree, never go on to launch a career, or to be a husband or a father, a traveller. Not even have the chance to make mistakes or bad decisions and mess up.

'Insta?' Shan said. 'There's a shortcut.' She pointed to the app.

They looked. As Eesha had told them, there'd been no new posts to any of his accounts since last weekend.

He hadn't really expected to find anything instrumental — after all, everything pointed to the killing being unplanned, a random encounter with a stranger that ended in tragedy. Nevertheless, Leo felt the slump of disappointment.

His mind was already turning to next steps when Shan said, 'What about backup? The cloud. We know Tyler took lots of photos. I've a friend who's a photographer and everything she takes is automatically copied from her phone. She set it up like that. It means you don't risk losing anything. She showed me how to do it.'

She tugged at her blouse, obviously still hot.

'And you think Tyler might have done the same?'

'It'd make sense. Give me the mouse.' Shan navigated and opened the cache of photos and videos. A page of thumbnails loaded.

Shan pulled her hair up from the back of her neck, face screwed up with concentration, lip caught in her teeth.

She clicked on the first thumbnail, the top left of the page. A video. The moor at sunset. The light was stunning. The camera swung up.

Film of a bird of prey. It soared through the sky, and then plunged.

'Amazing camera,' Shan said.

'Like Lydia said,' Leo agreed.

The bird rose again, wheeled, and Tyler cried, 'Oh wow! Female hen harrier. Never seen one before . . . Awesome.'

Shan felt a swell of pity hearing his voice. The light tone, the raw excitement in his words. The voice of a dead boy.

As the bird circled and banked, the light caught it. Leo saw patterned stripes of brown and white on the underside of its broad wings and on the fanned tail. Yellow legs. The film ran on, the bird moved, hovered. Tyler murmured, 'Beautiful.' He zoomed in closer.

Then a crack of gunfire. The bird jerking. Another crack. The camera jolted, dipping, losing focus. Tyler shouted, 'No! Shit no! Fuck!'

'Oh my God,' Shan breathed.

Five seconds of shaky footage bouncing over the dark peat and the heather, swerving to glimpses of the scarlet and golden sky on the horizon, blurry, everything out of focus. Tyler panting.

'He's running,' Leo said.

'But not away. He's running towards,' Shan said.

The rustle of clothing, his boots on the ground. Tyler panting. Shouting, 'What the fuck have you done?' The film swinging wildly over the rough terrain.

Then swinging up.

The hairs on Leo's arms, the back of his neck, rose as he made out the composition.

A figure was silhouetted against the blinding sun and crimson sky.

A figure holding a shotgun.

* * *

Shan

Shan's mouth was dry, her pulse surging. *Oh my God.*

Tyler's breath loud. Shouting again, 'You can't do that! You killed her.'

The figure shouting. Hard to hear over the noise of Tyler's gasping for breath.

'No!'

'Give it! Gimme the phone!' The figure steadied the gun, aiming it at Tyler.

'No, you're not going to get away with—'

The man discharged the gun.

A clunk and the film went dark. She heard rustling, sounds of movement, then saw footage again, a shaky sweep of the ground, blurred heather. The film cut out.

161

Shan sat for a moment, absorbing what they'd just seen.

'Shit, Leo. He recorded it all! Everything.' Her heart was racing. She was shaky. She could feel the blood beat in her temple. *He saw the bird shot and he ran towards danger.*

'Play it again,' Leo said quietly.

She did. They watched in silence.

'Tyler dropped his phone at the end. The shooter picked it up. They turned off the camera,' Shan said. *Tyler lay there bleeding and his killer's first response was to stop the recording.*

Shan quickly ran through the sequence of photographs that preceded the video. Landscapes, sunset and skyscapes taken on his walk up from the campsite, a close-up of moss, one of flowers. Tormentil, Shan knew, like buttercups but only four petals.

Then she started the video playing again.

'This is why he was killed. Fuck, Leo.' She looked at him and he nodded.

'I know,' he said gravely.

She imagined telling Eesha and Randall about their son's last minutes. The thought of them watching those moments unfold, of the video being played in court as evidence, of them seeing he'd died for the sake of a bird, one he couldn't even save . . . The sheer bloody waste of it heartbreaking.

Leo looked pained, sharing some of her distress.

But as well as the distress was the hard, cold fact that these revelations were a massive step forward for the investigation. *Finally!*

'They took his phone with them along with his wallet and keys,' Leo said. 'Stop on the shooter, see if we can get a better look.'

She froze the film at the moment where the figure seemed clearest.

'I can't make out any features,' Leo said. 'It's practically a silhouette. Can we get it enhanced?'

'Let me try a quick photoshop,' Shan said. She opened her own laptop and downloaded the video, took a screenshot of the figure.

She was parched, she noticed now. She could feel a head-ache coming, a band of tension around her skull. 'Have we any cold drinks?'

'I'll check the fridge,' Leo said.

Shan used the various editing techniques she knew, altering contrast, brightness, colour saturation and sharpening the image. Saving each version, but the person's face remained a daub of shadow.

The setting sun in the photograph illuminated the sky behind and highlighted some of the land, catching the tallest foliage to the right of the figure. The outline of the shape of a shotgun was plain to see. Shan considered the body type: average height, slim build. Almost definitely a man: the voice had sounded male, and the DNA recovered backed that up. He was carrying something at the hip. A bag? Of course, you'd need something to carry your prey. Was that the hen harrier dripping blood?

Bent over the laptop, she was aware of the tension in her spine and across her shoulders. She studied the figure again in each edition. In the one where she'd emphasised contrast, her eyes snagged on a patch on the chest below the shoulder that looked paler, perhaps reflecting the light. With a kick she realised what it might be.

Leo came back in and handed her a glass. 'Dandelion and burdock's all I could find.'

Shan smiled. 'Not had that for years. Who brings dande-lion and burdock in?'

'I reckon it's David,' Leo said. Their station sergeant.

She stretched, raising her arms and feeling the tug of her muscles, then drank some of the fizzy pop. It had a sweet, herbal, almost liquorice flavour.

'Any luck?' He nodded to the screen.

'Not really. Maybe our digital guys can do better. But I found something. Look at this. See here, the colour difference. I reckon that's a badge or a logo.'

Leo demurred. 'Bit of a reach. It could just be a random mark. A dab of light.'

'Or it could be the Patefield crest.'

'Come on,' he chided her.

'Think about it,' she insisted. 'That person is holding a shotgun, they're on the Patefield estate. Going by their build, I think it could be Jason Tattersall or his brother Niall.'

'Shan, it could also be a local hunter or poacher. We can't possibly tell. Not from that.'

'We should pick them up.'

'Shan, listen—'

Why was he even hesitating? 'Tyler filmed it. It's a gift. We should—'

'We can't pick them both up on the basis that *maybe* one of them is guilty. We'd blow the whole case. It's a fishing expedition. You know the rules.'

She groaned. Hating that he was right. 'So what, then?'

'We run their DNA. If we get a match for either of them with the DNA on Tyler, we're home and dry.'

'OK. We go now, ask them.' She needed to act. To follow up on the breakthrough as fast as possible. The impatience a maddening itch.

'Fine. Will you make a copy of all these files?'

'Sure.' Once she'd done that she turned off the laptops, drained her drink then belched. 'Sorry! It always made me do that.'

A shadow darkened his eyes. Had she offended him?

'What?' she said.

Leo shook his head. 'Our Luke, he used to have belching contests with his mum.' He gave a half-smile.

'Not with you?'

'Nah. She can do it to order.'

There was a pause. Too long. 'How is he? You said Ange visited.' Shan was unsure whether to broach the subject.

Leo didn't respond immediately. Then, 'I don't know. Early days.'

He turned off the fan.

'Right.' An injection of energy in his tone. 'Let's hit the road. Take my car?'

'Yes.' She pushed back her chair.

'Hey,' he said. 'Good job.' He pointed to the computers.

'That's down to Tyler,' she said, the images of the bird in the heavens and the figure with a shotgun swirling in her head.

***

Leo

The Grange was deserted. The guests, their SUVs and four-by-fours, had gone back to their well-appointed houses in desirable locations. Leo wondered whether Helena and Rafe Duvall would separate, if she'd take the chance to leave him as she obviously wanted to. And if their business would survive the current crisis. Whatever happened, they'd not go hungry or homeless — he'd put money on that.

Duvall would pay his fine and perhaps complete a community order for possession of cocaine. But Milo Carr, who'd supplied him, could face jail time. Even if he was let off lightly, his family's future was significantly more insecure than Duvall's. Living on the edge, scrabbling to make ends meet. It wasn't hard to see why dealing drugs had felt like an opportunity, a risk worth taking.

Carrie Crowther drove up just after them.

'Everyone gone?' Leo said as she got out of her car.

'Yes. Next party's in tomorrow.' She blinked at the wind, wafted a hand over her eyes. 'Hope this has calmed down by then.'

'And staff?'

'A precious day off.'

'But not for you?' Leo said.

Carrie laughed. 'No. You neither, by the look of it.' She opened the boot of her car; it was stuffed with bouquets of flowers.

'Do you need anything?' she said.

'No, thanks.'

They left her to walk through the yard. There was a jeep parked outside Jason Tattersall's house. 'Looks promising,' Leo said to Shan.

When Jason opened the door, his face sharpened and he rolled his head. 'What?' he said coldly.

'May we come in?' Leo said.

'Why?' He wore a sleeveless T-shirt and cargo shorts, bare feet. He hadn't shaved. He looked tired, his thin face drawn, mauve shadows under his eyes. Not sleeping? Because of guilt?

'A little privacy, perhaps?' Shan said.

Tattersall made a point of looking round at Beaumont's house next door and then across to the rows of cottages. 'Nobody about, is there? And I don't want you upsetting our Becky.'

'We'd like you to provide a DNA swab,' Leo said.

'What for?' Leo heard his tone change, a note of anxiety, though he still held his antagonistic expression.

'Jason?' Becky's voice from upstairs inside. 'Are we going?'

'A minute,' he called back.

'To eliminate you from our enquiries into the murder of Tyler Prasad.'

'Crazy.' He scoffed. 'I was here, I told you that.' Thumb and fingers tapping a beat on the door jamb. Edgy.

'And this could prove it,' Shan said.

'And if I refuse?' He raised his chin, belligerent.

'We'd have to draw our own conclusions,' Leo said. 'And look into getting a warrant.'

'You'd best do that, then,' he said to Leo.

Bugger.

'You don't want to help us establish who shot an unarmed teenager?' Leo was irritated at all the obstruction they kept meeting. No one seemed to give a damn. Tyler was an inconvenience, bad news, but somebody else's problem. Or was Tattersall's animosity, his lack of cooperation, a shield? Could he be their culprit and had Becky lied to give him an alibi?

'I wasn't there. Whatever DNA you've got, it ain't mine.'

166

'Jason?' Becky called.

'Coming!' he yelled back over his shoulder.

'Your brother Niall,' Leo said. 'He lives in one of the cottages?'

'That end one. Why? You testing everyone?' His eyes were sharp, calculating.

Leo didn't answer. He nodded to Shan. 'Shall we?'

'He's gone shopping,' Tattersall said.

'You know when he'll be back?' Leo said.

'No idea,' he said flatly. He stepped inside and closed the door with a bang.

Leo saw Beaumont crossing the yard. Two springer spaniels at his heels. He raised a hand in greeting. Jaunty. Leo nodded in reply.

* * *

'Will we get a warrant?' Shan asked as he navigated down the narrow lane that led to the main road. Trees formed a tunnel over part of the route, casting dappled shade over the moss-smothered walls and the ferns that clung to crevices in the limestone. The temperature was significantly cooler here.

'Doubt it. Not unless the digital team can work miracles with the photo.'

'Shit!' she said under her breath. Then, 'I can ring Niall Tattersall. We have his number. And fix a time to see him. If he'll give us a sample and we rule him out, we're in a stronger position to formally question Jason.'

'I don't know,' Leo said. 'Fair few ifs in there. And we'd have to arrest Jason to formally question him and compel him to give DNA.'

'You're not sure we have enough for an arrest.'

'Certainly not. Niall might refuse a DNA sample too,' he said.

'We won't know till we ask him.' Shan pleaded her case. 'We're close Leo. We're so close. We've got the videos and the photo, and when forensics confirm that's raptor blood at the scene we'll have that too.'

A party of ramblers, most carrying walking poles, came into view at the side of the road ahead. They wore baseball caps or bucket hats and sunglasses. Some had rucksacks on their backs. Leo moved out to pass them. Lifted his finger off the wheel when some of them waved.

'Try Niall,' Leo said. 'It can't hurt.'

Shan dialled the number. It barely rang and she left a message, crisp, professional. 'Hello, Mr Tattersall, this is DC Young. We'd like to arrange a time to talk to you, if you could please get back to me on this number as soon as possible. Thank you.' Shan turned her phone over. 'He declined the call.'

'How d'you know that?' Leo said.

'It only rang a couple of times before voicemail.' She looked at him. 'News to you?' Humour tugged at her lips.

Yep. 'Steady,' he cautioned. Then, 'Damn.'

The road ahead was clogged with traffic. A handful of cars parked either side and a patrol car, blue lights flashing, was blocking the way through.

Leo slowed to a stop and got out to approach. A narrow, metalled lane ran up to the hills on the left. The concrete the same grey colour as the rocks that dotted the slope. Old stone gateposts, weathered with age, stood at either side of the entrance but any gate was long gone.

Leo recognised the officer. 'Rick.'

'Leo.'

'What's going on?'

'Bunch of protesters up there lying in the lane, restricting access.'

Ah, Jesus. Ange's crowd.

A gust of wind hit them full on. They turned their backs to it.

'Bloody dust,' Rick said. 'Your lad. Bit of a shitshow, really, wasn't it? I mean, first offence, twelve months for a bit of graffiti.'

Leo took a breath. Yes, he'd been devastated that Luke got a jail term, but what he'd done was way more serious than 'a bit of graffiti'. Leo had always suspected Rick of being racist — the company he kept among their colleagues, occasional comments — but he'd not been sure till now, nothing concrete.

Shan shuffled, straightened her stance. He sensed her disquiet.

'Whose land is it?' Leo asked.

'Part of the Craven Estate,' Rick said.

'Not Parkfield Grange?'

'No, but the two connect up beyond Syke Moss,' Rick said.

'You got a map?'

'I have.' Shan pulled one up on her phone. Leo would have preferred analogue. He had an Ordinance Survey in the car but he could always look at that in a minute.

Rick pointed out the boundary on the screen. Then showed them where the group had planted themselves.

'Right to protest, freedom of assembly. They've banners. Free the Fells.' Leo saw Shan react. 'Pain in the arse. Local journo's up there an' all. The estate want them moved pronto, they've a shoot this afternoon. I've asked for reinforcements.'

'What will you do?' Shan asked.

'Move them. Give them the option to move themselves first.'

Leo considered fleetingly whether to go and have a word, try and reason with Ange and her crew, persuade them to disperse now they'd made their point. But he could only see that ending badly. Their point would only be made when they'd disrupted the planned shoot.

'You should know that Tyler Prasad was involved with the campaign,' Leo said. 'Makes it all the more sensitive.'

'You saying we shouldn't move them?' Rick sounded defensive.

'I'm saying it's important to consider all the factors. And how it's going to look if things are heavy-handed.'

'For the sake of an afternoon shooting party,' Shan added.

'They stand to lose thousands, the estate,' Rick argued.

'Drop in the ocean to them,' Leo said. 'They'll be insured anyway, won't they?'

Rick looked uncertain.

'Just thought you should have all the facts,' Leo said. 'You might want to run it by Command.'

'OK,' Rick said.

'You let us through, then?' Leo said.

They were halfway back to the car when he turned and walked quickly back to Rick, who was leaning on his car, vaping.

Leo caught the smell of the e-cig as he neared, something sickly sweet like toffee.

'It wasn't just a bit of graffiti,' Leo said. 'It was a hate crime. They daubed those words on an Asian taxi firm and a mosque.' He could hear his voice rising and tried to temper his tone. 'I wish he hadn't got sent down, but more than that I wish he'd never done it. It was racist, xenophobic. How do you think those people felt turning up to work, to pray? They were lining up a synagogue next. Antisemitic.'

Rick had paled then reddened as Leo spoke. Now he scoffed.

Leo glared, daring him to make any rejoinder.

Rick didn't speak. Just raised his vape to his mouth and sucked in a steady drag.

The wind snatched his exhalation and wafted it away but not before Leo caught another whiff of the cloying odour, turning his stomach.

Shan didn't say anything as he joined her but gave a tiny inclination of her head, which he took to mean she'd heard the exchange.

'So is Ange up there?' she said as he started the engine.

'Yes, more than likely.'

'Oh,' she said, the single word laden with understanding.

'Oh, indeed. I've already got my son behind bars. I'd rather not see his mother follow suit.'

'Not a great look for career progression,' she said.

'Not great on any score.' He laughed, which was way better than the alternative.

Leo had navigated carefully through the gap, having turned his wing mirrors to avoid scraping any vehicles, when his phone rang.

A voice, urgent, intent, came over the speaker. 'Inspector Donovan. Phil Beaumont. You need to come quickly. It's Jason. Jason Tattersall's been shot.'

CHAPTER ELEVEN

Sunday

Shan

Shan kept Beaumont on the line while Leo drove. 'Are you safe at the moment?'

'I think so.'

'Is anyone there with you?'

'Ian Kerrigan.' The gamekeeper who towered over the others. 'Carrie and Anita.'

'Did anyone see what happened?'

'No. We just heard the shots.'

'OK. Have you called an ambulance?'

'Carrie's done that.'

Good. 'Is Jason breathing?'

'Yes. Ian's with him. They told us to apply pressure to the wounds.'

'Right, good. They'll advise you better than we can. Where are you all?'

'Outside, in Jason's garden.'

Shan recalled their first visit there. Jason's wife with her swollen legs, uncomfortable in the heat. 'What about Becky?'

Shan heard Beaumont call out and Carrie reply, 'She's at the pool.'

'Can one of you check she's OK?' Shan said. 'But be careful, check first if you can see her from the Grange.'

Her mind filled with an image of the pregnant woman floating, blood curling in feathers and plumes through the blue water.

'Anita,' Beaumont called, 'see if Becky's in the pool. Make sure she's OK. But take care, look from the house. If there's any sign of danger come back here.'

'What do I tell her?' Anita asked, her voice shaky, faint. Shan imagined her some distance from Beaumont.

'Oh God.' Beaumont lost his composure.

Shan answered, 'Tell Becky that there's been an accident. You try and stay calm.'

'You got that?' Beaumont checked with Anita.

'Yes. Y-yes.'

'We'll be there soon,' Shan said. 'Call us back if you need to.'

Shan shared a glance with Leo, his face sombre. He drove quickly, swinging the old Peugeot round the twists in the road.

'Who'd want to shoot Jason Tattersall?' she said.

Leo shook his head.

'Maybe it was self-inflicted. If Jason was responsible for shooting Tyler, then we come round asking for his DNA, he thinks we're onto him. He panics. Waits till his wife has left the house then does something desperate.'

Leo stared at her.

'OK.' She held up her hands. 'I'm speculating. Is that against the rules too?'

Leo didn't reply. Just reached for his water bottle and took a long draught.

* * *

Jason Tattersall lay on the ground in the shade of the beech tree. Ian Kerrigan and Phil Beaumont were on their knees either side of him, pressing towels to the wounds on his chest and shoulder. A litter of bloody cloths had flies crawling over them. Carrie was relaying information to the paramedics over the phone, calm and collected. A barbecue smoked in the corner, the smell of charcoal tainting the air and catching in Shan's throat.

'Is he conscious?' Shan asked the men.

'Don't think so,' Kerrigan said. 'He's not responding.'

'No one saw anything?' Leo asked.

'Only heard the shots,' Beaumont said. 'They sounded too close.'

'And no gun found here?' Leo said.

'No.' Beaumont stilled. Shan saw him grasp that Leo was implying this could be self-inflicted. 'No, no, it's not that,' Beaumont said emphatically. 'And whoever it was used a rifle, not a shotgun.'

Different from Tyler, then.

'Can we move the jeep?' Leo said. 'The ambulance will need access as close as possible.'

'I don't know if he's got the keys on him,' Beaumont said. He patted Tattersall's pockets. 'Nope.'

'I'll check the house,' Shan said.

She moved briskly through the patio doors at the back, scouring the worktops in the kitchen, the table, the shelves in the hallway. She found a bunch of keys there and let herself out of the front door. She climbed into the jeep and started the engine, backed it up and then turned and drove it into the car park and left it beside Leo's car.

A blast of wind, then another, ripped through the plantation, bending the spires of the conifers and making them roar. It snatched up dust from the yard and Shan was momentarily blinded. She recalled a sandstorm in Bridlington on a family holiday, a fierce easterly wind whipping up the beach, the sand stinging her arms and legs, grainy in her mouth.

'Help! Help!' Shouting came from the direction of the main house. A woman's voice. *Anita?*

Shan turned and ran towards it.

'Somebody help!'

Is the shooter here? Shan's training had drummed into her the protocol for any critical incident: First assess the threat. Do not approach where you might put yourself or anyone else at risk.

'Help, please!'

Shan ran on, coughing in the dusty air, and stopped at the corner of the house near the edge of the top terrace. She peered round and saw Anita with Becky Tattersall at the poolside. Becky on the ground. Anita squatting and shouting again. 'Help!'

Shan ran down the terraces.

'She's collapsed,' Anita said, voice frantic with panic. 'She climbed out and she was all right for a moment but then she fainted.'

'OK, take a breath,' Shan told the girl.

Shan knelt. The tiles were scorching.

Becky Tattersall, eyes closed, was moaning. Her breathing was laboured. Her bloated ankles were discoloured, a deep, bruised violet.

'Becky? Becky? Can you hear me?' Shan tapped her shoulder. 'Call an ambulance,' she told Anita. 'Tell them she's thirty-eight weeks pregnant and high risk.'

The sun was relentless, and when Shan looked across to the more sheltered part of the gardens, the terraces rippled in the heat.

While Anita dialled, Shan dragged over one of the parasols in its base, grunting with the effort, and arranged it to shade the woman.

Hurried footsteps and Carrie Crowther joined them. 'What happened?'

'She's collapsed,' Shan said.

Anita was speaking, pacing, shuddering despite the heat. 'I don't have a date of birth. She's in her thirties, I think.'

'Ask them how long they'll be, Anita,' Carrie said.

'She's not bleeding, not that I can see,' Anita said. 'How long will the ambulance take?'

Carrie bent over Becky. 'Becky? Can you sit up, love?'

'They'll be with us as soon as possible,' Anita relayed.

'No!' Carrie stood. 'I'll take her, I'll drive her.'

'But they said—' Anita began to object, on the brink of tears.

'The waiting times are awful. We all know that. If we can get her into my car, I'll drive her. It'll save time. It could save her and the baby.' She spoke with composure, assurance, rising to the occasion.

'Yes,' Shan agreed. 'I'll get help.'

She ran up the slope back to the Tattersalls' and told everyone what was happening, then she asked Leo to come and help them move Becky.

On their return, Carrie had already driven her car to the bottom of the narrow drive that encircled the gardens and parked as close as she could to the poolside. The car doors were open.

Becky was sitting up but looked dreadful, her face slack and drained, eyes woozy, a towel now draped around her shoulders.

Anita was encouraging her to drink from a water bottle.

'OK,' Shan said. 'Leo and me, we're going to help you get up and walk over to Carrie's car. She's going to take you to hospital.'

'No,' Becky protested. 'Jason?'

Shan wasn't sure what Anita had told her, what Becky understood, but their priority now was to get her to hospital.

'Jason wants you to be safe, you and the baby. So hospital now, OK?' She positioned herself at one side and Leo took the other.

'On three,' Leo said, 'we'll stand you up. Nice and easy. One, two, three.' They hauled her upright and began moving to the car. Shan could smell the chlorine on her, the bleach mingling with the scent of coconut suncream.

Becky strained to breathe.

Leo was taller than her but Shan was strong. Years of aikido had kept her in shape even if she'd let practice slide recently.

'That's good, another step, that's great.' Leo kept up a stream of encouragement as they half walked, half dragged the woman to the car. They eased her down backwards into the passenger seat, then Leo lifted her legs to swing her around. Becky moaned.

Carrie was already in the driver's seat. She started the engine.

'Good luck,' Shan said, stepping away. She was breathless. The wind buffeted them again, flinging strands of hair in her eyes and making them water.

Carrie drove away and the three of them set off back up the hill. Shan deliberately let Anita draw ahead.

'No sign of the shooter at all, unless it's one of them,' Shan said.

'Is that likely?' Leo said, arching an eyebrow. 'Let's see what's what.'

* * *

'Any change?' Leo asked.

Ian Kerrigan was tending to Jason with Beaumont watching.

'No, but he's still breathing,' Kerrigan said.

And bleeding, Shan thought, seeing even more of the bloodied towels.

Anita's mouth trembled. She sucked in a breath, her arms crossed tight as if hugging herself. She was only a kid.

'It's OK.' Shan put a hand on her forearm. 'Let me get you some water.'

'Thanks,' Anita sobbed. Beads of sweat glistened on her brow. Strands of hair from her ponytail clung to her neck.

Shan filled a glass at the kitchen sink and brought it out. Leo had moved a chair so Anita could sit down. 'You did really well with Becky,' Shan said. 'Given her the best chance.'

'Any vehicles missing?' Leo was asking. 'Or vehicles that shouldn't be here?'

Beaumont considered the question. 'Don't think so.' Then, 'Where's Niall?'

'He went shopping,' Shan said. 'Jason told us before.'

'But his car's back,' Kerrigan called over his shoulder.

'Where is he, then?' Shan said. Was Niall a victim too? Shot like his brother? 'Leo—' she locked eyes with him — 'let's check it out.'

The door to Niall's cottage was slightly ajar. A prickle of unease flared across Shan's neck.

'Niall?' Leo called out, toeing the door open.

They waited on the threshold, straining to hear any sound from within, but the racket of the wind smothered everything.

Leo nodded and they stepped inside.

Holding her breath, Shan scanned the small living room and the kitchen beyond, the adjoining door flung back. No body, prone or otherwise. Bags of shopping on the kitchen counter, a pile of crockery in the sink. Fruit flies speckled the window.

She moved to the open wooden staircase. 'Niall?' She turned to Leo and mouthed, 'OK?'

He followed her up. The top floor was empty too. The heat there stifling. Shan felt sweat break across her back, pool under her breasts.

'So where is he?' she said.

Back in Jason's garden, she told the group Niall was missing. 'When did anyone last see him?'

Beaumont shook his head.

'Last night,' said Ian Kerrigan.

'Anita?' Shan asked.

Anita flinched. Her face worked. 'I didn't, I did . . . I didn't,' she gabbled. 'I never saw him, I . . .' Her hands flew to her head, shaking, as if to cover her ears.

'Hey, hey,' Shan crouched beside her. 'It's OK. You've had a shock, a horrible shock.'

'I can't. He'll kill me too.' She was crying.

Shan froze. Everything tightening, a sensation like glaze crackling over her skin. *The silhouette with the shotgun.*

'They were shouting. Jason was like, "What have you done? Tell the police," he said and, "You killed the kid. Put the gun . . . put the gun down."'

'Jason said that?' Shan's stomach turned over. Her mouth was dry, full of dust. Everything seemed brighter, louder. She was aware of the men behind her, everyone alert, listening. Kerrigan cursed under his breath.

'I can't!' Anita said, terror in her eyes. Her nose was swollen, red. Her lips too.

'Where were you?' Shan said.

'I didn't see. I didn't see anything.' She pressed her hands to her head, closed her eyes.

'Anita, where were you?' Shan touched her shoulders, gently, trying to offer some support, some comfort.

'Anita?' Beaumont sounded odd, almost a plea. He stared at her. Pulled off his rimless sunglasses.

'Anita?' Shan said. 'Where were you?'

'Up there.' She glanced up to the bedroom window of the adjoining house. The window was flung open. Her cheeks were tearstained, mascara flecked off in black dots around her eyes, like coffee grounds.

Shan looked to Beaumont, who drew his hand slowly down his face, smearing daubs of Jason Tattersall's blood on himself as he did.

'In the bedroom?' Leo said.

'Anita had just—' Beaumont spluttered. 'Just called round to—'

'I was waiting for you!' she screamed.

'Oh, bloody hell,' Kerrigan supplied, disgusted. Still nursing the wounded man.

'And your wife?' Leo asked Beaumont.

Beaumont looked beaten. All his bonhomie, his hail-fellow-well-met persona, drained away.

'She's away,' Anita said. 'Her mother's poorly. Heatstroke.'

Shan remembered Anita's smiles, from that first time when she brought coffee to Beaumont in the estate office and the way she startled and blushed on the terrace. *I'll find you later about those shifts?* Beaumont was what, maybe twenty-five years older than Anita and married. Anita was seventeen. Not a great look — shagging the staff while his wife was at her mother's sickbed.

'You heard shouting and the shots but you didn't see anything? You didn't look out of the window?' Shan said.

'No.'

'And you don't know where Niall went?'

'He'll come for me, he'll kill me,' she said wildly.

'It's all right. He's gone. He's gone,' Shan repeated.

Shan looked up at Leo. 'We need to find him.' She turned back to Anita. 'Listen, I'm sorry you went through that, I know it's frightening but telling us was the right thing to do. Now, we're going to want a statement from you after this, OK? So I want you to try and remember everything you heard. Yes? Everything.' Anita nodded, her breath hitching and tears falling down her face.

'That bastard,' Kerrigan said. 'The fucking bastard.'

'So, has he left on foot?' Leo said.

'He must have,' Kerrigan said over his shoulder. 'And he'll avoid the roads. He'll know you're looking for him.' He stood up, a hulk of a man. 'Phil, you take over here. I'll get Peg.'

'Peg?' Shan said.

'One of t'dogs, best tracker.'

'Niall's armed,' Leo said.

'Yeah? Well, so am I. Or I soon will be,' Kerrigan said.

'I can't let you do that,' Leo said. 'What we need to do—'

'How are you gonna stop us?' Kerrigan was seething, mouth a grim line. Looking like a Viking warrior with his bulky build and full beard.

Leo sighed, rolled his head. 'Listen—'

'You need to know where he is. This is best way,' Kerrigan said hotly. 'How else are you going to find him out there?' He flung out an arm.

It made sense.

'We call in armed response,' Shan said to Leo. 'Meanwhile, Peg can lead us in the right direction.'

Leo wavered.

'If we get sight of him we *don't* approach, *no one* uses a weapon.' She looked towards Kerrigan for agreement.

'No one gets within range,' Leo said.

'Fair enough,' Kerrigan said.

'What is the range?' Shan said.

'If he's still carrying a rifle, he can cover three hundred yards at a pinch.'

'We assume he is,' Leo said. 'No one gets within three hundred yards. No one else is getting hurt.'

'I'll fetch t'dog,' Kerrigan said.

'You'll stay with Jason?' Shan said to Beaumont, who was kneeling at the injured man's side.

He nodded. He looked subdued, awkward. His phone crackled, '*Can you tell me how he is?*' the call handler asked.

'His pulse is weaker, I think. But I'm no expert,' Beaumont said.

Shan hoped the ambulance would come soon. Jason had lost a lot of blood. She thought of Becky in hospital alone. Her husband being admitted to A&E. Her brother-in-law a murderer, a fugitive.

Shan recalled Niall Tattersall's friendly demeanour. His feigned concern. '*How's it going?*' His fake sympathy. '*This kid — his poor parents.*' His false alibi. '*I dropped in to see Becky. She's stuck there. In this heat.*'

The wind blew smoke from the barbecue her way and she coughed, tasting the acrid residue.

While Leo began the necessary calls, alerting Control to an armed suspect at large, asking for the armed response unit to be engaged and for Tattersall to be added to the watchlist for ports and airports, Shan fetched their water bottles from the car and topped them up in the house.

She joined Leo in the garden. 'Did you tell Control about the protest too?'

'Yes. They need to get them off that moor. I've tried Ange but she's not picking up.' Shan saw the worry in his eyes.

'Niall's alibi?' Shan said quietly.

'Becky.' He scowled.

'Why?' Shan said. 'Why would she do that?'

Kerrigan reappeared, a brindled spaniel at his heels and a gun at his side. He carried a polo shirt. 'I got this from his car.' The three of them walked out into the yard. Kerrigan held the clothing to the dog's nose. 'Where's Niall? Seek him. Seek him. Good girl.'

The dog wagged its stump of a tail. They followed her through the yard, Kerrigan encouraging the dog. She nosed the ground, trotting across to Niall's house and then back around the yard.

The man's scent must be all over this place, Shan thought. A dense web of trails. But the dog kept nosing the ground and then led them through the gap between the cottages and the yard and onto the start of the moor.

'This way,' Kerrigan confirmed. 'She's got his scent.'

Shan scoured the land. Amid the heather, the cotton grass shivered and the dried brown reeds bowed in the wind. There was no one in sight. Just acres of upland baking in the searing heat.

CHAPTER TWELVE

Sunday

Leo

The dog struck out, leading the way, seemingly sure of the trail. She travelled at a swift pace, forcing them to keep up. Every now and then Kerrigan commanded her to stay and the dog paused while they closed the distance. Then, 'Walk on', or 'Seek,' and the dog resumed tracking. She had a thick coat and Leo wondered about the heat. Surely it must bother her?

He scanned the uplands but couldn't see any figures. The heather trembled in the wind, and here and there, at scoured patches where the peat was degraded, silt was whipped up in puffs of powder.

A *chuck-chuck* sound came from close by, followed by the whirring of wings, and a pair of grouse flew up from their cover of heather. The dog ignored the birds, focused only on the hunt.

Leo was going over the turn of events, worrying at it like a tangle of knotted rope. Could they have done anything differently? Better?

His phone rang, interrupting the treadmill of his thoughts.

He stopped to take it, turning his back to the wind the better to hear. 'Leo Donovan.'

'Good afternoon. This is Marta Franklin from the wild-life crime unit. I believe you have information for us about an incident—'

'Sorry, this isn't a good time,' Leo said. 'I'll get back to you as soon as I can but, yes, we've proof of the killing of a hen harrier.'

The woman on the other end groaned. 'Proof?'

'Video footage. Look, I really have to go. But I will get back to you.' He hung up.

Kerrigan and Shan had waited while he took the call. 'Wildlife crime,' he told them.

Kerrigan didn't react. Leo wondered what his views were on the illegal killing. It remained an endemic problem on grouse moors in spite of protestations from the hunting and shooting lobby that there was zero tolerance for raptor persecution. It was common knowledge there was tacit approval among many gamekeepers and their employers, a culture of looking the other way. After all, grouse equalled money and the gamekeeper's role was to maximise the number of birds. The estates were vast and monitoring such crimes very difficult.

'Has Niall shot protected birds before?' Leo asked as they resumed walking behind Peg. The dog kept her head down, intent on her role.

'It's illegal,' Kerrigan said, which wasn't much of an answer. Then he added, 'Look, I'm not saying it never happens, but to kill someone over it and then to turn round and shoot his own brother — that's fucking mental.'

'Did they get on?' Shan said, raising her voice to be heard above the wind. 'Niall and Jason.'

'Not so's you'd notice. You know how some brothers are, always sniping and having a go. There were plenty of that. Niall had a chip on his shoulder, fixing to badmouth Jason if owt happened that he didn't like. I told him where to stick it more than once. He should have been grateful.'

There was a ditch in their path, not unlike the gulley where Tyler's body had been hidden. A couple of feet deep and twice as wide. They had to step down and then up the other side. The channel was dry and the chocolate-coloured peat cracked, scraped bare of vegetation.

'Grateful why?' Shan said.

'There's precious few jobs round here, hardly owt that gives you a roof over your head as well as a wage. Rents are off the scale. You've incomers snapping up old barns for conversions, property market's crazy. Jason basically got him the job, told him when there was a vacancy and how to apply. Jason was off his head to do all that. Niall's got a bloody awful track record. Been sacked from half the places he's worked.'

'How come?'

'Skiving, making trouble, you know — stirring things with the other staff, unreliable.'

'Why would Jason help him, if they were always at loggerheads?' Leo asked.

'Reckon he felt sorry for him. Felt he owed him, family duty shit. And Niall started out all chummy, but he were just waiting to show his true colours. Snake. He's a snake.'

A thought struck Leo. 'Is Niall in a relationship?' Perhaps he was heading for sanctuary with someone he was close to.

'No,' Kerrigan said. 'He doesn't seem that interested. Still carrying a torch for Becky, I reckon.'

'Becky and Niall?' Leo said, stunned.

'Aye. High school sweethearts. Until she dumped Niall for Jason.'

'Ouch!' Leo said. No wonder there was such bad blood between the men. And Becky had given Niall his false alibi. Because she was still fond of Niall? Or frightened of him?

But Niall hadn't been visiting Becky like she said, he'd been up here, hunting raptors, running into Tyler Prasad. If Becky hadn't lied, they could have focused on Niall. This latest violence might never have happened.

Kerrigan coughed, a bout that shook his large frame.

'You OK?' Leo asked.

'Asthma. This doesn't help.' He raised his eyes to the skies. Leo could hear him wheeze. 'Maybe you should—'

'No. That bastard shot my mate. I'm going nowhere,' Kerrigan said with feeling. 'Jason is a good bloke, you know. A good mate. If he doesn't make it . . . That fucker.'

'We don't approach him,' Leo said.

Kerrigan met his eyes. 'I know,' he said gruffly. 'Pity that.'

Leo felt an eddy of unease. Could Kerrigan be relied upon to do as promised and stay clear of Niall? Could he reign in his emotions?

Leo was thirsty. The dust in the air seemed to make it even drier. He swigged from his bottle, swilling the water around his mouth before swallowing. A stronger gust of wind and he was reminded of a holiday he and Ange had when she was expecting Luke. The hot wind had greeted them as they stepped off the plane in Mykonos and didn't let up for the rest of the week. Ange had resorted to wearing a headscarf under her sun hat to stop her hair whipping her face. Big bellied and beautiful, she'd spent as much time as she could in the sea. After the first day they'd walked from the resort to a smaller pebble beach, so they weren't sandblasted into the bargain. The *meltemi*, the wind was called, an annual occurrence that often stopped the ferries and sailing boats.

Ange had taken her sketchbook with her and captured some of the sights in coloured pencils. The sweeping bay, the old silvery olive groves, a taverna covered with bougainvillea and grape vines, sunset over the little harbour. Leo had found it impossible to imagine how their lives would change in the next couple of months. The thought of being a father had excited and terrified him in equal measure. That memory saddened him now. He tried to shake the feeling. Luke's arrival had been a joy, the years that followed a revelation. Leo's connection with his son was close and loving. Leo had been involved in his care as much as the job allowed him to be. He shouldn't let the trouble of the present taint the past like this.

They passed a scorched area, a huge rectangle of blackened vegetation, charred stalks and roots. A site of controlled burning.

Something stung the back of his neck, a sudden nip. A bite? Leo slapped at it. His skin was tacky with sweat.

'Curlew,' Kerrigan called. He pointed up. The distinctive birds with their long curved beaks flew above them — four in all, large wings flapping.

Was this a fool's errand, Leo wondered. Tattersall had a good start on them, must be close to half an hour. 'Are there places he could hide up here?' he asked Kerrigan.

'Take your pick. Old mine workings, potholes, caves, a bothy. But if that's his plan, Peg'll soon ferret him out.'

They breached the ridge of the moor. The land stretched out from the tops in a plateau to the west, a couple of miles at least, Leo thought. To the east the ground fell downhill before rising again to meet the sky.

'There!' Shan yelled, pointing across the moor. 'There! That's him!'

* * *

Shan

At such a distance the figure was small but could clearly be seen scaling the hillside, moving nimbly and carrying a backpack.

'That's him, all right.' Kerrigan was looking through the scope on his rifle. 'And that's Craven land over that far brow.'

'Call it in,' Shan said to Leo.

They kept walking while Leo phoned. 'No signal,' he said. 'Shit.'

'It's patchy around here,' Kerrigan said. 'Keep trying, you'll probably connect again.' He panted as he spoke, hand on his hip, leaning forward. A whistling sound when he breathed in.

Shan kept Tattersall in view, watching as he skirted an outcrop of rock. A jumble of huge limestone boulders. She held her breath when he disappeared from sight. Had he gone to ground? But then he emerged beyond the stones and kept climbing.

'It's ringing,' Leo said. When his call was answered he relayed the location, asking that the information be passed to armed response. 'Can we get the chopper up too?'

Shan heard him ask if the access road to Craven Estate had been evacuated. No doubt thinking of Ange and the protesters.

'Underway?' Leo said, dissatisfied. 'Underway' was not completed.

Tattersall had almost reached the top of the far ridge. He stopped, to catch his breath perhaps, then turned. The small figure froze.

'He's seen us,' Shan said.

'How d'you make that out?' Kerrigan said.

'I'm sure,' she insisted. Shan knew to trust her instincts. She pulled out her phone.

'What are you doing?' Leo asked.

'Calling him.'

Kerrigan scoffed. 'What for?'

Shan ignored him. She turned to shade the glare on her screen and bent her head to try and gain some shelter from the relentless wind.

The man was on the move again but he slowed and answered the call.

'Niall, it's DC Young again. Shan. I'm here with DI Donovan and Ian Kerrigan.'

He didn't reply but Shan could hear his breathing, rapid and ragged.

'We know what happened, Niall. We know about Tyler and the hen harrier and Jason. Jason is badly hurt. Running away now is not going to fix anything. It's going to make everything worse. I want you to relinquish your weapon and come back with us.'

'In't gonna happen, sweetheart,' he said. And the line went dead.

'Shit,' Shan said.

Kerrigan coughed again.

'I'll have a go,' Leo said.

Shan gave him the number and Leo dialled.

Tattersall was still climbing. The skies held a peculiar ginger tint from the dust cloud. The sand was thicker now.

Shan could see it coating Leo's hair and her hands. The wind rattled through the vegetation, a constant percussion.

'No answer,' Leo said.

'Keep trying?' Shan said.

'Can't hurt,' he agreed.

On the fourth attempt, with Tattersall now at the very top of the ridge, a matchstick man in silhouette against the orange sky, Leo finally got a response.

'Niall, Leo Donovan. You need to know an armed response unit has been scrambled and they'll be here soon. They train for situations like this. We'll also have aerial coverage from drones and the police helicopter. There's no way you're going to be able to hide. Or get away. The best thing now is for you to come with us. Give up your weapon and come with us. We want to end this without anyone else getting hurt.'

Shan saw Leo flinch, then shake his head, pocket his phone. 'Told me to fuck off.'

Kerrigan hawked and spat on the ground.

On the far horizon, Tattersall disappeared from view.

'What's over the other side?' Shan asked.

'Another valley, pretty steep,' Kerrigan said.

'Any idea where he's headed?'

Kerrigan shook his head.

'Any residents or settlements in the area?'

'The lodges for Craven will be about three miles as the crow flies.' He gestured straight ahead. 'Nowt to speak of any nearer.'

'He's got a good start on us,' Leo said.

'As long as we can keep him in sight,' Shan said, moving off. That was the point, after all. 'Is there any cover over there?'

'Not much,' Kerrigan said. 'A copse further down. Some plantation in the valley, though most of that's been felled. It's mainly open country for the grouse. Wait, Peg!'

Again the dog halted until they caught up.

Shan flexed her hands. Her fingers were swelling with the heat. Was she dehydrated? She drank but not as much as she'd like, careful to save some water for later. She should have worn a hat, put more sunscreen on, but there hadn't been time.

They made their way across the valley. Flies, black with milky wings and orange on their legs, crawled over the vegetation. Most of the streams that riddled the vale were bone dry. In one larger channel a thin skin of water seeped sluggishly though the mud. Leo wondered how it still held water. An underground spring perhaps?

They began the ascent at the other side. It was hard going. Kerrigan kept wheezing and coughing and Leo had to stop a few times. His arthritis was obviously giving him gyp on the steepest sections. Shan was sweating everywhere from her scalp to her feet. Her skin felt dirty, sticky with sand.

A few yards from the summit the dog started whining. Peg was circling, ears flattened, cringing and fawning.

She looked scared. Banjo did this sometimes when threatened by aggressive dogs.

'What's she doing?' Shan asked Kerrigan.

'Summat's up,' Kerrigan said. 'Peg. Here, Peg.' But she was backing away, reluctant to obey, cowering.

'What's it mean, her doing that?' Leo said.

Kerrigan shook his head. 'She's spooked. I don't get it.'

While he tried to coax the dog, Shan kept climbing, lungs and calves burning with the effort. The rise was almost perpendicular. She had to hold on to wiry bracts of heather for purchase, sometimes move on all fours, feet skidding on the loose gravel that peppered the path.

She reached the top and stood, heart thumping painfully, dizzied, blinking to clear her vision.

The sky darkened, dozens and dozens of grouse flying at her. They filled the sky, passing rapidly overhead, wings beating fast. *What the—*

Fire!

Her stomach plummeted. She couldn't breathe.

Fire! The slopes were ablaze, black smoke and vivid orange flames leaping across the land, sweeping up towards them. Rapacious, deadly.

'Fire!' she screamed. 'The moor's on fire!'

CHAPTER THIRTEEN

Sunday

Leo

Leo could smell the smoke before he reached the top of the ridge.

Shan was on her phone. 'Wildfire on Syke Moss in Swaledale. Near the south-eastern boundary of the Patefield Grange Estate. Fire's moving north.'

Leo climbed the last few feet, the pain in his knees like daggers with each step.

Oh good God!

The blaze was sweeping up the hillside. The roar of it filled his head.

'Ian? Ian?' Shan was calling.

Kerrigan, still down the slope with Peg, was doubled over coughing.

'Take her, go back,' Shan called.

'We need to get out of here,' she said to Leo. Her eyes were wild, mouth stretched in fear.

The clouds of smoke were closer already, obscuring some of the valley. Flames leaping and dancing, sparks swirling through the air.

'We can't run,' Leo panted. 'You can't outrun a fire.'

'We can't stay here, can we?' Shan said.

'We'll go along this way.' Leo pointed to the ridge running west. If they stayed at the top, at least they could see what they were dealing with.

'No,' Shan said. 'We go back down the way we came. Listen, fire travels more slowly downhill. It can buy us some time.' Her voice was shaking with urgency.

The fire had gained substantial ground. The crack and moan of it filled the air, flames arcing and jumping, snatching at the dry vegetation.

'Now!' Shan shook his arm.

The conflagration burst up the hillside. Embers landed on Leo's head and his arms and he swept at them, his heart beating fast, too fast. He couldn't believe the speed at which the fire was advancing.

He turned. The smoke poured over him and he was blinded. Nothing but dense clouds. He was choking on the tar. The racket of the fire was deafening, a jet howling over the moor.

'Shan?' He couldn't see her, couldn't see the way. 'Shan?'

He put out a foot, feeling for the path, and slipped. He fell, wrenching his foot, and slithered down on his back. He yelled in surprise and pain. His water bottle flew from his hand.

He couldn't breathe. There was no air, only the thick, charcoal smoke. His foot hurt. Flames spurted on the ground beside him, crackling and sizzling in the heather. He tried to call again but couldn't get any air. He grunted, winded.

Got to move. Go! Go down.

He felt feeble, no power in his limbs.

Need to move.

Stay low to the ground, smoke rises.

He felt limp, and heavy. So heavy.

Just a minute. Need a minute.

Was he still on the path? *Where's the path?* He patted at the ground with his fingers.

'Leo!' Shan, hoarse. 'Come. Come. Turn on your front, Leo. Move round, facing down here. Can you turn on your front?'

He tried, lungs burning now, a searing down his wind-pipe and the burnt carbon taste when he breathed.

His eyes filled. *I can't do it. It's no good. I can stay here, let go. Let it all go. Luke, everything.*

'Leo!'

A draught of wind snatched the smoke up and for a moment he glimpsed Shan, lying on the slope directly below him. Her face marked with smuts.

'Come on!' she yelled, then began to cough. 'Leo, just move.'

He rocked from side to side and then hauled himself into a sitting position. Moving onto his knees sent a wave of pain up his left leg and he thought he'd pass out. He vomited, a sour wash of bile that gave scant relief.

Shan was still coaching him, urging him on. 'Good, that's good. Now come. Come on.'

He leaned forward, weight on his hands.

He couldn't see her. He swept his arm out and felt her boot. She moved her foot in response then pulled away.

He crawled after her, his hands scraping on the grit of the path. His lungs on fire. *I won't make it,* he thought.

The fire was roaring at his heels, hungry, clamouring. He was too hot. His mouth parched, tongue stuck to his palate. So thirsty.

The smoke roiled and eddied. The ground swung. He was spinning, fading.

Help.

Please help.

Ange?

* * *

194

Shan was trying to take in as little air as possible, but even so, each shallow breath felt like it was full of glass fibre. The smoke rolled around them, but at ground level it was a little thinner.

She turned to check for Leo. He'd been just behind her. But now? *Shit!* He'd stopped.

She turned and pulled herself up the incline. His head was on the floor. Heart clattering in her chest, she touched his neck, feeling for a pulse. *Don't die on me*, she prayed. *Don't you fucking dare.*

There was a faint beat, wasn't there?

'Leo.' She shook his shoulder. 'Leo.' She tapped his cheek.

He whined a breath.

'Move!' she bawled, setting off another bout of coughing.

He hadn't even opened his eyes. A burning strand of heather landed on his back. Shan tamped it out, ignoring the smarting on her hand.

She wrestled off her backpack and pulled out the water. Only a few inches left. She pushed at him. 'Lift your head up, Leo. Drink this. Drink.' But he lay still.

Please, please don't do this. The fire had almost reached them. They had to move.

She yanked at his chin, pushing his head to one side, peeled back his lips and poured some water in. He spluttered.

She took a sip herself, then pulled off her shirt and soaked it with the rest of the water. This she tied round Leo's nose and mouth, then she shoved him again, repeatedly, violently, until he groaned.

'Move! Crawl, Leo. Come on!'

He came to, began to do as she said. She waited for him to pass her then moved after him, hitting out at his feet whenever he seemed to slow. Sometimes he howled when she hit him and she realised that one of his legs was hurt.

The fire was on them, engulfing them, savage. Setting alight the tinder at either side of the track. Sucking up all the air. There was nothing but scorching heat and the stench of burning. Her eyes were streaming.

It's too late. You're too tired. Just rest. Rest now.

No! No!

She shoved Leo's boot again. Yelped as pain bit into her own calf. Her trousers were alight. She rolled on the narrow track to starve the flames. Gasping and sobbing, she kept going. *Fuck this*, she said to herself. *Fuck you, fucking fire.* Her vision swam. She felt lava in her chest.

Too late, you see.

No!

Leo had stopped again. She hit him but he didn't react. She inched towards him, her forearms scraping against the stony ground. *This is hell. We're in hell.*

She could smell the dentist. The drilling of teeth. She screamed as acidic pain burned above her left eye. Her hair was on fire, crackling and flaming. She batted at her head. The smell was sickening.

She drew level with Leo, keeping close by his side to avoid the blazing heath.

The smoke billowed, a dragon rippling over its land. As it lifted, she saw an outcrop of boulders. Hope.

'Here! Keep going, Leo. Move!' She yanked on one of his arms. He responded and heaved himself forward.

Grunting and coughing, she led them to the large rocks. Found a narrow gap between two of them. Pushed him. 'In there! Get inside.'

He moaned and choked but moved all the same. The shirt still tied around his face was black with smoke. She edged in after him.

The dark space was cramped, smoky, but the rocks wouldn't burn. The only way they could both fit in the space was with Shan lying half on top of Leo.

'Head down.' She had to say it twice, to make sure he could hear, her voice so thin.

Outside, the inferno shrieked like a raging tornado.

It'll pass. The fire will pass.

I don't want to die, she thought, eyes stinging. *Oh please, I don't want to die.* The terror was in her, dark, monstrous. She couldn't stop coughing and every spasm tore at her belly muscles.

I want to live. And I want . . . I want Erin. Oh God, I want Erin. I'm so sorry. She wept without tears and the world burned.

*** *

Leo

Leo coughed. *Christ, that hurts.* He was trapped. Something pinning him down. He groaned and tried to move. He raised his head and cracked it against stone, the blow jarring his teeth. He gasped and that set him off spluttering again. He couldn't see much of anything.

A tomb? He was buried.

The weight above him shifted. It was alive! *A monster.* Dread sluiced through him.

A burning smell. He whimpered. *Ange? Is the house on fire?*

'Leo?' A hoarse whisper.

When he breathed there were knives in his back. Had he been shot?

It was a nightmare. A dream.

'Stay here a minute,' the voice croaked.

Wake up, he instructed himself. *Wake up!*

Someone else was coughing.

He couldn't see. He'd been gagged. He tried to move his arms to pull away the gag. Was it a hood? Had he been kidnapped?

'Grass like you, you want to watch your back.'

His body juddered as the thing above slithered over him, sending pain up his leg. 'Ow!'

'Leo.' The voice again. Shaking his leg.

'No!' he yelled, but it was soundless.

'Come out, Leo. Come back this way.' His head hurt. Everything hurt. He needed to sleep.

'Leo!'

Shan? It's Shan!

He flexed his feet and screamed at the spear of pain.

Bracing himself on his elbows and forearms, he edged backwards a few inches at a time. Every breath a rusty creak.

'That's it, come on,' she whispered.

His bad foot hit an obstacle. He strangled a cry and retched.

'Come on, nearly there,' Shan said.

He pushed and pushed, hot with the exertion, until finally the dark fell away and he was outside.

He looked up. It was snowing. Black snow. Flakes floating all around.

The stink of burning was overwhelming. His eyes smarted and watered.

He rolled gingerly onto his back, turned his head. There was Shan. On her knees. Her face flushed and soot-streaked. Black clots beneath her nose and round her lips. Her hair was all burnt on one side above the ear, the patch of skin at her temple blistered in bubbles. Angry red.

She wore a bra, smeared with dirt. Her trousers were torn and scorched. There was blood on one of her hands.

'Water?' she said.

He shook his head. He'd dropped it when he fell.

Painfully, he rose up onto his elbows. The land as far as he could see was charred, bitter black stalks and curls of white ash. A lunarscape. An apocalypse.

He coughed, tore at the cloth round his face. It came away. Her shirt.

'Keep it on,' she said. 'Here.' She shuffled to him and tied it on again.

'Can you walk?' she rasped.

'I don't . . . my ankle.' He pulled at his trousers. The joint had ballooned. The skin tight, discoloured.

'Well, you'll have to fucking hop then, won't you!' she said, suddenly fierce.

What the f— He laughed. God, he laughed. It hurt but he couldn't stop. That set him off wheezing. There was prickling in his throat, wadding in his lungs. He was laughing and choking and he was weeping. Great ugly sobs. Black snot on his hands.

* * *

Shan

Shan coughed and spat. 'That is rank.'

She got to her feet, unsteady. Her forearm itched but when she rubbed it the flare of pain, sharp stinging, stopped her. Another burn. Her hand was bleeding too, gashes where she'd torn the skin on something.

She turned slowly, eyes narrowed against the drifting smoke. A hellscape. Here and there, ribbons of smoke rose from lingering fires. Everything was monochrome, no greenery, no purple flowering heather, just cinders, ash, charred twigs.

The birds had flown from the inferno, but Shan realised that all the other creatures — the small mammals, the beetles, the moths, the spiders and grubs — would have perished.

She shivered even though the air was thick with heat.

'Any sign of Kerrigan?' Leo said. He sounded awful, a hacking cough and droning breath.

She scanned the area looking for the man or the dog. Shook her head.

'Ian?' she called but her voice was weak, grating. 'Ian?'

The only sound was the hiss and crackle of small flames, still gobbling up the last of the fuel.

Each breath hurt as though her windpipe had been stripped raw, scoured with drain cleaner.

She pulled her phone out. Her hand was dripping blood. She wiped it on her trousers then woke her phone.

No signal. She tried dialling anyway, 999.

'Can you get a signal?' she asked Leo.

He tried, his fingers trembling as he worked his phone. She looked away.

'Nothing,' he said.

'They'll be looking for us,' she said, aware she was trying to reassure herself as much as anything. 'You stay here, I'll go fetch help.'

'No,' Leo said. 'We should stay together.'

'But you can't—'

'We stay together.' He was trying to be firm about it but the squeak of his voice undermined the effect.

He moved onto his knees, hissing breath through gritted teeth, and placed his hands on the nearest rock to lever himself upright.

He swayed and she stepped forward, thinking he'd faint. He held up a hand, still trembling.

Her shirt hung around his neck now, like some bizarre bandanna.

'Just need to find my stride.' He tested his weight, breaking off when he was seized by a fit of coughing.

'OK.' He stepped forward on his good foot, then dragged the bad one, twisted at a peculiar angle, to catch up.

He flinched as he shifted weight but he persisted, taking another step.

Shan's head was pounding. She was so thirsty, her throat ached, her tongue felt like a husk in her mouth.

'Do you think Niall got away?' she asked.

Leo regarded her, his eyes red-rimmed, face blackened. She remembered photographs of miners shot in black and white, their rugged features seamed, careworn.

'Depends where he was when it started,' Leo said.

'He was there. He started it.'

Leo blinked, seem to consider what she was saying. 'Niall did?'

'He set it to stop us. The wind was blowing our way, fire travels uphill. He gets his lighter out, a couple of flames is all he needs, and off he goes.'

'We don't know that.' Leo frowned.

'I do.' She was right. She knew she was. She moved past him.

'You can't be sure,' Leo said.

'Ninety-nine percent.' It made a brilliant diversion, she thought bitterly. Buying him time, altering the focus of the emergency services. All the police efforts concentrated on saving people. On dealing with the fire. Yes, the police would still be on the lookout for him, but they'd be stretched too thin now. Tattersall could easily hole up in a barn or hide out down in the valley and wait them out.

We were so close, she thought. The frustration tight in her chest.

What do we tell Tyler's parents?

Slowly, they trudged along the footpath through the ashes, stopping every few yards.

Shan felt sick, shaky. She kept seeing the fire again as it raced and bellowed, barrelling towards them. She bit her tongue to stop from crying.

Just walk. Someone would be searching for them. The mountain rescue or the fire brigade. They would, wouldn't they?

Close to the bottom of the valley, Leo fell. A scream wrenched from him as he tumbled.

She moved back and lowered herself beside him. 'We'll rest a bit.'

His face was contorted in pain. 'Your hands are all puffed up,' he said eventually.

They were like sausages. 'Dehydration. Did we see any water anywhere on the way?' She couldn't remember.

'Over there, I think.' He waved in the direction they were headed. 'More like mud.' He growled, clearing his throat.

'I'm not fussy,' she said.

She heard a sound. *A bark.* Her skin prickled. *Peg?* 'You hear that?'

'What?' Leo said.

'A bark? A dog barking.'

Leo shook his head.

'Listen,' she said. They waited. Her ears were ringing, white noise sizzling in her head. Had she imagined it?

She hung her head, elbows on her knees.

After a few minutes, Leo said, 'Shall we find that water, then?'

She helped him to his feet. Once he was stable she tried for a signal again. In vain.

They'd only gone a few steps when Shan caught movement in the distance, a streak of white by some low stones. She stared, focusing. She was wondering whether it was burnt stalks quivering, then — *Peg!* The dog's brindle colours acted like camouflage in the razed landscape.

She called the dog, heard an answering bark, but the animal didn't move. Hurt perhaps.

'You were right,' Leo said.

'Ian?' Shan called.

Silence.

They made their way across the vale, through the cinders and dust, clouds of smoke occasionally closing in and limiting their view.

'I reckon she's gone for the water too,' Leo said. 'It's roundabout there.'

As they drew closer, Shan saw what she had thought were some stones resolve into the shape of a person.

'Ian's there,' she said. 'See?'

'That?' Leo said.

'Yes.' Shan ran ahead. Stabbing pains tore through her lungs with the exertion.

Peg barked as she approached. The dog was circling close to the man.

Kerrigan was lying on his front. Face to the dirt.

Reaching them both, she saw Peg had burns on her legs and chest, the fur scorched away. The rest of her coat was stippled with soot. 'Good dog,' Shan said. 'Good dog.'

Shan crouched down. 'Ian. Can you hear me, Ian?' She shook his shoulder. His clothes were dotted with scorch marks and burn holes.

She felt his neck, underneath his beard, searched for a pulse. Found nothing. Her guts tightened.

She needed to turn him over. She positioned herself to hold his shoulder and the belt at his waist and pulled, ignoring the sting of her cut hand. She strained but it was impossible. He must be over twice her weight.

She tried again.

When that failed, she concentrated just on heaving his shoulder, using both her hands. With a long grunt, she managed to haul him up onto his side then roll him so his upper body landed heavily on his back. He didn't waken.

Panting, she moved to pull his hips and legs round until he lay fully stretched out.

She pulled open his mouth, felt with her fingers. His airway was clear of obstruction. His tongue was dark, nostrils black.

She listened, ear close to his nose, but couldn't hear anything above the hiss of static in her own ears. She studied his chest for movement. Her first-aid training kicked in on autopilot even though beyond that, beneath that, she could hear herself screaming.

She straddled him. Locked her fingers tight and began to pump his chest, counting the beats and willing his heart to start. Her sore hand bleeding afresh.

The dog, watching all the while, whined softly.

* * *

Leo

Shan was doing CPR on Ian Kerrigan, panting with the effort it took.

Peg barked at Leo. He put his hand out and she sniffed it, then she switched her attention back to Kerrigan.

'You should get some water, if you can find any,' Leo said to Shan. 'I'll take over.'

Leo's foot screamed with pain as he manoeuvred himself into position over the larger man. His ankle was throbbing, burning. His vision kept blurring, he felt light-headed.

It was hard to keep the beat as fast as it should be — his arms were too weak — but he settled into some sort of rhythm. His muscles ached with cramp, lactic acid searing inside. After thirty beats, Leo pinched Kerrigan's nose shut and breathed into the man's mouth twice before beginning the sequence again. Everything tasted of charcoal, black and gritty. He found it difficult to concentrate and lost count at least once.

Here in the valley bottom there was less smoke, though the air still reeked, a long way from fresh. Leo imagined all the particles they'd already breathed in.

He thought of the riverside by their house. The times when the water ran full and lively. The cool, clear, soft air along the bank.

He was so dry. *Clemmed*, his mother used to call it, when she was really thirsty.

He wondered how old Ian Kerrigan was. They'd have a note somewhere in the staff records Beaumont had given them. Was he married? Kids?

'It's over that way.' Shan was back. 'Aim for the dip in the horizon, there's a puddle in the bed of the stream.'

'Water?' His voice had almost gone.

'Well, it's wet but you wouldn't want to bottle it.' She coughed. 'Any response?'

'No.' Leo stopped pumping.

Shan helped him up so he could bear most of his weight on his good leg.

'Take the dog too,' Shan said.

Peg was lying, panting, tongue lolling out of her mouth.

'Come on, Peg,' he said. 'Drink. Drink of water.'

She was reluctant to move. He kept calling to her as he slowly moved away. Promising her a drink. Eventually she followed.

Leo didn't think that Ian Kerrigan would make it, but you didn't give up. You kept going with CPR until help came or you were too exhausted to continue. He hoped it wouldn't be the latter.

Ange? Was Ange safe? Had they got off the moor in time? He wasn't sure how far it was to the site of the protest but a fire like this could cover miles, spread at a tremendous pace. He'd just seen that for himself. He couldn't bear it if . . .

Reaching the water seemed to take a lifetime. With each breath he could hear a rattling in his chest. Like cellophane.

At the shallow stream bed he saw the silty liquid glinting dully. An oily film on the surface. Peg lapped at it.

Leo stooped over and cupped his hands to scoop some up, the dribbles running through his fingers and down his wrists. It tasted of earth, had the density of coffee dregs. But like Shan said, it was wet. He repeated this half a dozen times, wondering if there were diseases in it but too thirsty to care.

Peg ran back to Kerrigan.

Leo followed slowly, biting down through each painful step.

The silence was unnerving — no birdsong, no rustling of little creatures, no running water.

Shan was sniffing when he reached her. It took him a few seconds to realise she was crying.

'Shan? Hey, Shan?'

She looked at him, sooty lines on her tear-streaked face, mouth turned down in misery. 'I messed up, Leo,' she said. Her words were jerky, echoing the rhythm of the CPR.

'Come on now, we did all we could—'

'No,' she said. 'With Erin.' Her tears were falling onto her hands, onto Ian's chest.

Leo waited, listening.

Shan gave a hard sniff. 'I couldn't . . . I didn't . . . I just trashed it, everything we had and—' She sucked in a breath, wiped her cheeks then bent to breathe air into Ian's lungs.

Leo searched for the right thing to say. 'Maybe it's not too late?' He offered. He tensed in case he'd misjudged. He cleared his throat. 'If you really love her.' His cheeks grew hot. 'If you want to—' *Shit! What? Keep going? Stick together?*

Shan resumed CPR, then froze.

So did he.

They both heard it. The *chokka-chokka* sound of a helicopter. His heart jumped and adrenaline flooded through him.

'Give me my shirt,' Shan said, getting up so quickly she lost her balance and staggered. 'Swap places.'

It took him a second to realise he had it draped around his neck. He pulled it loose and held it out. She snatched it up and began waving it above her head, eyes scanning the murky sky above in hope.

* * *

Shan

The helicopter hovered into view and Shan waved her shirt in as big an arc as possible. Surely they'd see her. *Please? Please?*

The noise grew deafening as it flew closer, the drumming of the motor an insistent heartbeat.

Shan watched. This close they must have seen her. Shan could make out the pilot. *Thank God.* They'd soon be out of here.

'No!' she shouted in dismay as the helicopter passed directly overhead and kept going.

She jumped up, brandishing her shirt, trying not to cry, but then the aircraft banked and turned. Flew nearer, came closer, lower.

The down-draught from the rotors lifted ash and dirt from the ground, swirling it in a dust storm. She had to shield her eyes. The helicopter settled directly above them, hovering. The vibrations shuddered through her. A disturbing sensation, as though the ground might split and swallow her up.

Nothing seemed to happen for long minutes.

Leo sat back, coughing violently.

'Here!' she shouted. She went to him. 'My turn. What are they doing? Why are they just hanging there?' Like some malevolent hornet teasing them.

Leo was straining to breathe. She saw he couldn't talk.

She waited for him to move. Clumsily, he dragged himself away from Kerrigan and sat heavily with a groan.

Shan took his place and started compressions. There was little colour in Kerrigan's face.

The helicopter moved, twirled around, rising then dropping down again, zigzagging over the area, and she realised they were looking for somewhere safe to land.

Perhaps fifty yards away, where the ground was at its most level, the aircraft came swaying and dipping, closer and closer to the ground.

Shan narrowed her eyes against all the grit being blown about.

The thunder of the rotor blades slowed and stopped.

She looked across to see two figures emerging, wearing jumpsuits and helmets, with large packs on their backs. They crossed the terrain quickly and ran to Shan.

'He's not breathing,' Shan said.

'OK,' the first woman said, pulling on disposable gloves. 'I'm Joanie, I'm a doctor. I'll take over now.' She kept talking as they changed places. 'This is Adeola, she's our emergency paramedic.' Adeola was getting equipment out of one of the bags.

'Shan Young, Detective Constable, that's my DI, Leo Donovan. This is Ian Kerrigan, a gamekeeper. And his dog.'

'You were all caught in the fire?' Joanie asked.

'Yes. In pursuit of a murder suspect. We weren't together when the fire hit. Leo and I got separated from Ian.'

Adeola handed water bottles to Shan and Leo. 'Drink as much as you can.'

'Any idea how long he's been like this?' Joanie asked.

'No.' Shan opened the bottle, chugged at the water, clean and cold. Wonderful. The relief.

'OK, we're going to try and start the heart with the defibrillator,' Joanie said as Adeola passed her the equipment.

Joanie moved to one side, applied the paddles to Ian's chest. 'Clear,' she warned.

Ian Kerrigan bucked as the charge hit. The medics examined the monitor. 'No activity.'

'Again.' The second shock didn't work either. Adeola set up an oxygen mask that she pumped as Joanie resumed CPR. 'We're going to transfer him to hospital now. And you two, you're obviously suffering from smoke inhalation. Any other injuries?'

'Leo's sprained his ankle,' Shan said.

Adeola looked over, Leo raised the bottom of his trousers. 'That looks sore,' Adeola said. 'We can take you both.'

'And the dog?' Shan said, suddenly anxious that Peg might have to fend for herself.

Adeola smiled. 'And the dog.'

Joanie conveyed the plan to the helicopter over their radio.

'Any word on Niall Tattersall? Our murder suspect?' Shan asked.

'Nothing,' Adeola said.

'Other casualties?' Leo asked.

'Not that we know of,' Adeola said.

Another figure descended from the rig carrying a long bundle which Shan guessed was a stretcher.

Everything tilted. Shan was woozy, suddenly too exhausted to stand. She plonked herself down.

They rigged up the stretcher and moved Ian onto it, strapping him down.

Will they be able to lift it? Shan wondered.

She needn't have worried.

After that things moved swiftly. Ian was taken into the helicopter in the cocoon-like stretcher. They provided Leo with crutches to enable him to walk to the aircraft. He looked so grey, Shan thought. It wasn't just the ash.

Peg was taken on board next and then Shan.

Joanie and Adeola were positioned either side of Ian Kerrigan and continued to perform CPR and administrate oxygen. Shan and Leo were at the tail end of the helicopter with Peg. They were buckled in and the door shut.

The pilot started the engine and the rotors began to move. The noise was ear-splitting. Shan felt it drilling through her from the crown of her skull to the soles of her feet.

With a lurch, they left the ground.

In another world, at another time, there might have been some thrill, a sense of excitement in the experience. But all Shan felt now was sick and frail and hollow. Opposite her, Leo had his eyes closed, his head dipping onto his chest.

He'll be all right, she said to herself. Then the bottle he was holding slipped from his fingers. Shan stuck out her foot to stop it rolling. Joanie noticed. She moved over and checked Leo's pulse. She locked eyes with Shan and nodded reassurance.

The horrors of the last hours were spinning through Shan's head. Jason bleeding on the grass, the ferocity of the fire, the fear that she might die, never make it off the moor. All of it swallowing her.

Shan could feel herself flying apart, shivering and shaking. Cold numbness creeping through her, smothering the terror.

CHAPTER FOURTEEN

Sunday/Monday

Leo

Leo couldn't remember much about arriving at the hospital. Fragments lingered: the helicopter landing, Ian being stretchered across to the entrance, someone asking Leo to sit in a wheelchair.

He'd lost Shan.

Now he waited in a cubicle, an oxygen mask over his nose and mouth. His boots and socks in a bag.

Last time he was here, Luke had crashed his motorbike. He'd lain there, pale and in pain, a fractured collarbone, tibia and wrist, with Leo at his side, praying that he'd be OK. And snooping on his son's phone, finding the evidence that would help incriminate him.

Luke had been born here too. Ange labouring through a long spring night, screaming and groaning, swearing at Leo, shouting at him to change the bloody music that they'd brought along.

Luke had arrived with the dawn chorus. Slithering out in a rush, red and wrinkled and smeared with white wax. A shock of black hair, like Leo, not ginger like his mum. Leo had burst into tears, could barely see to cut the cord. He'd held his son while Ange delivered the placenta. *His son!*

And now Luke was trapped in some stinking prison cell. Frightened, alone. *I nearly died.* The fact of it was a wall of water smashing into him. *He hates me and I nearly died. I'd never see him again. My boy. Oh, my boy.*

Leo startled as a man came into the cubicle now wearing navy scrubs. 'Leo Donovan?'

Leo tried to gather some composure. Nodded.

'Can you tell me your date of birth, Leo?'

It took him a moment to remember, panic gripping the back of his neck. *Tired. Just tired.* He pulled the mask aside to give it.

'I'm just going to check your blood pressure. And we'll take some bloods to see what's going on. You're booked in for a chest x-ray — there were some nasty crackles when we had a listen — and for an x-ray on the ankle, but there's a long wait. It could be a fair while.'

Leo followed instructions, stretching his arm as the cuff inflated and then balling his fist and watching the needle go in the crook of his arm.

'All done. Drink as much as you can.'

The room was stuffy and all Leo could smell was the stink of his clothing. Like a campfire. Black grime ringed the creases of his knuckles and round his fingernails.

Ange? He needed to know if she was safe and tell her where he was. That madman had set the fells alight — all the people who might be hurt.

He found his phone but it was off. When he tried to turn it on nothing happened. He fiddled with it, pressing all the buttons in turn, then together.

Frustration boiled up in him, frustration and fear, and he hurled the handset across the room. It hit the opposite wall with a satisfying crash as the door opened again.

'Leo?'

Shan! Standing in the doorway. *Oh, Shan.* Tears burned behind his eyes. 'Hi.'

She looked over to his phone, slid her eyes to him.

He tried to stand to go and fetch it, forgetting his dodgy ankle, yelped and sat back quickly. He pulled down his mask. 'My phone's dead.'

'Well, if it wasn't already it will be now.' She picked it up. Turned it to show him the screen, a spider web of cracks.

She coughed. Glanced at the open door. She had a faded hospital gown on. 'You OK?'

'I need to call Ange.'

'They've probably done that, Leo.'

'Yes?'

'When we got here, they asked for next of kin.'

'So she's all right?'

Shan hesitated. He searched her face for a clue. 'Well, I think so,' she said gently. 'But I don't know for sure. They just took the details and said they'd inform them. There's a payphone by the lifts. Mine's out of charge now.'

'OK. Cash?'

'Or card.'

He tried to swallow but his throat was raw.

'That looks awful.' She waggled her foot at his. His ankle was mottled in lurid navy and red bruises, even more swollen.

There was a dressing on Shan's head above her temple. Another on her hand.

'You waiting for tests?' she said.

He nodded.

'Same. I hate these places.' She shuddered.

'Niall? Is there any word?'

'No. I tried Control earlier,' Shan said. 'No verified sighting. I guess everyone was busy. I told them where we were and what was happening.'

Leo wondered if Niall had been overcome by the fire. Or if he'd fled. And which would be worse.

'Ian?'

Shan shook her head. 'I don't know. It didn't look good.'

'Other casualties?'

'Not that I've heard.'

'Jason will be in here somewhere.'

'And Becky.'

So many people hurt, Leo thought. All because of Niall Tattersall.

'I'd better go before they catch me,' Shan said. 'I'm a couple of doors down.'

'How did you know where I was?'

'Followed the bonfire smell.' She gave a smile. 'Nah. I heard them call your name, just now.'

He was still tearful and he didn't know why. And weighed down. An unbearable weight.

'See you later,' Shan said.

He didn't trust himself to speak but dipped his chin as she left.

After a few minutes he rolled himself in the wheelchair down the corridor. That took some effort, the muscles in his arms drained and sore from performing CPR.

Partway down, there was a young man on a trolley, his eyes closed, his face paper white, a drip in his arm. And further along, an elderly woman in a wheelchair with a carer beside her patting her hand. The woman was talking, jabbering really. Leo only caught the odd word.

He saw there were instructions for the phone and prayed they wouldn't be as complicated as the automated car parking machines that had drivers round the county flinging up their arms in frustration or turning to each other for help.

Once he'd figured it out, he rang their landline. He didn't know Ange's mobile number by heart. Did anyone learn those numbers? It seemed so stupid now, reckless, that he hadn't.

He waited for her to answer, imagining her irritation that he wasn't home yet. Was it only last night they'd eaten tapas?

The phone rang and rang.

She might be in the shower, or out in the studio.

Or hurt?

Don't!

If she's safe, why hasn't she come? he thought as he returned to his cubicle. Surely she'd heard about the wildfire. Wasn't she worried for him? Hadn't she guessed he might have been close to the danger given their case was centred on Syke Moss?

He was piqued.

Oh, get over yourself.

But maybe she'd tried to ring and not got any reply. His phone was dead. She could well be freaking out just like he was. She might have tried to find him, rung the hospital. How would he know? No one here would have time to carry messages.

He was so hot. Hot and thirsty. He drank more water, then put the oxygen mask back on. The gnawing pain in his ankle now hurt even when he kept it still.

How far had the blaze spread? To the Grange itself? There were farms around the estate, like the one where they'd parked on that first day. Had they been spared? And their livestock, the sheep?

If his phone had worked he could have checked the news. He could've spoken to his colleagues and found out what was happening.

The lighting was harsh. Could he turn it off? Turn it down? He'd look in a while. *Take a minute first.* He closed his eyes. *A bit of a rest.* The noise he made as he breathed made him think of trees soughing and creaking in the wind. He lay cradled in their branches.

Swaying.

Rocked to sleep.

'Leo! Leo Donovan!'

He startled awake, his chin itching from drool. Something over his face. He batted at it.

'Steady. Steady.'

Hospital. A porter there. 'We're taking you down to x-ray now.'

'What time is it?'

'Ten past six.'

With brisk efficiency the man removed the mask and wheeled him through the hospital to the lift. He didn't make small talk, which Leo appreciated.

When they reached the x-ray suite, Leo was parked in a waiting area beside three other people. A woman with a striking orange tan and lots of tattoos who had her arm in a sling, and a man with a small child on his knee. The child was whimpering, his wrist tucked close to his body, the joint swollen. Trampoline, Leo guessed. Luke had broken his arm on theirs, in spite of the safety net. How old had he been then? Seven? Eight?

The child and his father were called through.

Leo wanted a piss. But he didn't want to miss his place.

The minutes ticked by. There didn't seem to be anyone to ask, although staff emerged and disappeared in rooms off the waiting area, studiously avoiding the four of them.

Leo coughed. A rattling, hacking noise. He sounded like a smoker, forty a day untipped. Like his grandfather. Did they still make untipped cigarettes?

The woman with the sling turned her face away. Probably thinking he had a bug.

'Sorry,' Leo said.

She gave a quick smile.

He was about to try and reassure her when her name was called. She stood up and went with the nurse.

The coughing had brought him close to pissing himself, so Leo followed the signs to the toilets and used the disabled cubicle where he could transfer from the wheelchair using the support bars. His urine was dark, an amber colour. Sharp smelling. From dehydration, he guessed.

At the sink he was appalled by his reflection. He was still filthy from the fire. Scrapes on his face, his hair dusted with ash, sunken cheeks. He looked years older. He looked like an old man.

He washed his hands and face but the grime around his nails was ingrained.

Back in the waiting area, a nurse looking fed up barked, 'Leo Donovan?'

'Yes, sorry. I—'

'Through here.'

Chastened, he wheeled himself into the room.

The radiographer checked his name and date of birth and got him to sit on a table with his bad leg stretched out. They draped a rubber mat over his upper leg and positioned the x-ray machine before going into the adjoining room to operate the device.

After a few minutes, the radiographer came back in. 'Fractured ankle.'

'It's broken?' And he'd been thinking it was just a sprain.

'It is. It's not severe, you won't need surgery. It should heal in six to eight weeks. Paracetamol for the pain. Orthopaedics will provide you with a boot and you'll need crutches. I'll send those details through.' He yawned. 'If you wait outside, a porter will be along to take back.'

'Thank you,' Leo said. His mind went to Luke again — the way he'd limped away in the dock. *I'm sorry. I'm so sorry, Luke.* He *knew* it was the right thing to do but that didn't mean he didn't regret it in every sinew of his being. To be party to sending his boy behind bars. What sort of father did that? Ange understood. 'You're a good man,' she'd said at the time, though she'd wept.

It was a long and tedious wait for the porter. Leo was tempted to go back on his own but he'd no doubt get lost and annoy the staff, who were doing their best. They all looked as wiped out as he was.

When the porter left him in his cubicle, Leo drank more water then went to try the phone again. The boy on the trolley was still there, and the muttering woman. Another two stretchers had arrived. One bore a large woman using an oxygen mask, a bandage on one forearm, a drip in her hand.

There was a man whose face was turned to the wall. He was groaning in long, low moans.

Leo dialled again. The phone rang and rang. Where was she?

He should ask at reception. See if she'd been admitted. *Oh God, Ange. Please, please, Ange.*

His heart hurt, his breath was too tight. The phone rang on and on. He moved to hang up, then, 'Hello?' She sounded guarded, hostile.

Jesus! 'Ange?'

'Leo? Where've you been?' she snapped. 'Why aren't you answering your phone?'

He bristled. 'Where the hell have you been? I've been trying—'

'In a police cell,' she said.

'What?'

'I was arrested, Leo. I just spent the night in the cells. I've only just walked in.'

'Who arrested you?' he said.

'Well, the police actually,' she said, caustically.

'Yes, I know but . . . Was it Rick?' The encounter with the man still fresh in his mind.

'Yes. Rick the prick. He accused me of threatening behaviour. I never threatened him, Leo. I told him not to touch me. Well . . . in a manner of speaking.'

Leo sighed. 'What did you say, Ange?'

'Whose side are you taking!'

Leo closed his eyes. 'Did they charge you?'

'They said they were going to, but then, I don't know why, I don't know what happened, they let me go.'

'OK. That's good.' *She's OK. She's safe. Oh, thank God.*

'You sound weird.'

He didn't answer.

'Leo? Are you all right?' Her voice softened.

'Just about.' He swallowed. 'I was caught up in the wild-fire on Syke Moss.'

'Jesus, Leo! Where are you now?'

'Hospital. Fractured ankle and smoke inhalation.'

'I'll come and get you,' she said quickly.

'No, wait. They need to fit a boot and check my breathing's OK. Let me call you when I'm done. When I need a lift.'

Another patient, dragging a drip, paused a little way away, waiting for him to finish on the phone.

'And you're all right, yes?' Ange said.

'Yes.'

'And Shan?'

'She's fine.' He pictured Shan, crying over her broken relationship. Her persistence, her determination to escape the fire. Hectoring him to move. Saving him. 'She's pretty amazing actually.' He'd tell her the rest later.

'Oh, God, Leo. I can't believe—'

'I'm OK. It's OK. I'll be fine,' he said. 'I love you.' His voice was husky, full of smoke and tears.

'I love you too,' Ange said.

***

Shan

They'd not been happy with Shan's initial observations and wanted to keep her in overnight.

'Sometimes it can take twenty-four to thirty-six hours before the extent of any damage from smoke inhalation is clear,' the nurse had said, removing the stethoscope from Shan's back.

She was still coughing. Each time, she felt the tear in her stomach muscles.

'We'll keep you on oxygen and monitor your blood gas. Hopefully you'll be able to go home tomorrow,'

Home? Where? she thought. *Back to Dad's?*

'Can I get something to eat?' Shan said, aware it had been hours, breakfast the last thing she'd had. Her stomach was eating itself.

'Yes,' he said. 'There are vending machines at the end of the corridor. Now, we haven't got a bed available at the moment and to be honest it's unlikely anything will materialise while you're here. Even if it did, I'm afraid you wouldn't have priority.'

'No, of course,' she said.

'So I'll see if I can rustle up a blanket.'

Shan looked around. 'I stay in here?'

'Or the corridor.'

'Here then, if I can.' At least it gave her a little privacy.

She eyed the trolley, the only other furniture in the cubicle apart from the hard plastic chair, her bed for the night.

She thought to ask Leo if he wanted any food but found him asleep in his wheelchair, snoring heavily. Down the corridor she bought herself an anaemic-looking cheese roll from the machine along with some ready-salted crisps, a Galaxy bar and a can of coke. There was far more choice among the confectionery and fizzy drinks than there was among the food.

She'd dozed fitfully. The noises, people moving about, sudden cries, a cleaner at work, someone groaning in pain, the rumble of trolleys and the constant electric hum that droned on underneath everything, coupled with flashbacks to the day, had made proper rest impossible.

She went to the toilet in the early hours. Her muscles had stiffened and getting off the trolley, even just walking, she felt a deep aching. *A bath.* She imagined a bath, a good soak. She'd not had one for months. Who wanted a bath in a heat wave?

They'd told her to avoid getting the dressings on her head and arm and hand wet. There were smaller, lighter burns on her leg where her trousers caught fire. They'd probably sting in water. What if she put salt in? Would her dad have enough to spare?

She washed as best as she could, one-handed.

Going back, she met Leo being wheeled from his cubicle.

'Orthopaedics,' he said. 'It's broken.'

'Broken!' He'd walked across the moor on a broken ankle.

'Ange is OK,' he said. She could see the relief in his expression, in the set of his shoulders.

'Good. That's good.'

It wasn't that long afterwards that Shan was seen again, a different medic. She used a stethoscope to listen to Shan breathe.

'OK. I think you're good to go. This—' she passed her a leaflet — 'tells you what you need to do to deal with the after effects of smoke inhalation and what to do if any of the symptoms get worse. And the dressings, keep them clean and dry. Any questions, check the NHS website, all the information you need is there. Bin in the corner there for your gown.'

'Thanks.'

The medic gathered up the oxygen and left her to get dressed.

She was still wearing her socks and underwear. The rest of her clothes and her boots were in a plastic sack. The smell when she got them out was overpowering. Her shirt was stiff and streaked with blood and soot and grime. Her trousers had melted where they'd burned, the knees frayed and torn. She dragged them on. She must look like she was wearing some sort of Hallowe'en costume. She picked up her backpack.

Leo's cubicle was empty. She didn't want to leave without telling him.

She could wait, go sit in the corridor perhaps if they needed to use her cubicle. She left the door ajar and sat on the plastic chair.

The time seemed to crawl but her mind wouldn't stop whirring.

Ian. What about Ian?

Not knowing was eating away at her. Decided, she made her way to reception and showed her police ID to the woman there. 'I brought a patient in yesterday, airlifted with mountain rescue from the wildfire. Ian Kerrigan. Please can you tell me how he's doing?'

The woman took in the state of Shan and her clothing, and nodded.

'Date of birth?'

'I don't know.'

The receptionist used the keyboard, checked the screen. Typed again, pushed her glasses up her nose. Peered closer.

Shan knew before she said a word, saw it in the way her face slackened.

The receptionist glanced to the side, presumably checking she couldn't be overheard disclosing sensitive information. 'Pronounced dead on arrival. I am sorry.'

Shan blinked. 'Thank you. Thanks.' She hadn't expected him to make it but there had been an obstinate flicker of hope, which now guttered out. 'And erm—'

The phone on the desk rang. Shan waited while the receptionist took the call. When she'd finished Shan asked, 'Could you also check for Jason Tattersall. Yesterday as well. A gunshot wound.'

The woman's eyes widened.

'I know,' Shan said. 'Hard day.'

'You have a date of birth?'

'No, sorry.'

Had Jason died in his garden? Shan didn't know how long it took the ambulance to reach him. Even if he'd been unresponsive the paramedics would still have brought him in, making every effort to resuscitate him.

'Here we are. He's on surgical intensive care,' the receptionist said.

Alive!

'Is this about that Tyler . . . Patel. The other shooting?' the woman said.

'Prasad. Yes, it's connected.'

The woman shook her head, mouth pinched. 'Awful.'

'Yes,' Shan said.

The receptionist craned her neck, looking beyond Shan. 'Sorry, I need to . . .' Someone else was waiting for assistance.

Shan thanked her and moved away.

Go now, she told herself. *Tell Leo if he's back and then get out of here.*

221

But Becky Tattersall? And the baby?

You can ring and find out when you've charged your phone.

Coward.

What about her false alibi for Niall? She could leave that until Becky was discharged. But what if Becky knew where he was? Had heard from him?

Swearing under her breath, Shan followed the signs to the maternity unit.

She flexed her hands, tense, felt the aching muscles and the sting of the cuts on her left hand. 'Ask, then go,' she mumbled as she approached the ward entrance.

There was an intercom at the doors.

Shan pressed the button. 'Detective Constable Young. I'd like to speak to the ward sister.' *Is that right? Should it be matron?*

The buzzer sounded and she went in. The corridor led to a central nurses' station at a crossroads between the different wards on the unit.

She paused for a nurse pushing a patient out of one of the treatment rooms near the entrance.

'Thanks,' the patient said, glancing up. Then, 'It's you!'

Becky Tattersall.

She looked as though she'd been crying, her skin blotchy, lips puffed up.

And no baby. Shit! But maybe she hasn't had it yet?

'Oh God! It's not Jason, is it?' Becky said.

'No, no. Not Jason,' Shan said.

'He was shot,' Becky said, her voice breaking. 'They said Niall—' She broke off, clutched at her chest. 'He's had surgery but they don't know . . .'

'No. I'm sorry,' Shan said.

'Let's get you back,' the nurse said to Becky.

Becky wiped her eyes. 'OK.' Her calves and feet were still swollen. Her hair greasy. 'Come and see,' she said to Shan with a tremulous smile.

Before she had time to respond, the nurse wheeled Becky past the desk and into a ward on the right. Four beds. One occupied. Besides each a clear plastic cot.

'This is Archie,' Becky said, reaching to pick up the infant.

The baby was pudgy, bald. A deep dent ran across its forehead. Eyes like black beads seemed to fix on Shan.

Becky kissed the baby's head and breathed in as if she was smelling a flower, then looked back to Shan. Her eyes swam. 'I just need Jason to . . . You know? It's my fault. When you asked if Niall had been with me . . .' She squeezed her eyes shut.

'Why did you tell us that?' Shan said.

She glanced at Shan then away, her chin touching the baby's head.

'He swore he hadn't done anything wrong. I believed him. He's never lied to me before. I felt sorry for him.'

'How come?'

Becky sat on the edge of the bed, wincing as she lowered herself, still cradling her son. 'Things were really bad between Jason and him. I told you they had a big row that day. Jason wanted Phil to sack him. He told me as much. He wouldn't have him in the house.'

'Because of you and Niall, your history?'

Becky looked startled, guilty. 'What? He didn't know about that.'

Shan was confused. Kerrigan had said it was common knowledge that Becky had dumped Niall for Jason.

'I swear he didn't!' Becky said. 'No one did. How did you find out?'

With a swoop, Shan understood. 'You and Niall were still seeing each other?'

'Hardly ever,' Becky defended herself. 'I tried not to but . . . I love him,' she said. 'I love Jason too. I wish I didn't. It's such a mess.'

Well, it sure is now.

'What do I tell Jason, if he pulls through? That I lied because I still love his brother?'

The woman in the other bed turned, groaning softly, and Becky froze. But the patient carried on sleeping.

Becky said quietly, 'He'll never forgive me. And what do I say about Archie?'

'Archie?'

Becky swallowed. She closed her eyes for a long moment. 'Niall and I . . . well, the dates fit. It's possible.'

Shit! She wasn't sure who the father was.

'Do I tell him?' Her face wobbled with distress.

'I don't know,' Shan said. *And I'm the last person you should be asking for relationship advice.*

Archie began to fuss, squeaky cries.

'Will I go to prison?' Becky said. 'For lying?'

Shan was tempted to tell her that her false testimony had not only led to her husband being injured but the death of his friend Ian Kerrigan.

'Perverting the course of justice is a serious offence,' Shan said. 'But it won't necessarily mean jail time.'

'But it could. Oh God!' She rocked forward and back. 'And Niall?'

'He's on the run. Have you heard from him?'

'No.'

'Have you tried to contact him?'

'No.' Shan thought she saw a glimmer of unease in Becky's eyes. Was she still lying?

'If he contacts you or you can think of anywhere he might be hiding, you must tell us.'

'I will.'

Would she? Or would she continue to protect her lover?

'I'll see you soon, to follow up. Here.' Shan found a card in her backpack, smudged with ash. 'My number. Let me know when you're discharged.'

'I am sorry,' Becky said again, the baby's cries getting louder and more insistent as Shan walked away.

She lost her way twice trying to get back to Leo's cubicle. When she found him he was wearing an ortho boot.

'You won't be skipping up the office stairs for a while,' Shan said.

'We can stay on at the Dairy,' Leo said.

'If it's not burnt down,' she said.

'Of course. Or we can work at mine. I can't drive.' He tipped his head at the boot.

'They'll sign you off sick.'

'Not if I can help it,' Leo said. 'But if you need to take—'

'No. No. They said I can go,' Shan said. 'So tomorrow, let's pick it up tomorrow if they let you home. I'll fetch whatever we need and come to yours.' Work was the best thing, surely. She couldn't imagine sitting around at her dad's doing sweet FA. She'd go crazy.

'Good. But if you feel—'

'Back at you.' She took a breath, braced herself. 'Leo — Ian Kerrigan. He didn't make it.'

'Ah, no.' Leo sighed.

'But Jason's in intensive care. He's had surgery. And Becky's had a little boy.' Shan was wobbly. Her head buzzing.

He gave a laugh, eyes brightening.

'But listen . . .'

'I'm all ears,' Leo said.

'Becky and Niall, they were cheating on Jason, now and again. The baby could be either brother's.'

'Blimey. Didn't see that coming.'

'I said we'd talk to her again. He's going to be desperate — Niall. Setting the moors on fire, could have killed anybody. Might have. We don't know yet.' Walkers or farm workers or anyone else might yet be found dead in the ashes.

Leo agreed. 'He's dangerous. Very dangerous. People have been told not to approach, but if someone fancies a go . . .'

'Don't.' She could imagine the carnage.

'We have to stop the fucker, Shan.' Leo didn't often swear.

'Deal,' she said.

'Go,' Leo said. 'You look like you're about to fall over.'

She raised her hand in farewell.

'And Shan . . . thank you. If you hadn't pushed me, yelled at me, if you hadn't found those rocks—' He clamped his mouth shut.

'It's fine.' She felt herself blush. 'I'll see you tomorrow.'

In the fresh air, she stood to one side of the entrance doors, trying to figure out how to get to her dad's. He'd still be away, so he couldn't pick her up and her car was at the police station. A bus would take her to Leeds city centre and she could get another from there. But she wanted to be home soon. Get clean, eat something, sleep. Try and settle her jangling nerves. A taxi would likely cost fifty quid and she'd have to check if they'd accept card payments. Then she'd have to sort out getting from Leeds to Settle in the morning.

She eased off her backpack, looking for the bottle of water, glanced back and—

Erin! Coming out of the hospital.

Shan dropped her bag.

Erin stopped dead. 'Shan?'

'What are you doing — are you all right?' Shan's eyes ran over Erin, searching for signs of injury or illness. 'Why are you here?'

'Why do you think?' Erin looked scared. Blue eyes haunted. 'You were in the fire.' Erin shook her head. 'Look at you.'

Shan's mind flinched away, not wanting to light on the memories. Not yet. Not here.

'I couldn't get through to you,' Erin said. 'I was worried. I tried your dad.'

'He's in Bristol.'

'Yes. I said I'd come and find out and let him know.'

Shan waited. Was that it? Erin running an errand to reassure Shan's dad? Favour complete, would she go now?

Don't! Please don't go.

'Is that a burn?' Erin touched her own temple, mirroring the site of Shan's dressing.

'Yes.'

There was a pause. Shan didn't know what to say. Head empty.

'You always wanted to try an undercut.' A spark danced in Erin's eyes.

Astonished, Shan laughed. Which made her cough. 'Sorry,' she wheezed. 'Smoke. How did you know I was here?'

'They said on the news. About the fire and how a man had been admitted to hospital in a critical condition and two police officers with injuries. I just knew it had to be you.' She gave a shake of her head. 'Jeez, Shan.'

'It's a lot,' Shan admitted, tearing up. She blinked. 'I'm sorry . . . for everything. I do want . . . I want to make things—' Tears dripped down her face. 'Shit!' She swiped at them.

'Let's go home,' Erin said. 'Yes? We can talk when you're ready. But we must talk.' Her eyes were intent on Shan's, sharp and sapphire bright.

'Yes,' Shan croaked. She bent to pick up her bag. 'Yes, I'd like that.'

Shan didn't know what the future might hold for the pair of them. But one thing she did know, she wanted Erin in her life, she wanted her back, she never wanted to lose her again.

CHAPTER FIFTEEN

Monday

Leo

Leo insisted they stop at a phone shop on the way home.

'In that state?' Ange said. 'Why don't I take you back and then—'

'No. Mine's buggered and I need it for work. For everything.'

'It can wait another hour—'

'Ange!' He broke off coughing, gulping in air.

Ange shook her head with irritation but did as he asked.

The woman in the shop transferred everything over, downloaded his stored data and set it all up so he was good to go.

He had two missed calls from Randall McKenzie.

Back at home, Ange made him a sandwich and a cup of tea and demanded he shower before anything else.

He sat in the kitchen in his dressing gown, dizzy with exhaustion, racked by coughing spasms, and phoned Randall.

Ignoring the savage prickle in his throat, he explained they'd identified the man responsible for killing Tyler.

'The guy on the news,' Randall said. 'We saw that. "Wanted in connection with . . ." And not a word from you. I said to

Eesha, that must be . . . Why didn't you tell us? We had to hear about him like that. You promised!'

'Randall, I'm sorry. But we were caught up in the wildfire. We were pursuing him when the fire took hold.' His voice kept losing power, becoming whispery. 'My phone was ruined and we've been in hospital overnight. I've called as soon as I possibly could. I'm so sorry.'

Had he lost their trust again? *Please, say something? Please?*

'Are you sure he's the one?'

'Yes. We can come tomorrow to see you and talk to you. Tell you everything.'

He'd no sooner hung up than his immediate boss, DCI Matthew Booth, was on the line.

'How are you, Leo?'

Leo clammed up, the simple question unleashing a flash of fear, the primal terror of death that had devoured him up on the moor. And a backwash of guilt at the cowardly resignation that almost cost him his life.

He cleared his throat. 'OK. Fine, considering.'

'You don't sound fine. And DC Young?'

'She's OK. Some minor burns and—' Again he had to stop. Seeing Shan, blistered and burned, face streaked black with ash, standing in the hospital cubicle. Brave. Resolute. Leo blinked fast. 'We're good,' he said. 'Any sightings?'

'Nothing. Nothing that checks out, anyway. Drones still covering the area. Patrols on the surrounding roads. Most of the fire's burned itself out. Still a few areas the fire service are dealing with.'

'And casualties?' Leo asked.

'No. Thank God.' Matthew's tone changed — more forceful, brusque. 'So, I propose we approach Lancashire, see if they can lend a hand for a week or two until you're ready to take back the reins.'

'No. No way! I'm ready now.'

'I really don't think—'

Leo rode over him, 'Matthew, he's out there. He could kill again. He *will* kill again if he's threatened. He won't hesitate. He's ruthless.'

'And we are all looking for him,' Matthew said sharply. 'I'm not putting you and DC Young straight back into work after what you've been through. Your welfare—'

'What about Tyler Prasad? His parents? Ian Kerrigan's family.' He loathed the prospect of kicking his heels with Tattersall roaming the county. Another team would take days to get up to speed.

Matthew didn't respond at first. Leo could hear him breathing. 'Two days sick leave.'

'But listen—'

'No, you listen: two days and you keep the case or we get occupational health in, see what they think, carry out a full assessment before a return to duty.'

'Friday, you were on at me insisting how important this case was, how swiftly we needed to act. It's even more urgent now—'

'Leo, just do as I say, yeah? That's not a suggestion.'

'Understood.' Leo hung up, frustration boiling in his guts. *And tomorrow?* He'd just promised to visit the Prasads.

He climbed to his feet, struggled with the crutches to cross to the sink and drink some water. He looked out at the garden, the sweet peas and petunias frazzled, leaves crisped, flowers shrivelled. Ange wouldn't have been able to water anything last night, locked in a police cell.

No way was he going back on his word to the Prasads. Matthew needn't know anything about it. And he could spend the rest of the time until Wednesday as productively as possible, prepare next steps, start looking at the case they'd put together for the CPS, create a schedule of tasks and prioritise them. Then he and Shan could hit the ground running first thing Wednesday morning.

He called Shan to tell her how things stood. Her partner answered. 'Shan's phone, Erin here.'

He recalled Shan weeping as she compressed Ian Kerrigan's chest. *'I messed up, Leo. With Erin.'* Something must have happened to bring the pair of them together again. He was glad of it.

'Hello. It's Leo — I was hoping for a word with Shan.'

'She's in the shower but — ah, she's here now.'

He heard Shan take the phone. 'Hi.'

'You're back home?' Leo said.

'Yeah. I am.' A smile in her voice. Then she coughed.

He relayed Matthew's stipulation to her.

'Wednesday?' She was horrified.

'I know,' he said. But already he'd found himself more accepting of the situation. The last thing he wanted was to make any mistakes, and it would give them a little breathing space. 'I agreed. Well, he didn't give me much choice. But — and this is between you, me and the gatepost — I'd already arranged to see Randall and Eesha tomorrow and I'm going ahead with that.'

'You can't drive,' she said.

'Ange can.'

'Blurred lines,' Shan said. 'I'll pick you up.'

'Shan, if Matthew gets wind—'

'You going to tell him?'

'No, but—'

'Right, then. Ten o'clock?'

'Ten.' He smiled to himself, savouring her tenacity.

'Any news on Niall?' she said.

'No.'

'We've got to find him, Leo. We've got to stop him.'

'I know. Anyway, glad you're home again.'

'Yeah,' she said warmly. 'Yeah, me too.'

* * *

Tuesday

Leo

They'd just entered the city limits in Lancaster when Leo's phone rang. Not a number he recognised. He thought fleetingly of Rose Sherringham's tirade, defending what her son

Jack and Luke had done, and the warning from Counter Terrorism.

'Leo Donovan,' he answered.

'Fire Investigation, Andy Lingard.'

Leo switched to speaker so Shan could share the call.

Lingard needed them to talk through their pursuit of Niall Tattersall and pinpoint locations and times.

'We first saw the fire at half past three,' Shan told him, leaning towards Leo to answer but keeping her eyes on the road. 'That's when I called the emergency services.'

'And how much distance was there between you and Tattersall at that point?'

'About a quarter of a mile?' She glanced at Leo, who nodded in agreement.

'You didn't see anyone else in the vicinity?'

'Not a soul,' Leo said.

'No freak lightning?'

'No,' Leo said.

'At what point were you aware of the fire?'

'When we reached the ridge that divides the two estates,' Leo said. His throat locked as he recalled the wall of flames and smoke racing up the hillside.

'You almost died!' Ange had said when they'd sat and talked last night, Leo recounting their ordeal. She'd hugged him, hard, which hurt his aching body, but he didn't care. 'I nearly gave up,' he'd admitted, feeling ashamed. 'If Shan hadn't—'

Ange had pulled back, fixed her eyes on his. 'But you're here. You're here — you didn't give up!' she'd said fiercely. 'You didn't! I love you so much.'

'Right, I think that's it for now,' Lingard said, bringing Leo back to the present.

'Do you think it'll be possible to say whether Tattersall started the fire?' Leo asked.

'I'm hopeful, though it may be a case of "in all probability". No accelerant use, no witnesses or forensics beyond identification of likely point of origin and the pattern of spread.

We should be able to finalise the report in the next couple of days. I'll be in touch. Bye.'

'If Fire Investigation deliver, we can add arson to the charges of murder and attempted murder,' Shan said. 'Aggravated arson.'

'Yes, destruction of property.'

'And endangering life. And what about Ian Kerrigan? He was killed as a result of the fire.'

'True. But the defence could argue that Tattersall didn't intend to cause any person harm at that point, that he was simply trying to create an obstacle so he could make good his escape,' Leo said.

Shan complained, 'That's not right.'

'I know.' It felt unjust that Tattersall might not pay for the death of his colleague. 'We'll have to wait and see how things pan out.'

* * *

They met outside in the garden. All of them expressed shock and concern when they saw Leo and Shan's injuries.

'We're fine,' Leo said, though the hacking cough that overtook him somewhat undermined his assertion.

'And another man died?' Eesha said, once he was quiet.

'Yes. Ian Kerrigan, he came with us in pursuit of Niall Tattersall. He suffered from smoke inhalation and cardiac arrest.'

'And the man who was shot?'

'In intensive care. He was Tattersall's brother. He found out what Niall had done, that he'd shot Tyler, and tried to get him to turn himself in. I'm so sorry you had to hear about it like that.' Leo still felt awkward at letting them down.

'And this Niall, he's still on the run?' Eesha said, the name bitter on her tongue.

'Yes.'

'And if you don't catch him?' Padma said.

'He remains a wanted man,' Leo said.

There was a silence.

Randall covered his eyes.

Eesha reached out, stroked the leaves of the lemon verbena plant in the pot beside her. Leo caught a whiff of the sherbet scent.

'We won't stop looking,' Shan said.

'Actively?' Padma said, sounding sceptical.

'Yes,' Shan insisted.

'He's wanted for murder and attempted murder,' Leo said. 'We know he's armed. He's a dangerous criminal. Finding him will be a priority.'

'So what happens?' Randall said. 'We just wait?'

'I'm sorry,' he said.

'We bury our boy,' Eesha said. She looked over to Leo and Shan, her face stark. 'He'll have a woodland burial. We'll plant an alder tree. One of his favourites.'

Padma bobbed her head in agreement.

'And we're setting up a fundraiser in his name for Free the Fells,' Eesha added. 'I don't know if Ange told you, we're going to hold a vigil.'

Leo pictured the moor, blackened and barren. Desolate.

'Not on Syke Moss,' Eesha added, as if she could tell what he was thinking. 'We're still looking for the best site. Lydia, the filmmaker who was working on the project with Tyler, she says there's land above the campsite where they stayed that's unspoiled.'

Leo recalled the photographs Tyler had taken on his final walk up there. The landscapes, the skyscapes, the little yellow flowers and the close-up of moss. A young man on the brink of adult life, relishing the countryside, savouring the wildlife. A world he was fighting for.

'We'd like to come to the vigil, if that's OK,' Shan said, then shot a quick glance at Leo. *Am I right?* He blinked in agreement.

'Yes,' Eesha said. The other two concurred.

Randall saw them out, Shan went first.

Leo paused on the doorstep and turned to him. 'I am sorry.'

Randall dipped his head. His face was drawn with misery. 'I can't bear this,' he said. 'I can't.' His eyes brimmed with tears. 'My son — but what else can I do? How does anyone—'

Leo reached out and grasped his shoulder, squeezed it firmly. He felt vibrations under the skin, the quivering of the man.

Leo let go. Exchanged a look of understanding, his own heart aching for them all.

And longing to see Luke again. The gulf between them tearing him apart.

* * *

Wednesday

Shan

First stop on Wednesday morning was to speak to Jason Tattersall. He'd been moved to a general surgical ward and was waiting for space in a rehab unit. He'd survived surgery but his injuries were likely to be life-changing. Becky was being discharged home with the baby.

Shan felt a lurch of anxiety as they reached the hospital. Snapshots from the fire came flooding back, and panic and dread with them: Leo unmoving, not knowing if he was still breathing, screaming at him to move. Her blinded by the smoke, gasping for air, disoriented, no idea which way to crawl. Pumping Ian's chest, feeling pitifully weak. The agony of thirst that had her sipping at silt. Thinking she'd never see Erin again or her dad. Hating herself for her fear.

In the hospital car park, the sun bore down piteously on the serried ranks of cars. Blinding reflections bounced off glass and metal.

Stepping out and moving to open the passenger door for Leo, her foot sucked at the ground. The tarmac melting, glossy black.

Jason was alone in a side room just large enough for his bed and the two chairs that Shan brought in from the corridor. He looked shrunken, Shan thought, sitting in bed, propped up on pillows. Shrivelled and dull, as if there was little life left in him. The room was baking, the smell of bleach and plastic and something metallic thick in the air.

'We won't keep you too long,' Leo said. 'But we'd like you to tell us how you ended up here. What do you remember?'

Jason shook his head, slowly. A trail of saliva glistened at the corner of his mouth. Shan fought the urge to offer him a tissue.

'Nothing,' Jason said, his voice reedy.

'What's the last thing you remember before hospital?' Leo said.

'Pool.' He swallowed, wincing as though it hurt. Shan heard the spasm of his throat, the snick of cartilage and mucus.

'The pool?' Leo prompted.

'Becky had a swim.' His eyes brightened. 'Baby,' he said with relief or delight.

'Congratulations,' Shan said.

'Have you seen him?' Leo said.

'Aye.' His eyes still shone.

'You remember anything after the pool? Going back to the house?'

He seemed to consider the question. 'No.' He moved one hand to scratch at the small dressing on the back of the other. The site of a canula, Shan assumed. A vivid bruise covered the whole of the back of that hand. A dark rose blooming.

'Becky told us,' Jason said, eyes dim again.

Shan's mouth went dry. 'Becky told you what?'

Did he know Becky had been sleeping with Niall? That she'd given Niall a false alibi. That Archie might be his brother's child?

Leo met her gaze, intent too.

'Niall.' Jason frowned. A spasm of emotion rippled across his face, making him blink. His lips tremored.

236

'Shot,' he piped. 'Shot.' Confusion and pain at that betrayal rang clear. His one-word answers made Shan wonder if he'd sustained some brain damage, perhaps starved of oxygen with the blood loss he'd suffered.

'Shot?' he said again, a question now, looking from Leo to Shan. Beseeching.

'Yes, that's right,' Shan said. 'I'm so sorry that happened to you.'

'He's gone?'

'He's missing,' Shan said. 'We're doing all we can to find him.'

Jason turned his face to the side. 'He wants putting down,' he said. 'Bastard.' He closed his eyes. Shan sensed he was trying not to cry, the muscles of his face taut.

'Thank you,' Leo said. 'We'll leave you in peace.'

'He doesn't remember any of it,' Shan said as they walked along the corridor.

'Trauma can do that. Steal memories, burn holes in the brain. Some people reckon it's a form of protection. Silos off the unbearable.'

'How's he going to cope when he finds out what Becky's done?' Shan wondered aloud. 'Even if she doesn't say anything now, if we go to trial then her alibi for Niall is going to be part of our case.'

Shan slipped her sunglasses back on as they approached the automatic doors to part. She tried to imagine a future for Becky and Jason and the baby. And failed. Could only see it wreathed in guilt and blame, corrupted by the legacy of betrayal and violence.

* * *

Leo

Shan drove them up to the Grange after notifying Anita Nash, Carrie Crowther and Phil Beaumont that they wished to gather formal witness statements.

The Grange had been spared damage from the fire but a lot of the grouse moor was completely destroyed, a no-man's-land of scorched earth.

Bookings had been cancelled for the rest of the season. Beaumont had secured Niall Tattersall's cottage and would give them the key.

They made their way to the Orangery, where the three colleagues were waiting. The place was echoey, sound bouncing around all the hard surfaces. The sun glanced off the glossy leaves of the fruit trees. New blossoms had opened, perfuming the air. An idyll at odds with the conversation they were about to have.

'We've just seen Jason,' Leo told them. 'He doesn't recall being shot.'

Beaumont shook his head.

'Becky's back with the baby,' Carrie said.

'Thank God you drove her to the hospital,' Shan said.

'Can you tell us about Ian?' Beaumont said. He looked solemn, tired. 'You were with him?'

A clattering sound outside interrupted them: window cleaners with telescopic brushes were setting up.

'Oh God. I completely forgot,' Carrie said. 'Sorry. We can go through to the lounge.'

They crossed the vestibule to an enormous room set out club style with furniture grouped in several seating areas. Oxblood-leather chesterfield sofas and button-back wing chairs were placed around carved coffee tables. It smelled of furniture polish and cigars, though Leo imagined it'd been years since anyone smoked in here. The oak parquet flooring held a dull sheen. And suspended from the coffered ceiling were three brass chandeliers with candle lights, strewn with chains of yellow glass. Stained-glass panels of heraldic shields ran along the top of the windows.

A fireplace dominated the longest wall. The hearth featured a stuffed peacock, tailfeathers fanned out in display. A richly carved surround and mantelpiece showed heraldic beasts and hunting scenes wrought in the glossy brown wood.

Oil paintings of the Grange itself, and portraits of people, horses, even a dog, ringed the walls. Among them hung displays of stuffed animals. An otter with a fish, a beady-eyed golden eagle with a ferocious-looking beak and talons, two fighting cocks with silver spurs on their legs. Another stag's head.

Outsized Chinese vases, dense with colours, held fronds of dried pampas grass, bulrushes and giant thistles.

A colonial globe adorned one corner while another housed an aspidistra in a great copper urn. The unkillable plant, Leo thought. Unlike the animal trophies that littered the place.

Once they were settled, Leo returned to Beaumont's question about Ian Kerrigan and talked them through the sequence of events on the moor. Peg tracking Tattersall, Ian bothered by his asthma, lagging a little behind. The conflagration making it impossible to see each other. The pair of them getting separated from Ian and the dog.

'Shan and I sheltered in an outcrop. When it was safe to move again we headed back this way. It was Peg we saw first, she'd stayed with him.'

'Oh,' Anita said softly, eyes filling.

'She's back here now,' Beaumont said. 'I went to fetch her from the animal shelter.'

'We tried to resuscitate Ian. We performed CPR until the mountain rescue arrived,' Leo said.

Carrie gave a heavy sigh and pressed a hand to her French plait.

'Was he married?' Leo asked.

'Engaged,' Carrie said. 'She was away with friends, an early hen do. They were getting married here. She's devastated.'

Shan groaned in sympathy.

'Victim support will be in touch with you all to see if there's anything they can help with,' Leo said.

'Great,' Anita responded. 'Good.'

Leo sensed that relations between Beaumont and Anita had cooled. There was a studied politeness in the way they listened to each other, a reserve in their body language. He hoped it was over. An affair with a married man, one of her bosses, when she was just starting out in life wasn't a healthy choice.

And how would Mrs Beaumont feel when she came back from her mother's sickbed in the wake of these tragedies to hear the sordid details of what had been going on in her own home?

'What possessed him?' Carrie asked Leo. 'Niall, I mean. How does someone go from being a normal bloke to . . .' Dumbfounded, she didn't finish the sentence.

There wasn't any answer Leo could give.

How different it might have been if Niall had let Tyler go, knowing he'd face criminal charges, or if Niall had never hunted the hen harrier in the first place, or if he'd never got a job with his brother.

But in Leo's experience Niall would now be plagued by guilt, by the horrific reality of having taken a life. He would carry the events of Syke Moss wherever he went, however far he ran, however deep he tried to hide. Like a cancer, the guilt and shame and the trauma would grow and fester. Niall Tattersall might not be locked up yet but he would never be truly free.

CHAPTER SIXTEEN

Wednesday

Shan

Anita and Carrie withdrew while Beaumont went over his testimony. Then they talked to Anita.

'Can you remember much of the argument you heard?' Shan asked once Anita was settled.

'Yes, you said to try and do that, so I wrote down what I could.' She held up her phone. 'But it's been going round and round in my head ever since anyway. Just over and over.' She looked troubled.

'It's difficult, I know. But it's a good way of processing what happened. It's healthy even though it feels awful,' Shan said. *And exactly what I didn't do after I lost the baby.* Shan gathered herself. 'So you were upstairs at the Beaumonts' and the window was open?'

'Yes. I heard voices. Niall was there and Jason told him you wanted to see him. Asking for DNA. That you must have found something on the body. And Niall said, "Like what?" And Jason didn't know, but he said something about traces and how it was on all the true crime shows that Becky liked.'

'Then Niall asked Jason to lend him some money, he was going away for a bit. And Jason was like, "What you on about? You can't just take off. We've ten Guns booked in tomorrow."'

'But Niall wouldn't leave it.' Anita halted. She took a shaky breath.

'Take your time,' Shan said.

'Right.' She read her phone. 'Yes, he said Jason was his brother and he should give it him. And Jason said he must be joking. Then Jason goes, "What the fuck have you done?" Sorry.' She apologised for swearing.

'That's fine,' Shan said. 'Everything you remember.'

'I got it then.' Shan saw the fear simmering in her eyes. 'I knew what they were talking about. The murder, like. I was so scared.' She gulped a couple of breaths. Shan waited, quiet.

'Niall started on about a hen harrier and he'd have lost everything and he'd no choice. He kept saying he had no choice, that Tyler wouldn't give him the phone. And Jason said he had to tell the police — no, that was later.' Anita corrected herself, checked her phone and nodded. 'Niall said he could have been sent down for killing the bird and Jason said, "Well, you fucking will be now. You've killed him, you've killed a kid." He said Niall was mental. And that's when Jason said about telling the police. Niall didn't say anything but Jason was going, "You've got to tell them." I think . . . I think Niall ran off 'cos Jason was shouting after him. Then his phone goes, Jason's, and Jason answers — it was Becky and he said he'd be down in ten minutes.'

To the pool, Shan guessed.

'Then it was quiet but I heard Niall come back and he says, "I want the money, whatever you've got. And the keys to the jeep."'

'Jason told him to put the gun down.' Anita's voice rose in distress. 'He said, "You going to shoot me 'n' all?"'

'And Niall said how Jason had always had it easy. He was always throwing his weight around ever since they were kids. Swinging his dick.' Anita blushed. 'I didn't know what to

do. I was so scared. Niall said, "You owe me. Money. Keys."
Then Jason was saying Niall was always crap at everything and
everything he touched turned to shit and he was a loser and if
he wouldn't turn himself in then Jason would. And Niall said,
"You don't want to do that. Give me the phone."'

She sniffed. 'And Jason called him a pathetic little creep.
Said he hadn't the balls.' She raised her eyes to Shan. 'He shot
him.' Tears stood in her eyes. 'He just shot him.'

Shan touched her shoulder. 'Thank you. I'm so sorry you
had to witness that. And then to go through it all again. You
did really well.'

* * *

Shan left Leo to interview Carrie while she went with Beaumont
to search the area around the main house in case Tattersall had
made his way back to home territory.

'We'd look like idiots if Tattersall turns up in a shed on
the estate,' Leo had pointed out to Shan earlier.

'We'll start with the ice house,' Beaumont said.

They crossed through a small wood at the back of the
Grange. Beams of sunlight shafted through the canopy, illuminating pollen and dust and flying insects as they made their
way to the building. The entrance, a curved stone vault, was
above ground.

'There was a pond, where the swimming pool is now,'
Beaumont said. 'They'd bring the frozen ice from there in
the winter and store it in hay, deep underground. Fell out of
favour once refrigeration came in.'

The wooden door had long since rotted, the edge that
remained looked as though it'd been chewed away, and the
doorway was wreathed in brambles, nettles and twisting bind-
weed with its white trumpet flowers. All clotted with spider
webs.

It didn't look to have been disturbed but, determined
to be thorough, Shan made her way through, crushing the

thorny branches and vicious stinging nettles underfoot, and stepped inside, stooping to clear the arched roof. Beaumont stayed close behind.

Over the threshold, she paused to listen. There was no sound from below.

She lit her torch, and swept the cone of light down the stone stairway. Dead leaves, curled and crisp, littered the steps. She caught the sour smell of stale air. Birdsong from outside was muffled then almost gone as she descended, swiping away the cobwebs.

The square space at the bottom bore witness to visitors long gone. Old bottles with wire stoppers, the labels mildewed away. The remains of a small fire. More leaves.

The place felt like a tomb and Shan shivered. She was glad to turn and climb out.

Two other stone buildings, their purpose lost in the mists of time, were deeper in the wood, close to each other. Neither had a roof any longer. The first was full of fallen stones, decrepit.

The second was favoured by a flock of crows, who scattered in alarm as Shan and Beaumont approached. The walls were spattered with guano. This one held a rotting mattress, colonised by couch grass and ferns. There was a pile of debris in one corner, pint-sized milk bottles, a crumbling log, a plastic tarpaulin, rusted food cans, a broken garden fork.

Shan nudged the pile with her boot, and woodlice, bright orange centipedes and two enormous spiders scuttled away. She bit down on a scream.

'Anywhere else?' Shan asked Beaumont.

'There's an old bothy but he'll not be there. It's close to some of the snares and those are still being checked regularly.'

'Who by?' Kerrigan was dead, Jason in hospital, his brother an outlaw.

'We brought in a couple of locals, beaters who know the estate.'

'I'd still like to have a look,' Shan said. 'Make sure.'

Beaumont was about to speak — to object? — but thought better of it. He led the way to the conifer plantation with the bright, medicinal smell of pine sap. Shan could see the sticky resin glistening on trunks. Underfoot lay a soft layer of bronze larch needles and assorted pinecones which crunched as they walk. A blackbird was singing. And Shan heard another shrill, trilling cry that she couldn't name.

She asked Beaumont if he knew the bird.

'Crested tit,' he said. 'They like the conifers.'

They emerged onto moorland. Scrub here, grasses rather than heather. The building stood a couple of hundred yards away.

'What's that smell?' Shan said. A grotesque reek assailed her, like sewage or rancid meat. Or a body she'd once found on a welfare check when she was a response officer in Leeds. A lonely old man who'd died watching television. Heart attack. The smell and the image of his putrid body had never left her.

Now the stench made her want to retch. She covered her nose. Sweat pricked her armpits, the back of her neck.

'Stink pit,' Beaumont said. 'It's by the bothy.'

'Stink pit?'

'We leave dead vermin there to attract more. There's snares all round here to trap them. You still want to go?'

'Yes,' she said.

A footpath tracked through the grass. As they drew closer a bevy of jackdaws rose squawking from the carrion. The revolting stench grew thicker. Shan had to breathe but each sip of air made her guts heave, her throat spasm.

The contents of the pit came into view. Shan glimpsed the muddy red fur of a fox, something black beside it. The image resolved, the black was a cat, desiccated. A mass of flies swarmed over the corpses, feasting on the flesh. She recognised other creatures: birds, rabbits, the guts of something. A piece of flesh was rippling, heaving with cream-coloured maggots.

'You just leave them like this?' Shan said, sickened by both sight and smell.

'That's the idea,' Beaumont said. 'It's a lure, see? To reach here the vermin pass the snares.' He pointed ahead, just beyond the pit. Shan saw a jerking movement, a rabbit ensnared by its neck, wire glinting in the sun.

'I'll put it out of its misery,' Beaumont said.

She watched him bend and remove the animal from the snare, stretch it out then wrench the head sharply.

He slung it into the pit.

In silence they walked on to the bothy.

This had less of a derelict air. No rubbish inside. But a couple of upturned plastic crates faced the doorway.

'It serves as a hide,' Beaumont said. 'You can sit here and pick off anything that the snares don't catch.'

'Let's go back,' Shan said. Sick of it all. The death, the killing, the gore. The pitiless heat. Rotting meat and men with guns. Sick to the core.

* * *

Leo

Becky Tattersall was already back at the house. When her mother opened the door, she told them Becky was resting.

'We do need to speak to her,' Leo said.

She gave a swift nod and stood back to let them in.

There were boxes and suitcases in the room, a baby carrier, packs of nappies.

'Moving?' Leo asked.

'Becky's coming to mine.'

'Can we take your address? It's likely we'll want to speak to her again.'

She supplied them with details of her home in Hawes.

She went upstairs to rouse her daughter, then made tea while they waited for her.

They sat in the kitchen, where days earlier Anita Nash had recounted the argument between the two brothers. The curtains were closed now. Leo imagined Becky didn't want to look out at the garden where Jason had been attacked by his brother, Jason's blood probably still visible on the grass.

* * *

When Becky appeared she looked drowsy, her eyes puffy, hair matted.

'Mum, will you go up?' she asked.

'I could put the monitor on?'

'No. Please?'

Leo assumed Becky wanted privacy.

'Oh, OK.'

Becky joined them at the table. She sighed as she sat.

'How's the baby?' Leo asked.

'Fine. Good.' A flicker of warmth in her response.

'You getting any sleep?'

'No. Even if he'd let me, it's too hot.'

Leo nodded. 'We've seen Jason this morning. He doesn't remember what happened.'

Becky gave a nod, eyes sliding away. 'They don't know how long he'll have to wait in there. For rehab.'

'Becky, we want to go over the events on Wednesday evening when Tyler Prasad was killed,' Leo said.

'I already told you all that.' She directed her comment at Shan.

'We need to get it in writing. A formal statement,' Shan said.

Becky described Jason coming home in a foul mood because he'd had an argument with Niall. Jason swore it was the last straw, that Niall wasn't fit to do the job. He vowed he'd talk to Phil about firing him. She told them about Jason leaving to go pick up the parts from the garage in Richmond.

'And then?' Leo asked.

'That was it. Jason got back just after nine.'

'And Niall?'

'I didn't see Niall that day.' She avoided eye contact.

'He didn't visit you — as you previously claimed?'

She shook her head, mouth working.

'When did you next hear from Niall?'

She exhaled loudly. Twisted at the wedding band on her finger. 'On Friday he rang. He told me, if you asked, to say he came round here on Wednesday. He swore he had nothing to do with the murder, that I knew he'd never do anything like that, but the police were on him and if I said he was with me between seven and eight then they'd leave him alone and not waste their time when he was innocent.' She paused, still fretting at her ring. 'So when you came, that's what I said.'

'You gave your brother-in-law a false alibi?' Leo said.

'Yes.'

Once the details of her account were typed up, Leo asked Becky to enter a signature.

'Have you heard from Niall since?' Leo asked.

'No.'

'Have you tried contacting him?'

'No! I wouldn't.' She drew back, a spark of repulsion.

'Becky, you may be required to testify to what you've told us in court,' Leo said.

'But then everyone would know! Jason . . .' Horror lanced in her eyes. 'Do I have to?'

'You can refuse to answer a summons but that risks you being held in contempt of court. And given you've already misled the police enquiry, it's not something I think you should consider,' Leo said. He spoke slowly, giving the words weight, hoping she would grasp the seriousness of her situation.

Becky bowed her head, elbows on the table, fingers braced around her forehead. Eventually she turned to stare at Shan. 'You said I could be charged with perverting the course of justice. Will that be up to the courts?'

'Anything you can do now to help us find Niall could be used in your favour,' Leo said. 'If he's been in touch—'

'He hasn't! You can check my phone.'

'What about friends? People he might ask for help?' Leo said.

'No one would do that,' she said. 'And he wouldn't risk it.'

'Family?'

'Same. There's not many of them, and after what he's done to Jason. Let alone . . . Look, we don't even know if Niall's alive!'

'We don't know that he isn't,' Shan said.

'Where do you think he'd go? How he'd manage?' Leo asked.

'He's probably living rough. He's practical. That wouldn't be a problem. Not in this weather. He might have gone abroad,' she said.

'He'd be stopped at the border,' Leo said. 'The family farm, the one that was sold to the estate — did Niall ever take you there?'

'No. He barely remembers it. I think it's a stables now.'

'When did you meet Niall?' Leo asked.

'At school. Same year group.'

'And when did you start going out?'

'Not until year 12,' she said.

'Which was?'

'Erm . . . 2013.'

'And that lasted?' Leo said.

'Four years.'

'Then what happened?'

'Jason happened. Do we have to do this?' she pleaded.

'It helps us to understand the dynamic and what's brought Niall to this point.'

'Yeah, my fault. I know that,' she said hotly.

'Becky, it's not your fault that Niall shot Tyler.'

'But it's my fault he shot Jason, isn't it? If I'd just told the truth—' She choked back tears.

'2017?' Leo prompted after a beat.

'Niall and I were in a bit of a rut. Arguing. Falling out. Jason seemed so much more together and he was really kind

249

to me and . . . one thing led to another. I never meant to hurt Niall. I really didn't. I think he knows that.'

'How did Niall react?'

'Well, he wasn't happy about it,' she said sarcastically.

'Was he violent?'

Her mouth snapped open as if in instant denial. Then she relented. 'It was just a fight. Brothers fight. He was hurt. He took it out on Jason.'

'Not you?'

'He'd never hurt me.'

He just shot your husband, Leo thought. *That not count?*

'Were there other times he was violent?'

'You say "violent",' she complained, defending Niall. 'He just didn't like being messed with. He'd stand up for himself.'

Attack as a form of defence.

'Like when? What sort of thing?'

'I don't know — just if someone was on his back, putting him down, making him look stupid. Getting in his face. He'd snap.' She shrugged. The threat of tears replaced by nonchalance.

'No one ever reported him?' Leo knew Tattersall had no criminal record.

'You're making it out to be bigger than it was. Men fight now and again. Always have, always will. It's just natural.'

Leo wanted to shake some sense into her, thought of her raising her son with the same philosophy, the easy acceptance of aggression. He thought of Tyler, the sickening waste of a young man's life.

And of Luke finding some warped sense of belonging in threatening people seen as 'other'.

Becky gave a heavy sigh, rubbed her eyes. 'Since you and Jason married you've continued to see Niall?'

'Not at first, but then . . .'

'How often did you have sex together?' Leo said.

'Why does that—'

'Just answer the question,' Leo said gently.

'Every few weeks, maybe. We had to be careful. More if Jason was away or if we could get away. I tried to end it, properly, for good. So many times. But I couldn't do it. I just couldn't,' she appealed to them.

'And in between meetings, was there contact? Messages? Texts?' Leo asked.

'Yes.'

'Regularly?'

'Yes.'

'How often?'

'A few times a week.' A ripple of regret crossed Becky's face. 'I know I shouldn't have, it was awful, but—'

A wail rose from upstairs, piercing, surprisingly loud.

Becky started. 'Oh, shit!' She crossed her arms over her breasts but not before Leo had glimpsed the damp patches.

She turned her face away, embarrassed.

'Go feed him,' Leo said. 'I think we've got what we need for now.'

* * *

Shan

It was common sense that the more a hunter understood their prey the greater chance of success.

The same held true for a manhunt.

Beaumont had given Shan the key to Niall Tattersall's cottage and they went straight there.

The bag of shopping on the counter had attracted a trail of ants. The fruit flies had multiplied, and a wasp buzzed furiously at the kitchen window. The air was stale, a hint of something putrid — food scraps rotting in the bin perhaps, or bad drains.

The cottage was a modest size, sparsely furnished, living room and kitchen on the ground floor, the open wooden staircase leading up to two bedrooms and bathroom above. Low beamed ceilings and small windows.

In the living room sat a TV with games consoles on the rug in front of it. Shan saw cases from *Call of Duty* and *FC24*. There was a bulky sofa upholstered in faded brown corduroy and a side table with a couple of crushed beer cans and a Yorkshire rose ashtray which held a few cigarette ends. They could take one of those for DNA testing if Shan couldn't find a hairbrush or toothbrush.

A shelving unit in the alcove housed papers, bills and invoices. DVDs, old Star Wars films, the Lord of the Rings trilogy, Batman movies. A couple of novels, Lee Child and Andy McNab. A wired speaker sat abandoned, presumably from his laptop or tablet, which was missing.

A glossy magazine lay on the sofa: hunting and fishing. Cover photo of people gleaming with health. Kitted out in plus-fours and tweed jerkins, sexed up with mirrored shades.

By the door, a pile of shoes, a coat rack with jackets on.

Pictures on the wall included an aerial photograph. Shan looked closer at the roofs of the buildings. 'This is the estate.'

'There was a trend for those, I remember,' Leo said. 'The local paper used to advertise.'

Another frame held a collage of family photographs.

'That must be the parents, and the grandparents,' she said. The older formal wedding picture bore the stamp of a studio in Skipton.

The narrow, sharp-faced features of the brothers echoed those of their father and grandmother.

'And here, that's the parents with Jason and Niall,' Leo said.

The younger boy was in his mother's arms, a sheepdog by her feet. Jason stood in front, his father's hands on his shoulders. Jason was beaming. A world away from the nervy, terse-speaking man they'd interviewed when they first arrived at the estate.

'Do you think Jason knew Becky was cheating on him with Niall? And that's why he was dead set on giving him the push?' Shan said.

Leo considered it. 'I doubt it. Subconsciously perhaps. But I can't imagine him not confronting Becky, and his brother for that matter. Being cuckolded in a situation like this, a tight little community — you'd be so humiliated.'

'Cuckolded?' Shan teased.

'Does the job.' Leo smiled.

The wasp careened through the living room and batted against the front window with an angry, whining buzz.

'This is where the family moved after they sold the farm,' Shan told him. 'These might be his parents' pictures. It can't have been easy for him. Jason and Becky just over the way, playing happy families, Jason bossing him about at work. Why stay?'

'You heard what Beaumont said, Kerrigan too. Locals can't afford to live here. He'd no capital, he'd be leaving a job with guaranteed accommodation. To go where, do what?'

'And if he left he'd have to accept he wasn't going to win Becky back,' Shan said.

'He thought that might happen?' Leo looked at her.

'You'd have to, surely. I'll look upstairs, see if there's a hairbrush or toothbrush as well,' Shan suggested. 'You do the kitchen.'

The bathroom was in need of renovation. No shower, only a stained bathtub, the taps fitted with a rubber shower attachment. A toilet with a cracked seat. A chipped sink.

Basic toiletries in a wire rack. Razor, shaving foam, shampoo, athlete's foot powder. Shan snapped open an evidence bag and collected the toothbrush that lay on the sink surround.

The spare bedroom was small and filled with a jumble of empty cardboard boxes and the items of spare bedrooms everywhere: a hardshell suitcase, an exercise bike, an acoustic guitar furred with dust, a George Foreman electric griddle. Shan recalled her parents buying one of those when they first came on the market. That had ended up in their spare room too. She opened the curtains. A collection of dead flies and moths peppered the windowsill. The glass was thick with grime, inside and out.

From the window in the main bedroom, Niall had a view of the moor. The same stretch that she and Leo, Ian Kerrigan and Peg had crossed when they began their pursuit. Untouched by the wildfire and undisturbed by the sound of gunfire, it looked serene. A sea of purple heather and tawny grasses.

Shan felt unsteady for a moment, tasting again the terror that unfolded that day. The ferocity of the flames, the all-consuming roar of the blaze, the air choked with smoke and soot. The visceral fear that she would die there.

Shaking the memories off, she turned and surveyed the room: double bed, bedside table, wardrobe and drawers all in the same pine wood. Clothes discarded on the floor.

A hairbrush on the drawers and a mirror above. Shan bagged the hairbrush too. Belt and braces.

She found nothing of interest in the wardrobe or drawers. Casual clothes and his work outfits all, apart from a black suit in a dry cleaner's bag. Weddings and funerals.

On the bedside table was a small gooseneck light. In a shallow drawer she found a packet of paracetamol, a bottle of cough linctus, Olbas Oil.

In the cupboard below, *The Institute* by Stephen King. A bundle of greetings cards.

Shan flicked through them. Birthday cards from Becky, a Valentine's also from Becky. A postcard she'd sent from Cyprus dated 2014. A glossy photograph, Niall and Becky, glowing, fresh-faced under a sixth-form prom banner.

Half a dozen other snaps looked like they'd been printed at home from digital files. A slight bleeding of the colour and the photo paper curling at the edges. Becky in babydoll lingerie leaving little to the imagination. A close-up too, Becky gazing straight at the camera, a gleam of warmth in her expression, the beginnings of a smile.

Others showed the two of them outside, selfies. Standing, arms around each other, under a tree. The edge of a rope ladder visible. On open moorland at the edge of a tarn. Sitting in the doorway to a derelict field barn. One of the same location in wintertime with snow on the ground. Niall in a puffer jacket, Becky a black parka, standing beside a snowman.

Keepsakes.

Shan took them down to Leo.

'We could show these photos to Becky, see where they were taken, if Niall might have gone to any of them?'

'Yes,' Leo said. 'We'll go tomorrow, straight after the vigil.'

'I'll call the stables. I know they'll have been covered in the drone search. But he could have steered clear until that ended and then sought refuge somewhere like that.'

Shan looked up a number for them on her phone and dialled.

'Saunders Riding School,' a woman answered.

'Yes, hello. This is Detective Constable Shan Young. I'm involved in the search for Niall Tattersall.'

'You think he might have come here?' the woman said.

'Just checking every eventuality. From your website it looks as though the stables has a busy programme.'

'We do, yes.'

'Is there someone on-site twenty-four seven?'

'That'd be me.'

'And have you any security installed?'

'Yes, CCTV. We have a perimeter gate too. Locked out of hours.'

'Has there been any cause for concern, signs of intruders, suspicious incidents?'

'No, nothing like that. But if we did notice anything I'd be in touch immediately. The idea of him roaming around.' The woman made a shuddering sound.

'Nothing,' Shan told Leo. 'But we can tick that off.'

'Three days, he's been out there. Three nights,' Leo said. 'No money — nothing. The longer he's on the run the more desperate he's going to get. Every time the phone goes I think it'll be another shooting, another victim. We've got to stop him before that happens.'

'I know,' Shan said. *Why did I buy into it*, she thought, *Niall's act as the caring, helpful bystander? Why couldn't I see the truth? 'If only I'd—'*

'Hey,' Leo said. 'Hindsight's a dead end. Eyes forward, eh?' He smiled and she gave him a wry salute.

CHAPTER SEVENTEEN

Thursday

Shan

Shan woke to pins and needles in her right arm. It was too hot to be spooning. She must have fallen asleep like that, curled round Erin, holding her close.

She eased her arm free, their skin tacky with perspiration. When Erin murmured but didn't wake, Shan kissed the nape of her neck. She felt the slow wash of desire licking through the pit of her stomach, through her breasts and thighs. Maybe later.

She rolled onto her back and felt the sweat drying.

She'd slept deep and dreamless. Her first proper sleep in the days since the fire.

Daylight was spilling along the top of the curtain. She checked her phone. It was only half six but she was awake now.

In the shower, she washed her hair, careful to be gentle around the burn. It was a relief to have the dressings off.

Afterwards she rubbed cream onto the patch, reaching from the top of her ear to her eyebrow and above into her hairline, where the new skin was red, tight and shiny. It was hard to tell if it would scar permanently.

Erin had cut her hair, shaving the right-hand side to match, leaving it longer on the top and back. Giving her that undercut she'd always fancied trying.

'Gorgeous,' Erin had pronounced. 'Pixie face.'

Shan, facing the bathroom mirror, had raised an eyebrow. 'You're meant to be the pixie.'

'Always room for one more.' Erin hugged her from behind, nuzzled her cheek.

They had begun to talk a little about their relationship, about how losing the baby had blown everything up, alienated them from each other.

The first step from the guide Erin had found online had been to each talk uninterrupted about how they felt. Just about themselves while the other person listened. Then the listener had to summarise what they'd heard. There was no place for argument or defensiveness, interruption or correction.

'And that's it?' Shan had asked when Erin explained the exercise. It sounded so simple.

'For now. We'll take it slowly.'

They talked sitting side by side on the sofa. It had been hard hearing Erin lay out how she'd felt: sidelined by Shan, her own grief unacknowledged, irrelevant, unloved. 'I felt you were punishing me and that everything I tried to say or do was wrong and cruel or stupid.' Shan kept wanting to respond, to clarify things or challenge her, rather than just sit and take in what was being said. And when it was Shan's turn to speak, she felt wretched. She hated having to take the lid off her emotions and poke around, waking those feelings of anguish, picking over her misery, her sense of failure, her desire to run from it all, far, far away.

Afterwards, she didn't feel relieved or cleansed or particularly positive. Erin did seem to understand what Shan was saying, and when Shan became upset and blurted out, 'I lost the baby because I didn't deserve to have it. I'm not good enough, Erin. I wasn't good enough when I was a baby myself, when I was abandoned, and I'm not now. I don't think I ever will be,' Erin had listened with tears in her eyes and perhaps for the first time seen how insecure Shan really was.

Shan had hated every minute of it. But if this was what had to be done, she'd do it. And if it didn't work, didn't bring them some of the peace and happiness they'd known before, then maybe she'd suggest talking to a professional, like her mum and dad had done.

Erin was coming with her to the vigil for Tyler today. The funeral would be private, family and closest friends only. But the vigil was open to all.

* * *

It was already busy when they arrived. A steady stream of people heading up the footpath from Keld in the sunshine. The day was calm, no wind, no Saharan dust. The path was just about accessible; anyone using a wheelchair or pushing a buggy would be able to attend, as would Leo, still on crutches. And the campsite provided parking.

Not far up the hillside was a plateau, once the site of lead mines, perfect for the event. The family had made it clear that the afternoon, a mass picnic with music, was to be in celebration of Tyler and of the work he'd been committed to.

As they climbed, Shan's nerves felt like eels seething in her belly. Her heart seemed to lose its rhythm, to skip and thud. She slowed.

'Shan?' Erin looked at her, slipped off her sunglasses. 'You're shaking.'

Tyler, smooth brown skin scattered with dots of blood, seeds in his black hair. Eyes destroyed. Ian Kerrigan coughing, bent double. Jason, the blood seeping from his wounds. Tyler, wrist twisted. The fire racing, roaring. No air.

Erin pulled Shan aside to let people pass. 'Sit down.'

Shan's heart was bursting.

She lowered herself to the ground, hands in the heather. The rough warty feel of the stalks. The sweet, musky scent of the flowers.

Erin rubbed her back, slow circles. 'Just breathe.'

Shan stared down at the plants, at a spray of cotton grass moving lightly with the passage of people. A shiny black fly. The smell of earth baking.

The pain in her heart ebbed away. 'I'm OK.'

'We don't have to stay.'

I do. 'No, I want to. I'm all right. Near enough.' She looked around. 'I haven't been up here since . . .'

'I know. Think about it, Shan. You lose the baby, then you work this horrible murder, just a kid. There's another guy gets shot, and you deal with all that and then the fire. You could have died.' Erin's voice wavered but she continued calmly, 'And Ian Kerrigan, you tried to save him. But you lost him. That's enough trauma for a lifetime.' Erin gripped Shan's hand. 'We can go home now, just say the word. Be kind to yourself.'

Shan looked at Erin, was thankful for her understanding. But being here today meant so much, she couldn't walk away, didn't want to. And she knew that facing this, coming up here on the moors, was part of the journey she needed to make.

'I know. But I want to do this. I think I'll be OK now. If it gets too much, I'll . . . I promise.'

'Stubborn,' Erin complained. Then she smiled. She stroked Shan's arm, leaned in and kissed her. 'OK. Here, have some water.'

Shan drank and then they resumed their journey.

Pennants, long rectangular banners suspended from bamboo frames, ringed the picnic site. Made with collage, appliqué, printed photographs, graffiti, they carried messages about the land, wildlife, nature, diversity, the planet. *THIS IS OUR RAINFOREST*, read one, the letters stencilled on a batik image of the moorland. A banner in the middle displayed an enlarged photograph of Tyler. Similar to the one Shan had seen before but an individual shot this time. Both hands making peace signs. He beamed a wide smile. He wore a bucket hat and the T-shirt that they'd found him in. He was so young.

'That's just beautiful,' Erin said.

Here and there in the gathering were smaller pennants and flags, placeholders for charities, pressure groups, local community organisations. Some groups wore matching T-shirts: a cycling club, a ramblers' group, climate protesters, a church contingent. There was a large party of teenagers, dressed in green and white. Shan wondered if they were Tyler's schoolmates.

Lots of people had brought their dogs along. Shan thought of Peg, the way she'd stayed with Ian, her singed fur.

Was Molly Unwin here somewhere? With her parents, or her friends? *She loved him to the moon and back.*

A folk band were playing, fiddle and flute and drum, a woman singing.

Shan and Erin found a space to sit and spread out the blanket they'd brought.

'Hungry?' Erin asked.

Was she? She still felt jittery, her guts cramping, but maybe the food would settle that. 'Yes,' she said.

Erin doled out chunks of ciabatta, a pot of hummus, slices of cheese and cherry tomatoes.

Shan saw Eesha and Randall with Padma in a large group. She'd go and say hello at some point. Though she felt inadequate. The job half done. Yes, they'd uncovered the truth, but while Niall Tattersall evaded justice it wasn't enough.

She spotted Ange walking between the groups, stopping to talk to people, coordinating the afternoon.

'Shan?'

She turned, shielding the light from her eyes, to see Lydia Siemens.

'Hello.' Shan moved to get up but Lydia said, 'Don't. You're fine.'

She sat down and Shan introduced her to Erin.

'I'm Deaf,' Lydia said. 'But I can lip-read. This is lovely.' She signalled around at the gathering. 'But . . .' She pulled a face.

'Lydia was working with Tyler,' Shan explained to Erin. 'She's making a film.'

'It's nearly finished,' Lydia said. 'I wanted to ask if you ever found Tyler's phone. If there's any photographs I could use. Anything he hadn't had the chance to post on Instagram.'

Shan's stomach clenched. She felt sick thinking of what they'd found when they checked the cloud.

'We didn't, no.' She decided not to elaborate, the images and videos were evidence, not something that could be shared. And they assumed that Niall had got rid of the phone the same day he hid Tyler's body.

'Is the film about the protests?' Erin asked.

'Sort of. About the land, why it matters, how it could be better used.'

'To plant trees?' Erin said.

'No, no,' Lydia said. 'Trees would dry out the bog, they'd steal the water. What we want is to preserve the peat bog, restore it, but also diversify the wildlife. All this—' she waved an arm — 'is precious. We must conserve it. It's a massive carbon sink.'

'And the grouse?' Erin said.

Lydia rolled her eyes. 'Industrial-scale grouse breeding and slaughter is not part of the plan. It distorts the whole ecosystem. People bang on about jobs, economic benefits. It's crap. It could easily be matched, increased with alternative projects.'

'Like whale watching instead of whale hunting,' Shan said.

A sudden barrage of sound drew everyone's attention. A samba band. Drums and shakers and whistles beat a ferocious rhythm. Children flocked to follow them through the site. Lydia said her farewells.

Shan finished her bread and found the apples, handed one to Erin.

The samba band stopped processing and people formed an audience to watch their set piece, dancers performing to the drums. The music changed in pace and rhythm, built to a crescendo. Applause and whoops greeted the players.

Shan caught sight of Leo with the Prasads. 'I'm going to go say hello. See Leo. And the family.'

'I'll wait here,' Erin said.

Shan passed a child, her face painted with butterfly wings, and then a family who had brought a portable gazebo and were circled in the shade underneath it. Another couple were crouched down trying to calm a screaming toddler, the child on the ground, back arched, legs kicking, face red with fury. *That could be us one day*, Shan thought. *Why would I want that?* Her stomach dipped with guilt. Was she looking for excuses not to consider having a child with Erin? She'd have to face it head on eventually, she accepted that. But she was still confused. Uncertain. And hurt from losing the pregnancy.

As she walked, she smelled suncream and caught a whiff of onions from someone's food.

Eesha noticed Shan approaching and came to greet her. 'All the people,' she said. 'Thank you for coming.'

'No, of course. It's brilliant,' Shan said. More musicians were gathering, people carrying trumpets and trombones, saxophones. Metal gleaming in the sun.

Leo waved to her and she nodded hello.

Randall joined them. He stooped to greet her, then turned to his wife. 'Ange says now would be a good time.'

'I must go,' Eesha said. 'I'm giving a speech.' She pulled a rueful expression.

'Good luck.'

Shan returned to Erin.

There was a crackle of sound from a PA system, a squeal of feedback, then Eesha, standing on a natural stone platform at the edge of the area, began to speak.

'Welcome, everyone. And thank you so much for joining us today. We are here to celebrate our marvellous, kind, funny, brilliant, passionate son, Tyler. As some of you know, Tyler was a big Liverpool fan.'

A few voices cheered in solidarity while others gently groaned.

'He loved gaming too and cycling, but his greatest joy was the natural world. Tyler was here working with Free the Fells this summer before he started at university. He loved what he was doing and we're glad to say that the project will continue with funds raised in his memory. We hope the campaign will go from strength to strength.

'I want you all to take some time now to remember Tyler, to think of Tyler. But not in silence.' She paused, and when she resumed her voice was louder, bolder. 'Because we will not be silenced. We have come together to make noise, to demand change, to find peace and justice, equality and freedom. So please, raise your voices. Hum like bees, cry like birds, howl like wolves or sing like the whales. Or if you prefer, click your fingers or pat your hands. For Tyler. For all of us. For this world, our home, and every living thing.'

Eesha began to hum, wavering at first, then stronger. Each note two or three seconds long. Standing beside her, her sister Padma harmonised. People caught on quickly. Soon the air resounded with sound, vibrating harmonies forming and dissolving, some people tapping, a sound like rain beneath the tune. Shan had a lump in her throat.

Erin took Shan's hand and squeezed it. The music grew louder, more powerful. Shan could feel it resonating, thrumming through her chest.

Eesha used her arms to conduct, to bring them to the pinnacle. Then cut them off. Silence fell.

A dog barked and a child squealed with laughter.

A moment.

Two.

A trumpet sounded. Slow, haunting notes, a melody which echoed round the plain. Shan recognised the tune: 'What a Wonderful World'. The rest of the brass band joined in. But Shan heard another sound in the mix. She stood up on tiptoe trying to see what it was. Asked Erin if she knew.

'It's a sitar,' Erin answered.

People were mesmerised, captivated as the poignant song, with its message of joy and love, swelled and grew. Uniting them all.

* * *

Shan

Becky was glum, seemingly numb, when she let them into her mother's house.

It was a pebble-dashed semi on a small estate of a dozen properties, built originally as council housing for renting to locals in need. No doubt many, if not most, would have been snapped up back when the law was changed to allow tenants to buy their homes.

There was resignation in Becky's voice as she asked, 'What is it now?'

'We'd like to show you some photographs that we brought from Niall's. If you can tell us where they were taken,' Shan said.

'All right,' she said.

The baby was asleep in a Moses basket on the sofa. Becky sat beside it, put her feet up on the same leather footstool they'd seen at her own home. Had she brought it with her — or did mother and daughter have matching items?

Shan imagined them on shopping trips together. Felt a pinch of jealousy. Once something she and her mum did.

Leo moved to stand behind Shan.

There was an overpowering sweet, peppery smell in the room. Was Becky wearing perfume? Then Shan saw the plug-in air freshener. It would be scenting the place with chemical aromas, 'Summer Meadow' or 'Coastal Escape'.

'This picture?' Shan showed her the one by the tree.

'Yes. The treehouse. Jason and Niall built it.'

'Treehouse?' Shan's skin tingled. He could be in the tree-tops. A perfect place to hide.

'It had a roof and everything.'

'Where is it?'

'I don't know if it'll still be there. That's what, nearly ten years ago?'

'Where is it?' Shan repeated.

'It's down near Syke Low. You can walk from there to the footbridge. Then there's a track up.'

'Did you go there often?'

'No. I don't like heights,' she said flatly.

Shan wondered if Becky was depressed. Not uncommon after a baby was born. *Would I have been — if . . .?* She yanked her attention back to the present. If you added into the mix the traumas that Becky had gone through, was going through, it was understandable she'd be low. Or had something happened? Had Becky told her mum the full story and felt her disapproval? But maybe her mum supported her. Understood Becky's mistakes.

'And these?' Shan said, showing her the pictures at the barn. A ghost of a smile crossed her face at the winter scene. 'That's the old barn on the way to Thwaite.'

Archie murmured and Becky stopped, watching him.

'Becky?' Shan said after a minute.

'Yes?' She looked at Shan, apparently befuddled.

'What about this?' The picture by the lake.

Becky's lips parted. 'Oh,' she said. 'That's at the tarn.' Her cheeks pinked. She coughed.

Shan sensed it held meaning, saw yearning wash through Becky's eyes.

'A special place?'

Becky scoffed. Shook her head. 'We went there a lot, the first year or so, that's all.'

Shan wasn't sure what to ask her next but wanted to hear more. 'Go on.'

'We stayed there, camping out. I'd say I was with one of my mates and Niall did the same.'

'Your parents didn't approve of the relationship?' Shan said.

'Not that. Just, we were on our own there, nobody to tell us what to do. We could get pissed or high, stay up all night, it didn't matter.' A look of sorrow softened her eyes. Then drained away.

'How do we find it?'

'It's the middle of nowhere,' Becky said dismissively.

'Nearest place?' Leo said.

'Above Catrake Force.'

'Yes?' Leo said, asking her to elaborate.

'There's a path up to the rocks. You go right at the rocks and keep on the top of the ridge. Then there's a dip, where the tarn is.'

'No roads? No dirt tracks?' Leo said.

'No.'

'Anywhere else that the two of you used to go?' Shan said.

'No. He might be dead, you know,' she said bluntly. Grief, fleeting, crossed her face. 'After everything that's happened.'

'What makes you think that?' Shan said.

'Dunno.'

Shan hoped she was wrong. She wanted to find Niall Tattersall and bring him in. See him face justice. The Prasads, Ian Kerrigan's family, Jason — they all deserved that.

* * *

Shan's car was roasting, so she opened the doors and suggested they wait a moment. 'Let's see if we can work out where they are, the treehouse and the tarn.'

Leo got his map out and straightened it on the car bonnet. The sun glancing off the paper made it hard to see.

'This here is the wood Becky talked about.' He tapped the map. 'There's the footbridge. So somewhere up here will be the treehouse.' He followed the road to Thwaite. 'And here — that's the barn.'

'Right by the road,' Shan said. 'Bit risky if you want to keep out of sight. And the tarn?'

'Here,' he pointed. Shan peered, deliberately shifting to cast her shadow over the map and make it easier to see the blue oval. 'It's miles from anywhere. But we could get close enough to the treehouse, on this road.' Shan traced the route. 'At least we could see if that track's been used recently, if it's completely overgrown or blocked off or if there's a bloody yurt glamping site there at least. That way we won't waste anyone else's time. And we can drive past the barn.'

'We should just report these locations.'

'Leo! How do we know she won't message him, warn him? I think she's still crazy about him. We take a look, then we can call it in. We'll know if either of them is worth following up.'

The sun beating down made the scar on her forehead itch.

'Shan, there's no way I'm letting you stride off into the wild blue yonder with a desperate armed man on the loose.'

'Letting me?' She glared at him.

He looked at her, sighed. 'You know what I mean—'

'Just a recon. If we see any signs, we can call it in. We just take a look — that's all I'm saying.'

A long pause. *Say yes. Say yes.*

She waited.

'Extreme caution,' Leo said with emphasis.

Shan grinned, releasing her breath.

CHAPTER EIGHTEEN

Leo

They found the footbridge a short walk from the lane where Shan had stopped. She'd parked close to the wall to allow other traffic to pass and clambered out of the passenger door after Leo.

It was hard to tell if the footbridge had been used recently. There was no mud nearby to display footprints. The beck below had dried up, the shallow stream bed now a swathe of Himalayan balsam. The invasive plant had choked out the local flora, all tall green stems and waxy fuchsia-pink flowers, sweetly scented.

Up the bank opposite was a scene of desolation. It reminded Leo of the scarred landscapes where forests had been logged. But this was messier, more chaotic. Trees listing, fallen, split open, limbs torn loose. Hurricane? It took him a moment to understand, as he noticed the black lesions on some of the trunks, the wilting leaves on those trees still upright.

'Ash dieback,' he said to Shan. 'Have you got the photo?'

She took it from her bag.

Leo heard the familiar cry of a chiffchaff from on high and a chaffinch too. Noticed movement on the ground under the trees, a robin fossicking for worms.

Leo studied the tree in the photo where Becky and Niall had posed. The blue, polypropylene rope ladder. 'That's an ash too.' He tapped the photo.

'So it'll be dead?'

'Some of them survive.'

'There!' She pointed. 'Next to the holly. That's it. See the ladder?'

The tree was close to the top of the slope and would have been hidden from view before the disease had hit.

Leo brought out his binoculars, removed the lens caps and adjusted the focus. 'Yes, that's it.'

The blue ladder hung from the platform base of the tree-house but the walls and roof had collapsed, a heap of rotting planks, some of which hung precariously over the edges of the cabin floor.

'So—' he capped the binoculars — 'I don't think he's here.'

'No. The barn, then?'

He lifted his crutch from where he'd balanced it on the rail of the footbridge.

A damselfly with an orange and black body and lacey wings hovered over Shan's shoulder.

She noticed it and laughed. 'Dragonfly!'

'Damsel,' he corrected her.

'You're being picky.'

'I'm being accurate.'

'I'd a thing about dragons as a kid,' she said. 'What's the difference then, dragon and damsel?'

He began to explain as they retraced their steps to the car. Shan climbed in.

Leo groaned as he got in after her. *In pain?*

'Are you OK?' she said. 'Do you want to call it a day?' She sounded dismayed.

'I'll survive,' Leo said.

Drawing close to the barn, they could see it had been renovated, solar panels on the roof, triple glazing no doubt, outbuilding with sedum roof. Leo wondered how they managed to water it, given the drought. An electric car in the driveway.

Shan pulled into the roadside. 'Eco-house,' she said, defeated.

Something niggled at Leo. The same sensation he'd had when Shan had mentioned how the wood might have been converted to yurts. *What is it?*

'Listen — the tarn,' she said. 'If I went on foot in hiking gear—'

'Turbines!' Leo said. He stabbed at the map. 'I knew there was something. I'm pretty sure they've built a wind farm here, over to the west, which means there'll be access roads there now.'

Her face brightened. 'We could check. Leo, please?'

'I don't—'

'If there is a road . . .' She entered the grid reference on her phone. 'Look! You're right.'

A tractor approached from the other direction, pulling bales of hay.

'Please. Look, it may be a dead end but we have to try.'

He weighed it up. It wasn't far to drive, and it would mean they could tie up this particular part of the search.

'OK.'

Shan opened directions to the wind farm in her maps.

Leo leaned over to compare the updated version to his map. 'We should park on that access road there, at the top,' he said. 'If I'm reading the map right, then those contour lines mean that stretch is above the tarn. So we won't be easily visible if he's actually there. Although he may hear us coming. Anyway, from there we can survey the area, look for any sign of habitation. This here—' he pointed to his own map — 'is the nearest right of way, a public footpath.'

'How far from the tarn?'

'Three hundred yards maybe,' Leo said.

'So if he was at the tarn, he couldn't be seen by anyone along there.'

'That's right.'

* * *

Shan

They neared the destination, turbines visible across the hilltop. Static, no wind today.

Shan followed the grey gravel track and slowed as they drew level with the lake. The body of water reflected the blue sky above. Ringed by straw-coloured grass and jumbled piles of stone, it would make a perfect Dales watercolour.

There was no sign of habitation. And no tree cover of any sort.

Shit!

'Nothing,' Leo said. 'Well, we've done what we can. We should be able to turn round at the top.'

Could he have escaped? There were murderers who had been on the most wanted list for years and not been caught. Could he have found someone to create a new identity for him, a fake passport? Altered his appearance, changed his name and slipped away on a ferry to Spain or a flight to Amsterdam? Possible. But likely? A man who had lived his whole life in the same area, out in the sticks?

As she put the car into gear, Shan's eyes snagged on a stone feature in the side of the hill. *Not a cave but . . . worth checking out.*

Cresting a steeper section, they reached the plateau and she parked. Walkers were visible on the footpath in the distance.

'Why have you stopped?' Leo said.

'Show me the map,' she said.

Brow knotted, he passed it to her.

'Here — look. *Shaft disused*,' she read out. 'It's an old mine, Leo! I could see the archway in the hillside.'

'And?' An ominous note in his voice.

'He could be sheltering there. It'd be perfect. I can look—'

'No way!'

'From here—' Shan waved her arm — 'go to the edge. There might be — oh, I don't know, a fireplace or water carrier or something we couldn't see from the road.'

'Or nothing,' Leo said.

'Yes, all right. Come on, Leo. What harm can it do?'

She waited, listening to him breathe. She knew he wanted to protect her, would have gone with her if he wasn't on crutches. At last he said, 'OK, but keep low when you get there.'

She got out of the car. The ground was uneven and rough, tussocks of grass, with hollows in between.

Shan picked her way over the grass, alert, concentrating on looking and listening. As she neared the edge she got onto her hands and knees. Crawled forward and finally lay down, feeling the stalks pricking through her clothing.

She could see the tarn spread out below. And the piles of stone which were presumably from demolished buildings associated with the mining operation.

But she had absolutely no sight of the mine entrance at all. She strained to catch any sound but could only hear birdsong and faint rustling in the grass.

Even if she could have seen the entrance, unless they were lucky enough to catch Tattersall coming or going, how could they know if he was using the place?

'This is stupid,' she muttered.

They needed to actually search it.

Frustrated, she returned.

A large group were now walking the footpath. Perhaps twenty of them in brightly coloured summer clothes. Two dogs barking and running up and down the line.

'It's useless,' she complained to Leo. 'I can't see a thing. It's the wrong angle. We need to look inside.'

273

'*Somebody* may need to look inside. But it isn't going to be us.'

'Shit!' Shan swore under her breath. 'That's it, then?' She knew she sounded petulant but she was close to tears. She'd wanted this to work. And like a kid, she'd imagined if she wanted it enough then it just might happen.

'We go back,' Leo said. 'We call it in. Ask an armed response unit to investigate.'

'You think they'd do that? Seriously? Based on an old photograph of his first love nest?' She shook her head; it was too thin, it wouldn't happen. It'd been a stupid idea. She was clutching at straws, but what else had they?

'We can only ask,' Leo said.

Sullen, wanting to kick or punch something, Shan drove the car back down the road. At the bend by the tarn she halted, twisted to look back at the mine entrance again.

'We can't even tell if it's blocked,' she said, slowing the car. 'We could just—'

'No,' Leo said.

'Jesus, Leo!' She slammed the heel of her hand on the steering wheel.

He didn't speak.

She swallowed her fury and released the handbrake, pulled away.

Straightening out of the bend, she saw a walker in front of them, heading downhill. Baseball cap, small rucksack. She was about to steer clear when her whole body jolted, electric shock, brain racing, adrenaline surging.

Niall! Recognition scorched through her. *Niall Tattersall!* It *was*. She knew it was. The build. The gait. Hands empty. No gun.

She hit the brakes, killed the engine, jerked the handbrake on, and jumped out of the car, ignoring Leo's shout.

She raced down the hill.

Tattersall looked back, fear sharpening his face. He began to run but Shan was closing in, close, then closer. Lungs burning, her thighs stretching.

Shan pelted after him.

He was fast but she could match him. Arms pumping, heart thudding, she drew closer. Then she was on him, roaring, her hand reaching out to grab him.

He wheeled round, one fist swinging for her face. She dived, rolled. But he clipped her cheek. The impact, dizzying, sent a thick wave of pain through her head.

He kicked out but she scrabbled out of the way. She spun round to kick back, aiming her heel at his kneecap. Her body finding moves from her aikido practice. But meeting only air as he leaped and ran again.

She was up and after him. Determined to bring him down.

Chips of gravel flew up from the track as he sprinted ahead of her.

A stitch stabbed her side, a slice of agony, but she pushed through. Sweat on her back, between her breasts, along her arms.

Again she sped after him.

Her breath hurt, a flame in her windpipe, knives in her lungs.

She gained on him, and he began to zigzag, dodging. She read the pattern, put every ounce of her energy into keeping up. Reaching him, she threw out her foot, hooking his ankle, and he fell heavily, roaring in anger.

Shan bent his arm back to immobilise him.

She sat on his back, panting, unable to speak.

He bucked beneath her, trying to throw her off, but she was dead weight.

When she could breathe she yanked his arms back, wrists together and pulled the cuffs from her pocket. Snapped them on.

She shuffled back, climbed to her feet. She swayed, blinked hard, light-headed. Her vision swam. Her cheek throbbed.

'Get up!' She yanked at him. 'Get up. Get the fuck up.'

He stood. A grazed cheek sported beads of blood, which trickled into a scrawny beard and moustache. Sunburn blistered his nose.

Leo was limping down the hill on his crutches.

'It's fine,' Shan called, waving him back.

'A'right, Niall?' She swallowed, the thrill of satisfaction ballooning in her chest. 'We've been looking for you.'

She began the caution, 'Niall Tattersall, I am arresting you for the murder of . . .'

One of the turbines rose behind him, two of its great arms pointing to the sky in a wide embrace.

She'd done it.

They'd done it.

They'd bloody done it!

* * *

Leo

Leo listened to Shan arrest Tattersall with his heart swelling, relief replacing the fear and panic he'd had moments before as she'd hared after the man. Even though the words were procedural, a set formula that Leo had heard many times, there was a weight, an emotional heft to Shan's delivery. Carrying the story of all that had led them to this point.

He was so proud of her, all she'd done, everything she'd had to cope with. And he was bloody furious at the risk she'd taken.

He waited in the car with Tattersall while Shan went to examine the mine.

She came back with two evidence sacks full of booty. Proof that he'd been living there. 'Got the rifle,' she said to Leo, triumph bright in her eyes.

The journey back, with Tattersall in handcuffs in the rear seat, was mostly done in silence. There was a salty, fatty smell and the tang of stale cigarette smoke coming off the man.

Tattersall never said a word. Head lolling back against the seat, he appeared to doze. Had he any idea how his brother was faring? Did he know Becky had given birth? Making him an uncle or possibly a father.

At the station Leo watched Shan, as arresting officer, book him in and request that his clothes be bagged up for evidence. Niall might have been wise enough to wash or dispose of the clothes he was wearing when he shot Tyler, but when he shot Jason he'd had to flee immediately. His clothes might well bear traces of his brother's blood. The lab would soon be able to tell them.

Leo shifted on his crutches, the gnawing pain in his ankle grating. Another two hours until he could take more painkillers. But he felt as if the boulder that had been pressing him down had lifted. He could stand straighter, breathe more easily.

* * *

Dusk had fallen as they left the station and soon it was full dark. There were few settlements on the road back and little light pollution. It was a clear night and Leo gazed at the sky, a river of stars, some faint sprays of silver dust, others diamond bright.

'That was stupid, you know.' He couldn't keep quiet any longer.

'Stupid?'

'It was dangerous, reckless. You put yourself—'

'Hang on! I could see he wasn't armed — his hands were empty. I'd never have done that if he'd been carrying,' Shan insisted.

'We agreed to do a recon and then we'd pass it on,' Leo said.

'So I should have just let him swan off? Waved hello as we drove past? He's in a cell now, Leo. If I hadn't—'

'You could have been hurt.'

'I can look after myself,' Shan said hotly. 'Do you think I didn't deal with that and worse when I was response in Leeds? And we've got him. It worked.'

'Don't you ever do that again!'

'I'd do it tomorrow in the same situation. I'm not going to apologise for it. It was the right call. You should be pleased.' She scowled at him, furious.

'Watch the road.' Yes, he was pleased but she didn't seem to understand . . . if anything had happened to her . . .

A few minutes' silence, then he said, 'I am pleased but—'

'No buts. We nicked him.'

'I know.'

He watched the sky while she handled the twists in the road.

'The Milky Way,' he said eventually.

'Can you see it?'

'Yes. You can keep your eyes on the road, though.'

'Ah, there!' she said. They were driving uphill, and over the brow ahead the bowl of the night sky was clear, a vast painting. A ribbon of scattered quartz on black velvet.

'Whoa!' she breathed.

'Most people in the country never see that nowadays,' Leo said.

They passed a derelict field barn, a For Sale sign at the roadside: *12 acres*.

Last night's dream came back to him: he and Ange had moved, he was wandering round their new home, a warren of damp rooms full of broken furniture. Mould blooms on the walls. Rotting red velvet curtains. No windows. No garden. He was panicking: *What are we doing? I want our old house back. This is horrible.* Water had bubbled up underfoot, foul smelling and icy. Part of the roof collapsed close by, lathes and plaster and tile crashing to the floor. Ange had looked at him, appalled. 'Why have you done this?'

Shan had her window open an inch. The night held the heat of the day. Leo could smell hay and the whiff of manure.

He spotted a hedgehog flattened on the road, a tuft of quills making it possible to identify it in the beam of the headlights.

Leo called the Prasads. There was no answer on Randall's number and Leo didn't want to leave a message, so he tried Eesha.

'Hello? Leo?'

'I have some news.'

'Go on.' Her voice held trepidation.

'We arrested Niall Tattersall today.'

'Oh!' she gasped. 'Randall! Randall!'

Leo waited until he could hear that the couple were together.

'You've caught him?' Randall said.

'Yes. He was holed up in a remote location. We were able to apprehend him there.'

He could hear Eesha crying.

'We'll be interviewing him tomorrow and I'm pretty sure we'll be charging him then too.'

They wouldn't be adding arson to the charges. Not unless Niall Tattersall voluntarily confessed to starting the fires that contributed to Ian Kerrigan's death. Word had come back from the CPS that the evidence wasn't robust enough, as Leo had predicted.

'And then what happens?' Randall's voice was strained.

'He'll make an appearance at the magistrates court, where the case will be referred to the Crown Court and he'll be detained pending trial.'

'There will definitely be a trial?' Randall said.

Leo knew how double-edged that sword was. The prospect of getting to the truth and securing justice weighed against the burden of hearing every harrowing detail of Tyler's murder.

'If he pleads not guilty we go to trial. If he enters a guilty plea then there's no trial but he'd be sent for sentencing at the Crown Court.'

Randall exhaled. 'OK. Thank you.'

'I'll let you go,' Leo said. 'And we'll talk again tomorrow.'

'Thank you,' Eesha said, her voice high and unsteady.

Leo gazed out at the dark fields. Now and again the headlights chanced on sheep, daubs of white in the fields. The Milky Way still swung above them, a girdle of stars.

He rolled his shoulders and stretched his neck, preparing to make the next call.

Becky listened to the news and Leo's explanation of the next legal steps. He could hear Archie fussing in the background, frail whimpers.

'And how soon would it be? A trial, if there was one?' Becky asked.

'Could be well over a year,' Leo said.

'*What?*'

'Yes, I'm afraid so.'

Here she was struggling with all the demands of a newborn. Her husband wounded instead of by her side. Most times a baby would be a sign of hope, but in these circumstances would Becky's relationship with her son be tainted, forever tangled with betrayal, with the shadow of Niall?

* * *

As Shan dropped him off and drove away he met Ange coming out of the house. 'We got him,' Leo said. 'Picked him up this afternoon.' Mixed in with Leo's fatigue was the thrill of elation, the fizz of triumph.

'Right.' Ange seemed distracted. She looked harassed.

'What is it?' Leo said. *Luke?* His guts dropped. *Please! Please, no!*

'Billy, he's not right.' She gestured over the lane to their old neighbour's house. 'He's talking rubbish. Packing random stuff in a suitcase.'

'Infection?' Leo recalibrated, his heart finding its rhythm again.

'That's my guess. If we went to A&E, he'd have to wait hours.'

'And it's not a life-threatening emergency,' Leo pointed out.

'No, right. We can get the district nurses in first thing. Meanwhile . . . will he sleep?'

Leo shrugged.

'I don't even know if he's eaten. I'm going to try and sort him out. Get him to go to bed,' she said, puffing out her cheeks, hand in her hair. 'It's endless, isn't it?'

'What?' Leo said.

'Life.'

'Not really, no,' Leo said, fixing her with a look. Everybody dies. *And some people die way too soon.*

She blew him a kiss, sarcastically, then crossed the lane.

By the time she came back, Leo had hauled himself upstairs on his crutches and was washed, changed and in bed reading *The Edge of the World* by Michael Pye, a history of the North Sea. Normally anything like that would have him gripped, but he found it impossible to absorb the text. His mind kept sliding back to the man in custody and what tomorrow might bring.

Billy had settled, Ange said, and she hoped he'd be all right till the morning. 'If he takes it into his head to light the gas or run a bath . . .'

'You've done what you can,' Leo told her.

'Is it enough?' she said, stripping off her clothes.

It was something he was asking himself about the case. If Niall Tattersall held out for a trial, surely the evidence would convince a jury. But then again, juries were notoriously unpredictable, and witnesses often unreliable, their memories compromised. The defence would make every effort to undermine them, cast doubts on their testimony. He thought of Anita on the stand, how tough that would be for her. *But we have the video. The photograph. The forensics. The DNA from the toothbrush ties him to the murder. Surely . . .*

Ange climbed into bed.

'What time will you leave?' he asked. She was visiting Luke again, Leo still in exile.

'About one.'

'OK.'

'Good luck tomorrow,' she said. 'It's brilliant you've got him.'

'Yes. Sleep well,' he said.

'I can hope.'

'You did the windows?' he checked.

'I did.'

'D'you see the Milky Way?'

'Yes, so clear. Beautiful,' she said.

He switched off the bedside lamp. Tugged at his pillow and lay back.

After a moment, he heard Ange stir, whisper, 'Shit!'

'What?'

'I forgot to turn off the fan in the shower,' she complained.

'Just this once?' He encouraged her to let it slide.

'Maybe.'

He could sense her struggling with the decision.

'Nah. Save the planet, eh?' She got up, padded off.

All of us, he thought, seeing it burn, watching it drown and doing our best. Recycling, cutting down on meat, on flights, saving energy. But the polluters, gas and oil, the money behind them, still hell-bent on wringing every last cent from the business no matter the cost to the place we call home.

CHAPTER NINETEEN

Saturday

Shan

Shan was anxious, her stomach in knots, a band of tension around her head. They were waiting for Niall and the duty solicitor to be escorted to the interview room down the corridor. She was too hot; the room didn't have any ventilation or natural light. Their morning's work had been done under the glare of downlights.

We're prepped, she reassured herself. We know what we're doing. They had all the documents prepared, evidence stacked on the desk or loaded onto her tablet.

But one mistake . . .

Shut up!

Shan and Leo had talked about how to structure the interview, and he suggested they share out the lead role in different sections.

'Seriously?' Shan asked.

'Way to learn. Put that training into practice.'

Could she do it? Do it well?

'If it's too much . . .' he said when she hesitated.

'No. No. I'll do it. I want to.'

The custody officer called through to tell them all was ready to go in interview room one.

Shan swallowed and took in a steadying breath as they rose. She tried to calm her mind in the short walk down the corridor.

Niall Tattersall barely seemed to register when they entered the room. Next to him sat Nichola Fearns, the solicitor.

Niall looked smaller than Shan remembered, scrawny. His hair was tangled, oily. No place to wash or groom himself hiding out at the mine.

He wore the standard-issue grey tracksuit he'd been given last night.

Again she recalled talking to Niall in the bar at the Grange. His apparent support for their work, and later when he spun them the tale about visiting Becky and checking snares, his expression of sympathy for Tyler's family. Stone-cold liar.

Shan set the video recording and Leo began by introducing everyone in the room. He read out the caution. Then, 'Mr Tattersall, Niall, you've been detained here on suspicion of the murder of Tyler Prasad on Wednesday the thirteenth of September, and the attempted murder of Jason Tattersall on Sunday the seventeenth of September. This interview will address those offences. Do you understand?'

Niall was expressionless. He dipped his chin.

'Please could you answer aloud for the recording.'

'Yes,' Niall said.

'What can you tell us about the events of the thirteenth of September?' Leo asked.

'No comment.'

Shan's hopes slumped. It wasn't unusual for a suspect to answer like this. In fact, in the majority of situations the solicitor would advise them to do so at initial interview to prevent them incriminating themselves and to allow time to look at defences against any charge. But Shan had hoped that Niall would engage now he'd been picked up. That he'd accept it was all over. Bar the shouting, as her dad liked to say. And that he'd find some relief in admitting to his crimes.

They'd still be able to charge him, but a confession — what she'd give for that.

'Did you shoot Tyler Prasad?' Leo asked.

'No comment.'

With calm, forensic precision, Leo laid out the evidence they had in front of Niall, starting with the video of the hen harrier from the scene.

Shan saw a spark of shock dart through the man's eyes as he watched. No doubt he thought he'd destroyed it when he disposed of Tyler's phone. He turned his head away.

'This was you, shooting the bird,' Leo said. 'Wasn't it, Niall?'

'No comment.'

'And this still from Tyler Prasad's video. That's you, isn't it?'

'No comment.'

Leo proceeded, outlining the nature of Tyler's wounds, the cause of his death, the type of firearm used. 'You told us you were in the yard checking snares at 8 p.m. on that day. That you'd been with your sister-in-law at her home before that. But you'd actually been up on Syke Moss at that time, hadn't you? Where you had killed Tyler Prasad.'

'No comment.'

'We know you asked Becky Tattersall to lie and provide you with an alibi for the time of the murder.'

Leo saw Niall flinch at that but quickly recover.

'You shot an unarmed teenager and tried to conceal his body. Isn't that the truth?'

'No comment.'

Leo challenged him with the DNA evidence. His DNA found on Tyler's clothing and skin, proof that he had touched the young man.

'You killed this boy because he filmed you shooting a protected bird, a hen harrier. Isn't that the case?'

'No comment.'

There was no spark or heat in his replies. They were rote, numb. The air that came off him was one of withdrawal. *Still hiding*, Shan thought.

Having exhausted the questions about Tyler's murder, Leo handed the baton to Shan.

She drew back her shoulders and took a slow breath in. *You can do this.*

'Niall, we have witness testimony that on the seventeenth of September you confronted your brother Jason in the garden of his home, demanding money. An argument followed, during which Jason accused you of killing Tyler Prasad and told you to turn yourself in. When Jason refused to help you, you left and returned shortly afterwards with a firearm. You threatened your brother and when he wouldn't do as you demanded, you shot him, didn't you?'

Shan saw Niall's mouth tighten, his lips tremble, as she finished speaking.

He didn't answer.

'Niall?'

He stayed mute.

'You left your brother wounded and fled across Syke Moss. When contacted by phone, you refused to surrender and be taken into police custody. Is that correct?'

He was staring at the table now, refusing to respond.

Shan studied him, the thin, sharp-featured face, the wispy beard. His lips were cracked and peeling. White flakes on vivid red skin. She noticed the pulse in his neck jumping.

She thought back to Anita's account of the argument, the way Jason had disparaged his brother. And the view Ian Kerrigan expressed, how the brothers were 'always sniping and having a go', that Niall had a chip on his shoulder and still carried a torch for Becky. She recalled Becky talking about Jason coming home steaming on the Wednesday after a big row, determined to see his brother sacked. And her description of their illicit affair. The family dynamic — could she use that to push some buttons, break through his defences?

'I don't think you set out to harm your brother. But I think you found yourself in an extremely stressful situation. I'd been in touch with you and you knew we were getting closer. Perhaps Jason told you we were wanting a DNA sample. You knew that could prove you killed Tyler. Your instinct was to run.'

His mouth twitched, beard jerking. He was with her now. He was hearing the truth. Surely he'd cave.

'But Jason wouldn't help and he started badmouthing you, insulting you, humiliating you. Again. Like he'd always done. Putting you down. Bullying. Sneering. The man who'd stolen Becky from you, who wouldn't even have you in the house. He'd taken her, hadn't he? Now he was going to make sure you lost everything else.

'You snapped, that's all it was. You lost control. You just wanted him to stop, didn't you Niall? To listen to you for once. But he wouldn't. So you stopped him. You shot him, didn't you, Niall?'

She waited. Her tongue pressed against the roof of her mouth. She could feel her own heartbeat, heavy in her chest.

'You shot Jason, didn't you, Niall?'

He took a breath in, stuttering.

Say it!

She counted the seconds.

Say it!

He raised his eyes to hers. She watched the pain, the shame, recede, and the blank indifference return. The barrier back in place.

'No comment,' he said flatly.

She'd failed.

* * *

Monday

Leo

A crowd of reporters greeted them outside the single-storey courts building. They were clustered around the flight of wide shallow steps that led up to the entrance. The capture of Niall Tattersall had made national news, and public interest was high in this, his first court appearance.

Yesterday's headlines had trumpeted his arrest. *SYKE MOSS KILLER CAUGHT*, and *MANHUNT SUCCESS — PRASAD SUSPECT IN CUSTODY*.

Randall, Eesha and Padma were already in the foyer. So were Carrie and Phil Beaumont. Becky had stayed away. 'I don't want to see him. Not unless I have to.'

'Of course,' Leo had said.

Leo and Shan greeted them. The mood was hushed, leaden with significance. They didn't have to wait long to be called into the courtroom.

Weeks earlier, Leo had sat in the very same court watching Luke lose his liberty.

At Saturday's prison visit, Ange had found Luke even more subdued than the first time. The reality setting in?

'I asked if he was feeling low and he looked at me like I was thick. "Can you see a doctor, maybe get a bit of help?" He shut me down: "Don't make a fuss."' Ange's eyes shone with tears.

'I told him about you — and the fire, how you almost—'

Leo had clasped her hand in his own.

'He looked at me, like maybe I was making it up or something. Then he said, "But he's OK?"'

Leo's throat had closed. *He cared enough to ask.*

'I'm worried about him,' Ange had said.

Leo was too.

'He should get time in the gym soon,' she'd said. 'Maybe that'll . . . oh God, Leo, I don't know. What can we do?'

'Hey.' He'd hugged her tight, chin on the top of her head. 'We do all we can. We keep showing up. Well, you do.'

And me? Will he ever let me back in? Does he think I'll give up trying? I won't, Leo had sworn to himself. *I'll never stop trying, as long as I draw breath.*

The benches filled up. Leo caught sight of Lydia and Ange and a bunch of others in a group, some he recognised from the vigil. Anita came in and Carrie waved her over.

Leo identified members of the press, two familiar faces who covered the local area, but there were others who he assumed were from farther afield.

When they went to trial they could expect many more of them. News crews from everywhere. The case of a teenage boy shot on the wild moors, an attempted fratricide and a killer on the run, held particular fascination. Unusual and compelling. Terrible.

The room was stifling and he felt sweat break out around his hairline, in the centre of his back, under his arms.

The magistrates entered and the whispered chatter ceased. They took their seats at the bench. The coat of arms on the back wall above them.

Niall Tattersall was escorted into the dock by a guard.

Leo felt the tension in the room, the ripple of reactions, as people laid eyes on the accused.

'Please tell the court your name, address and date of birth.'

'Niall Tattersall, 3 Patefield Grange Mews, ninth of January 1988.'

'Today you are charged with the following offences. That on Wednesday the thirteenth of September you murdered Tyler Prasad contrary to common law. How do you plead? Guilty or not guilty?'

Eesha and Randall were staring at Niall. Ange put an arm around Lydia.

Leo felt the heat, suffocating. His throat caught, he coughed as lightly as possible.

The moment stretched on. The atmosphere tight, everyone holding their breath. Leo sat rigid, his hands gripping his knees.

'Mr Tattersall,' the magistrate said, 'do you plead guilty or not guilty?'

Leo closed his eyes. He felt trickles of sweat drop down his sides. Heat in his skull.

'Guilty,' Niall said.

Adrenaline flooded Leo's body. Gasps and cries ricocheted round the space, bouncing off the ceiling and the wooden benches.

Shan, at his side, startled in surprise. She looked at him, eyes wide.

I know, he mouthed.

He saw Randall embrace his wife. Padma touch her back from the other side.

The magistrate waited for calm.

'And in the charge of the attempted murder of Jason Tattersall on the seventeenth of September contrary to common law, how do you plead? Guilty or not guilty?

'Guilty.'

Yes!

Anita had her head down, shoulders heaving, in tears. Carrie had her hand over her mouth. Phil Beaumont sat back, staring at the ceiling, face grey, eyes closed.

Lydia and Ange were clutching hands.

There'd be no long months waiting to fight for a conviction. No days in court for those people left behind.

In time those same people might want to know more, to hear more from Niall, to gather the details in all their stark brutality and their pitiful mundanity, so they could knit together a picture of exactly what befell their loved one.

In time Niall Tattersall may or may not cooperate with those approaches.

That was all for the future.

'You will be remanded in custody and committed to Crown Court for sentencing,' the magistrate pronounced.

Niall, almost robotic, was accompanied by a guard back down to the cells. He hadn't once made eye contact with anyone present. Shielding himself, Leo presumed. Insulating himself.

Leo saw again the video of the hen harrier's flight, heard Tyler's excited commentary. Then the crack of the shotgun and the boy's shock and horror.

If only.

Oh God. The guilty plea was a good result. But if only it hadn't ever happened. None of it.

Ange turned to look at him, wiping tears from her face, nodding. Job done.

* * *

Shan

Outside the court Shan joined Leo and the family, who were making statements to the press.

Leo spoke first. 'We are satisfied that we have been able to bring the person responsible for the cruel, senseless murder of Tyler Prasad and the brutal attack on Jason Tattersall to justice. The loss of someone as young as Tyler is heartbreaking. A young man of great talent and promise, his life was stolen from him. His future savagely cut short. The fact that Jason Tattersall suffered life-changing injuries on the day that his first child was born is the second tragedy. These were truly shocking attacks. I would like to thank everyone involved in the investigation for their painstaking work.

'Our thoughts are with Tyler's family and friends, and Jason's family and friends. And I would like to thank them all for their dignity and endurance throughout this distressing investigation. No family should ever have to go through what they have been through. Their lives have been devastated, torn apart, and the events in court today, while welcome, can never change that fact.' Leo paused than went on, 'I would also like to thank Ian Kerrigan, a gamekeeper who bravely gave his life assisting us in trying to apprehend the offender. Thank you.'

Eesha spoke next. 'We would like to thank the police for everything they have done.' She smiled at Shan and Leo. An acknowledgement of how far they had come. Of trust won. 'Tyler was our sun, moon and stars. Our heart of hearts. He died up on the fells, exploring the world he so passionately wanted to protect. Nothing . . .' She froze. Tears slid down her cheeks.

Randall waited, bent towards her, offering support. She fought to continue. 'Nothing can bring our boy home, but we will do all in our power to carry on the struggle in his name. In his steps. With his love and his humour and his understanding. We love you, Tyler. We always will.'

Shan blinked hard.

When the cameras stopped flashing, the groups separated. Randall, Eesha and Padma thanked them in turn, clasping their hands, tearful.

'Good luck with your son,' Shan overheard Eesha say to Leo as they parted.

Carrie and Beaumont and Anita approached.

'Is that it?' Anita asked. 'He's pleaded guilty, so we won't have to come to court to be witnesses?'

'That's right,' Shan said.

Anita shuddered, made an attempt to smile. 'Come on,' Carrie said gently. 'Let's get back.'

Shan watched the Prasads walking down the street, people filming them with their smartphones.

Forever, she thought. The whole of the rest of their lives without Tyler.

She lifted the hair from the back of her neck. The day was hot, muggy, bright but overcast. The grass outside the courts brown, dried up.

'I never expected him to go guilty,' she said to Leo, still reeling, an edge of hysteria making her feel giddy.

'Me neither,' Leo said, shaking his head.

'Why did he?'

Leo considered the question, eyes squinting in the harsh light. 'Perhaps he realised he had no possible defence. That the game was up.'

'Or this felt easier?' Shan thought of the dynamic between the brothers. 'A trial would have put him in the limelight, humiliated him, forced him to account for his actions. None of what he did was premeditated, it was in desperation, for self-preservation. He'd mucked everything up — again. He didn't want his failings publicised like that.'

'You could be right,' Leo said. 'Don't think we'll ever know.' He paused, then, 'So, next job is getting those reports sent through to the Crown Court.'

'Most of it's ready.'

'Yes.' He exhaled loudly, shifted on his crutches.

'You won't be able to get up Syke Moss for a while yet.' She gestured to his boot.

On their previous case, the first time they'd worked together, Leo had taken her to revisit the site where remains had been found. He called it squaring the circle, something he did whenever an investigation was resolved. Going back to the beginning.

'Not for a while,' he agreed. 'But it'll still be there when I'm fit.'

'It's a date,' she said.

* * *

Erin was home already when Shan got back. Pasta sauce bubbling on the stove.

'You were on the news,' Erin said.

Shan grinned. 'He pleaded guilty. And I. Am. Knackered.'

'Eat and sleep?'

'Shower, eat, sleep.' She crossed the room quickly. Kissed Erin. 'Thank you. Thank you. Thank you,' she said, something like joy bubbling up inside her.

'It's only ragu.'

Shan laughed, punched her in shoulder. 'For having me back. For everything. I love you so much, you know.'

Erin hugged her.

There was a sizzling, hissing sound. Shan started. Turned to look for water boiling over. For something burning. She held her breath.

Nothing.

But the noise grew. Roaring. Her skin crawled. *Fire?* A thump of fear. Acid in her veins. *Flames crackling, choking smoke, the stink of charring, taste of soot . . .*

No . . . It's—

'Rain!' she gasped. 'It's raining!'

She grabbed Erin by the hand and opened the door onto their tiny backyard. She pulled her outside. The rain hammered down, splashing off the flagstones, filling the gutters, streaming down the walls. Soaking the pair of them to the skin. Shan threw back her head, mouth open. Rain. *Sweet, sweet rain.* Tasting of air and stone and water.

* * *

Leo

Leo had the patio doors open, the better to savour the downpour that was drenching the garden, stippling the pond, dripping off every leaf and stem, bouncing off the patio. Making the grasses and flowers dip and nod, filling the water butts. Pouring over the roof of Ange's studio.

The light was on out there. After checking on Billy, now dosed up on antibiotics courtesy of the district nurses, she'd wanted to catch up with material for Tyler's fundraiser.

Leo breathed in the rich humus smell. *Life.* The air was cool, clear, rinsed clean.

Flood warnings were out in many parts of the country, where the bone-dry land was unable to soak up the sudden deluge. Places already damaged by erosion, intensive farming, artificial drainage, the removal of natural tree cover. The water plunging down the hills. Torrents filling the rivers. Bursting the banks.

Another reason to defend the peat bog, to preserve and develop it. Ange had told him, 'It's a sponge. You muck about with it and all the water runs into the valleys. It doesn't just store carbon, although that's the most important point, it's a flood defence.'

He closed his eyes, listened to the symphony of water, hissing, drumming, pattering, rushing.

Then he picked up his pen and — with both hope and fear — began to write, *Dear Luke* . . .

THE END

APOLOGY

I have taken outrageous liberties with the geography of the Dales, inventing places and changing some real locations for the sake of my story, but I hope I've captured the unique beauty of the landscape, the backdrop to so many outings and holidays in childhood and since.

Eagle-eyed readers who have also read *The Fells* may have noticed that while Leo and Shan's stories follow on quite closely from that book, the wider world has taken a leap forward of a few years. I had my reasons!

ACKNOWLEDGEMENTS

Thank you so much to my writers' group — Livi Michael, Sophie Claire and Jennifer Nansubuga Makumbi. Your support and feedback make such a difference and our meetings are a real pleasure. Many thanks to Kate Lyall Grant, Laura Coulman and the whole team at Joffe — you're brilliant! Finally, thank you to everyone who acts to protect our wonderful planet, our wild places and our natural world.

THE JOFFE BOOKS STORY

We began in 2014 when Jasper agreed to publish his mum's much-rejected romance novel and it became a bestseller.

Since then we've grown into the largest independent publisher in the UK. We're extremely proud to publish some of the very best writers in the world, including Joy Ellis, Faith Martin, Caro Ramsay, Helen Forrester, Simon Brett and Robert Goddard. Everyone at Joffe Books loves reading and we never forget that it all begins with the magic of an author telling a story.

We are proud to publish talented first-time authors, as well as established writers whose books we love introducing to a new generation of readers.

We won Trade Publisher of the Year at the Independent Publishing Awards in 2023 and Best Publisher Award in 2024 at the People's Book Prize. We have been shortlisted for Independent Publisher of the Year at the British Book Awards for the last five years, and were shortlisted for the Diversity and Inclusivity Award at the 2022 Independent Publishing Awards. In 2023 we were shortlisted for Publisher of the Year at the RNA Industry Awards, and in 2024 we were shortlisted at the CWA Daggers for the Best Crime and Mystery Publisher.

We built this company with your help, and we love to hear from you, so please email us about absolutely anything bookish at feedback@joffebooks.com.

If you want to receive free books every Friday and hear about all our new releases, join our mailing list here: www.joffebooks.com/freebooks.

And when you tell your friends about us, just remember: it's pronounced Joffe as in coffee or toffee!